NONE
STOOD
TALLER

NONE
STOOD
TALLER

From the ashes of the Blitz to the D-Day landings.
One Woman's Remarkable Story.

Peter Turnham

A CIP catalogue record of this book is available from the British Library.

Cover design and interior formatting by JD Smith Design

ISBN No: 978-1-9160979-4-0 (ebook)
978-1-9160979-5-7 (paperback)
978-1-9160979-6-4 (hardback)

Publisher: P&C Turnham
www.peterturnhamauthor.com

Acknowledgments

To my wife Carol,
my spell- and grammar-check,
my editor and IT consultant,
my indispensable other half.

Dedication

For my grandchildren:
Florence
Caitlin
Arthur
&
Jacob

The future is yours.

May your generation never repeat the mistakes of the past.

Peter Turnham
September 2020

Table of Contents

Dear Reader

I didn't dream as a self-published author that "None Stood Taller" would become a bestseller. It has enjoyed success beyond my wildest imagination. And then, in order to bring the story to its natural conclusion on VE-Day, and to allow the characters to properly develop, a three-part series has resulted. I thank everyone who helped to make that possible, and of course I thank you, the reader. It all started with a simple idea: take a woman from the East End of London, leave her with nothing when her home is destroyed during the Blitz in 1941, and then send her out to find her way in war-torn Britain. That was when I realised it wasn't my character Lily who needed to find her way in war-torn Britain - it was me!

During my research I found many extraordinary people who did extraordinary things. People such as Vera Atkins, who contributed so much towards setting up and running Section F of the SOE. Or Joan Bright who ran the secret intelligence centre in the Cabinet War Rooms under Winston Churchill. I can't take the credit for my character Lily Heywood; she already existed in those women. Lily owes more to Vera Atkins than she does to me.

The same can be said for my character Dotty. Thirty-nine women served in Occupied France as SOE field agents. Dotty owes more to those thirty-nine than anything in my imagination. Her SOE operations in Occupied France and Germany that appear in the third book may be fictitious, but the details of those operations, like everything else in this series, are grounded in reality.

If there is a single reason for the success of these books, it is that readers connect with the characters. I effectively lived the lives of these people; in many ways I feel I was there with them! These books result from that shared experience. I can't tell you how gratifying it is when readers tell me they have shared that same experience. Over ninety percent of people who read this first book go on to read the next in the series. This is what makes it all worthwhile.

Writing would be nothing without you, dear reader, I couldn't continue without your support. Your comments and reviews are my lifeblood. Now I must move on and find another Lily, or Dotty, another historical context, another story. This is an immensely hard act to follow. I hope you will join me on that journey.

Best wishes.
Peter Turnham
September 2022

https://www.peterturnhamauthor.com
peterturnham.author@gmail.com

Introduction

In 1945, when Victory in Europe had been declared, a grateful nation honoured its brave and fallen. Not everyone was recognised; for some, like Lily Heywood, the veil of secrecy surrounding her work for the Special Operations Executive (SOE) was so pervasive that it continued long after the war. For Lily and her colleagues in SOE Station M, there were no medals pinned to their chest, there was no recognition. Instead, they meet every year on the anniversary of D-Day, the invasion which was such a vital part of their work. On June 6th 1980, at their annual reunion, Lily decided that after 35 years of silence the time was right to share her wartime memories. She chose her godson, Charlie, to confide in. He knew that his parents and his godmother played an active part during the war but was unaware of the remarkable story Lily has to tell.

War was declared in 1939 when Germany invaded Poland. No-one realised at that time the full extent of the horror which was about to be unleashed upon them, or how close the nation would come to defeat. The ignominious evacuation of the British Expeditionary Force from Dunkirk which began on May 26th 1940 was as much a personal tragedy for Lily as it was a tragedy for the nation.

During the ensuing 'Battle of Britain,' the RAF was all that stood between a thousand years of history and the tyranny of Hitler's Third Reich. Few pages in the annals of British history glow with more pride, than when *so much was owed by so many to so few.* The courage of the 'few' turned the tide against the aggressor. The German Luftwaffe failed in its objective, only to return with an even more sinister strategy. It will attempt to break the will of the British people by raining death and destruction upon its great cities.

September the 7th 1940 marked the start of the German bombing campaign which became known as the Blitz - a terrible period when the spirit of the people was to be tested to its limits. Lily was living in Stepney, in the East End of London. Her proximity to the London docks placed her in the most dangerous place in Britain. She starts her account of the war at the point where her life was about to change irreparably. It is March 1941, a time when large swathes of the East End of London lie in ruins. It is a scene of wanton destruction which Charlie cannot begin to recognise nor comprehend.

Few people are unscathed, most have lost friends or relatives, thousands have lost their homes. Before the Blitz is finally over, it will take the lives of over 40,000 people, half of whom will be Londoners. Despite the hell which has been visited upon them, letters are still delivered, the buses still run; this is the spirit of the Blitz, and it cannot be broken. People like Lily are determined to go about their daily lives as usual. Sheltering in the Tube Station each night is her only concession to the enemy. This is the daily existence which Lily tries to describe to Charlie.

Chapter One
Stepney London March 1941

"It was a terrible time, Charlie; we lived in constant fear of our lives, death was all around us."

"It's difficult for me to visualise, Lily, but you say you carried on as if all was well?"

"We did; I went to work each day, and I spent every night in the tube station. Each morning we came out to see yet more death and destruction."

"How did you cope with it; how can you witness all that death and destruction without it affecting you?"

"I don't know, we just did. I saw terrible things, Charlie; it still haunts me, there are things I can never forget. As bad as it was, we knew we had to continue, it was our way of fighting back. Hitler wanted to break our spirit; well, I can tell you, Charlie, the Germans didn't have enough bombs to break our spirit in the East End! The more of our people they killed, the greater that spirit grew."

"I've read about the spirit of the Blitz. Such collective courage is difficult to comprehend; no wonder we call you the greatest generation."

"I'm not sure that's an accolade we deserve, Charlie; we just carried on. Defiance for us meant exactly that - we remained determined to go about our business. Death came searching

dread when her children are in harm's way is like no other fear a woman can feel.

"What do we do, Lily?" she asked in a raised voice.

"We'll be fine, but just to be sure, let's all sit under the stairs."

Linda's under-stair cupboard was like mine next door, just large enough for us all to get into. Like everyone else she had cleared away some items previously stored there, just in case. The boys were only four years old and didn't fully realise what was happening, so we tried to make it feel like a game for them.

We searched around the confinement of our under-stair hideaway, looking for something to amuse them. Linda put a coat over the floor mop so it looked like hair spilling out over the collar. I put the handle of a tennis racket up one sleeve and we pretended the mop man was chasing the boys. The drone of distant bombers grew ominously louder, so we used the mop man to full advantage, making as much noise as possible.

It sounded like the Docks again; the explosions were making the windows rattle. I blamed the mop man for shaking the windows - Johnny and Adam thought it was a brilliant game and pulled at the sleeves excitedly. A stick of bombs fell close enough for us to hear them whistle through the air - it was terrifying. For a moment we sat there on the floor, frozen in silence, just looking at each other with fear in our eyes. Linda instinctively grabbed Johnny while I held Adam as tightly as I could.

An explosion blew out the rear windows and we heard some crockery on the dresser crash to the floor. The boys were now screaming in terror. Then we heard the whistle of falling bombs again. In those final few seconds, we both knew what was going to happen.

There was a tremendous explosion, shaking the house to pieces. Things came crashing down onto the stairs above us. As terrifying as it felt, it wasn't a direct hit and for that awful split second, I allowed myself to think we were safe. Then I realised I could still hear a falling bomb! That was my last memory.

I have no recollection of the final explosion; I found out later that the bomb exploded next door; it fell directly into my house. Had I been at home and not next door with Linda, I would have been killed. The blast destroyed my house and the two adjoining houses on either side.

I have no idea how long I lay there; I must have been unconscious. I just remember that suddenly I couldn't move or see anything. It was so difficult to breathe, I didn't know if I was dead or buried alive; I couldn't think clearly at all. The worst thing was the dust in my mouth and lungs, it crunched between my teeth and filled my eyes. Thank heavens I was not properly conscious, or the horror of being buried alive would surely have filled me with terror. It is likely that I would have choked to death in my panic. The first coherent memory I have was someone shouting, "There's one alive; over here!"

I was buried beneath rubble; the staircase had collapsed over me, and somehow it had protected me from the full weight of bricks and masonry. I could feel the men moving the rubble above me but couldn't move a limb. That was when I really started choking on the dreadful dust in my mouth and lungs. My head was painful and I could hardly hear anything other than the ringing in my ears. I just assumed I must be gravely injured and felt sure I was about to die. The men quickly pulled away the remaining rubble, and I found I still had my arms and legs. They pulled me out, and it amazed everyone that I was alive.

Having put me onto a stretcher, they hurriedly carried me away towards a waiting ambulance. I remember holding one man's hand, trying in vain to thank him. The ambulance crew washed the dust out of my mouth and eyes, while they methodically checked me over for serious injuries. Incredibly, except for cuts and bruises and my aching head, I was in one piece.

"I thought we were wasting our time here," one of the crew said. "I didn't expect anyone to walk away from this house!"

I had no feeling of elation that I'd survived, just bewilderment. As my aching head cleared, my first thought was of Linda and the twins. That was when reality forced itself upon me, as it all became horribly real, filling me with terror again. The ambulance crew tried to restrain me, but I managed to break away from them. I struggled back into the rubble that was once Linda's house. I stumbled and fell but climbed over to where the same three men were trying to clear away more of the bricks and masonry.

They looked up at me with some alarm, one of them putting his hand up to stop me from going any further. It was too late; I could see Linda lying there amongst the rubble. She just looked as if she was asleep, still holding Johnny lying motionless in her arms. Her face, her clothes, everything was grey, an awful, all-consuming grey. It felt as if colour only existed in life; in death there was only grey. The one exception was the bright crimson blood trickling from the corner of her mouth, her last gasp of life clinging to its vivid colour in defiance of the all-pervasive dust.

Nothing could have prepared me for what I saw that day. Every part of my body seemed to react in an instant, I wanted to scream and cry, but nothing happened. Slumping to my knees, I gently touched Johnny's face, and then as if a closed door had suddenly opened, I thought - where was Adam?

"*Where's the other boy?*" I screamed.

"You don't want to see him, you really don't," one of them said.

"*Where is he? Where is he?*" I kept shouting.

Reluctantly, they pointed to a spot some yards away. I looked down to where they had cleared the rubble, and little Adam was lying there. I only knew it was Adam because I could see Johnny lying lifeless in his mother's arms. The bright glistening colour of what was once a young, vibrant life seeped into the rubble, being consumed by the dispassionate grey dust. One moment, two lovely boys were playing with the mop man; the next, they were lying in the dust, broken and lifeless. It was the most horrific thing I have ever seen.

As long as I live, I shall never be able to banish that image from my mind; it has haunted me my entire life. I looked right into the eyes of death that day, and death stared defiantly right back at me. I don't think it intended me to walk away from that encounter. Somehow death lost its clammy grip on me, but as I turned away, it left me in no doubt that it lay in wait for me around some future corner. Rather than causing tears, it just left me feeling numb; it was more than I could cope with; I had to shut it out. Death and destruction were all around me, but I was no longer a part of it.

I have no idea how I climbed over the rubble, but now I could struggle no further. The ambulance crew had to carry me away. They could not believe I didn't need to go to the hospital, eventually deciding they would take me to the local rest centre. I remember little; it felt as though it was all happening to someone else, as if I was merely an onlooker.

Just at that moment, Mrs Johnson appeared; she was a neighbour from further down the road. Her familiar long overcoat flared out behind her as she hurried towards me. It was an old army coat that she had altered and dyed dark blue. She marched up to the driver who was helping me into the ambulance. Placing a firm grip on his arm, she looked him straight in the eye, stopping him right in his tracks.

"Is she badly injured?" she demanded to know.

"No, she doesn't appear to be; we're taking her to the rest centre," the driver replied.

"In that case, you can leave her with me, dear, we take care of our own around here," she said with great authority. "Come on, Lil, you're coming with me, luv."

The driver didn't reply, he just did as he was told. Faced with Ivy Johnson in full flight, that was probably an excellent idea! With that, she put her arm around me and marched me off down the road. I don't suppose we had gone more than a few yards when I felt another arm slip round me. It was Rose from the opposite side of the road.

"Chin up, Lil, you're better off out of that damp place," she said.

I can't remember walking down the road, I just recall sitting in Mrs Johnson's kitchen, and her putting the kettle on, with Rose holding my hand.

"I'll go back and find out if they've taken Linda to the rest centre," she said, her voice filled with concern.

Gripping her hand, I tried to tell her not to go back, but I was unable to bring myself to utter the words. I just looked at her. She looked back at me and we had an unspoken conversation; her eyes welled up and her bottom lip trembled.

"And the boys?"

I said nothing; I didn't have to. Rose turned away and walked into the kitchen. When they both returned with cups of tea, it was as if nothing had happened. Linda and the twins were gone; time for grief was a luxury which only existed in peacetime.

"It's her poor husband I feel for," Mrs Johnson said, contorting her lower lip.

"It's just awful," Rose replied, "her Alan's on HMS Gloucester, so goodness knows when he might come home. I'll make sure he knows, poor devil. Do you know when your Gerry's back on shore leave, Lil? Make sure he knows what's happened before he gets home."

"I don't know when he's due back; he's only just re-joined the ship," I said.

Then it occurred to me; had he not been at sea, Gerry might have been at home that night. I shuddered at the thought and pushed it from my mind.

"You can stay with me, Lil, for as long as you like," Mrs Johnson insisted, "me and Arthur's got plenty of room. We can make up the settee for you."

"I've got some spare clothes and blankets, Lil, you'll be okay," said Rose.

"You're both so kind but what I really want is to go home to my parents," I said.

Mrs Johnson and Rose were both very kind to me. They cleaned me up as best they could, Ivy brushing the dust out of my auburn hair while Rose got me one of her old skirts to wear. I hadn't realised I was showing everyone my undies.

"You'll get over this Lil, don't you worry," said Rose.

"Of course you will," said Mrs Johnson, "a lovely young girl like you, you've got your entire life ahead of you."

It didn't feel like that for me; at that moment, it felt more like my entire life was behind me. My neighbours' response when confronted with death and destruction was typical of Londoners, especially East Enders. It became known as the spirit of the Blitz. It was why Hitler could never defeat us.

They both walked with me to Stepney Green Station. We passed another four bomb sites on the way, in the road behind ours. These must have been the other bombs that Linda and I heard falling. Apart from people clearing debris from the road, none of us gave the broken houses much of a second thought, much less the broken lives of the poor sods who once lived there.

The entirety of one terraced house lay as a pile of rubble, and yet the house next door stood defiantly with its rooms exposed for all to see. A double bed clung to its precarious existence, teetering on the edge of oblivion. No doubt that bed had a story to tell, maybe nights of grand passion, or perhaps sad nights of cold detachment. It only seems to be real if you know the people involved. To us, this was just another bomb site; the bed was just a bed.

Kids were climbing over the smouldering rubble, searching for shrapnel trophies to take home. They were all breathing the dust-laden acrid air as if it were perfectly normal. The postman went about his round as usual, smiling and shouting over to us, "Morning, ladies!" as he pushed his bicycle around the worst of the rubble. The only concession people made was to walk on the other side of the road if fire had recently destroyed a building, catching the unfortunate inhabitants inside. The smell of burnt people is just too unbearable.

It was not far to Stepney Green, but I would not have got to the station without help. I doubt I could even have bought a ticket; Rose bought it for me. I can't imagine what I would have done without Ivy and Rose. Fortunately, once I was on the train, it was a journey I knew well and didn't have to think about it.

Stepney Green to Stockwell doesn't take long, but it was the most surreal Tube journey I am ever likely to take. People must have noticed my grazed face and legs, my dusty clothes, and the distant look in my eyes. Nobody stared at me; they just smiled an understanding smile. Everything about the Tube seemed reassuring; this subterranean world just carried on regardless of what was happening above. Here, at least, the horrors of wartime London seemed to exist in another place.

As the train rattled along, I noticed there were some soldiers in uniform. They looked clean and smart, carrying their kit, all the while laughing and joking among themselves. I assumed that their leave was probably over; maybe they were returning to their regiments. There were two other servicemen sitting separately, their uniforms looking bedraggled and unwashed, as they just stared blankly into the distance. An airman sat reading a letter, then he looked up with a troubled expression, crumpled the letter, and returned it to his pocket. One or two older gentlemen concentrated on their newspapers, while several women, mostly East End girls like me, were just going about their business.

It was all perfectly normal except, for me, that day was anything but normal. It was only at night when the two separate worlds came together: transport by day, and subterranean shelter by night.

A woman said, "You all right, dear, you look a bit shaken up?"

"Not really," I replied.

"Anything I can do, luv?"

She didn't ask why; she didn't need to. The offer of help was kind, but this was how it was, especially in the East End. I shook my head, not letting anything distract me. Getting home to my parents was all I could think about, I couldn't cope with anything else. When the train arrived at Stockwell, the same woman got off with me.

"Are you sure I can't help you, luv, where are you going?"

I told her where I was going and she said she was heading in the same direction. I don't suppose she really was going in my direction at all, but she insisted on coming with me. I hardly spoke to her and wouldn't even recognise her if I saw her again, but I will never forget the kindness of that stranger. I wonder now if I would have made it without her; I was in such a state of shock, I hardly knew what I was doing.

Chapter Two
Stockwell

I seemed to have no say in the matter; like a moth to a flame, I was being drawn inexorably towards the reassurance of familiar things. I thanked the stranger as best I could, and she let go of my hand. The unassuming red-brick terraced house in front of me beckoned like an outstretched hand. I struggled as always with the little front gate, lifting it from its latch. The stone hedgehog sat in the usual place; its only purpose was to watch over that tiny patch of garden. Perhaps most reassuring of all was the green-painted front door. Here at last was the salvation I had struggled so hard to reach.

Despite all our differences, the house I grew up in was the only place in London which felt normal, and the only place where I would feel safe. I don't know how I got through that morning, every step seeming to require yet another act of willpower, another demand on my diminishing spirit. That far at least I had succeeded but despite my best efforts, it was a battle I was in imminent danger of losing. I couldn't wait a moment longer; my resolve grew weaker with every faltering step towards the door. I so desperately needed to just let go.

The lion-head door knocker, freshly painted black, shone resplendent in the early afternoon sun, its former rusty self now consigned to my childhood memory when it had always been just beyond my reach. It seemed to look down at me with a welcoming smile, inviting me to reach out towards it. I momentarily rested my weight against it, to regain my balance.

Two loud knocks, and I stood back with my head bowed, looking down at my trembling hands. All the suppressed memories of the past twelve hours waited menacingly, like an uninvited intruder, just on the edge of my consciousness. It would only require the slightest opportunity for them to torment me again.

It felt like an age, but it was probably only seconds before the door opened. One glimpse of my mother's face and my resolve to keep going just melted away; those ghastly memories came flooding back. I was living in a world of unspeakable horror, but standing in front of me was love, warmth and comfort. I poured myself into her arms and burst into tears.

"Oh Lily, what's happened?" she asked, a sense of alarm in her voice.

I couldn't speak; I tried to, but just couldn't draw breath. I felt as if I was shivering with cold, my legs giving way beneath me.

"*Jack, come quickly,*" Mum shouted, the alarm in her voice escalating towards panic.

Dad must have sensed her alarm and ran from the kitchen, knocking over a cup of tea. This was completely out of character for my father; he was a sergeant in the last war, and usually nothing flustered him. He took one look at me clinging limply in my mother's arms and just did what my Dad always did; he took control of everything. Having scooped me up in his arms, he carried me into the house as if I were no more than a dusty old raincoat.

"What's happened, Lily, are you badly hurt?"

I could hear him talking to me, I could see his lips move, but somehow it seemed unreal. His comforting voice was like a dream I didn't want to wake up from. I felt that, if I spoke at all, it would suddenly make this whole situation real.

"She's in shock," he said, "quickly now, get blankets and a hot water bottle, and I'll get the brandy."

I remember them wrapping me up in blankets in the armchair, and Dad making me sip the brandy. It took my breath away for a moment, but it stopped me breathing so rapidly.

"We'll need plenty of hot tea," he said, and as Mum rushed off, he shouted after her, "and lots of sugar, Pam."

He cupped my bruised and grazed face in his big reassuring hands and kissed my forehead.

"You're safe now, Princess, I've got you."

When I was little, I remember my father as being a rather distant figure. We were not really that close, but if ever I bumped my head or grazed a knee, my Dad would pick me up and say those same words. As a child I had needed those reassuring words more than most, and I was desperate for them now. I tried to drink the tea but my hands were still shaking, so Mum held the cup for me. Dad seemed to know instinctively what had happened.

"You've been bombed out, haven't you, where were you, are you sure you're not hurt?"

"I don't know why I'm not dead," I said, "it was terrible."

"You don't mean you were at home," Mum asked, "why weren't you down the Tube?"

I tried to answer her but must have made little sense, as I tried to tell them I had been babysitting the twins next door for Linda. They did their best to console me, but nothing could ever erase those memories.

"Oh Mum, I can still see the look of terror in Linda's eyes."

"Is Linda all right, and the twins?" Mum asked.

"They're dead, Mum, they're all dead!"

"Oh God no, not those lovely boys."

"Tell us what happened, luv," Dad said, "how close did the bomb fall?"

"It fell directly into my house, and if I hadn't been next door with Linda, I would have been killed."

My parents listened to my sorry story with a look of horror on their faces. It was more than Mum could bear, and she broke down in tears.

"Oh my God, we almost lost you as well," she sobbed, clasping both hands to her mouth.

She was trying hard to stay in control, but a dreadful feeling of pain and sorrow inhabited that house; it lay barely hidden in every dark recess. It only required the slightest prompting for it to emerge from the shadows. Dad said nothing, just squeezed my hand, but the distressed expression on his face said it all.

It had been less than a year since my brother Ian was killed at Dunkirk, and the pain of his death had not receded for a second. It hung over my family like a pall of suffocating smoke. I had lost nobody that close before, so had nothing to prepare me for the awful feeling of grief. He was my younger brother, a part of me that can never be replaced. To feel any greater pain seemed incomprehensible to me, but I discovered that sharing my parents' grief was even more devastating.

I knew neither of them would ever be the same again, especially my mother; I doubted any of us would. My presence in these circumstances inevitably invited the spectre of Ian's death into the void that we each had inside us. Dad, however, did his best to deal with one situation at a time.

"Just tell us what happened," he said, trying to conceal the tremor in his voice.

I told them as best as I could, telling them how kind Ivy Johnson and Rose had been, and how the stranger on the Tube walked with me from the station. As I was recalling the morning's events, I looked up at my parents, to see they were hanging onto my every word. Mum poured me another cup of tea as Dad cleaned up my various cuts and grazes. It was only a speck, but the sight of the blood on the towel suddenly brought back the terrible image of Linda and the boys, and I burst into tears again. My Dad had a reputation as a hard man and always looked as if he hadn't a compassionate bone in his body, but the reality was the exact opposite as far as his only daughter was concerned.

"I've got you, Princess, you're safe now," he whispered.

I felt safe in his arms and abandoned any attempt to remain in control; I just let go. He said nothing – there was no need to - he just had to be there. My recollections of that afternoon and evening are vague. I remember Dad carrying the tin bath in from outside, putting it in the kitchen where the steaming gas copper was heating the water. I remember a loud knock on the door. It was two air raid wardens - Dad was in charge of the local group.

"Not tonight," Dad said, "I'm sorry, my Lily's in trouble."

"Anything we can do, Jack?" came the reply.

"No, it's okay, but I've got to be with her tonight. Can you report back to me later?"

I knew he shouldn't have done that, which is probably why I remember it. When the water was hot, Mum helped me into the bath, and it felt good to wash that dreadful day away. For a moment, I scrubbed frantically, desperate to loosen death's dusty grip on me, but gradually the warmth eased my pains. I sat there until the water was cold and my skin wrinkled.

Finally, feeling clean again and wearing some of my mother's clothes, I sat with them and tried to eat something. I was so tired, all I wanted to do was go to bed. Mum was insistent that I should write to Gerry as soon as possible.

"I know, I'll do it tomorrow," I said. "I wish he was here with me now, but you know what would have happened if he had been home."

Mum thought about it for a moment. She realised what I was thinking, and just raised her eyes toward the ceiling for a moment. Dad looked distracted and kept looking at his watch, and then as the air-raid siren sounded, I realised why. My heart jumped in my chest - "*Oh God, not again!*" Dad could see the panic in my eyes. Knowing I would react badly, he immediately put his arm around me and held me tightly.

"Okay, no rush, plenty of time to get into the shelter," Dad said in his most reassuring voice. He hastened to check that his blackout was perfectly in place, and then he glanced back through the kitchen door. "Buggered if I'm leaving that jar of Bovril behind, not going to let those bastards get my Bovril. Pop that in the tin, will you Pam, and quickly get that piece of cheese you've got in the larder."

Their air raid drill was well-rehearsed, the tin always at the ready to take any food leftovers with them to the shelter. The gas masks were in their place on the hall table, as was a Thermos flask of hot tea which Mum had quietly prepared without me noticing. My head was full of that awful wailing sound of the siren. As we stepped out into the garden, the sound was suddenly louder. If Dad hadn't been holding me so tightly, I would have covered my ears and screamed.

Three or four steps into the absolute blackness of the night and the siren wound down. By the time we reached the Anderson shelter, it had stopped. I'm not sure what was worse, the terrible wailing, or the silence. The only things we could see in the absolute blackness of the night were some distant searchlights combing across the night sky. The only sound we heard was one of Dad's ARP colleagues shouting at some unfortunate neighbour.

"Put that bloody light out!"

I remember when Gerry helped Dad to build the shelter. Not content with the instructions which came with it, they built a brick wall at the back, and a double brick wall at the entrance; the space between was filled with earth. The rest of the garden was hollow because they piled all the soil up over the shelter, and Dad complained that it was not good for his vegetables.

Everything was there, ready for us. Dad had built bunk beds, there was canned food and dried milk, spare clothes, a jerrycan full of water, candles, an oil lamp, another tin for important documents. The government told us the spacious Anderson shelter would accommodate up to six people but at 6ft 6in x 4ft 6in, it was claustrophobic for one person, let alone six. The blankets were damp, everything was damp, and that night it was freezing cold.

We sat in a dreadful anticipatory silence, watching our condensed breath rise in the flickering candlelight. We just looked at each other, listening for the sound of approaching death and destruction. There was no playing at being the mop man, no attempt to make light of the situation; we all knew the drill. With my heart racing, I clung to the only vestige of control I had left. The first explosions were only a distant rumble, but the moment I heard them, I shook. First it was my hands and then, as the bombs came closer, it was my entire body.

There was an ack-ack battery near to the house; the sound of those guns was just as frightening as the bombs. Again and again, as they fired, we could feel the vibration. For a while, it continued relentlessly as the bombers went overhead. Dad kept reassuring me that we were perfectly safe in the shelter, but no comforting words could stop me from shaking.

Then we heard the drone of the bombers again, a distant rumble at first which gradually grew louder and louder, and then the sound of more ack-ack, followed by ever-closer explosions. The bombs were close enough to make the ground shake, and the candle flickered as a remnant of the shock wave found us there huddled together. Dad lit the oil lamp.

There was a period of silence; for a moment I thought it was over, but it was just a cruel illusion. Some ten minutes later, we heard the drone of a second wave of approaching bombers. The ack-ack guns opened up again just as the sound of falling bombs was growing louder. The cacophony of noise appeared to reach a crescendo, as my grip got ever tighter on the blanket which I was holding over my head. That terrifying sound was as nothing compared to the moment the bombs exploded. The shelter shook violently; I felt the pressure of the shock wave hit my chest, and the oil lamp swung on its hook. All I could think about was that awful image of Linda and the boys being buried alive.

I lost whatever self-control I had left. I pulled my legs up into my chest, put my hands over my ears and screamed. I remember little else until it was over; I don't even recall hearing the all-clear siren. Dad carried me out of the shelter and back towards the house.

"Thank God, looks like the house is okay," Mum said; the relief in her voice was palpable. "Get her inside as quick as you can, Jack."

I just remember Dad carrying me effortlessly inside and up the stairs to my bedroom, where he laid me down. I could not understand why Mum was so keen for me to get into my nightdress. She tried to save my embarrassment by saying my borrowed clothes needed to go into the wash. Dad returned with a hot water bottle, telling me a cup of tea was on its way, but I just sat there shaking.

"I'm so sorry, Dad, I don't know what's happening to me."

"Don't you worry, Princess. I saw some of the most courageous men I ever served with react like this in the trenches; it's shell-shock."

"What's that?"

"The MO explained it to me; it's just your body's reaction to the stress, you can't turn it off."

"But look at me, I'm shaking like a leaf."

"I know you are, Princess, but I promise you *will* get over it. Let me get you something."

With that, he stood up and went back downstairs. I heard the back door open and close with its distinctive clunk. A few moments later he was back, sitting once again on my bed. He held a brown leaf from the sycamore tree in the garden and placed it on the blanket.

"Be grateful you're shaking like a leaf, Princess, this leaf isn't shaking, is it?"

I looked at the leaf and then at Dad, suddenly realising what he was so graphically telling me. Linda and her lovely boys were gone. My brother Ian was gone. So many people were gone, but I was still here.

Chapter Three
Picking up the Pieces

I slept fitfully, with the sound of falling bombs and the awful image of Linda and the boys haunting me. Dad left the house early to carry out his Air Raid Warden duties, so Mum and I had breakfast together. It didn't amount to much, just a slice of bread with a bit of margarine and Golden Shred. Above all, it was the cup of tea that I most urgently needed.

"We must get you some new ration books," Mum said. "That's one of the first things we need to get sorted out, your father will know what to do."

She was right, life had to go on. Now that I had none of the little extras which Gerry brought home from the Docks, it was up to me to pick up the pieces. So many people were in the same position. But when you have lost absolutely everything, the feeling of helplessness can be overwhelming.

"You must write to Gerry and tell him what's happened. You can't have your husband coming home and finding the house destroyed," Mum insisted.

I worried every day about Gerry, never knowing where he was, or what danger he was in. All I knew was that he was on board HMS Hood. Gerry had been beside himself when he was assigned to the Hood. It was the biggest and most powerful battlecruiser in the world, so I consoled myself thinking surely that fact alone would keep him safe. Now that the bombing had started, he would be as worried about me as I was about him. 'Please God, keep him safe,' I mumbled under my breath.

"See if you can't find a telephone box that works," Mum said, "you need to get in touch with your firm and tell them when you'll be back."

My job had been the last thing on my mind, but I could see what Mum was doing; I needed to take back control of my life. I tried to write a letter to Gerry, but the writing was so terrible with my shaking hands, I worried that Gerry would instantly read between the lines and assume all was not well. For the sake of another day, I thought I would wait just a little longer and type it at work.

The prospect of leaving the house made me feel anxious. Mum could see I was apprehensive. It was silly, and I knew I had to get over it.

"Come on, luv, the fresh air will do you good, it's a lovely bright day," she said, "and take my coat from the hall stand; it's quite fresh outside."

The coat was too big for me, but I put it on, anyway. It smelled of the rosewater Mum used as substitute perfume. I pulled up the collar and breathed in the smell - it's strange how something I had hardly noticed before could suddenly become such a comfort.

The moment I opened the front door, the sunlight confronted me - a stark reminder that this was another day. I stood in the warm cocoon of home, looking out onto the harsh reality of the wider world before me. For a moment, I stood in my own hinterland, unable to go forward, trying not to go back. Two steps out, and I closed the door behind me. I looked back at the lion-head knocker for reassurance. It momentarily made me smile, the memory of when I was too small to reach it still fresh in my mind.

The stone hedgehog just looked at me, inert as ever. Perhaps that was its charm, bound to the ground by its mossy overcoat, immovable, dependable. Dad used to assure me we had no slugs in the garden because the hedgehog came alive at night and gobbled them all up. I had always believed every word of whatever my Dad told me. A few more steps and the little gate resisted my attempts to open it as usual.

I did not know where the bombs had fallen the night before, though it was close by. I expected to see the aftermath with all its attendant horrors laid out before me. To my amazement and relief, our road looked perfectly normal; it must have been one of the adjacent roads which was hit. It was a bright crisp March day, and people were going about their business as usual. I couldn't understand it. My lovely friend Linda and her boys were dead, my home was rubble - how could it be that the sun was still shining and these people were oblivious to the horror I'd lived through. I could see the people and feel the sun on my face, but I felt resentful of the normality of it.

The nearest phone box was on the corner nearby, but you never knew if it would work or not. When it did work, you somehow felt you had won a prize, creating an involuntary need to punch the air in celebration. Every step towards it was like an event in its own right, one event followed by another. Step by step, I approached the telephone box, all the while considering where to go next, in case it didn't work. Miraculously, not only was it working, but nobody was waiting to use it.

I breathed a spontaneous sigh of relief. I pushed my coins into the slot, dropping one on the floor, so then I had to struggle in the cramped box to reach down to pick it up. Finally, I could dial the number of the firm where I worked. Marcia answered the phone as usual, but for a moment I forgot to press button 'A.' Eventually I remembered to press it and as the coins fell into the box, I could hear Marcia's reassuring voice.

"Thank God you're okay, Lily, he's been beside himself with worry!"

"Is he worried about me, or is it just that he can't manage without me?" I said, trying to sound cheery.

"He's worried about you, Lily, you know what he's like."

I knew full well that George would be worried sick about me so told Marcia to reassure him, I would be back in the office the next morning. George served with my Dad in the First War; he was Dad's commanding officer. I know they went through a lot together, especially at the Battle of Passchendaele. Dad carried George to safety when he was wounded, saving his life. I'm not sure anyone else can understand the bond that kind of thing creates between two men. Considering the large social divide between them, it probably accounts for the unlikely friendship they formed after the war.

He was such a regular visitor, almost like a member of our household, I had always regarded him as almost a second father; he was 'Uncle George' to me. When I look back now, it was an unorthodox relationship, but I didn't question it at the time; nor did I question it later when he offered me a job in his business for which I was wholly unqualified. I loved him like a father, and when I now look back from later in life, nothing has changed the bond we shared.

I stepped out of the phone box, feeling pleased with myself. It wasn't much, but I had achieved something. When I looked up, I noticed Dad walking down the road towards me. He didn't notice me at first, just seeming to stare into oblivion; it had been a long morning for him. He was carrying his helmet under his arm, drawing hard on a fag. His grim face ashen grey, and there was no bounce in his stride. The moment he saw me he made a reasonable attempt at a smile, but I could see something was troubling him. He put his arm around me and we walked home together.

"A lot of destruction in Grantham Road," he said, with little or no emotion in his voice. "It was more than one bomb, half the road's gone, eight dead. I found the Roberts family all dead in their shelter."

Dad didn't mention Grantham Road again, nor the eight people who had lost their lives. I knew he was friendly with the Roberts'; he used to play bowls with Bob Roberts before the war. We walked silently together, passing two middle-aged women going in the other direction.

"Morning, Jack, that was terrible last night, wasn't it?" one of them said gravely.

Dad hardly responded, just a muffled 'yes', and a nod. I was aware enough to realise he was holding back a lot of emotion. As the sound of their footsteps receded into the distance, I glanced back at the women. I noticed the long shadow I was dragging along the pavement behind me, and I despised the sun for shining so brightly.

My walk to the telephone box and back had only occupied twenty-five minutes, but it felt as if I had been out all morning. The moment I walked back into the house, I slumped into one of the kitchen chairs and put my head in my hands.

"This is no good, Lily," Dad said, firmly, "there isn't time for this. I'll take the day off work; I'm taking you back to Stepney. We need to go to the Food Office there, to get your new ration books and documents. And I'll have a quick look at your house just in case there's anything worth salvaging."

He was being stern with me, but I knew he was right, and so admired his strength and fortitude. He had just witnessed something utterly horrific, he'd lost a friend, and yet he was concerned for me. I had to get a new identity card, and ration books, and then I had to register my ration books with the local shops in Stockwell. Until then, I would share what rations Mum and Dad had.

I also needed to go to the bank which we used for work; even though they knew me, I would still need an identity card. There was a lot to do, but I was in expert hands. Dad made it a part of his job to help bomb victims get back on their feet, so he knew exactly what to do.

We retraced my journey of the day before. The Tube train

was as reassuring as ever, but this time I didn't feel so conspicuous. There was the usual huddle of humanity carrying on
with business as usual. No doubt behind each face there was
another story to tell; few people in my part of London walked
free of the shadow cast by the Grim Reaper. Despite the heartache concealed inside, we all just got on with whatever we had
to do. I coped with it all until we finally approached where my
house had been.

"Good God! How did you walk away from this?" Dad said
in amazement.

I couldn't bear to look and turned away; I just couldn't go
anywhere near it. It was only a scruffy little red-brick terraced
house, and Rose was right, it *was* damp. One of the rainwater
gutters leaked, leaving a trail of damp all the way down the
wall where various enterprising flora had set up home. We told
the landlord many times, but nothing was ever done. Gerry
said he would fix it, but then Gerry said he would fix a lot of
things. He also said he would fix the door to the privy, and
he didn't get around to that either. When it snowed the week
before, it was blowing in around the door like a blizzard, and
my clothes were full of snow before I realised it. Believe me,
you did not want to spend a long time in there.

We had not been married long and couldn't afford much
furniture; we just had a few hand-me-downs from both sets
of parents. Our tiny house had little to commend it, but the
thing was, it was *our* little house. How dare that bastard Hitler
take it away from us! As for Linda's house, I can never see a pile
of rubble again without reliving that dreadful image.

There was nothing there to salvage; even if there had been,
it would have already disappeared. It wouldn't have been the
neighbours, we stood by each other in the East End, but there
was always the odd stranger to be seen, lurking about in the
wake of other folk's troubles. I suppose they are like the weeds
that found a foothold on the wall of my house - opportunists
who only need the right conditions to thrive. People like

my Dad, who had been through the last war, were unable to understand it.

We did everything we needed to do in Stepney, including the endless waiting in the Food Office. There seemed to be an almost continuous stream of humanity queuing to replace their lost documents. We looked like a line of flotsam washed up on the high tide mark - numerous people standing in everything they owned, staring ahead but seeing nothing. Few of them had any conversation; just one person's story would have described us all.

I found it all mentally and physically tiring by the time we got home; it had exhausted me. Mum was pleased to see me back with my replacement ration books; getting enough food to eat was not a trivial matter. Although I had gone straight to the local shops to register my new books, it was too late in the day to buy any food worth having.

Following my trip to the bank, I had also bought some clothes. With so little choice then, most of what I bought was second hand. It was more than I wanted to spend, but I couldn't continue to wear Mum's cast-offs. Clothes were important to me, and at least they were not subject to the ration system - not yet anyway.

I liked the new fashion of wearing trousers, so I found a couple of nice pairs, and some skirts and blouses. I also found some hand-knitted short sleeved jumpers. Someone must have knitted the jumpers for herself or for family; beautifully made, they had pride locked into every stitch. They had obviously never been worn, and I shuddered to think of why they had found their way into a second-hand shop.

It was late afternoon, and the last of the bright sunshine clung tenaciously to the rooftops opposite. As a day is born with the arrival of the sun, so it dies as the setting sun surrenders to the dark forces of the night. Somehow, I got through that day, and I was now determined not to surrender to those dark forces which lay ahead. I remember thinking another sunrise was waiting for me the following morning, and I wanted to see it.

Mum was busy doing the best she could to prepare something for us to eat, so I set about helping her scrub potatoes. They were the one vegetable still reasonably plentiful, and Mum had a thousand things she could do with them, sometimes even making potato pancakes. She had bought three sausages and a cabbage for that night's dinner. My Mum was a wonderful cook. I just wished I had her enthusiasm and talent for it. She would rummage around in a larder that wouldn't support a church mouse and then, as if by magic, something miraculous would appear on the table.

That night it was toad-in-the-hole, which she perched on top of a bed of bubble-and-squeak. She placed it in the middle of the table on a large china dish. The thick brown gravy spilled out of the batter and ran around the edge of the dish, and I could see the pride in her eyes as she denounced it as just another meagre meal. She did all the work and then Dad set about it with the carving knife, cutting it into perfect portions, after which Mum praised him as if he had produced it all himself.

There was something about the meal that night. I'm not sure what it was, but for a moment I had a tear in my eye and a lump in my throat. The ritual with the carving knife and the predictable 'This looks wonderful, luv', to which Mum would say, 'Oh, it's not much, best I could manage.' She always belittled her efforts but was unable to conceal her considerable pride. My parents had a rocky start to their marriage. It had a nasty effect upon me as a child but beneath it all, I knew they loved each other.

We were not the most united family, but the dinner ritual was the one occasion when we were a family together. This was a scene being played out across Britain, but this was *my* family, and suddenly I realised the significance of it all. This was what we were fighting for, this was the British way of life; it was my family's way of life. In 1940, Mr Churchill had said, "*We shall defend our island whatever the cost - we shall never surrender.*" He was damned right!

Dad quickly finished his dinner with one eye peering at the clock. No sooner had he wiped his plate clean with a slice of bread, than he had to leave. He picked up his helmet and gas mask to prepare for his ARP duties. Mum said nothing, but I knew it terrified her each night that he went out. Dad would always give her a hug and a kiss goodbye; now, for the first time, I realised the full significance of that hug.

As an air raid warden, Dad's job was to check the blackout in the local roads and to help anyone left in the open to find a shelter. He and his team knew everyone locally, doing an invaluable job but all the while he was helping and directing other people, he himself remained at the mercy of the falling bombs.

Sometimes he made it back to our Anderson, but more often he ended up in the public shelter three roads away. He would never admit it, but I knew sometimes he didn't get to a shelter at all. No wonder Mum was so worried; no wonder every hug was significant. I don't know how they did it; most of the wardens were part-time volunteers. Dad would work for hours at night, and often in the early morning. Then he would have some breakfast and go to work at his job with the Council in the building department.

We were halfway through the washing up when the siren sounded. I was expecting it, I had been living with it for months, but still I shook as Mum and I carried out the usual procedure. I think I did a good job of appearing calm, but beneath the surface I was in turmoil. It was one of those nights when the bombs fell elsewhere. We could hear the distant rumble of exploding bombs, and all the while we felt guilty for being happy that it was some other poor sod being killed, not us.

When it was finally over and the all-clear had sounded,

we went back into the house where Mum's spirit lifted immediately. No local bombs meant Dad was okay, so his absence was nothing to worry about. It was late, so we chatted together while we waited for him to return. I mentioned Ian, as we so often did. I found it immensely painful to talk about him but somehow, we just couldn't help ourselves. The large photograph of him on the mantelpiece was usually the trigger which prompted a recollection or memory. He was only two years younger than me, but I always felt very protective of him. We had learned to depend upon each other during our tough childhood years.

Ian was with the 2nd Battalion, The Royal Warwickshire Regiment. Among others, they fought the heroic rear-guard action which held the Germans at bay while the troops were evacuated from the beaches of Dunkirk. We were told he was gravely wounded, one of the few rear-guard soldiers carried back to the beach for evacuation. It was the last day of the evacuation, on 4th June 1940, when he was lost. We didn't know exactly what happened but we knew from reports that two stretcher-bearers got him as far as the Mole. Perhaps it was too late, perhaps the last of the little boats had gone, or perhaps they even made it onto a boat - we had no idea.

All we knew was that in amongst all the confusion we lost him, together with those two brave stretcher-bearers. They were all lost without a trace, so we have no grave; there's nothing - he only exists in our memories. Whenever I think of Ian, inevitably I think of those two men who tried so valiantly to save him. What greater sacrifice can there be; they died trying to save my brother. If either of them had a grave, I would kiss the ground they lie in.

The pain never goes away; the period of disbelief and denial gives way to resignation, but the pain remains the same. We tried to remember the wonderful memories - he always had something funny to say, was full of humour, and his smiling face is the face I try to remember. The photograph of him on the mantelpiece was typical of Ian, clowning about with an enormous smile. This is the point where the happy memory turns sour. When the end came, he wasn't clowning about, nor was he smiling; we can only imagine his terror in those last seconds. This is the pain we live with.

Chapter Four

Back to Work

The following morning the sun rose again. It couldn't expunge all that had gone before, but the light heralded a brand new, unblemished day, and I found I was pleased to see it. If Dad hadn't knocked on my bedroom door, I would have slept on, so it was with bleary eyes that I sat down with them for a slice of toast. I still felt very shaky, constantly aware of my heart beating.

"How are you, luv?" Dad asked, worried about me.

"Fine, I must get on, it's more of a journey to get to work from here."

"You're not fine at all, but maybe going to work will help you get over it," Mum said, as she spread a thin layer of marmalade on her toast.

"Pass me the marmalade will you, luv," said Dad.

In so many ways it was just another day in that dreadful war, but for me it would be a challenge. I had to get over to the Royal Docks at West Ham; the journey had been easier when I was doing it from Stepney. Our office was right next to Victoria Dock, on the second floor of one of those tall red-brick Victorian buildings which symbolised the prosperity of that period. I looked down on the Dock from my office window.

Before the war, it was always a hive of industry as ships

came and went, with cranes constantly lifting goods either to or from cargo holds. Dockers were seen everywhere, loading, lifting, stacking, or even riding the jib of a crane. Occasionally I would catch sight of Gerry, and he would wave his docker's hook in the air - the ubiquitous tool which all the dockers carried.

Above all, I felt as if I was part of something important. As shipping agents, we were a vital cog in the economic engine of the country, organising everything on behalf of the shipowner. I would take care of their paperwork, arrange their dock time, and ensure their cargo was always in the right place, at the right time. Ship owners depended on me and after many years, they no longer questioned my arrangements; I was fully in charge of my remit.

The bombing had changed the Docks profoundly, and day-to-day business had to work around the damage. It was an ever-increasing struggle; ships didn't want to be in port during the night. Even arriving at the office almost on time that morning felt like an achievement; I was quite pleased with myself. The bomb damage around the Docks was so terrible, I was amazed that we conducted any business at all. It really spoke volumes about the London spirit. The latest overnight raid had left yet another trail of destruction, but once again our office was spared. I walked up the stairs, looking forward to seeing familiar faces.

George gave me such a hug, as did Marcia.

"When you didn't turn up, Lily, I really feared the worst," George confessed. "I knew it must have been something serious."

I described what had happened but was unable to bring myself to mention Linda and the boys as I reassured him that I was all right. Then, to my complete surprise, Marcia appeared carrying a tray of tea and biscuits. We sat down, smiling at each other; this was something we never did, not first thing in the morning!

"What's all this, Marcia, you never treated me like Royalty before!"

"I really feared the worst, Lily, I'm just so relieved you're all right, we both are."

"Can I have tea and biscuits like this every morning, George?"

"As far as I'm concerned, Lily, you *are* Royalty. You can have whatever you want! I don't mind admitting this place ground to a halt without you here."

"There you are, George, that wasn't so bad, was it? You finally admitted you can't do without me!"

We all laughed. I did struggle at first when I arrived there as a teenager, because I couldn't call him 'Uncle George'. Even though I was now twenty-seven years old, I still thought of him as my Uncle. He always treated me like the daughter he never had, we had a wonderful bond between us. George knew full well that I would do anything for him. He had a disastrous marriage, the poor man; I'm not surprised there were no children. This was why he spent so much time with us in Stockwell. He finally left her and set up home by himself, so sad. Marcia had long since lost her husband, and I always thought she had a soft spot for George; she had been with him right from the start and they seemed to support one another.

Over the next few weeks, we established a pattern of life. I went to work each morning, always exhausted after a night with little sleep, a genuine problem for everyone. On the Tube in the morning, it was commonplace to see people dropping off to sleep, often sailing past their station. Everything about my job was getting more and more difficult, with ships being lost at sea and freight often days or weeks late. Communications were interrupted or even non-existent, and I grew tired of organising Dock time and transport, only to have to do it all over again.

As the shipowners' representative, they would heap all their problems onto us, and the more troublesome things became, the more they relied on me. Before the war, I used to enjoy my job, and mostly I had the shipowners eating out of the palm of my hand. Things changed during the chaos of the war, and I was growing weary of shipowners asking me the same question, "So what are you going to *do* about it?" Mostly, there was nothing I *could* do.

I knew I wasn't coping as I used to; I would get home tired and exhausted, always in fear of the next raid. Every night, Dad would say, "I'll see you later," while Mum and I prayed he would return. Every night the same fear, the same trip to the 'Andy', never knowing if a bomb had your name on it. I tried hard to cope with it all, and was starting to get on top of it, but I just could not seem to put my terrors behind me. Night after night, I sat shaking in the shelter. Mum was overly concerned about me, and one day it all came to a head.

I arrived at work as usual, only to find it gone! George, Marcia, an Air Raid Warden and all the staff were standing there on the other side of what was once the road. There was absolutely nothing left standing, just rubble everywhere. When such familiar surroundings are razed to the ground, it's difficult to adjust - I wasn't even sure exactly where our building had been.

I stood with a blank expression on my face, just like George and Marcia, unable to comprehend what I was looking at. The Victorian building had stood there since 1855, witness to the once-growing prosperity of the nation. Every brick probably had a story to tell but lying there on the ground, none of it made any sense; all the history and the memories had been erased. The past had let go its association with the present; now it was just the forgotten past.

It had been a heavy raid on the Docks, with the devastation far-reaching. We were told it was one of those landmines they dropped with a parachute. The Warden knew all about landmines, and seemed to revel in the details, saying this had been one of the big ones, 2200 pounds of explosive. They explode at roof height, so that the blast wave rips through the buildings, rather than penetrating the ground. The result was obvious to see.

"I think it was offices here," the Warden said.

"It was," I replied, "shipping agents."

"That's right, I remember. I've seen you before, haven't I, did you know the place?"

"It's where I worked."

"Oh, I'm sorry, but at least you weren't there when it happened. I've got to press on, take care, luv."

The Warden went on his cheery way and left us standing there. We said little, just staring at the rubble in disbelief, as if some irrational thought were telling us this was all an awful dream from which we would shortly wake. George had set up his business there in 1924 after the First War, so this was the end of an incredibly significant part of his life, and it showed. He had tears in his eyes; even the junior girl was in tears. This was her first job, and she had only been with us for two months.

"What will you do?" I asked George.

"I can't start again at my age," he said, with a sad look of resignation in his eyes. "It's always been my intention that you would take over the business when I retired. I think I've just retired Lily!"

I was more than a little taken aback. "You mean you want *me* to take over the business. Why would you give it to me?"

"Who else would I pass it on to, Lily?"

"I couldn't do that, it's your family business."

"And you're my family, Lily; besides, you virtually run the place single-handed, anyway."

I was only just coping as it was; I didn't think I could manage any more pressure.

"You know how hard it's been since the war started," I said tearfully, "and it was hard enough before that. How can you run a shipping agency when half your ships lie at the bottom of the ocean? I couldn't do it, George, not starting all over again, not without you."

Then something happened that quite took my breath away. Marcia put her arm in George's and said, "Let's just go home, George; come on, it's time we put our feet up."

The inference was obvious; she meant them going home together.

"Are you telling me you two are living together? All the years I've known you both, and I didn't know - how on earth have you kept it a secret?"

They were both very middle class and tied up with social protocol, and Marcia looked embarrassed. "Oh dear, I'm so sorry George, what have I said?"

"Oh, it's too late now," George replied.

"The thing is, Lily, we had to keep it a secret, even from you. You know George is still legally married?"

"Well yes, I think so."

I knew George's wife had been difficult about their divorce. Dad had told me - it was a long time ago. I think I probably just assumed they had divorced.

"It's the shame, Lily, we can't have people knowing we're living together, not like that."

"Well, goodness me! I've been working with a pair of clandestine lovers all these years, and I had no idea! Come here, the pair of you, let me give you both a hug."

"Do you mean you're not disappointed in us, Lily?" Marcia asked.

"Disappointed, don't be ridiculous, I'm delighted for you both."

What a momentous day it had turned out to be, I had just lost my job, but I couldn't help smiling. They made me promise not to tell Mum and Dad, but happiness was such a fleeting commodity during the war, I didn't think they had anything to be ashamed of. I told them they shouldn't waste a moment longer worrying about it.

Marcia suggested we should go down the road to the nice little tea shop and have a cuppa. It was obviously the quintessential British thing to do; all our lives had changed irrevocably, so what the situation required was a cup of tea! I told our handful of staff members to go home, and we turned our backs on the bomb site and walked away. Only after several paces did we momentarily stop to look back.

"I suppose we knew it was likely to happen," George said philosophically.

"Doesn't really prepare you though, does it?" I replied, trying my best to hold back a tear.

The tea shop was a lovely little place, but that day there was bomb damage close by; they had a broken window, and rubble right outside the door. It was business as usual inside, and we found a quiet corner table away from the broken window.

I suspected that Marcia was not sure if she felt upset about the office or jubilant that she could finally discard the burden of their secret. George was devastated, adamant that he couldn't face trying to rebuild the business. He said he'd been thinking about retiring soon anyway, and this was the right time for him to put on his slippers. Looking at the pair of them, I thought that was the right decision and George, especially, was too upset to do anything; I felt desperately sorry for him.

"Okay, leave it to me George, let's go to your place and get the records you keep at home. I can use your telephone, and I can send telegrams. I'll contact the owners whose ships are in transit and cancel the future contracts. The outstanding accounts need to be sent; I'll pay the wages to the end of the week and make all the loose ends disappear."

"My God, Lily, you really are amazing!" George said, trying hard not to break down. "I feel I've let you down, this is *your* future more than it's mine."

"No, you haven't let me down George, this is the right time for me to move on."

"Do you mean that Lily? I couldn't live with myself if I thought I was letting you down."

"I mean it George, I really do, I'm not sure I could run a shipping agency without you; perhaps I need a fresh challenge."

"You so underestimate yourself, Lily! I know you feel I only took you on because I think of you as family, but you're wrong. I saw that sparkle in your eye long before you came here as a typist. You didn't get where you are because I gave you a helping hand; you're an amazing woman, Lily. You should be so proud of yourself - with your abilities, there is nothing you *couldn't* do. I wish I could make you see that; just look at what you've done for this business. We all know I would have sunk long ago without you. Whatever is left in the account after we settle everything, I want you to have it all, Lily, it's yours by right."

I just didn't know what to say; I knew he really appreciated all I did for him, but he had never expressed it quite like that before. I don't think I *could* have said anything even if I knew what to say! The three of us just sat with our arms around each other. George had made up his mind; he'd had enough. I knew I'd had enough, and Marcia just wanted the two of them to be happy. In the strangest of ways, Hitler had done us all a favour!

It was an interminable day. When I finally got home, I was completely exhausted. What made it worse was knowing that I had several more days like it ahead of me. I'd had nothing to eat, and was starving hungry, but barely had the strength to put fork to mouth. Mum and Dad were shocked, but not entirely surprised to hear about the day's events. Their prime concern was that we were all okay. Inevitably I spent too long talking, and for that moment at least, I lost track of the time.

The siren started wailing earlier than usual, well before I could finish what Mum had prepared for me. It took me by surprise, but the harsh reality of the wailing sound had a way of focusing your mind. The war was dictating every aspect of my life, and I didn't know if I should scream or cry. I decided

I wanted to scream but instead we just picked up our things and marched outside towards the 'Andy'. Dad went off with the other wardens while Mum and I stooped into the shelter. In so many ways I was reaching the end of my tether, and what I desperately did not need was a local raid that night, but that was precisely what we had.

We sat together in silence, waiting for the bombers to come. Mum opened the food tin containing our various leftovers - it raised a momentary smile as we picked our way through it with our fingers. There was a packet of Smiths crisps with its little blue bag of salt. That was as close as we came to a treat, sitting there in the cold and damp of an Anderson shelter.

As the time passed, there was a moment when we thought we might be let off. That abruptly changed moments later when all hell broke loose. The shelter shook violently, and all the while a relentless thumping came through the ground from the ack-ack guns. On two occasions, I felt the shock wave of an explosion hit my chest. I moaned through my teeth, '*For God's sake, I just need some sleep*'. No sooner had it started than it was over; the all-clear sounded but I just remained where I was, shaking.

The next thing we heard was Dad shouting from outside, "Are you okay?"

Mum shouted back, "We're fine, luv". Her next question was, "Is the house okay?"

Dad reassured us that the bombs had fallen three roads away. Our road was unscathed yet again, just a few broken windows.

"Thank heavens, let's get Lily inside," Mum said.

We groped our way back in the dark, and sat around the kitchen table drinking tea, while they both just looked at me.

"I can't see you like this, Lily, it really upsets me, I worry about you all the time. If anything happened to you," she hesitated and paused for breath, "well, you know we wouldn't survive that, don't you, not after Ian."

"Mum's right, luv, it's too dangerous around here; besides, you're just not coping, are you?"

Dad was right, I was not coping, but I wasn't about to admit it.

"We have little option, do we," I said.

"Me and Mum have talked about it, luv, we'd like you to go down to Middlebourne and stay with your Gran. You'd be safe there and it will give you time to recover."

"You mean you want to get rid of me again!"

The moment I said it, I wished I hadn't. I knew it wasn't the case and now was not the time for old grievances. I could tell from their expressions that feelings still ran high even after all the intervening years, but Mum wisely chose not to dwell on it.

"One day, Lily, when you have children of your own, you'll understand the fear of losing a child. I know you lost the baby, but a miscarriage is not the same thing. We don't worry about ourselves, but we live in dread every time there's a raid. We can't lose you, luv, we just can't."

"Mum's right," Dad said, "you have to get yourself better, and we have to know you're safe."

"What about you then, why should you risk your lives here?" I said.

"Can you seriously see your Dad giving in to Hitler, and leaving his home, where we've lived for over thirty years! As long as we have each other and we know you're safe, we can cope with the bombing. Besides, what better time now that your job has gone?"

I had no idea what to say. My Gran was an enormous part of my life, I loved her to bits, but I was a Londoner, an East Ender, I wasn't at home in the country. We talked about it until we were too tired to talk any more. I knew I needed to get away from the bombing, and I desperately needed a proper night's sleep.

Despite our differences, my parents would do anything

for me, yet I could see the burden of worry I was imposing upon them. Reluctantly, I ended up seeing it from their point of view and to their obvious delight, I agreed, saying I could always come back. Before I knew what was happening, telegrams were being sent, and arrangements were being made.

I kept my word to George, making all the loose ends disappear as best as I could, and those I couldn't, I passed on to other agencies. We had very few records left, but I think I dealt with most things. When it was finally over, I had no regrets at all. It was the right time for me to move on. I suspect George thought there would be a sizable amount of cash left in the bank account, but there were more outstanding creditors than he realised. I just took my wages from the account and left what remained.

He used to argue otherwise but I know that, without the opportunity he gave me, I would have remained just another girl from the East End. I shall never forget what he told that young, headstrong teenager, when he said, "Others might run, Lily, but *you* can fly." That was such a pivotal moment in my life, nobody had ever believed in me before. We had a final get-together at their house, to go over the paperwork. Obviously, we would see each other again, but it was the end of an era. It would be a very emotional goodbye.

"This is the moment I've tried to prepare you for, Lily," George said, "but it's so hard to let you go."

George had done everything to prepare me for life, my debt to him was enormous.

"Marcia, you know, don't you?" I asked. "You know how much George has invested in me?"

"Yes, I do Lily, if you mean the private boarding school, then yes I know everything."

"When you say you know everything, what is it you're not telling me, Marcia?"

She looked at George as if she had said the wrong thing. He looked back and his expression confirmed that she had. I wasn't sure what to say. My relationship with George wasn't remotely like a 'friend of the family' relationship; even as a fourteen-year-old I realised that. He took a no-hope East End girl and transformed me into what I am today. He lavished private education on me and when he realised my talent for singing, he introduced me to the opera, and then arranged singing tuition for me. He treated me in every respect as if I was his only daughter.

There was one obvious question I had always wanted to ask him. It was the most important question I could ever imagine but I just couldn't ask it, never feeling fully prepared for the answer. Marcia knew the answer to that question, I could tell she did. I even think she wanted to tell me. There was a period of silence between us. It was not one of those embarrassing silences; it was a lovely moment. They said nothing. Words were unnecessary.

"I owe you absolutely everything George," I said, "there's nothing I can say that could even begin to express my gratitude. All I can say is thank you."

"There's no need to thank me Lily, you give me the credit for what is your own achievement. I didn't make you who you are today, you did that. I just gave you the tools to do it with. The one thing I cannot give you is self-belief. I've known you since the day you were born, Lily. I know you felt unwanted; I know you felt abandoned, but none of it was your fault. Keep fighting those demons, Lily, and you'll go on to greater things."

"I'm trying George, really I am."

"I know you are, you'll have a wonderful life Lily, that's all I want for you."

"I won't disappoint you, George, I promise."

George was right, I struggled with low self-esteem, but he planted a seed of self-belief in me. I hoped together we would watch it grow. It was such a heart-breaking moment; we were all struggling with our goodbyes. I hugged them both for the last time. George and his faithful Marcia stood by their front door as I walked down the path and onto the pavement beyond. I closed the gate, waving to them one more time. The moment I turned my back, I burst into tears.

-oOo-

And so it was that, in April 1941, Mum and Dad went with me to the railway station, and you would have thought I was emigrating to Australia! We stood there on the platform, surrounded by my luggage, with our arms around each other. Mum and I were in tears, and when I looked at Dad, even he had a tear in his eye.

"You've got something in your eye, Dad," I said jokingly.

"Let me see," Mum said, as she handed him her handkerchief, "you're not as tough as you make out, are you, luv!"

"It's just a bit of soot from the train - it's got into my eye."

We all laughed. I wasn't travelling far but knew that, despite our differences, I would miss them terribly, and I knew they would miss me. I waved out of the carriage window continually as the train moved forward, while they followed along, keeping pace with the train as it gently pulled away. Inevitably they came to the end of the platform. Mum was waving frantically, biting her lip, while Dad kept complaining about the damned soot in his eye.

"I'll write as soon as I can," I shouted.

As my carriage pulled away from the shelter of the station, a great cloud of smoke and steam came barrelling down over the window. Mum and Dad disappeared from view, so I quickly slid the window up to exclude the smoke from the carriage.

That was when I realised, I had closed the window on an entire chapter of my life, and another waited for me at the end of the line.

Chapter Five
Middlebourne in Kent

My mind was full of the image of Mum and Dad waving me goodbye. It disturbed and upset me to watch them fade into the distance; it was adding to my lengthy list of such occasions. Gradually, I settled down in my carriage and gazed out of the window. My mind was somewhere between my inner thoughts and the passing scenery, unable to concentrate on either. I shared the carriage with only two other people - an elderly gentleman engrossed in his newspaper, and a woman in her forties who appeared ill-at-ease and restless. She sat opposite me and smiled an acknowledgement which showed that she chose not to speak to me. I smiled back and averted my gaze towards the window.

The initial part of the journey out of London was a constant reminder of the war, with the speed restrictions, not to mention the very visible bomb damage. From a local neighbourhood perspective, it was surprising how quickly we all accepted such destruction as the new normality. The wider vista presented to me by the moving train was quite another matter. The scale of the destruction was terrifying, and I realised any attempt to normalise it was misplaced. The shocking reality was a stark reminder that we were fighting to preserve our culture, our way of life. What if we lost that fight?

As the train progressed and pulled away from the built-up areas, a sense of genuine normality returned. The occasional army truck was visible on the roads near the track, and I noticed a few servicemen on the train moving along the corridor past my compartment but otherwise, my view of the countryside looked as reassuringly normal as it always had. The woman opposite me produced a book from her bag, and apart from the occasional glance out of the window, she concentrated upon reading it.

I realised she must be a regular traveller, that the passing scenery held no surprises for her. She wore a very stylish pale blue trench coat, wide pointed lapels with two rows of buttons down the front. The carriage was not warm, and so she sat with it on, buttons undone and open fronted, revealing a contrasting check lining. Her wide-brimmed hat sat on the seat next to her. She had one hand holding her book while the other fidgeted with her long bead necklace. I must have looked very ordinary in comparison and assumed she had made the decision that I would not be worth talking to.

The train clattered along the track, as I and my fellow travellers swayed from side to side in unison. The lady opposite looked peeved when we passed over a junction where the additional clatter and sudden jolt disturbed her concentration. We pulled into Sevenoaks, the train gradually screeching to a halt. Several people disembarked, while only a few were standing on the platform waiting for the train.

A young man, a rare commodity in those days, approached the carriage door. He was scruffy and dishevelled, with a cigarette hanging from the corner of his mouth. As he reached out with his hand towards the door handle, the woman opposite me raised her eyes from her book, looking at him with an expression that I could only describe as revulsion. As he glanced up at her, his hand dropped back towards his side and in a continuous movement, he walked on towards the next carriage. She intrigued and annoyed me in equal measure.

Having been looked down upon by people like her for most of my life, I felt for the young man.

I recognised the last few miles as we approached my station, so it was time to concentrate my thoughts, to get ready. The train slowed down and the brakes squealed loudly as the sign for Tunbridge Wells West appeared, moving past my carriage window. I started to struggle off the train with my luggage, but within moments I had two airmen assisting me. It was fortunate they were boarding the train; I sensed I might have had trouble getting rid of them otherwise. They were like bees around a honey pot, but I was grateful, and they made me smile. My fashionable travel companion also disembarked. She had no luggage to struggle with, and walked past me adjusting her hat, her only concession being a slight nod of her head.

It was a delightful surprise to be met by my cousin Jim, who just appeared out of nowhere, giving me an enormous hug.

"Hello, Lily, you look more lovely than ever, girl - give me your cases."

"I didn't expect you, Jim, that's kind of you."

"No problem, luv; besides Gran would skin me alive if I'd left you waiting for the bus!"

We both laughed, I knew exactly what he meant. When Gran wanted something done, she always made sure it *was* done. Jim pretended to struggle with my cases, complaining all the while about the weight of them. He was a big burly fellow, and I very much doubt he would have noticed even if they *were* heavy!

As we left the station entrance, I looked up at the imposing clock tower, so familiar to me. It felt like a symbol of my family connection with Kent and Middlebourne. Jim led me towards a tractor and trailer which I expected to walk straight past, it not occurring to me this might be my transport!

"You'll be all right in the back of the trailer, won't you, Lily?"

"Yes," I replied, desperately trying not to look annoyed.

Jim threw my cases into the trailer with a single hand on each of them. As I contemplated climbing up after them, I noticed my travel companion sitting in the back of a limousine, with a uniformed chauffeur sitting at the wheel. They pulled away and swung around right next to us, as she smiled a half smile and raised her hand with a dismissive wave. I momentarily closed my eyes, waiting for her to disappear; how, I wondered, do women like that always manage to be so damned superior? I had risen above it all until that final humiliating moment.

I clung tightly to the sides of the trailer as we bounced along the country lanes towards Middlebourne. This was an altogether unfamiliar world which I had almost forgotten, with hardly any people, no bomb damage, and no actual sign that we were at war at all. The only thing I noticed was that all the road signs were missing. London felt like another page of a book; it was there, but completely separate to the page I was on.

Breathing a sigh of relief as we drew closer to the village, I realised that I was breathing fresh air. The air in London during the winter was filthy, full of coal smoke. After a while, you became so used to it that you never even noticed it - not until you breathed fresh air again.

The roads were rough, and Jim's driving was not considerate, giving me visions of being thrown out of the trailer at any moment. It covered me in straw and what looked like mud, at least I hoped it was mud. Despite the trauma of the last leg of my journey, I couldn't help but smile when we finally arrived.

It was a lovely thatched cottage, white rendered on the outside, covered in climbing roses, with leaded-light windows. The thatch curved over the two loft windows like eyebrows. Having spent so many of my past years there, it was a treasure trove of childhood memories; I even attended the local village school for a while. Sometimes I was with Ian and occasionally it was just me and Gran, but they were all fond memories.

Both the front and back gardens were enormous compared with those at Mum and Dad's tiny house. Beyond the back garden, the fields rolled away into the distance. As a child, I had a wonderland to play in, which extended as far as I could see. I remembered when the garden was bursting with colour, with hollyhocks and foxgloves lining the path to the door. There used to be flowers everywhere, now it was all vegetables.

And then, there she was, white-haired and slightly stooped, walking down the little path to greet me. Now my image of the cottage was complete; without Gran, it would be just another building. She was so pleased to see me, just as I was to see her, and we gave each other an enormous hug.

Gran was my Mum's mother, and an East Ender to the tips of her fingers. She fell in love with a countryman and ended up living in Middlebourne. But as they say, 'you can take the woman out of the East End, but you can't take the East End out of the woman.' Grandad had been gone a long time, but there had never been any doubt about who was the head of our family, the matriarch. Mum did the exact opposite of Gran, growing up in Middlebourne, only to fall in love with an East Ender, moving home to be with him in London.

"Oh, it's wonderful to have you stay, Lily, I can't tell you how pleased I am." She stepped back to look at me. "You really are a sight for sore eyes, luv, does Gerry know how lucky he is?" Then she hesitated, as she looked me up and down. "What's all this muck on you?"

A quick glance at the trailer and the answer to her question was immediately apparent. Jim had just come back with my cases. He was over six feet tall and built like a brick-built-privy. Keeping her balance with a hand against the fence, Gran reached up as high as she could and just as he was putting the cases down, she gave him a friendly swipe across the back of his head.

"What's *wrong* with you, Jim Smedley, why didn't you clean out that trailer? This isn't just anyone, this is my Lily!"

We were all used to this from Gran. "You tell him, Gran," I said.

Jim took his reprimand like the big man he is, and we all laughed. As I was brushing the straw from my coat, Spencer the black Labrador noticed my presence and bounded out of the house. Named after Spencer Tracy, Gran's favourite film star, he was a relative newcomer to the household. The last time I saw him, he was still an adorable puppy; now he jumped up at me with youthful enthusiasm, only adding to the mud on my coat. Gran reprimanded him in her usual style, and Spencer arched his back and lowered his ears as he scuttled off back into the house.

As he went in, there was the sound of a commotion, and then the old cat Boris came rushing out, fur standing on end. I loved Boris - he must have been ten or twelve years old, and obviously not remotely compatible with Spencer Tracy.

In no time at all, I was sitting in Gran's wonderfully familiar kitchen enjoying tea and cake, with Spencer's head on my knee. This was not just any cake; this was Gran's famous fruit cake! Spencer watched my every movement, hoping for a dropped crumb or two.

"I've baked it special for you, Lily," she said.

The look of pride in her eyes made me smile; it was exactly the same expression as my Mum's. I could see Jim skulking around, eyeing the cake.

"Don't you even think about it, Jim." She turned him around and gave him a shove towards the door. "He's a good boy, I love him really," she said, with that irresistible smile of hers.

Jim winked at me as he left for home, which was just two houses down the road at my Aunty Mavis' house. "I'll see you later, Lily."

He had a long courtship with a woman several years previously which, for some reason, broke up, and he'd stayed single ever since. His married brother Bob was living not five minutes away. Then there was Gran's other sister, my Aunty Mildred, close by in the next village. I often wonder what my great-grandparents were thinking when they named two of their daughters Mildred and Mavis, especially when I tell you my Gran's name was Margaret. Mildred had two daughters and a son, more cousins, and they all lived not far away. Mavis' husband, Uncle Ted sadly died only a few years ago, as did Mildred's husband, Uncle Colin. Middlebourne is very much my family, a second home for me.

Gran was full of questions. How was I, how were Mum and Dad, how was Gerry, when was he coming home on leave, how was George, and what had happened to his shipping business? I had to explain it all, and she hung on to my every word. She didn't know my friend Linda, but I told her about that, and how badly it affected me. You always told Gran everything because she seemed to have experienced it all herself and understood everything. Whatever your problem was, Gran could always soothe it away.

"Terrible thing, the sight of death." she said, "and violent death is even worse. It's not just the loss of your dear friend Linda, it's the loss of your own immortality. Did you leave her lying there thinking death was waiting for you, just around the next corner?"

"Gran, that was exactly what I felt, how did you know?"

"The longer you live, the more you see, and the more you see, the more you know." Then in the next breath she said, "I've lived a long time."

She had - the oldest of the sisters, she was nearly ninety. Mind you, you would never have thought so. Her mind was as sharp as a drawer of cutlery. Gran was a truly remarkable woman; she virtually ran the Parish Council. She was secretary of the Choral Society; in fact, she was a prominent figure in just about anything that happened in Middlebourne and the surrounding area.

She was also known as the voice of Middlebourne, and it

had nothing to do with the Parish Council. My grandmother's singing voice was the most beautiful I have ever heard. The Choral Society held a large open-air concert every year and people came from miles around to attend; there was never any doubt who they had come to listen to. We inherit everything from our forebears; special gifts or abilities can be passed through families for generations. People tell me I have a special gift, and if that is true, then I know exactly where it comes from.

"I've got two Land Girls lodging with me," she said, "it'll be a bit of a squeeze; you'll have to share. When Gerry comes home on leave, the girls will just have to go up into the loft room. There's two beds, I've told them you're my granddaughter, so Dorothy and Fiona will just have to share, and you can have the other bed. They're nice girls, you'll like them."

I hadn't stopped to consider that I might have to share a room and wondered how I would get on with these girls, Dorothy and Fiona.

"What do you plan to do, luv, are you going to join the Land Army?"

"Crikey, I've not even thought about that! I suppose I must get some kind of job."

"You won't get any other work around here, not unless you travel into Tunbridge Wells. You could always join ENSA and sing for the troops."

"Oh, come on, Gran, I'm nowhere near good enough to do that!"

"I've told you before, luv, you *are* that good. That's why you had all those singing lessons; I've heard no one sing like you, Lily."

"Well, I think I'm probably better suited to be a farm worker. What do they pay you - you *do* get paid, don't you?"

"Oh yes, they're paid really well, and it's just gone up this March; my girls get paid thirty-two shillings a week now. I think that's fair, and I only charge them fifteen shillings a week for food and lodgings."

"Thirty-two shillings a week," I repeated what Gran had said.

"I know, it's not bad, is it?"

"Gran, that's terrible! I was earning five times that much with George."

"I can't believe it, you earned that much money!"

"I worked hard, Gran, and it was long hours."

"No wonder George wanted to retire, that's all I can say! Besides, you get a nice little uniform as well when you sign up for the Land Army. Anyway, whatever you decide to do, you need to get your ration books registered with the local shops or you'll go hungry. Oh, and mind, you might be my granddaughter, but you must muck in with the girls. There's all the cooking, and the laundry, not to mention the cleaning and shopping, I'm not running around after you."

"Yes, Gran."

What I wanted to say was that I was a married woman, not twelve years old any more. The thing was, when she treated me like a child, I kind of liked it; it was oddly reassuring. Gran showed me to my usual bedroom, and left me to settle in. I opened the door expecting it to look as it always had, but it was filled with the belongings of the other occupants.

One side of the room was relatively tidy, with the clothes neatly folded and orderly, but the other side looked like a jumble sale. Clothes covered everything in the room, and I could detect two distinct wearers.

On the untidy side, there were bright blouses and skirts, and fancy patterned dresses, not to mention some embroidered knickers, and a fancy bra the likes of which I had never seen before. The other clothes were kept much tidier, with more expensive, classic-cut dresses, a pleated skirt, and knickers that came up to the waist. I sat for a moment just looking around, wondering about my two roommates.

I had very few clothes to bring with me, but where to put them would obviously be a problem. Not wanting to start off on the wrong foot by moving all their clothes around, I just placed mine on the bed that I thought might be mine. The furniture I remembered was still there; a dressing table, the wardrobe with a mirror on each door, and the two old wicker chairs, except the seats now had loose cushions to protect you from the protruding strands of willow. The extra items were two chest-of-drawers, and a long clothes rail which looked like it had come from a shop.

The familiar view from the window looked out over fields and hedgerows, so different from Stepney. I remembered exploring those fields, my hair in pigtails, and my knees always grazed and covered in mud. Gran would tell me off for getting my clothes filthy and then, the next moment, she would pick me up and make me feel like the most special little girl in the world.

I remembered walking up the stairs to bed with a candle holder in my hand, desperately hoping the candle wouldn't go out; the flickering shadows on the walls were full of menace to a young girl. Gran would make light of it all, saying, "Let's go up the apples and pears, and see your old Uncle Ned." Needless to say, it was the same old 'Uncle Ned' which I was now sitting on.

The only significant change in the house was electricity, with Gran still regarding it as some new-fangled invention. The only concession she was prepared to make was the wireless which we brought for her from London two years ago, before they declared war. Dad proudly installed it, and we all stood around it with beaming faces. Gran wanted nothing to do with it until she heard a voice she recognised coming out of the strange box.

"That's Gracie! I'd know that voice anywhere," she exclaimed, "what's Gracie Fields doing inside this thing?"

These were lovely memories. But just as I sat there smiling, I heard footsteps coming up the stairs, and a woman burst into the room.

"Oh shit, I didn't know you wus 'ere yet! You're the old girl's granddaughter. I should've tidied up a bit."

"Hello, I'm Lily."

"Call me Dotty. Dotty by name, Dotty by nature. Bloody 'ell, look at you, 'ow do you keep your 'air looking like that?"

"Well, I try to make a bit of an effort."

"Christ, what must you think of me then?"

I had quickly assumed that Dotty was not looking at her best. She wore a brown bib-and-brace that was covered in goodness knows what, and her rolled-up sleeves revealed tanned arms which were also covered in something. A head-scarf covered her hair, but nothing could conceal her brash manner and cheeky smile. She was every bit an East Ender, just like me.

"What *is* that stuff you're covered in? It smells awful!" I dared to ask.

"Oh this? This is pig shit; you soon get used to it."

There was something about her – she had instantly filled the room the moment she entered it, and I immediately liked her. She pulled off her headscarf to reveal her short dark hair, neatly cut, very stylish, and it suited her sharp facial features and big brown eyes.

"Pleased to meet you, Lily, you're from London. East End, I'd bet, which part?"

"Stepney."

"*No*, really?"

Her cheeky smile was contagious, and I found myself captivated by the sight and sound of her, despite looking preposterous, dressed as she was. I would have been embarrassed to meet someone while dressed like that, but Dotty appeared to be oblivious to her appearance.

"Where are you from then, Dotty?"

"East Ham, just down the road from you, small world init?"

She stood there, hands on her hips, unable to sit down due

to the pig muck on her overalls. I knew she must be tired and weary, but nothing would stop her talking. Dotty wanted to know everything about me, and quickly found we had a lot in common. She was irrepressible - when I mentioned anything that she could associate with, she would almost scream with excitement. "I know that place," she would say, "yes, I've been there."

Looking at her, standing there as she was, a strange thought came into my mind. Not so long ago, Gerry had brought home a box of oysters from the Dock. I'd never had oysters before, and thought they looked awful, covered in barnacles, mud and seaweed. Gerry insisted we had to clean them up and try some. He pressed a knife into one of them and prised open the shell; I just could not believe such an unpromising object could be worth the trouble. There inside, tucked away to one side, was a pearl, a bright shining, iridescent pearl. This was Dorothy.

"We'll get on fine, you and me, Dotty," I said, "but there's just the one thing."

"I know, but you get used to it, trust me," she laughed as she stepped out of her overalls.

"Do you want a bath tonight, Lily? I reckon you better go first if you do; we have a system, you see, cleanest goes first. Fi's been repairing the stables today, so she's okay; I think we can guess who's going to be last!"

The prospect of sharing a tin bath with a bunch of filthy farm workers was not particularly appealing. As for being the last in line, that really did not appeal at all, although it didn't seem to bother Dotty in the slightest.

"I'm fine," I said, "you carry on."

The copper was in Gran's scullery, and the tin bath hung on the wall. It was always freezing during the winter, never seeming to matter how much coal you put under the copper; the room always stayed just as cold. I guessed that bath nights were not just once a week for farm workers, and in the cold of Gran's scullery, they probably didn't take very long. Fiona had gone straight into the scullery from work and was out in a trice; she soon joined me preparing vegetables in the kitchen.

She was a different proposition altogether compared with Dotty. Fiona was tall, elegant, and very middle class, not remotely fitting my image of a Land Girl. She lifted a heavy pan onto the range, but that was nothing compared to the weight she bore on her shoulders. If you came from a four-story townhouse in Chelsea, it was obviously demeaning to be lodging with a girl from the East End. Now she had the unpalatable prospect of lodging with two of us. I almost felt sorry for her. She was well-educated, polite, and spoke terribly nicely, and that was good enough for me; we had no need to be the best of friends if she didn't want to. She was, however, very gracious in the way she greeted me.

"Hello, Lily, I'm Fiona. Your Grandmother speaks so kindly of you, I've been looking forward to meeting you." From that moment, we just talked continually. She was charming.

In the country, things were a lot different in the kitchen. I couldn't believe the abundance of food we had available. We had a leg of lamb roasting in the oven, and I couldn't even recall when I last saw a leg of lamb, let alone ate one. The smell of it was like nothing I could remember; I had never felt so hungry.

"We don't get this every day," Fiona said. "I can see Margaret's pulling out all the stops for you; you're her favourite!"

I wondered if she begrudged me that dubious title, but just smiled to myself. Then, just as I put the last of the sprouts into the pot, Dotty breezed into the room.

"Look at this then, do I clean up well, or what?"

She certainly did clean up well. Dressed in a nice skirt and knitted jumper, I could see she was one of those women who had the knack of always looking stylish. She put her arm around me as if we had known each other for years.

"This must be a nightmare for you, Fi, you've got two of us Cockney girls to contend with now!"

Fiona could see the funny side of the irrepressible Dorothy. I wasn't sure it was even possible to take offence, whatever Dotty said.

"I suppose you're right, Dorothy," she said, "I'll just have to make the best of it, I suppose; just don't expect me to talk like you!"

As Fiona was laying the table, Dotty whispered into my ear. "It's that rod up her arse that does it. Actually, I think she's all right, she don't take herself half as seriously as she makes out; it's a bit of a pretence, if you ask me."

Fiona half overheard. "Is she going on again about me having a rod up my bottom?"

"No, dear. I didn't say 'bottom', I said 'arse'."

We didn't see that Gran had entered the kitchen. She gave Dotty a clip behind the ear, and said, "Don't you use that kind of language in my kitchen, young lady!"

We all fell about laughing, including Fiona. Dotty was right about her; it was all a bit of a pretence; I had misjudged her. She came from a different part of town, and the class system held us all rigidly in our own place. But we were both victims of it in our own way - I suspect I was equally guilty. Our conversation didn't stop, and all the while the smell of roast lamb filled the kitchen. I could hardly wait for it to come out of the oven and the moment it did, Dotty set upon it with a carving knife.

I had never seen women eat so much, and so quickly; it was the best meal I had eaten in years. What a pleasure it was, sharing that meal together, I felt it was something special. Gran sat at the head of the table presiding over the three of us as if we were schoolchildren, and I suppose, to her, we probably were. Every time Dotty was about to say something she shouldn't, Gran gave one of her looks, just as she used to do to me when I was a child. The fact that Dotty was twenty-four years old seemed to make no difference.

"Quite right, Margaret," Fiona said, "you might even make a lady out of her."

"Not much chance of that, is there, Gran?" Dotty replied.

"I'm not your grandmother, Dorothy."

"I lost my Gran years ago, in fact I can't really remember her, so now that we've got Lily, I'm going to adopt *you* as my Gran instead."

They both started calling her Gran; I liked that. Gran must have liked it as well because she would have told them off otherwise. Dotty went on and on about all the places we had in common, many of which Gran could remember. Dotty could make a visit to the newsagent sound like a trip to the funfair, candy floss and all. I sat smiling at her, then she suddenly got up from the table.

"Oh Christ! I've got to go out the back for a wee! It's so bloody cold, I'm gonna freeze my tits off out there."

"*Dotty*, I've told you before," Gran said, "*don't* use that kind of language in my kitchen."

"Quite right, Gran, I'll have a good curse when I get outside."

It seemed Spencer Tracy understood the word 'outside' - he was out of his dog blanket and on his paws in a trice, pestering Dotty. Spencer's favourite preoccupation was to stick his head between your legs as hard as he could.

"For pity's sake, *not now*, Spencer, not when I'm busting for a wee."

Dotty rushed outside with Spencer snapping at her heels, and even with the door closed, we all heard her shouting at the dog.

"Oh, piss off, Spencer."

The rest of us had tears of laughter in our eyes, and Gran rocked back and forth in her chair.

"That girl will be the death of me!" she laughed.

"I complain about her," Fiona said, "but really, she's a treasure, isn't she?"

I was warming towards Fiona by the minute. Dotty was right, her superior attitude was just a pretence. I had been surrounded by girls like Fiona at boarding school. It took me a long time to realise that a superior attitude does not *make* you superior.

"She is," I replied, "she must have been quite a challenge for you to cope with."

"She was; don't tell her, but actually she was so kind to me when I arrived here, I couldn't help but like her straight away."

Dotty came back rubbing her chilly hands together, the faithful Spencer right behind her.

"He doesn't need to go out again, I think he cocked his leg against the lav door."

"I've told him not to do that," said Gran.

"What did he say?" replied Dotty.

Come the end of a wonderful evening, I kissed Gran good-night, and Dotty and Fiona did the same.

"What's all this, you silly girls, be off with you!" Gran said, her smile filling the room.

We went up the 'apples and pears' together, and I reminisced with them about some of my childhood memories of the place, and they asked me lots of questions. I sat down on my bed and they both sat down on the other bed as we talked.

"Oh, God! I've just realised I'm sharing with you, Dotty," Fiona said, half serious and half smiling.

"Could be worse, Fi, it could be that randy bastard Spencer."

I could hardly get my nightclothes on for laughing. Finally, as we sat in our beds talking, I thought nothing would ever stop Dotty from talking.

"Tell me all about this feller of yours, Gerry, what's he like then?"

I don't suppose I said more than a dozen words before Dotty was asleep.

"Peace at last," Fiona said.

This was the start of an incredibly special friendship between the three of us, a friendship which was to last the rest of our lives.

Chapter Six
The Land Army

Without an air raid, it was the first night I'd slept through for months. I woke to find Dotty up and dressed, and Fiona already gone.

"Come on, Lily, being late for breakfast is a capital offence around here!"

With that she, too, had gone. I rushed downstairs as quickly as I could; Fiona was just coming in through the back door with a bucket of water from the pump.

"You can share my bucket, Lily, if you want to wash in the scullery."

I thanked her for what hardly sounded like the best offer I'd ever had. At least in my little house in Stepney we had the gas Ascot to provide some hot water. The alternative, however, was to wash outside in the trough, so I accepted Fiona's offer.

Dotty had prepared breakfast. A great vat of porridge was bubbling away on the range, and the smell of wood smoke filled the room, seeming to linger between the beams on the ceiling. Once again, there appeared to be no shortage of food, and no shortage of appetite. Dotty and Fiona continued to amaze me with the amount they could eat.

"What are your plans, Lily?" asked Fiona.

"Well, I've thought about it; I think I'll join you girls - I'll join the Land Army."

"I'll talk to Reg," Fiona said, "he's always complaining that he doesn't have enough farm labour; you have a word with Jim - he knows about getting you signed up."

"What are you smiling at, Dotty?" I asked.

"I can't wait to see you covered in pig shit, Lily! You really *will* be lady muck then!"

They left, laughing aloud. I looked at my lovely hair in the mirror and considered Dotty's words. Undaunted, I went to see Jim and just as Fiona said, he knew all about it.

"You must register with the Post Office," he said, "or, if you're in a rush, I can take you to the local WLA Headquarters."

"When can we go?" I asked.

He ran a tractor repair business, and they classed him as a 'Reserve Occupation'. Cousin Jim was a lovely man, always kind to Gran, and now he didn't hesitate to extend that kindness to me. He mentioned the trailer, looking at me quizzically, and I looked back with the most disdainful expression I could muster.

Nothing was said, but soon he came back to pick me up in a delivery van he was servicing. The local WLA headquarters was in Tunbridge Wells, which was a bit of a drive, but Jim got me there in no time. I enrolled and assumed that was it, but not a bit of it - I was told I had to go for a medical. That was arranged for two days later and even then, it was not over - I also had to go for an interview.

This was all delaying things, but it was the first time in goodness knows how long that I had relaxed. I worked hard, cooking and cleaning for Gran and the girls, but I didn't feel any pressure. I was fully occupied yet felt no stress, and above all I was getting some sleep. Finally, I had to go for the interview at the Institute of Agriculture in Tunbridge Wells.

Once again, it was Jim who came to my rescue, driving me there in the same delivery van.

"Are you sure about being in the Land Army, Lily?" he asked, as we made our way there.

"Of course, why not?"

"Not for me to say really, Lily, but you don't look to me like you're cut out for that kind of work."

"What do you mean, why shouldn't I be able to do it?"

"No reason, but we all know you're the bright one in the family. You could do anything you wanted."

"Well, maybe, but I just want some time to relax a bit and have some fun. I've forgotten what fun is."

"You'll get plenty of that with Dotty! Maybe you'll make a fine Land Girl."

"I'll try, Jim."

With that, we arrived at the Institute, and Jim parked the van outside. He wished me good luck as I made my way into the building. It took me a while to find where to go, and then I had to sit and wait my turn. Finally, I was called into a large room by a shrill voice that called out, "Heywood, come in."

The moment I clapped eyes on her, I recognised her immediately. It was the same pompous arse of a woman who sat opposite me on the train. I think she recognised me too, because she adopted the same condescending expression the moment that she saw me. My heart sank, and I immediately expected another humiliating encounter. She looked at my application form, and the first thing she said was that they were really looking for single women.

"Do you mean I've been wasting my time applying?"

"Well, it is unusual."

"My husband is in the Navy, he's been away for weeks, I have no idea when he will come home on leave, and when he does, it will only be for a temporary period."

"Well, in that case some might say that you should be at home preparing the house for his return."

"I can't believe what I'm hearing. Do you seriously think I should stay at home and tidy the house? Let me tell you something, I don't even *have* a home, they've blown my house to smithereens, and they blew my best friend and her children to smithereens along with it. It's easy for women like you, sitting here in Tunbridge Wells, making cakes for the Women's Institute. I will *not* let Hitler defeat me, I want to fight back, and I can't do that by tidying the house or baking cakes!"

She physically recoiled, and sat back in her chair, as I waited to be told to leave.

"Well, my dear, you certainly know your own mind. Not that it is any of your business, but I also want to do my bit. This is only one of the jobs I volunteer to do for the war effort. And do not make the mistake of thinking I am not affected by the war either. My son was killed at Dunkirk, and my husband is a high-ranking officer serving in the Army. I don't need a lecture from someone like you!"

"They killed my brother at Dunkirk," I said, without thinking.

"Oh, my dear, I'm so sorry, I really am, you've had more than your share of hardship."

"No, it's me that's sorry, I didn't mean to imply that you only bake cakes, I'm just so desperate to do something to fight back."

"We need women with your spirit in the WLA. We *will* defeat Hitler, you know - I rather think you could defeat him by yourself," she said with a smile.

I learned a valuable lesson that day. The war touched everyone, and no-one had a monopoly on the misery it imposed on the country. I was accepted right away and quickly issued with my uniform.

That evening, I put it on for the first time, wanting to surprise the girls when they came home. I had the olive-green cotton corduroy breeches that the girls called 'whistling cord' because of the noise it made when you walked. I put on the long sleeve version of the fawn cotton shirt, together with the green and yellow striped WLA tie. I tucked the green sweater into the breeches and pulled up the long woollen socks. Then, just for fun, I put on the felt brimmed hat.

They arrived home tired and filthy, to find me standing there like a tailor's mannikin. We had a riot that evening; what fun we had. I'm sure we made Gran feel younger, she didn't stop laughing with us.

"You're supposed to look like a farm worker, not a bloody fashion model," said Dotty, with a wry smile.

"At least that's something you'll never be accused of Dotty; I've never seen a fashion model covered in pig shit!" Fiona said.

"*Fiona*, did I hear you say *shit?*" responded Dotty, mischief written all over her face.

"Oh, my goodness, I did! You see the dreadful effect you're having on me!"

"No, that can't be me," replied Dotty, "I wouldn't say a thing like that, it must be Lily."

We were in such high spirits that night that even Dotty didn't fall asleep straight away when we went to bed. All they wanted to do was ask me questions, so we sat up talking. Fiona asked me if Gerry and I intended to have children, and for some inexplicable reason I told them my little secret.

"I was in the club when we got married, which was the only reason we married in the first place. Then, just a month later, I lost it."

"Oh, my goodness, that's terrible!" Fiona said.

"Do you mean it was terrible she lost the baby," Dotty asked, "or do you mean it was terrible she slept with him?"

Dotty had a way of not mincing her words. Fiona, on the other hand, was nothing if not a prude, explaining that she was shocked on both counts. I admitted it was all a bit of a disaster, except for the sex.

"That part was pretty good," I said.

"Oh Lily, how could you?" exclaimed Fiona.

"You and me need to have a little talk tomorrow, Fi!" Dotty said.

With that, we all laughed some more until Dotty started

her usual snoring. I had made light of the miscarriage, but at the time it affected me badly. This was the first time I talked about it without becoming upset.

The following morning, I tucked my hair up into a head-scarf and looked as much like a farm worker as I could - not that I really knew how a farm worker was supposed to look. We finally sat together looking at each other over our bowls of porridge, and Spencer sat with his head on Dotty's knee.

"What are you smiling at, Dotty?" I asked.

"I can't remember when I looked clean and smart like that," she said.

"I'm afraid it won't last, Lily, you'll end up looking like Dotty!" laughed Fiona.

"Surely not?" I replied.

We all reported bright and early for work at Reg's, and what a day it was. The nerve centre of the farm was an area of mud and cow muck which stretched out between the farmhouse and some large sheds. The sheds were empty of cattle now, as they had recently been turned out onto the fresh grass. The mud and cow muck appeared to be like a river, although there was no perceivable movement. It all appeared to be heading in the same direction, towards one building in particular.

"What's that building over there where the river of muck is going?"

"Oh, that's the milking parlour; twice a day Reg brings the girls in for milking. He will have already done it this morning while we were still asleep," said Fiona.

"What time does Reg start, then?"

"He'll start calling the girls about 4.30 am, 'cos he likes to have his breakfast by 7.00am so he's ready for us at 7.30," replied Dotty.

I think they could see from my expression that I hadn't realised the commitment required. The stench was dreadful, but when I contorted my face like you might to close the open end of a paper bag, the girls looked at me with amusement.

"How do you bear this smell, it's dreadful!"

"What smell?" replied Dotty.

"You get used to it, Lily; after a while, you don't even notice it," Fiona said with a smile.

I noticed they both walked with no regard for the deeper areas of muck; it covered their boots. I approached it as if I were entering a minefield. This was all a violation of my sensibilities, but the harsh reality was that the muck wouldn't change. It was my sensibilities which would have to change.

Dotty stood with her hands in her pockets, and a smile on her face, moving up and down on the balls of her feet, making squelching sounds in the muck. Fiona, equally happy, pushed the muck away with the outside of her boot, like a child playing in the sand.

Then the farmhouse door opened, and Reg appeared. He was rather as I imagined, initially a little fearsome, well into his sixties and weather-beaten for at least sixty of those years. He wore dungarees tucked into his boots, a flat cap, and a threadbare jacket. Reg looked up to see the new girl standing there, probably looking as out of place as a pork pie at a bar mitzvah.

As he approached me, his craggy face was expressionless. He shook my hand, and his hand felt like a gnarled tree stump. He peered out from beneath his grubby flat cap, eyeing me up and down.

"I can see you've not done this before, Lily, so I suppose I'd better put you on something easy to start with."

Reg's idea of an easy introduction to farming was clearing ditches. I didn't want to be a disappointment to everyone, determined to do the best I could. The girls made their way toward their own tasks, while Reg picked up some implements and set off across the field. He didn't say very much, so I just followed on behind until we reached the edge of the field, defined by the ditch. It appeared to be a long way down, and I just stood there looking at Reg.

He slithered down into the ditch with effortless ease. When I tried to imitate him with a bold step forward, I found my feet in the air and my backside skidding down the bank of the ditch. At the bottom, sitting half in the wet mud and half on the slope, I felt like a complete fool. Reg looked at me with what I took to be an expression of utter derision.

Just as I thought he would tell me off for being so hopeless, a hint of a smile emanated from the corner of his mouth. It didn't propagate very far, and then it was gone, but at least he had shown a flicker of humanity.

"You're supposed to be digging the bloody ditch, not sitting in it!"

He offered me his hand, and pulled me back onto my feet, and I was too proud to admit my backside was killing me. Reg then started to dig into the mud and sediment which had built up in the ditch, wielding the spade as if he had some unseen mechanical connection to his tractor. He threw the mud up the bank in a continuous movement, and in next to no time had progressed ten feet along the ditch.

"Right then, Lily, that's all there is to it, you should get all this section finished today."

With that, he hopped up the bank and left me to it. He made it look so easy and I thought, if a man of Reg's age can do it, then it should be easy for me. I looked down at myself, already covered in mud; what else did I have to lose? I stamped the spade into the mud, and it sank up to my boot with a satisfying ease.

Having pushed and pulled the handle back and forth as Reg did, I then intended to lift spade and mud together in one continuous action, leaving the mud at the top of the ditch. Except that nothing happened, I couldn't lift it from the ground. I could lift half a spade-full, but when I propelled it skywards, the mud stuck to the spade, and both mud and spade left my hands simultaneously. I was a disaster; I just couldn't believe how utterly hopeless I was.

We had a half hour lunch break, and even the sandwiches felt heavy. The girls laughed at me; I was the butt of every joke Dotty could think of. I pressed on after lunch, and gradually mastered the technique. Wet the spade first, so that the mud slides off, lean on the handle with a straight arm, bend at the knees.

My improving technique was complemented perfectly by my diminishing strength. The result was that my initial progress was abysmal, and as I improved my technique, my progress remained abysmal. When Reg appeared at the end of the day, I braced myself for the worst. He stood there looking down at me, his face expressionless.

"You've not done a bad job, Lily, not as much as I hoped, but not bad."

"I tried to get to the end, Reg, but I just couldn't do it, I'm sorry."

"Oh, I didn't expect you to do it all."

"But you said I should finish the section."

"Did I say that? I don't remember, but never mind, give me your hand, luv, I'll take the spade."

The old bugger was human after all; he helped me out of the ditch with a genuine smile. The girls made fun of me as we walked back to Gran's - slowly. I struggled along the path to the front door. I wanted to lean on Dotty, but she was covered in something undesirable, while Fiona was back working on machinery, so she'd hardly raised a sweat. Spencer Tracy came bounding out of the door, thinking Dotty smelled adorable.

"Bugger off, Spencer," she shouted, "why don't you pester Lily?"

Spencer appeared to understand, and jumped up at me, his paws up to my chest. I instinctively tried to stop him, not wanting his muddy paws on me. Then I realised it was me who was making the dog filthy!

They decided I should be number two in the bath after Fiona that first evening. I was so slow getting prepared, I found

Dotty had jumped ahead of me. Even my face was covered in mud where I had wiped the sweat from my brow; I'd never seen myself looking so filthy.

I went into the scullery after Dotty to see the bath water looking decidedly grey with a floating scum which appeared to be impenetrable. Much as I hated it, I had to put a foot into it which was bad enough, but then I had to sit down! Despite everything, the comfort of the hot water was so welcome that I almost overcame my aversion to the scum. I wanted to just lie in the tub easing my aches, but the water quickly cooled, and I felt cold.

When I stepped out of the bath, I could hardly put one foot in front of the other. My legs had turned to lead, but I still had to do my bit in the kitchen. When we finally sat down for our meal, I suddenly realised why they ate so much; I was starving.

"You're eating that as if you haven't eaten for a week, Lily," said Gran.

"I know how these two feel now, hard work gives you an appetite," I replied. "Were you this weary when you started, Fi?"

"I was exactly the same, much to Dotty's amusement."

"Fi went to finishing school, Lily," said Dotty, "she learnt everything she knows about farming there."

"You joke about it, Dotty, but that's the reason I came here. My parents were keen for me to be a genteel and refined lady, and then the war started - can you think of anything more ridiculous than finishing school? I wanted to help and suddenly realised how pointless it had all been."

"Gran told us you went to school here in Middlebourne for a while, Lily." said Dotty. "I thought you lived in Stockwell when you were a kid?"

"I spent a lot of time here with Gran, so much time in fact that I ended up going to the local school for a while."

"Why was that then?"

"That's a long story, Dotty. Truth is my parents didn't want me at home."

"Lily, you know that's not true," said Gran, "it was a hard time for your parents, they just wanted to protect you from their problems, that's all."

"Wow, this is intriguing, tell me more," said an inquisitive Dotty.

"It would take too long Dotty; let's just say they had marital difficulties. It was a hard time for me and Ian."

"Who's Ian?" she asked.

"That's my brother, he was here too."

"What's he doing now, Lily, is he in the services?" asked Fiona.

"He's dead Fi; Dunkirk."

Fiona was very astute and could see the family thing was a sensitive issue for me. She quickly commiserated with me about Ian and changed the subject.

"I really hated finishing school, above all I hated boarding."

"I know what you mean, I didn't enjoy boarding," I said.

"You didn't go to boarding school, did you, Lily?" asked Dotty.

"I did, I went when I was fourteen."

"Crickey, I thought you were from the East End, Lily! East End girls don't go to boarding school," said Dotty.

"I know they don't, but I did. I owe it all to my Uncle George. He thought I showed promise, and he wanted to improve my education. I still had a lot of problems at home, and so Uncle George saw the opportunity to get me away from home at the same time."

"But that's wonderful Lily," said Fiona, avoiding my family problems. "Why didn't you like it?"

"I liked the education, they said I was an outstanding student, but I would never fit in, would I? I was the only girl there with an East End accent. They all looked down on me and tried to make my life hell."

"Oh no, that sounds awful," Fiona said, "how did you cope?"

"George told me I had to try hard and be the best I could, and I promised him I would. So when they made fun of me, I just had to show them I was better than they were."

"And did you?" asked Dotty.

"I suppose I did. When I took my School Certificate, I got a matriculation exemption. I was the only girl who did."

"What on earth is that?" asked Dotty.

"That means Lily achieved at least a credit in each of the five subjects in the School Certificate," Fiona replied, "and it means she could apply directly to a university with no entrance exam."

"Wow, you must be the smartest woman I know Lily," Dotty said, "no offence Fi."

"None taken Dotty, I didn't do half as well."

"And did you go to university? I don't know anyone who's been to university," said Dotty.

"George was really hoping I would, but so few women go to university, I would have stood out even more like a sore thumb. I just couldn't bear the prospect, not after how they treated me at boarding school. George was extremely disappointed, but he offered me a job instead in his shipping agency."

"Who is this Uncle George?" Dotty asked. "He's obviously got pots of money, I bet he's not from the East End."

"Dotty, that's so *rude*," said an embarrassed Fiona, "you shouldn't pry into Lily's family affairs."

"Have I said the wrong thing, me and my big mouth."

"No, it's okay Dotty. George was not my actual uncle at all; he was my Dad's commanding officer during the First War, and they became close friends. It was an unlikely friendship, really; George came from a completely different background. He left his wife, and he spent a lot of time with us; he was like another member of the family to me. Nothing about my childhood was normal in the conventional sense. There was always something there in the background that we never talked about. It was like having an elephant standing in the room which we pretended wasn't there."

"Was it an elephant or was it Uncle George?" asked Dotty.

"Dotty really, you mustn't ask questions like that," intervened Fiona.

"It's okay Fi, I don't mind, it's not talking about these things that's been at the heart of my family's problems."

Gran sat quietly without contributing to the conversation. She knew more than I did about George; she knew more about everything. Her silence on the subject was all a part of my family's conspiracy of silence. I looked at her, hoping she would say something.

"Well, I know I'm not supposed to ask," said Dotty, "but why did an uncle, who isn't an uncle, spend so much money on your education, and give you a job at the end of it?"

"George is a lovely man," said Gran. "He's both wealthy and generous, took a shine to our Lily and wanted to help her, that's all." She pondered for a moment before continuing. "You shouldn't blame yourself Lily, none of it was your fault. That was why he suggested the boarding school. You had no self-confidence at all until George took you under his wing."

"Are we talking about the same Lily, Gran?" asked Fiona. "I've never met a more confident person than Lily."

"You'll never know what a compliment that is, Fi. It's all a pretence I'm afraid, I get horrible anxieties; I have to fight it all the time."

"You amaze me Lily, nobody would ever know," said Fiona. "So tell me, do you ever regret not going to university; that would have been quite something, wouldn't it?"

"Not at the time, but I came to regret it later when I realised the benefits it might have given me. I tried to make up for it by going to an Evening Institute two nights a week, I wanted to do it for George."

"You really put us all to shame Lily," Fiona said, "all I got was a pass, and learnt how to arrange flowers."

"I suspect that's not quite true, Fi," I said, as we both looked at Dotty.

"No, don't look at me, all I got was a telling off from the headmaster."

"Why does that not surprise me," Fiona said.

"I was the fastest runner in the school though, does that count?"

"Of course it does, Dotty," said Gran.

We talked into the evening until, like Dotty, I could feel my eyes closing. When we went to bed, I understood why they went to sleep so quickly.

-o0o-

Our employer Reg was actually a friendly chap. He had been farming his eighty-five acres all his life, as his father had before him. For him, his farm was not just a way of life; it was in every sense all of his life. We women were just labourers, and didn't have any feel for the land, or the livestock. At least this is what Reg used to say. Initially he was right, but as the war years progressed, the Land Girls became proper farm workers. When the war was over, most women in the Land Army would say that those back-breaking times were the best years of their lives.

Reg was like nobody I had known before. I thought I worked hard at my job as a shipping agent, but Reg worked fifteen hours a day, six days a week, and then occasionally he would have a few hours off on a Sunday. No wonder he had a reputation for being a miserable old bugger. The poor man had no life other than working. And yet somewhere deep inside his tired and worn body, there was a kind and warm human being who I suspect Reg had forgotten existed.

The next morning when we arrived back on the farm, I quickly learned that Dotty had talents I would never have suspected. Nearly all the lambs had been born for that season, with only two ewes left to produce. I noticed Dotty looking at them in the pen.

"I think these two are ready, Reg."

"Go on then, Dotty, you know what to do."

I saw the last one born, with Dotty as midwife. I marvelled at her apparent experience, and her dedication to the ewe and the new lamb. The look on her face when she handed the newborn to its mother made a huge impression on me. This was a side to Dotty I had not seen before, nor even suspected could exist. Reg was overseeing his prodigy, and I could see he was proud of her, putting his arm around her shoulders.

"Well done, Dotty, you have a natural touch, my girl. I'll make a farm worker of you yet," he said.

Dotty could leave that tender side of her nature behind in a trice. "Don't get excited, Reg, us galley slaves will rise up one day, then you'll be in trouble!"

I hadn't realised either, how talented Fiona was. She could read a workshop manual and then take a machine apart as if she had done it a hundred times before. Cousin Jim was a skilled engineer, so Fi would always ask him about things she didn't understand. The two of them discussed engines like Dotty and I would talk about a dress. She seemed to revel in her newfound skills, and Reg had quickly come to rely on her. She hated heavy manual work, so perhaps this was her incentive to work on the machines.

I didn't have Fiona's technical skills, and I didn't have Dotty's capacity for heavy work. I wondered if I had any skills which could be useful on a farm. I could see immediately that Reg probably managed his farm exactly as his father had before him. His heart and soul were in his land and livestock; business management didn't really exist at all. Fiona was quick to point out how productivity would improve with some extra equipment, and I was appalled with things like the haphazard way Reg sold the milk from the small dairy herd.

I soon realised that he just accepted the price the Estate Manager Phillips gave him. Reg disliked this man and a derogatory term always followed or preceded his name, often quite a colourful one. I didn't need any great understanding about farming to see that Reg farmed with no real profit motive. His love and contentment of everything which surrounded him was enviable, but I feared that Reg's world was quickly disappearing. If he were not careful, he would disappear with it.

It was not my place to tell Reg how to run his business; he would not even want to know that he should run his farm as a business. I decided that I would have to continue clearing ditches and stacking bales. I grew stronger every day, and my body ached a little less as my fitness increased. I began to feel much better in myself and could even find I was covered in muck and not complain.

Above all, our spirits were high. Whenever we worked together, we couldn't stop laughing. There was always a highlight to any day, and usually Dotty would be at the centre of it. One day it was just me and Fi. Reg had us clearing stones from a field and suddenly we looked up to see a solitary Spitfire coming towards us. We knew it was a Spitfire long before we saw the familiar silhouette against the sky; the sound of the Merlin engine would make your heart soar. We thought perhaps the pilot must have been on a test flight - whatever the reason, he was flying alone above the farm.

When the pilot saw the two of us standing in the middle of the field, waving like demented idiots, he flew over us and dipped his wings from side to side. Then he circled round in a big arc and came back towards us again. He was diving exceptionally low and coming straight towards us.

Fi and I lay down on our backs with our arms outstretched like two crosses on the ground. He flew right over us, only yards above our heads. A tremendous rush of wind blew up the surrounding dust, and the roar of the Merlin engine made the air in our lungs vibrate. We jumped up the second he passed over us and waved hysterically.

Winston Churchill's words came into my mind as we waved goodbye to the pilot. "*Never was so much owed by so many to so few.*" Fiona pointed out that he shouldn't have done any of it; that was the kind of thing pilots got into trouble for. However, it was a wonderful experience, and we went home that day brimming with patriotic pride.

I continued to grow stronger every day, and although I still was not cut out for heavy manual work, there were days when I positively enjoyed it. Dotty was the one with all the strength and stamina; she would always do extra if one of us was struggling. Dotty was indomitable; nothing ever got her down.

The friendship between the three of us also seemed to grow stronger every day; we stood by each other without fail. The three of us became inseparable.

Chapter Seven
The Interview

In the few weeks since I met Fiona, she seemed to have grown in stature, gaining confidence each day. She possessed great charm and a wonderful elegance which she no longer tried to disguise. She was also really pretty, with lovely blonde wavy hair. Dotty would sometimes call her Jean Harlow. She was undoubtedly very content as well; I think discarding the chip on her shoulder had a lot to do with that. Like me, she quickly came to realise that class stereotypes had no place when we were digging ditches together. Of the three of us, she was undoubtedly the least suited to manual work, and it was Fiona who spotted an advert in the local paper for an administrative job at the big house. We discussed it anyway, despite the paper being several days old.

"I think I could do that," she said.

We both agreed. With her background she was far more suited to secretarial work than to farm labouring and machine maintenance. I suggested she should apply for it. Initially she was hesitant, but by the end of the evening we had convinced her to apply.

She duly sent a letter to the big house via the details in the advert and sure enough, a few days later a letter came back offering her an interview. We were all enthusiastic about it; just the prospect of her attending an interview in the big house was exciting.

The big house was Middlebourne Manor, the home of the Ninth Earl of Middlebourne. We had all seen the Manor from a distance. You couldn't miss it, sitting on the highest point, looking down on the village. Needless to say, the village looked up to the Manor.

I understood that the old Earl died not so long ago, and his son had inherited. Beyond that, I knew little - it was another world. Apart from occasionally seeing one or two of their servants in the pub, and the old Earl's yearly appearance at the village fete, nor did most other village people.

Come the day of the interview, Fiona worried about what to wear, and what she should say, and whether Reg would be annoyed. We calmed her down with the assurance that we would cover for her on the farm, that she looked lovely, and all she had to do was to be herself.

"Are you sure I look all right?"

"Fi, you look wonderful; just go, before you're late," I said.

"Okay, wish me luck."

She did look lovely, and she was such a capable woman. As we waved her on her way, I fully expected her to get the job. We couldn't wait for her to come back, but by the time she had gone home and changed, it all took an age. When she did finally appear back at the farm, we pounced on her with questions. Fiona was full of it.

The position was personal assistant to His Lordship, and it had quite gone to her head. His Lordship conducted the interview himself, making quite an impression on Fiona. Apparently, she found him to be charming, a little difficult to talk to, but apart from that, she thought he was wonderful.

We poked fun at her all evening. "Will you take tea, My Lady? Would you like your hair brushed, My Lady?" Dotty was in her element and for her part Fiona took it all in a friendly spirit.

A few days later, when we arrived back from a day's work, a letter had arrived; we all knew what it was. None of us washed or changed - we just stood in our filthy overalls looking at the envelope.

"Well, open it, Fi," demanded Dotty.

"What if I haven't got the job?" Fiona asked.

"Then Reg will be thrilled," I replied.

Fiona opened the envelope and tentatively removed the letter. Her face dropped; she had not got the job.

"If I'm honest, I'm not surprised," Fi said. "He was awfully specific about a lot of his requirements; I got the feeling there's a lot more to the job than he was telling me. It was clear that he's looking for someone special; someone who can provide inspirational leadership was the expression he used."

"But you *could* do that, Fi," said Dotty. "I don't understand why you didn't get it."

"I think I do, Dotty; he's looking for abilities they didn't teach me in finishing school. You could do it though, Lily."

"Me; don't be so silly," I replied.

"No, really Lily, I think he's looking for someone exactly like you."

"His Lordship wouldn't look twice at me, Fi, a woman from Stepney with an accent like mine. If *you* didn't get the job, I wouldn't get past the door."

"You have a poor opinion of yourself, Lily. I don't agree with you."

They were unable to talk me into it, so they dropped the subject. We commiserated with Fiona, and if she was disappointed, she didn't show it. We had largely forgotten about it, when a few days later, I received the shock of my life.

"You should have applied, Lily," Dotty said.

"Apply for what?" I replied.

"You said you used to manage a big business. You could manage His Lordship, couldn't you?"

"We discussed that Dotty; His Lordship wouldn't offer someone like me a job like that."

"No, you're probably right, but he'd be a fool if he didn't. Anyway, you've got an interview first thing in the morning."

"What are you talking about, Dotty?"

"I met the housekeeper, Mrs Morgan, I told her about you. She said His Lordship still hasn't found anyone, and if you turn up in the morning, she will ask His Lordship to see you."

"Are you serious, Dot, you're not having me on, are you?"

"*Me*, don't be daft, as if I'd do that."

"This is ridiculous, Dotty, I'll be thrown out!"

"Very likely, but at least you'll get a look inside."

"Oh, Dotty, what have you done, tell me you're not serious?"

"It's first thing in the morning. Me and Fi will cover for you; but you must go straight on to the farm afterwards. We've got to unload that lorry, so you can't be too late."

"Prepare a curriculum vitae," Fiona said.

"What's that?" asked Dotty.

"Oh, it's just a list of your qualifications and experience, but I really can't see the point Fi, he'll never offer the job to someone like me."

"I told you, I think he's looking for someone exactly like you. This low opinion you have of yourself, Lily, it's misplaced. Trust me, those boarding school girls were wrong."

"That's a kind thing to say, Fi, but I can't help it. I really do think it's pointless."

"Well, do me a favour and write out a CV anyway," she said sternly.

We talked about it all evening. I was a little cross at Dotty for placing me in what I thought was an invidious position, but they both remained adamant, I should attend the interview. The following morning I was up early because I had to look my best, so washed my hair and brushed it out, standing over the range. I put on a little powder and some lipstick, but I didn't want to overdo it. Worst of all, I had no option but to wear my uniform; I had to go from the Manor directly on to the farm. I worried and fussed about everything.

"I wish you hadn't done this, Dotty," I said.

"You'll be fine, Lily, you'll get the job, you'll see."

I wished I had Dotty's confidence. By the time I was walking towards the Manor, I was feeling nervous. What I did not expect was to see a soldier on guard at the entrance.

"Do you have business here?" he asked.

"Yes, I've got an interview with His Lordship. I have to see Mrs Morgan first."

"Okay then, walk on to the Manor. As you face the building, you'll see what looks like a separate section to the right, but it's all a part of the main building. Just walk along to the end of that section where you can turn left and you'll find the Servants' Entrance."

"Thank you, soldier; actually, I'm feeling nervous. It's not about the job so much; it's His Lordship, what's he like?"

"This is all new to us being here; I've only seen him once or twice. Just another stuffed shirt if you ask me. Nothing for a good-looking woman like you to worry about."

"Well, thanks, I need all the encouragement I can get! I'll let you know how I get on."

"You do that, luv, you can't miss me, I'm the idiot who has to stand here all day."

When I got to the Manor, its sheer size was daunting, I felt very insignificant. As directed, I went to the Servants' Entrance and knocked on the door, half expecting it to make a loud creaking noise as it opened. Within the setting of the building, that would have seemed appropriate. However, it opened silently to reveal a little silver-haired old lady.

"Hello, dear, can I help you?"

"I hope so," I said, "the housekeeper said I should come for a job interview."

"I see, wait here then, dear, I'll get Elsie for you."

I stood there looking around, naively expecting something grander than the rather run- down hallway I stood in. The ceiling was low, and it smelled damp. A woman came striding down the hallway towards me, and I assumed from her appearance that she was the housekeeper.

"Hello dear, I'm Mrs Morgan, you must be Lily. Your friend Dotty spoke so highly of you, I thought you should come and see His Lordship. I didn't realise you were a Land Girl."

"Yes, I'm sorry about this, I've got to go straight on to the farm from here, so I had to come in my work clothes."

"I see, oh well, never mind, let's see what His Lordship thinks of you."

That didn't inspire my confidence at all, but I followed her as directed. We walked along several little hallways until suddenly we entered an unfamiliar world. I was walking through the most enormous room, and then into an even more impressive room - it was too much for me to take in. There was such detail everywhere - paintings, carvings, the furniture. When I glanced up towards the ceiling, I couldn't take my eyes off it. Then we went into a smaller side hall.

"Sit here, dear, I'll tell His Lordship you're here, and someone will call you."

I sat down, feeling even more insignificant. There I sat for what felt like an age, becoming very impatient, thinking about the girls covering for me, but finally, a footman approached me.

"Follow me, Miss," he said, "what's your name?"

"Lily. Lily Heywood."

He led me to a door, which he opened, stepping inside. "Miss Lily Heywood to see you, My Lord." The room was not as lavishly decorated as those that I had previously walked through. It was nothing like as ostentatious; instead, it had all the obvious trappings of an office, although nothing like the office I used to work in. It was poorly lit, and although the window was large, the hangings obscured the sides of the panes. A man was sitting at a desk with a table lamp bathing him and the desk in a warm glow. There were piles of papers, and numerous maps on the wall. There were a few items of furniture, but this was a business-like room. He was engrossed in something. I just stood there like a schoolgirl sent to see the headmistress.

What should I do; should I say who I was, should I cough or something? I decided to just stand there, shuffling from one foot to the other, as I looked at him. He was only four or five years older than me. I had just assumed he would be older. He had dark brown, slightly wavy hair combed back from his forehead. From what I could see, he was wearing an immaculate double-breasted suit, waistcoat, and tie. His breast pocket handkerchief matched the tie, and to be honest he cut a very dashing figure. I could see immediately what Fiona meant about him; this must be His Lordship, I was thinking.

After what felt like an embarrassing eternity, he pushed some documents to one side, and gradually raised his head to look at me, revealing his face for the first time. He had wonderful features and lovely eyes. Those eyes were initially wide, warm, and welcoming, but then, in an instant, they narrowed into a quizzical expression.

"I'm sorry for keeping you, Miss Heywood, I'm very busy and you don't have an appointment, do you?"

"No, that's right, Mrs Morgan said she would arrange it for me."

"Yes I see, but why has Mrs Morgan directed you to me, I don't interview my farm workers."

"Yes, I'm sorry about the overalls, I'm in the Land Army. I couldn't avoid it, I'm afraid, but I'm not applying for a farm job."

"I don't understand, what are you applying for?"

"I thought I was applying for the position of your Personal Assistant."

"I'm sorry Miss Heywood, I require an assistant with an extremely high level of attainment. With the greatest respect, I am not sure you realise the qualifications such a position requires. There has surely been some kind of unfortunate misunderstanding. I can't imagine how this happened; I can only apologise that Mrs Morgan has inconvenienced you."

He reached for the servant bell and pulled it; I was about to be escorted from his office! I felt horribly humiliated, although it was exactly what I expected. I think I over-reacted, not coping well with the rejection.

"If there has been a misunderstanding, then I can assure you it has not been of my making. You know absolutely nothing about me, you have not even offered me the courtesy of asking me about my education and experience. You presume to make a judgment of me, when the only knowledge you have applied to that decision is your own prejudice. This does not speak well of you, My Lord. I won't thank you for seeing me, and there is no need to show me out."

He sat open-mouthed; it was obviously the only time during my brief interview when I had impressed him.

"Miss Heywood, may I ………."

I interrupted him. "No My Lord, I don't think we have anything else to say." I turned and walked towards his office door. "One last thing, it's not Miss Heywood, it's Mrs Heywood!"

I left his office still feeling humiliated. At least I felt quietly pleased with myself that I had spoken out calmly and rationally and had not allowed the situation to get the better of me. The footman asked if I was leaving.

"Yes, I think that's the general idea," I said.

He politely escorted me, and along the way we met Mrs Morgan again.

"How did it go, dear?" she asked.

I told her in no uncertain terms what I thought about His Lordship.

"Oh dear, he is very busy, you know, I think in his rush he must have misunderstood; that doesn't sound like His Lordship at all. I'm sorry you've wasted your time."

"Not your fault Mrs Morgan, but what exactly did you tell His Lordship?"

"I told him exactly what Dotty told me. She said you were the smartest woman she knew, and that you had managed a large multinational shipping company. That's right, isn't it?"

"Well, it's kind of right. I've got it all written here, but he didn't want to see it. Thank you for taking the trouble, Mrs Morgan."

"Let me have your reference, perhaps I can still show it to him."

I gave her my CV and went on my way, growing happier about the whole thing the further I walked away from the Manor. The soldier smiled at me as I approached the barrier at the estate entrance.

"Well, did you get the job?"

"Did I hell, you were right, he's just another stuffed shirt."

"What did I tell you? Never mind, luv, perhaps I'll see you in the village pub one night?"

"You never know, soldier!" I shouted back as I walked away.

I walked the rest of the way to the farm with my disappointment equally balanced against my anger about the way he had treated me. By the time I arrived, my anger had eclipsed the disappointment. I gave Dotty a scowling look, admitting the interview had been a disaster. We had no opportunity to discuss it during the day.

Come the evening, I really gave Dotty what-for. "What on earth did you tell Mrs Morgan? You really made me look like a fool, Dotty!"

"I just said you had managed this big multinational shipping business, and you read all these books, and you're the smartest person I know."

"But Dotty, that made it sound like I was in charge of hundreds of people, there were only nine of us."

"I tried to make a good case for you, Lily, and you *are* the smartest person I know."

"It would have been better if you'd said nothing, Dotty. He was expecting to see a business executive, only to be confronted with a Land Girl. He obviously thought I was a complete fraud."

"I only wanted you to get the job, I'm sorry Lily."

How could I possibly be angry with Dotty? Fiona thought it was hilarious which, really, I suppose it was. They wanted to know all the details, so I gave them a blow by blow account of the interview. Inevitably my account turned into a farce, and we couldn't stop laughing.

"Effectively, he threw you out then," Fiona said, with tears in her eyes.

"He tried to, and that was when I told him what I thought of him."

"What does 'utter disdain' mean, Lily?" Dotty asked.

"It means His Lordship treated Lily as if she was unworthy of respect," Fiona said.

"That's a good word, I'll try to remember it," Dotty said, with a smile that seemed to surround her entire face.

"So what did you say then?" Fiona asked.

"Well, I was polite, but I told him what I thought of him."

With that, we all erupted into laughter again, except for Gran, who sat glum-faced.

"You need to show some more respect, Lily, you can't talk to His Lordship like that."

Dotty jumped up and put an arm around her.

"Come on, Gran, you've got to see it from Lily's point of view. He'd shown utter disdain, you see - that's a good word - and he made a mistake when he did that to our Lily!"

"Too right, Gran, I think he had it coming," Fiona said.

Even Gran finally saw the funny side of it. "I don't know, you modern girls will be the death of me!" she said.

"At least you'll go down laughing, Gran," said Dotty.

Over two weeks went by - days of digging ditches, mucking out stables, and more hilarious evenings with Gran and the girls. I had long since put the whole thing behind me, until a letter arrived, and I could see it was from the Manor.

As I opened it with some trepidation, the girls had their heads in the way, so I could hardly read it. It said would I please attend His Lordship at 3pm the next day. Well, 3pm was a difficult time for me to escape the farm, but Dotty was still feeling bad and said she would do whatever was necessary to cover for me. They all decided for me, I should go.

The next day I slipped away from the farm and went home to change. I didn't bother to take an age to get ready, I didn't see the point, though I did make a reasonable effort, especially with my hair. Pretending to be confident, I walked towards the Manor with a spring in my step. The soldier at the barrier was the same young man I had seen the week before, and he recognised me immediately.

"Afternoon, Miss, have you come to see Mrs Morgan again?"

He couldn't suppress his cheeky smile; it must have been so boring, standing on guard. By the look on his face, I had the feeling I was the most distracting thing he had seen all day.

"Yes, it's about the same thing as last time."

He wanted to chat, but I needed to get on. When I knocked at the Servants' Entrance, Elsie Morgan came through to meet me.

"You've caused quite a stir, Lily, I can tell you!"

"Am I here to be reprimanded?"

"I'm not sure why you're here, but you should have seen the look on his face when you left last time!"

It mystified me why he wanted to see me; surely, we had nothing to say? The footman escorted me to his office, and I sat down outside to wait. I was quite prepared to give him another piece of my mind - he might be a Lord, but I was not about to let him or anyone else treat me as he did before. I assumed he would keep me waiting for ages, but he didn't. I had only just sat down when he opened the door personally.

"Mrs Heywood, would you please come in?"

He then walked back around his desk and sat down, and this time there was another chair in front of his desk.

"Please take a seat, Mrs Heywood."

He sat there for some time, seemingly agonising over what to say to me, as I just sat there waiting. Finally, he drew a deep breath, and lifted up his head to look at me.

"Mrs Heywood, it is a comparatively rare occasion when I make a serious error of judgment. It is an even rarer occasion when I make a complete fool of myself, but regrettably this is precisely the situation where I now find myself.

It would appear that my error of judgment has only been eclipsed by the sheer magnitude of my foolishness. I find I have behaved in the most reprehensible manner, exactly as you so adequately described. I would like in these circumstances to extend to you my deepest and most sincere apology; I am contrite, Mrs Heywood.

In my defence, I was under a lot of pressure that day, you did not have an appointment, and I freely admit I allowed the pressure of the day to affect my judgment. However, this in no way excuses my deplorable behaviour, I merely try to explain it. I have absolutely no right to expect you to extend your forbearance to the extent of forgiveness. However, would you consider me impertinent if I were to ask you to at least reconsider your opinion of me?"

This shook me to the core - this I did not expect - I expected a confrontation, so his beautifully worded apology completely disarmed me.

"I confess, My Lord, you've taken me by surprise. What's changed your opinion of me?"

"Many things; I read your CV, Mrs Heywood. You are an impressive woman, and I have never been so adequately put in my place as I was on the day of your interview.

After you left my office, I felt compelled to telephone Mr George Miller, your employer, and we had a lengthy conversation. His opinion of you, Mrs Heywood, is difficult to overstate. I asked him if he thought your capabilities would be adequate to this position, and it quite surprised him. He said such a position was not sufficiently challenging for you, he could not understand why you had applied for it.

So you see, Mrs Heywood, you were perfectly correct in your assessment of me; I knew nothing about you, and it was impertinent of me to think otherwise.

However, I know something about you now, and it is perfectly clear to me that you have exceptional talents, Mrs Heywood. You may, with some justification, consider me to be an unsuitable employer, and you may also feel that the position I offer is not sufficiently challenging to engage your very obvious capabilities. However, I would compound my litany of errors if I were not to offer you the position. Mrs Heywood, would you at least consider being my Personal Assistant?"

I was speechless, completely deflated. On the one hand, I loathed and despised the man but then, he was the most eloquent and impressive person I had ever spoken to. He was utterly charming, and it was also difficult not to allow his appearance to influence me. He wore a different three-piece suit this time, dark grey with a pronounced pinstripe, with every inch perfectly tailored to the contours of his body. He was impossibly stylish, and there was an immense and inescapable charm about him.

My head was spinning. I wasn't cut out to be a farm worker, and neither was I cut out to work for a Lord but knowing which of the two I would prefer, I realised I wanted to say 'yes'.

"I'm not sure, My Lord, I'm not sure I could work for someone who has shown me so little respect."

"I perfectly understand, Mrs Heywood, and I can at least show you respect now by reluctantly accepting your decision. I am immensely grateful for your time, and for the opportunity to apologise to you in person."

"No, I didn't say I *wouldn't* do it, I said I wasn't sure about it."

"I'm not sure I understand, Mrs Heywood?"

"I think you do, My Lord, I think you know I want to say yes."

"I try not to presume, Mrs Heywood, but I would, however, confess to hoping."

I suddenly realised - I was about to start a whole new chapter in my life.

Chapter Eight
Death Calls Again

We had Saturday afternoons and Sundays off so on the following Saturday afternoon, we went to the pub to celebrate my new job. We spent so much time in our WLA uniforms that it almost felt strange to dress up in our nice clothes, the contrast immediately making us feel feminine again. I washed and dried my hair, and it was on occasions like that when I was pleased that I hadn't cut it short. Fiona's hair would always look good because of its abundant natural curl, even after she had been wearing her headscarf all day. Fi always looked feminine and attractive, even in her WLA uniform.

Dotty, however, was the complete opposite. Her short dark hair and tomboy approach to life meant that she just seemed to look at home in filthy overalls, the only exception being when she removed her gloves, revealing an obsession with her nail polish. Come the weekend, however, a totally new Dotty would appear like an emerging butterfly. With her big brown eyes, and long eyelashes, red lipstick and those fingernails, she was attractive and overflowing with sassy charm. It was perhaps inevitable that any trip to the pub would be eventful with Dotty.

The local pub, The Forge, was charming in every respect.

It had obviously been the local blacksmith's forge at one time. It was a lovely old building, still with the original canopy over the fireplace, and the oak beams spoke of a time when smoke from the forge was a constant companion.

We found it quite full, with lots of local farmers, several Land Girls, and a bunch of airmen. Anyone in a blue uniform was a hero as far as the locals were concerned, the Battle of Britain having unfolded directly above the heads of the people of Middlebourne. They may have been powerless to affect the outcome, but the collective will of the people of Kent was up there with those young men in the cockpit. It was common to see locals buying drinks for the flyers, but none of this applied to Dotty. Dotty did what Dotty always does, and in the process embarrassed us all. She walked straight up to the group of airmen and stood there, with her hands on her hips.

"I know what *you* boys want!"

They fell over themselves to gather around her. "What do you have in mind, darling?" one of them said.

"What I have in mind is for you boys to buy me and my friends a drink."

It worked every time, and we all sat together around a table as Dotty orchestrated everything.

"What are we having, girls," she asked, with a provocative smile.

Gin was available during the war, but as mixers in the local pub were in such short supply, we were perfectly used to drinking beer. Armed with a glass each, Fi and I sat back to watch Dotty tantalise the airmen. They were a nice, well-mannered bunch of boys, with only one who could resist Dotty's charms. We all had our share of attention, not least me, but it is surprising the effect a wedding ring can have on a young man's ardour.

I thought one in particular was a lovely man, not as brash as some of the others. With his great charm and good looks, he was quite adorable. His name was John Albright, but his pals all called him Johnny. For some reason, Dotty's charms were not working on Johnny - his full attention was directed towards Fiona.

They kept buying us drinks, and Dotty's presence filled the pub, surrounded as she was by men entwined in the invisible web which she spun around them. Fiona, on the other hand, could not take her eyes off the adorable Johnny, who was staring right back at her. She hung on to his every word, just as he did hers. There was a very tangible spark between them, I could see it in their eyes. I had on rare occasions recognised that look in other people, but sadly it had always eluded me; Gerry and I just didn't have it.

When it came time for the boys to go, we stood outside hugging and kissing as if we were all lovers. It's what happened during the war, every kiss could have been your last. Dotty and I kissed them all, everyone except Johnny. He and Fiona just stood locked in each other's arms.

The boys finally drove off in an RAF car, arms waving enthusiastically out of every window. Fiona waved frantically even after the car had disappeared from view. Little did she know then, but the man she was waving to so fervently would be her future husband.

Dotty had drunk far too much, but insisted we go back into the pub.

"Let's have another beer," she said.

Somewhat reluctantly, Fi and I agreed and sat down again at the same table. The pub was now much quieter without the airmen, which only made Dotty sound all the louder. Just as we sat back with our glasses of beer, two men came into the pub, one in army uniform. He had lots of pips on his shoulder, obviously a high-ranking officer.

The other gentleman was tall and smart, wearing an immaculate, perfectly tailored dark double-breasted suit and waistcoat, military looking tie, and an inescapable air of confidence. It was His Lordship! I elected to look away and gestured towards Fiona. She glanced over for a moment, immediately recognised him, and did the same.

"Probably best if he doesn't see us," I said, "especially after all those beers."

"You're right," replied Fiona. "I hope Dotty says nothing when she comes back from the Ladies."

"Oh Christ, she won't know it's *him,* will she!"

"Oh no, she *wouldn't,* would she?

"Here she comes, we'll soon find out."

The route back from the Ladies meant she would pass right next to the table where His Lordship was sitting. He cut a dashing figure, so it was perhaps inevitable that he was far too attractive for a very drunken Dotty to resist.

"Well, hello boys, I know what *you* want," she said.

"I beg your pardon, madam, I do not believe we are acquainted," replied His Lordship.

Dotty swayed a little as she tried to focus her eyes on him.

"Quite right, and that's a situation I just know you want to correct. Am I right, or am I right?"

"Quite wrong, Madam, I have absolutely no desire whatsoever to be acquainted with you."

"Everyone wants to be acquainted with me, I'm Dotty! Dotty by name, Dotty by nature."

"You have made a serious misjudgement, Madam. I can assure you I would rather have Hitler as my father-in-law than be acquainted with you."

Fiona and I almost choked on our beer, desperately trying not to laugh. I'm not sure which of our emotions had command of the situation. It was hysterically funny, while also being excruciatingly embarrassing. However, Dotty wasn't done yet, bracing herself against a chair-back, and drawing in a deep breath while still trying to focus her eyes.

"I think what you just said was totally *dainful,* that's a big word isn't it? My friend Lily taught me that word, so what do you think about that, then?"

"We finally have the semblance of an understanding, madam. I most certainly do not deign to converse with you. My advice, madam, is that you inflict yourself upon a less discerning person."

For everyone's sake, I felt obliged to intervene. Either I would choke on my beer, or Dotty would dig an even deeper hole, so I stood up and walked over to his table. The second he saw me, the pair of them jumped to their feet.

"Mrs Heywood, what a delightfully unexpected pleasure. May I introduce General Broadbent."

"Good evening, Mrs Heywood."

"Good evening, General."

"Mrs Heywood is soon to be my Personal Assistant. She is ridiculously over-qualified, and I count myself extremely fortunate to have acquired her services."

"That's very kind of you to say, My Lord."

"I think we both know, Mrs Heywood, I have considerable ground to make up. A simple reiteration of the truth is not a bad place to start, don't you think?"

Once again, he had taken the wind right out of my sails. He could really be the most charming man imaginable. Dotty just stood there swaying, unable to let go of the back of the chair she was bracing herself against.

"Did you say My Lord, Lily?"

"Yes I did, Dotty, and you are making a dreadful spectacle of yourself."

"Oh my God, I've done it again, haven't I?"

Fiona quickly took Dotty by the shoulders and led her away after acknowledging His Lordship's smile of recognition.

"Yes, Dotty, that's what I would call really making a spectacle of yourself," she said.

"Friend of yours, Mrs Heywood?" asked His Lordship.

"No, not now, but tomorrow - probably yes. Dorothy is the person who caused all the confusion with Mrs Morgan, your housekeeper."

"That explains a lot, Mrs Heywood, not that it exonerates my behaviour, but a spanner in the works can have that effect."

"Dorothy has been an embarrassment, My Lord, for which I sincerely apologise on her behalf. I can assure you she is not normally drunk, and her behaviour this evening has been totally out of character. Dorothy is a very dear friend to us. She is actually a wonderful person - she lights up my life, and I would be saddened if you were not aware of that."

"Your defence of a friend is commendable, Mrs Heywood, and an endorsement from you is more than sufficient for me to reform my opinion of her. If the situation should arise, I would welcome the opportunity to become reacquainted."

Once again, his response had left me speechless; his generosity of character seemed to be boundless. How could this same man have treated me so badly during our first meeting?

"Would you care to join us, Mrs Heywood?"

"That's very kind, My Lord, but as I think you will agree, my friend Fiona and I probably should take Dorothy home before she makes an even greater spectacle of herself."

"Sound judgment, Mrs Heywood. I look forward to our new association in a week's time."

"Yes, My Lord, I am looking forward to it as well."

"Until then, Mrs Heywood."

I smiled graciously and left with the others. *Why did I have to sound so enthusiastic*, I thought to myself? I could have just said, 'see you then,' but no, I had to throw myself at him. I chastised myself all the way home.

"Gran will go nuts when she sees Dotty," Fiona said, "she doesn't approve of drunken behaviour at all."

"Serves Dotty right, if you ask me," I replied.

As soon as we arrived at Gran's, Dotty threw up in the garden.

"I was worried about you girls; seems I was right," said Gran. "Oh goodness, Dotty, you silly girl. Get her inside, the poor luv, I'll take care of her."

I had misjudged many people that day, including Gran. She put Dotty to bed while Fi and I had some supper. I just *had* to ask her about Johnny.

"I don't understand it, Lily, I couldn't stop looking at him, and I can't stop thinking about him."

"Do you know, Fi, I reckon he felt the same. Have you got his name and address?"

"You bet; did you think I would let him go otherwise?"

I smiled, because what I had seen flashing between them was a wonderful thing to be a part of. She talked about him endlessly.

Then she said, "Didn't you feel the same thing with Gerry?"

"No, not really, I wish we had. Truth is, Fi, I was in the club, we *had* to get married, and I think it's unlikely we would have married otherwise."

"You're not telling me you don't love Gerry, are you, Lily?"

"I'm not sure what I'm saying Fi, it's the drink talking. I just know we don't have that spark I saw between you and Johnny - I wish we did."

"What about you and His Lordship? Do you not realise how you look at him, Lily?"

"I don't, do I?"

"You certainly do! I thought you loathed him."

"I do, but he has this way of undermining me. As soon as I get cross with him, he says something, and I forget why I loathe him."

I could really talk to Fiona, often in ways that would have been difficult with Dotty. We laughed and talked until late and then finally went up to bed. As we approached the door, we could hear Dotty snoring loudly, and then farting.

"Oh, my goodness, I'm not sharing with Dotty, I'm getting in with you."

I agreed - we were so weary we could have slept on a clothesline. Just as we were dropping off, there was another loud fart, and we fell asleep laughing. The following morning the room stank, and as I opened the windows to let in the cold fresh air, Dotty looked every bit as bad as she deserved.

"Oh God, what's happened to me, what's happened to my mouth? I feel dreadful."

"It wasn't just your mouth that was the problem, it was your arse," I said.

Fiona was mortified. "Does everyone in the East End of London talk like you two?"

"It's not arse, dear, it's bottom; that's right, isn't it, Fi?" Dotty said.

Even first thing in the morning with a terrible hangover, Dotty could still have fun. She struggled downstairs, dressed only in her bra and knickers, went straight outside, and stuck her head fully into the trough. She had her backside pointing towards the heavens just as Jim was walking by.

"Morning, Dotty, I thought I recognised you."

"Oh, for God's sake! Morning, Jim."

She came back considerably more sober than when she went out.

"You're a tonic, Dotty, you really are," said Fiona.

We ribbed Dotty about that night for years after, but a far darker memory of the following day overshadows my recollections. We had just finished breakfast, and the conversation continually came back to Dotty's embarrassment. We were having great fun at her expense, when Aunty Mavis came rushing in, looking overly concerned.

"Have you heard the wireless, Lily?" she asked.

"No, why, should I?" I replied.

Her expression alarmed us all, and we assumed it was unwelcome news about the war. We rushed into the front room and turned on the wireless. The BBC Home Service was a discussion about growing vegetables, so I quickly re-tuned it to the Light Programme, to find it was broadcasting jazz.

"What are we listening for?" I asked Mavis.

"I don't want to worry you, luv, but I heard something this

morning about HMS Hood. I know your Gerry's on that ship, so I've sent Jim out to get the Sunday paper."

My heart immediately jumped in my chest; I was filled with an all-consuming sense of panic. I feared the worst and hoped for the best, but the feeling of desperation was overwhelming. I had to know! Gran and the girls gathered round me, everyone assuring me that Gerry would be fine, but no amount of assurance could quell my fear. The next fifteen minutes were the longest of my life. Fiona kept looking out of the window to see if Jim was in sight, and her pacing up and down only added to my tension.

Eventually she shouted, "Here he is."

Jim came in and I just knew from his expression that the news was terrible.

"Lily, I'm so sorry, luv, it looks really bad," he said.

Jim put the paper down on the table. It was the Sunday Dispatch dated that day, May 25th. The headline read *Hood Sunk, blown up, feared few survivors, states Admiralty.*

My world imploded, and I just screamed, *"No,"* over and over again. Those first terrible moments were a toxic blend of horror and disbelief, quickly replaced by something far more corrosive. Everyone hugged me at the same time; the more my body shook, the tighter they held me. As my cries and screams diminished, so a part of me diminished with them.

Jim read aloud the newspaper report. "The report says the Hood engaged the German battleship Bismark off Greenland on May 24th. It says it blew up; they've sunk it."

During those awful days that followed, there was inevitably the forlorn hope that Gerry would be one of the few survivors. Half of me knew it was a false hope, but I never let go of the hope. However, when my telegram finally arrived from the Admiralty, it confirmed, 'Lost, presumed dead'. I was prepared for it, but it was another of the blackest days.

There were 1418 men on board the Hood, and only three survived; it was a national disaster. The Hood was symbolic of the power of the British Navy. For twenty years, it had been the biggest, most powerful warship in the world. When Gerry found they had assigned him to the Hood, we were all delighted, thinking, if he was on the greatest warship afloat, he must be safe.

The week following the news was awful; death had found me again. First came the denial, then the disbelief, soon to be replaced by the terrifying void that your life falls into. I wouldn't have made it without Gran and the girls. Once again, we had no body, no funeral, and there was no cathartic moment to say goodbye. Each day just merged into the next. Reg said I should have as much time off as I needed, but towards the end of the week, I put on my uniform and asked Reg for the hardest work he could find for me.

I helped him to clear a fallen tree; Reg cut the branches while I loaded them onto a trailer. Even though each piece was too heavy for me to lift, I somehow lifted them anyway. Reg said little, seeming to understand my anguish. I didn't invite any conversation, feeling unable to reach out beyond the void I had fallen into. I think I felt that if I punished my body sufficiently, the reality of the pain might allow me to touch life again.

I worked most of the day, putting every ounce of my anguish and grief into every branch. I threw them onto the trailer until I was so exhausted, I just couldn't lift another branch and sank to my knees.

"That's enough, Lily, I know what you're doing, and I think you should stop now," Reg said.

Fiona saw me there on my knees and came rushing over to help me.

"Take her home, Fi, she can't keep on doing this."

My body hurt so much I could hardly move; Fiona strug-gled to help me to my feet. As she helped me across the field towards home, Dotty saw us from a distance. She instantly dropped her rake, running towards us as fast as I have ever seen anyone run. She grabbed me around the waist and put my other arm over her shoulder. I swear had Fiona not been there, Dotty would have picked me up in her arms and carried me all the way home.

I sat in a hot bath, the first one in it this time. In a strange way, the pain in my body relieved the pain in my heart. I felt dreadful, but differently. They all waited on me hand and foot that evening. It was Fiona who pointed out what I had forgotten; I was due to start at the Manor the following Monday.

"I'll tell them, Lily," said Dotty, "you need another week or so."

"No Dotty, I need to do it, I don't want His Lordship's sympathy."

They all argued with me but I knew, if I forced myself to do it, then I was forcing myself back towards normality. It was Saturday morning, and I wanted to get up for work, but I had really hurt my back. Gran tried to insist that I stay in bed, but I didn't want to be alone with my thoughts. It was not just Gerry; I kept seeing Ian, Linda, and the boys, I was sinking into a bleak place.

I just had to make myself get up and get dressed, and eventually I struggled downstairs, only to slump into the armchair. I seemed to be powerless to exclude those uninvited thoughts which kept tormenting me. Even Spencer Tracy couldn't distract me. My body ached and my spirit was broken, but I just kept telling myself I'd been here before and would find a way back. Then there was a knock on the front door.

Gran answered it and shouted, "It's Reg to see you, luv."

My heart sank, I assumed he was there to ask why I hadn't reported for work. Reg was renowned for being grumpy, his physiognomy was perfectly matched to his curmudgeonly disposition. So I didn't expect the Reg who walked into the room, carrying a bunch of flowers and a large tin.

"What's this, Reg?"

"It's just a few things for you, Lily, I picked these for you, and Flo has baked you a cake."

As I thanked him profusely, I think he realised I was thinking this was a Reg I had not seen before.

"You see, Lily, I knew what you were doing yesterday. I knew because we lost our youngest son during the last war, and I did the same thing you did, exhausting all my grief with the hardest work I could find. So I just want you to know, I do understand and want to wish you well for the future, Lily, because there *is* a future. I've lived most of my life grieving, but you're only just starting your life; don't do what I did. Take hold of your future, Lily, don't hide from it."

"Oh Reg, if I could move, I'd kiss you!"

"Don't worry about that, *I* can still move!"

Never in my wildest dreams would I have ever thought I would give Reg a hug, let alone kiss him. When I told the girls later, it started quite a revolution on the farm. Dotty, especially, never missed an opportunity to give Reg a hug and he, in turn, always protested vigorously, but as Dotty said, he always complained *after* the event! I learned a lot from my few weeks as a Land Girl, not least that old cliché about books and covers!

Chapter Nine
Middlebourne Manor

On Monday morning, I struggled out of bed. My back was still painful, but I washed and dried my hair, making myself look as good as possible; anything to distract me from my real disposition. The girls thought I was bonkers going to a new job while feeling like that, and they were probably right. Grief drains the body of both strength and will, I already knew that, but I already knew I needed to fight back. We all had to fight back during the war, and I drew on the collective strength of the nation.

I remembered my first morning at Mum and Dad's after they bombed me out. My first faltering steps towards the telephone box, my resentment that the sun was shining. This day felt much the same. It was a warm late-May morning, but the fading memory of winter still lingered enough to remind us of the contrast with those dark, cold months.

It was the kind of day which makes people smile, and that's what grief denies you. That kind of misery is like a filthy wet cloak which death has forced you to wear. You recoil from it, but you get to know it, and knowledge is everything. A single step is all you need to start a journey, so I struggled, a step at a time, but I managed. The soldier at the barrier was different that day; as I approached him, I prepared myself to explain who I was and why I was there, wishing I had no need to.

He stood to attention, saying, "Good morning, Mrs Heywood, please go straight through."

Taken aback, I just nodded and carried on, knocking on the Servants' Entrance where I waited. The same silver-haired old lady answered the door.

"Oh, it's you, luv, I'll just get my daughter Elsie."

Elsie Morgan appeared somewhat surprised to see me.

"What are you doing here, Lily, I mean Mrs Heywood? You're main entrance now."

"You mean I should go in through the Grand Entrance?"

"That's right, His Lordship has instructed the staff, but may I just say, Mrs Heywood, I'm so sorry for your loss; it's terrible."

I didn't ask how she knew, I could guess, and so I thanked her for all the help she'd given me, and went back outside, heading towards the main entrance. This all felt even more nerve-wracking. The Grand Entrance was so imposing, my heart was racing. As I approached, a footman stood looking down at me.

"Mrs Heywood?"

"Yes."

"Please follow me, Mrs Heywood."

I followed him into the Grand Entrance Hall. They built the Manor to impress and it was extremely imposing; I couldn't help but feel even more intimidated. I was expecting to be taken to His Lordship's office, but the footman opened the door into a wonderful Reception Room and announced me.

"Mrs Heywood, My Lord."

I stepped into the room feeling a mixture of emotions - grief, sadness, and anxiety, coupled with a glimmer of excitement. His Lordship sprang to his feet.

"Mrs Heywood, please come in, do sit down."

I sank deeply into a buttoned Chesterfield armchair, with His Lordship sitting opposite me. He was as immaculately dressed as ever but was lacking the usual slightly arrogant self-assurance which I had seen before.

"Mrs Heywood, I have been informed of your tragic loss. May I say how desperately sorry I am, please accept my heartfelt, deepest condolences. I have to say, Mrs Heywood, your very presence here today in these difficult circumstances, confirms to me that you are a most extraordinarily brave and courageous woman."

"I don't understand; how do you know, My Lord?"

"I understand now, Mrs Heywood, why you value your friend Dorothy Archer so highly. Miss Archer came here yesterday and specifically asked to see me. I might have refused, but she told my housekeeper that it concerned you. She graciously apologised for her conduct the other day, for which I insisted there was no need, then she told me about the tragedy which has befallen you. Miss Archer is concerned for your well-being, Mrs Heywood. She worries that you are understandably in a fragile condition and was equally concerned that I should show consideration. I tried to convince Miss Archer that knowledge of your awful tragedy was the only motivation I required to change my plans entirely.

What I propose, Mrs Heywood, is that we just sit and talk awhile. There will be many questions you will require answering, but unfortunately, I have to go to London later this morning, so I have asked my mother to take care of you. You will find her immensely helpful regarding the affairs of the household. I would like you to regard today as merely an introduction to Middlebourne Manor. You may start your new position tomorrow or the day after, or whenever you feel strong enough to do so. I now fully appreciate what you meant, Mrs Heywood, when you said Miss Archer shines a light in your life."

"Oh dear, how embarrassing!"

"It should not embarrass you in the slightest, Mrs Heywood; your presence here today and your very worthy friend's concern only combine to reaffirm my opinion of you. Would you care for tea, Mrs Heywood?"

This was not at all how I expected my first day to begin. Once again, he had taken me by surprise. He rang for the maid, and requested a tray of tea, then had an afterthought as the maid was leaving, also requesting some cake. I was totally out of my depth, not expecting any of this. My expectation was that I would be sent to an office somewhere and treated just like any other member of staff. The tea soon arrived, and the maid set it on a low table, asking if His Lordship wanted the cups poured, but he declined, saying he would take care of it.

"Allow me," I said.

"I'm not sure pouring tea is one of your duties, Mrs Heywood."

That gave me the ideal opportunity to ask the question I most wanted to have answered.

"What exactly *are* my duties, My Lord, and why am I not being treated like any other member of your household staff?"

"I like that, Mrs Heywood, straight to the point, and I will be equally forthcoming, but first I am required to ask you to sign this document."

"Sign a document - what on earth for?"

"It is a mere formality, I assure you, I am constrained by this same document."

"I'm not sure I follow you, My Lord."

"This is the Official Secrets Act which the law requires you to sign before I can even disclose the nature of your employment here. Furthermore, once you have signed this document, its conditions will bind you. Not to put too fine a point on it, Mrs Heywood, this binds you to absolute secrecy regarding anything you do, see or hear while you are in my employ here at Middlebourne Manor, and anywhere else for that matter.

The penalty, should you not conform to these conditions, ranges from a term of imprisonment to possibly hanging, capital punishment being restricted to treasonous offences."

"Oh, I'm pleased to hear that, about the treasonous offences I mean, but I'm still not sure I understand, My Lord."

"Trust me, Mrs Heywood, this is a necessary requirement."

For some reason I did trust him. If he said it was a formality, then I believed him, so I looked at the document, scanned through it, and signed it.

"Congratulations, Mrs Heywood, you have joined an exclusive club which offers neither perks nor benefits!"

I smiled as best I could, completely mystified about what was going on. He poured the tea with great finesse, seeming to enjoy the ceremony of it.

"Cake, Mrs Heywood? I highly recommend it."

I accepted the tea and the cake, but what I wanted was an explanation. He sat back with his cup of tea and looked at me.

"I work for a Government department, Mrs Heywood. I keep an office here, and another in the War Office. I manage the Joint Technical Board, it's just dull administration, but it's the nature of these things during wartime, everything has to be Top Secret you see."

"I wondered why there was a military guard."

"Yes indeed, silly regulations, very tedious. The thing is, I also have an estate to run here. There is an unavoidable interface between my two activities, and this is why I need you, Mrs Heywood."

"I see." I had no idea why I said that because I didn't really see anything.

"My father mismanaged the estate, as did his father before him. We operate a loose collective of businesses, with tenant farmers who each manage their farms as they always have done. We have forestry and shooting interests, property and tenant interests; my estate manager oversees these activities. My housekeeper manages the household affairs, and my butler

Jennings ensures the house and the staff run smoothly. Mother keeps the household accounts. Do you see my problem, Mrs Heywood?"

I didn't want to speak out of turn, so hesitated for a moment, to think about it. I decided His Lordship was not looking for a weak opinion, so I said what I thought.

"Yes, My Lord, I can. My brief time as a Land Girl has taught me a lot about how your tenant farmers run their farms. If I were to assume the rest of your estate affairs are managed in the same way, then I would have to conclude that the inefficiencies are not sustainable."

"Exactly right, Mrs Heywood, how perceptive you are - this is why I need you. My estate needs proper management, and every aspect needs to be looked at with fresh eyes. I am charging you with that responsibility. In my absence you have complete authority. Mrs Heywood, you may hire and dismiss as you see fit, you may change management practices as you desire."

It completely blew me away, not knowing what to say. How could I possibly do all the things he wanted of me? I felt it was beyond me.

"Why on earth do you think I can do all these things you want of me?"

He just sat there, his self-assured confidence returning, his smug smile starting to reappear. He reached over to a pile of documents and picked up a folder, handing it to me. I looked down at the vanilla coloured folder. Grubby, with turned-up corners, it had been subjected to much handling. It shocked me to see my name on the cover and the words Top Secret emblazoned across it. I looked at him, and then back to the folder, as he maintained his smug smile. Inside there were separate transcripts of interviews with various people, each with qualifying notes.

Uncle George's transcript was the largest, but there were many others - ship owners, haulage company owners, dock authority officials, customs officials, even dockers. There was even a brief statement from the woman who ran the tea shop in the docks. There were dozens of them, my school reports, and my lending library record. The most shocking was a transcript of my interview with the woman for my Land Army enrolment. Some sections were highlighted. Then I saw my brother's army record, and a statement from his Commanding Officer. Even my Dad's army record was there. My immediate reaction was outrage - how dare he do this to me? I knew he saw my eyes flash.

"Your reaction is understandable, Mrs Heywood, it is based upon your view of the world as you saw it before you came into this room. Working for a government department gives me access to this kind of thing, and for good reason. I need a person with exceptional attributes, not just qualifications, and I will be candid with you. When you first attended the interview, I gave you short shrift because I did not associate the attributes I required with a woman from your background. I have already apologised for that mistake. Mrs Heywood, I can assure you when the information about you accumulated, no-one was more surprised than I was, but do not for one second underestimate yourself as I did. I take advice with important decisions like this, and from the final selection of four people, intelligence experts and psychologists all agreed that you were outstanding."

Again, he had completely knocked the wind out of my sails. Initially I was outraged, and then the next moment I had no idea what to say.

"I don't know what to say, My Lord, I don't understand what you see in me. Even if I *could* see, how on earth is a woman from the East End going to command the respect you seem to think I should receive?"

"Perhaps you are a victim of your own prejudices, Mrs Heywood, just as you accused me. I have every confidence in you, why else would I entrust my estate to you."

"What about the soldiers, how do I treat them?"

"They are an unfortunate addition to my estate, but we have not been requisitioned; they are here at my invitation. As such, they are subordinate to the estate, and their rank is immaterial Mrs Heywood. You are in charge here."

"Does this position come with a salary, My Lord?"

"Of course, Mrs Heywood."

"May I ask what it is?"

"I have no idea; this is something within your own jurisdiction. You must pay yourself whatever you think appropriate. I would suggest you look at my estate manager's salary, and I suggest you triple it."

"Very well, My Lord."

I was not about to argue. I just sat feeling rather terrified and bewildered.

"Another cup of tea, Mrs Heywood?"

"Yes I will, thank you, allow me to pour."

As I approached his desk, I noticed the front page of an old newspaper that was lying there. He noticed how the headline captured my attention, and we both read the report. Enemy aircraft had sunk HMS Gloucester off Crete on May 22nd. This was just two days before they had sunk HMS Hood. The report listed 807 crewmen; they feared there were few survivors. Those that survived were picked up by the Germans, which His Lordship said was rather odd. He said we had other ships involved and he could not understand why they didn't pick up the survivors. He asked who it was that I knew on the ship and I couldn't avoid telling him it was Alan, Linda's husband, and that they were our closest friends; Alan and Gerry had both signed up at the same time. It was too much for me; this was the straw that finally broke me and he could see my reaction.

"Mrs Heywood, I have marvelled at the strength you have shown by coming here today and am aware that I have extended your resilience to its limit. I have no right to impose myself further upon you, not at a time like this. As you will see, I am not particularly good with situations like this, but my mother is very keen to meet you, so this is obviously an appropriate moment."

I felt I had embarrassed him; I could tell he had no idea how to deal with a lady in distress. He terribly politely excused himself, saying his mother would attend me. I didn't want to be attended by anyone, I just needed time to compose myself, but in the circumstances, I felt obliged to stay there and was awfully glad I did.

Some little time passed until a most elegant lady entered the room. I immediately assumed it was the Countess. I had no idea whether to curtsey, shake hands, or just say nothing, but I need not have worried. This most delightful lady approached me with a smile, offering me her hand.

"Mrs Heywood."

"I'm so sorry," I said, "please excuse my ignorance, how should I address you?"

"Well done, my dear! Most people in your position make an awful mess of a situation like this. Formally, I am the Dowager Countess of Middlebourne. Most people refer to me as Lady Middlebourne, or My Lady, and in less formal circumstances I prefer Lady Caroline."

"It's a great honour to meet you, My Lady."

"My son speaks highly of you, Mrs Heywood; he has asked that I help you in any way that I can."

"That is very kind of you, My Lady, I suspect I shall need all the help I can get. His Lordship seems to have placed me upon a pedestal from where I can only fall. I just hope to earn the trust he has placed in me."

"You have probably noticed, Mrs Heywood, that my son can be a little arrogant; however, you must overlook and forgive him for that. He is in possession of an enormous intellect, and his ability to assess people and situations can be quite unnerving at times. My son assures me you are more than capable of the task ahead of you, and he will not be wrong, I do assure you."

"I'm not sure if that's a comfort to me or not, My Lady!"

"It should be both a comfort and a compliment, Mrs Heywood. I have learned to trust his opinion. My son has also told me about your tragic loss, I am so sorry. Frankly, I am amazed that you came here today at all, I admire your strength of character. If there is anything at all that I can do, please ask."

"This has indeed been a terrible week for me and my way of dealing with such a situation is to fill my mind with alternative thoughts and challenges. To be honest, I'm in a dark place, and this job offers me light. I'm not at all sure I can do it, but I am attracted to the light, it's what I thrive on. So I wonder if perhaps I could see the domestic accounts?"

The Countess appeared to warm towards me, and I have to say I felt the same towards her. She immediately escorted me to what appeared to be the nerve-centre of the household, a small room where she kept the accounts, and where she would discuss issues privately with her housekeeper and butler. Not being sure what to expect, I was secretly thinking that her accounts could be a shambles. I wasn't a qualified accountant, bookkeeper, or anything else, but I had studied all aspects of accounting and managed all the affairs of the shipping agency. To my surprise, I found her accounts were well set out, everything done correctly. Her copperplate handwriting was a joy to follow.

"You love doing these accounts, don't you, My Lady?"

"I do, it is something in which I have always taken great pride."

"It shows; you must continue doing it."

We discussed all aspects of domestic affairs, as I looked at the breakdown into expenditure, wages, food, maintenance. I also noticed there was now a financial contribution from the War Office. There was a reduction in wages compared to previous years, which made the current accounts appear far more sustainable, and I realised the reason for that. The war effort now involved most of the young men and women who had previously served at the Manor.

Her Ladyship also gave me invaluable information regarding the servants. She said that she highly valued her housekeeper, Mrs Morgan, who could absolutely be relied upon. She also equally valued Jennings the butler, but he could at times be 'difficult'. She suspected he would have great difficulty accepting my authority. If I needed a reliable ally among the junior staff, she recommended young Florence. She had come from a problematic background, but she was a lovely girl. However, the estate manager was quite a different prospect; Her Ladyship did not have a kind word to say for him.

"My late husband could see no wrong in the man, but I don't trust Phillips. I'm not convinced he is an honest man; besides, he has a dreadful manner."

I made notes of all this information; to be forewarned is to be forearmed. I also made a note of things I felt I should look at, such as where they purchased food and provisions. Estate maintenance attracted a huge yearly expenditure, so I thought I should just cast an eye over that.

"Shall we adjourn for lunch, Mrs Heywood?"

"I think it best if we could just have a sandwich here, I would prefer to carry on."

Everyone in the family had traditionally stopped for mealtimes, so the concept of a working lunch was revolutionary for the Countess. She put a brave face on it, and we achieved an enormous amount that day. Come the evening, I realised I was no longer fighting back the tears. They were still only a memory away, but the distraction had held them at bay. Her Ladyship was exhausted; it had been much more than the Countess was accustomed to, so when she suggested we should call it a day, I agreed. My first day was over, I was still terrified, but I was quietly pleased.

"I don't know about you, Mrs Heywood, but I need a drink. You will join me?"

Her offer took me by surprise. I doubted that she had ever been prepared to share a drink with a member of staff before. I can tell you I was flattered by the offer. I thought about it because I wasn't sure how best to approach my new role. Should I be regarded as an insider, or would I be better to remain on the outside. Should I treat the servants as the family would, or should I try to work among them? If I accepted her kind offer, they would immediately see me as an insider. I had no experience to draw upon, so I decided to just be me, and see what happened.

"I would love to, My Lady," I replied.

We sat in the wonderful Drawing Room surrounded by three hundred years of opulence. The maid called me Madam, and I answered as if I had not noticed. Then I experienced my first encounter with Jennings, the butler. Approaching me with a gin and tonic on a silver tray, he was very correct, placing the glass on a table next to me.

"Your gin and tonic, Mrs Heywood."

I noticed immediately it was the way he said 'Mrs'. I could see Jennings would take some winning over. Social order in the great houses was steadfastly held to; everyone knew their place. My place had been the East End of London, and Jennings believed I was sitting on the wrong rung of the ladder.

"Thank you, Mr Jennings, I am looking forward to us working together."

"Yes, His Lordship has informed me. I understand the situation."

Her Ladyship thanked Jennings, and he politely left. She waited until he had closed the door.

"I think you can see the problem with Jennings. You will need to exercise all your people skills if you are to win him around."

"Don't worry, I know how to deal with Mr Jennings!"

"You have made quite an impression on me today, Mrs Heywood," she said.

"That's kind of you to say, but really I just need to keep busy at the moment."

"I don't mean to be disparaging, I'm really not like my son in that regard, but you both impress and intrigue me in equal measure. Would I be right to assume from what I have been told that you didn't come from an affluent background, and yet look at you! Where does it all come from, Mrs Heywood?"

"Yes, you're right, I don't come from an affluent background. I had an unusual upbringing, with a period of private education. I also have an uncle who has been very influential in my life, but really, I'm just a younger version of my grandmother. She had this same red hair, and she's everything I would like to be."

"Is she still with us?"

"Yes, she is nearly 90, going on 65, and I love her to bits. It's why I'm here at all. I'm staying with her, here in the village."

"But I thought you would be a resident here at the Manor?"

"His Lordship mentioned that. Perhaps occasionally, but I value being with my family and friends above all else."

"When my son described you to me, I thought it was hyperbole, I assumed a pretty face had turned his head. I was right about the pretty face, but oh my goodness, I can see what he means. I share my son's confidence in you, Mrs Heywood, I can tell his affairs will be safe in your hands."

"That is a kind thing to say, Lady Caroline, thank you. I'm having a bit of a crisis of confidence at the moment; His Lordship seems to expect so much of me, but whenever I doubt myself, I will remember your kind words."

I hadn't dreamed for a moment that I would get on so well with Lady Caroline. She was everything I imagined a countess would be. She had a wonderful elegance, coupled with a disarming charm. In the family portrait of her with her two children, she is eye-catchingly beautiful. It was always impossible to walk past the painting without becoming fixated upon her beguiling smile. The woman sitting opposite me was perhaps thirty years older but no less beautiful, and no less beguiling.

-oOo-

I arrived back at Gran's after the girls had come home, I could see them through the window as I approached. Spencer Tracy could hear a pin drop at a thousand paces, barking from behind the door even before I had even closed the front gate.

"Get down, Spencer, that's a good boy, *get down*. Dotty, can you call him?"

"*Spencer*, come here," shouted Dotty.

Spencer dropped his ears and reluctantly returned to the kitchen, to be praised by Dotty. I never understood how Dotty had such control over him. I sat down at the table with everyone, and Spencer was still desperate to come and greet me. He sat right next to me with one ear twisting back and forth, expecting a telling-off from Dotty. She in turn was looking rather sheepish, no doubt thinking I was cross with her.

"Before you tell me off, Lily, just remember I was concerned about you, I didn't want that man upsetting you."

"I'm not cross, Dotty, I know you meant well. It must have taken quite some nerve to approach His Lordship like that, especially after what you did in the pub!"

"That's what I thought," said Fiona, "it only goes to show, you really don't have any shame, do you, Dotty."

"What's done is done, that's what I say," Dotty replied. "Actually His Lordship was quite understanding, saying I'd no need to apologise. When I told him about Gerry, he seemed almost human."

"He *is* human, Dotty. He was kind to me, in his own way."

"Well, that's good, then," Dotty said. "I warned him, he'd have to answer to me if he upsets you!"

"I don't know how you get away with it, Dotty. You insulted the man, and then he referred to you as my 'very worthy friend'. I told him you shine a light in my life, and he said he could see why."

"You told him that?" Dotty whispered.

For once in her life, Dotty had nothing else to say; I had silenced her. Gran and Fiona sat smiling, as did I.

"What?" asked Dotty.

"Nothing, Dotty," Gran replied, "tell us about His Lordship, Lily."

"Let me change first, at least," I said.

"Bath's full, Lily, you're last one in, I'm afraid," Fiona said.

"You mean get in after Dotty, have you lost your senses?"

That evening was the first time since the news of Gerry that I actually laughed. It was not much, but it was a step forward. As I changed into some casual clothes, I couldn't help but reflect upon Dotty's reaction to me saying that she shone a light in my life. She was such an extraordinary, extrovert character, but I was realising I had failed to see beyond that, and wondered if, behind the facade, there was a vulnerable Dotty. I knew they would be full of questions, and so with one more glance in the mirror I went back downstairs. As soon as we sat down to eat, they were all over me like a rash, wanting to know everything.

"What's His Lordship like then, Lily?" asked Fiona.

"Yes, come on, Lily, does he always have that rod up his arse?" said Dotty.

"Bottom, dear; it's *bottom!*" laughed Fiona.

When I had finally stopped laughing, I tried to tell them.

"He's not like anyone I've ever spoken to before. I don't mean because he's an Earl; he's just different. The Countess told me that her son has an enormous intellect, and he does. When he talks to you, he's thinking so far ahead all the time, you feel you must run to catch up."

"You've met Her Ladyship as well?" asked Gran.

"Yes, she's a lovely lady. She was so kind to me."

"Forget the old girl," said Dotty, "tell us more about Lord Snooty."

"I know what you want me to tell you, Dotty, but honestly it's impossible to see him in that light."

"So you're not all gooey-eyed then?" Fiona said.

"Certainly not! He wouldn't recognise a gooey-eyed woman, anyway; he doesn't think on that level at all."

"Shame really, he's rather good looking, isn't he," Fiona replied.

"Can you girls not think of anything else?" Gran said. "I'm more concerned about the rationing! The meat ration has dropped again, it's only a shilling now, and some of that you have to take as corned beef. *And* now it's clothes as well."

"Oh no, not *clothes!*" I said.

"What about that leg of lamb we had the other week, Gran?" joked Dotty.

"That's different, luv, that's a private arrangement, and it's our own vegetables."

I smiled - rationing there in the country was different to London. Then there was rationing at the Manor; I could see that was a different thing again. We were all treated equally with the rationing system; it was just that some were a lot more equal than others. We never stopped talking all evening and Gerry wasn't mentioned once. I was unsure whether he should have been or not, but even family avoided mentioning it, for fear of causing upset. Perhaps I just felt guilty because I was talking happily, when maybe I shouldn't. The war didn't help; we had to show a stiff upper lip as far as war casualties were concerned. It was almost a case of not allowing Hitler to get one over on us.

Dotty's eyes were closing even as she stood drying the dishes. It was the end of a momentous day for me. I had no idea what the future held; I just knew my life had changed that day. Full of self-doubt, and not understanding why he had selected me for such an enormous task, I only knew that I wanted to take it on. By the time I went into the bedroom, Dotty was already snoring. Fiona raised her eyes towards the ceiling, in an expression of resignation.

"You don't mind me getting this job, do you Fi?"

"Good Lord no, I knew he was looking for something more than I could offer. I'm truly delighted for you, Lily; you can achieve things there that I couldn't possibly do. I think you'll be an enormous success, and you can always rely on us here."

"I'm frightened, if I'm honest. I hope I can do what he thinks I can."

"You will, Lily, you will."

I went to sleep happy, knowing that I had a wonderful support system around me.

Chapter Ten
A New Broom

There was a lovely winter coat for sale in a shop window in Tunbridge Wells, mustard yellow, long and very stylish, with a contrasting lining. I couldn't imagine where the shop found it; in a drab wartime Britain, it shone out like a beacon of hope. It was April when I first noticed it, obviously not a popular time to buy a winter coat, which was reflected in the price. When I went back to Tunbridge Wells for my last WLA interview, it was still there and I was unable to resist it, so I bought it.

On the morning of my second day I woke to find it was damp and dreary, nothing like the end of May at all. It felt more like autumn than summer, so it was the perfect morning to put on my new coat. With my long auburn hair, my wide-brimmed chestnut brown hat and bright long coat, there was no doubt I would stand out on that otherwise drab morning.

We had breakfast together, then the girls went in one direction, dressed in their farm clothes, and I went in the other, feeling like a world apart. I approached the Manor for my second day, knowing this was the start of a new venture. I was His Lordship's Personal Assistant, with authority over the entire estate! My problem was that I hadn't met that person yet - I was terrified.

I thought about what George had told me. I just had to conquer my inner demons. Those demons were telling me I could only fail, so I had to force myself on. The butterflies in my stomach felt like a flock of birds! The young soldier at the barrier stood looking me up and down as I approached. Finally he stood to attention, appearing hesitant, as if deciding whether he should salute me.

"Don't be ridiculous, soldier," I said, with all the authority I could muster.

"Yes, Mrs Heywood, sorry, Madam."

I could see that His Lordship had prepared my way in advance, but the man standing in front of me was having difficulty dealing with the situation. He looked like a nice young man who first and foremost saw me as an attractive woman. Wanting to smile at me obviously conflicted with his orders to treat me as his superior! It was a valuable lesson for me, and I hadn't even entered the grounds of the Manor!

"Let's be clear, soldier, I'm His Lordship's Personal Assistant. I am not, however, a commissioned officer in His Majesty's Army. You stand to attention, but you do not salute me, do you understand?"

"Yes, Madam."

"I'm not sure you do, soldier, I am not 'Madam'. You will refer to me at all times as Mrs Heywood. Furthermore, soldier, if I catch you looking at me again like you did just now, you'll find yourself on a charge. You know exactly what I mean, Corporal, and make sure the rest of your attachment understands that."

"Yes, Mrs Heywood. I'm sorry, Mrs Heywood, it won't happen again."

"Just make damned sure it doesn't, Corporal. You have a good day now."

I looked as defiant and authoritative as I could manage, while inside I was shaking. I was not remotely used to talking to people like that. I had built up respect with George and the shipowners, but demanding it was quite another matter. I started to question my whole approach: I always tried to look my best, but perhaps on that day especially, it was a mistake? I planned to treat the military differently to the household staff, seeing no alternative. However, treating the soldier like I had was far outside my comfort zone. It left me feeling very uneasy, not to mention shaking.

When I left home that morning, I felt attractive in my mustard yellow coat, and my wide-brimmed hat; but now I just felt conspicuous. I could see the footman watching me approach, then he straightened his back and only averted his gaze at the last moment. I knew nothing about him other than his first name, which was William. He was in his fifties and would have looked smart in his uniform anyway, but I could tell he was a man who took pride in his appearance.

"Morning, William."

He was taken aback. Servants like him were used to being invisible.

"Morning, Mrs Heywood," he said, with a smile.

"Dreadful weather, William, it's more like autumn today."

I invited a response from the poor man, but invisible people were not accustomed to responding, and he wasn't sure what to say.

"That's what I told my wife this morning. You wouldn't think it was nearly June, I said!"

"No, you wouldn't, William. Is your wife in service here in the Manor, as well?"

"Yes, Mrs Heywood, she is Her Ladyship's maid."

"Does your wife know how you look at women like me? It's not very becoming, William, you're old enough to be my father!"

He almost died of embarrassment. He wasn't a young hot-head like the soldier, and his shame was more than a sufficient reprimand for me.

"I'm dreadfully sorry, Mrs Heywood, it will not happen again."

"Make sure it doesn't, William. Now, enjoy the rest of your day."

I entered the Great Hall for the second time; here at least I would not look conspicuous. The magnificence of the room was overwhelming. The many family portraits appeared to be looking down on me with an inquisitive disdain. What, I wondered, would they have made of me? His Lordship's father and grandfather, the seventh and eighth Earls of Middlebourne, looked dreadfully austere.

The portrait of His Lordship must have been a recent one and made him appear warm and welcoming in comparison. The sense of family history was all around me, but it was the family portrait with Lady Caroline that I couldn't look away from. I stood admiring the portraits, not noticing the young maid who was scurrying about in the corner of the room. She stood motionless the moment I saw her.

"What's your name?" I asked.

She curtseyed, and said, "Florence, Madam."

"No, that's not right, Florence."

"It is, Madam, I'm Florence."

"No, you silly girl, you're not supposed to curtsey to me, and you call me Mrs Heywood."

"Yes, Mrs Heywood. I'm sorry, Mrs Heywood."

"You've got lovely hair, Florence, what do you wash it with?"

"I just use shampoo powder and I can't always get that now, but the secret is to use rainwater."

"Would you be able to get me some clean rainwater, Florence?"

"Of course, Mrs Heywood, just ask me, and I'll heat it up as well for your lady's maid."

"I don't have a lady's maid, Florence, and neither will I be having one. I'm here to work, the same as you."

"I'm not sure I understand, Mrs Heywood, but if you would like me to wash your hair, I would be pleased to. You have such lovely hair."

"Florence, you're a gem, and don't worry about your shampoo, I'll take care of that." She was sweet; I had only been pleasant to her, and in return she offered me a smile that brightened my day. I knew not all hearts and minds would be so easily won over.

I had not even seen inside my office yet; I only knew it was the door immediately next to His Lordship's office. As I walked along the hallway, I could see the door ahead of me, and could see a nameplate with my name on it. I needed a deep intake of breath; what on earth was His Lordship thinking of! It seemed even more ostentatious because His Lordship's office door only had a modest nameplate which said 'Private'.

I stepped inside with more than a little trepidation; it was a plain room, large, with a high ceiling. There was a fireplace on one wall with a marble surround, and a window on the other. I had a desk, a filing cabinet, and one or two items of sundry furniture, obviously previously superfluous household items. The lighting was an incongruous chandelier converted from candles to electricity. Sitting in pride of place on my desk were a telephone and an Imperial typewriter. It had all the hallmarks of an office equipped by someone who had never worked in one. I had the basics, but little else. I took off my coat, only to find I lacked a coat stand, and there was no mirror. I couldn't possibly exist without a mirror; so this became a most urgent requirement! The room was bare, lacking so many of the minor essentials, not to mention consumables. It was, however, an excellent start, and I could soon make it my own.

There was a timid knock on the door. It was the other maid.

"Would you like tea, Madam?"

My instinct was to say, 'that's kind of you, luv, yes please,' but I managed not to do that.

"What's your name?"

"Mary, Madam."

"Well, Mary Madam, I would like tea and two biscuits on my desk every morning at 8am, but today I would like two cups of tea and four biscuits."

She smiled - I was human, after all. "Yes, Madam."

When she returned with my tea, I asked her where she came from, what her background was. It wasn't much, but I wanted her to know I was interested in her. I wanted her to go back to the kitchen and tell the staff I was not so different to them, that I was approachable. I had made the decision that I could not pretend to be someone I wasn't. If I were to gain their respect below-stairs, I would have to do it from the inside.

"I'm not a madam, Mary, I'm Mrs Heywood. Would you ask Mrs Morgan to come and see me?"

"Yes, Madam. Sorry, yes, Mrs Heywood."

Mrs Morgan soon knocked on the door, with a worried look on her face. It seemed a request to attend my office was a cause for concern.

"Come in, Mrs Morgan, sit down, have a cup of tea with me."

I could see she didn't expect that, smiling as she sat down. I had decided to start below-stairs and work up. I would confront the various elements of my job, one at a time, starting with the kitchen. My first concern was the presence and therefore, the cost of the military personnel at the Manor. I also guessed that we had an inefficient, haphazard purchasing system, especially in that time of rationing. I learned a lot about purchasing power in the shipping industry, and the need to centralise it. I also knew Mrs Morgan would not be amenable to me organising her, so I had to approach the subject carefully.

"I was wondering how you're coping with all the additional food purchasing you have to do now that we have the military here. You must be rushed off your feet."

"I am, we can't go on as we are! It's the rationing; I just

can't order enough food, and it's impossible for Cook to cater properly."

"Do you still have to register all the ration cards with different suppliers?"

"Well, yes, I can't get round it."

"It's not fair, is it, not when London hotels are serving as much food as you can eat," I said.

"How do they do that?" she replied in astonishment.

"They have a different system. The Ration Board can issue a certificate to restaurants and institutions, allowing them to purchase more food."

"That isn't fair, not when we have these soldiers to feed. I wonder if we could get one of those certificates?"

"I hadn't thought of that, Mrs Morgan, but now that you mention it, perhaps I should approach the Rationing Board. What do you think, and perhaps we could even purchase from a central supplier? With the rationing and everything, that would make your job much easier, wouldn't it?"

Elsie Morgan smiled; she could see the sense in her own suggestion.

"You should have spoken to Her Ladyship sooner, Mrs Morgan, that's a grand idea. I can see why Lady Caroline values you so highly. While you're here, what can you tell me about Phillips, the Estate Manager?"

"Well….. I wouldn't like to speak out of turn, it's not my place."

"I've heard lots of things about Phillips from Reg at the farm," I said, "and if what Reg tells me is correct, then it would be a cause for concern. If you can help me, Mrs Morgan, I think we all have a duty to His Lordship to do the right thing."

"Well, if you put it like that, Mrs Heywood, I suppose you're right. The thing is, I hear stories from lots of people about Philips. People say he manages His Lordship's affairs in his own interests."

"This is what Reg told me. Philips tells him who to sell

his milk to, and at what price. It's the same with the lambs; Reg doesn't take them to market, because Philips tells him he already has the best price."

"Trouble is, Mrs Heywood, Philips has too much influence around here. People like Reg feel they have to do as he says, because they fear the consequences, otherwise."

"If that's the case, Mrs Morgan, I shall need to put a stop to it. Hitler didn't intimidate me with his bombs, so I certainly won't allow this man Philips to intimidate people like Reg. You leave this with me."

Things moved apace over the next couple of days. The local Ration Board was not a problem; the Earl's name carried a lot of weight in official channels. In the fullness of time, Mrs Morgan got her additional rations. They say an army marches on its stomach; well, the same can be said for a Manor House. Rationing had become such a part of life, the mere sight of an extra rasher of bacon raised morale among the staff enormously. After all, we were now a part of the war effort. We could also access more non-food items, such as soap and shampoo.

The Blitz looked as if it was finally over, with the last large-scale raid on 11th May. Hitler was turning his attention towards Russia with 'Operation Barbarossa'. I found I worried less about my parents. In the absence of continual air raids, I didn't have to worry about His Lordship either while he was in London. When there was a phone call for him, all I had to do was tell the caller he was at the War Office.

This left me with the time I needed to integrate myself into the household. I wondered if His Lordship might have planned things that way. I was building up a good rapport with nearly all the servants and quickly came to rely on Florence for any below-stairs gossip that I might need to know. Mrs Morgan was indispensable, just as Lady Caroline had suggested. I asked her to explain to me how the Manor had changed since the beginning of the War.

"It's not the same at all, Mrs Heywood; the Manor was

always full of guests. We had shooting parties nearly every weekend during the Season, and Lady Elizabeth had an almost constant stream of guests."

"I'm sorry, Mrs Morgan, who is Lady Elizabeth?"

"Oh, didn't His Lordship mention his sister?"

"No, I'm afraid not, but I saw the young girl in the family portrait."

"Lady Elizabeth could be a little wild, and some of her parties caused friction with her father, the Eighth Earl. When His Lordship became the Ninth Earl, he - shall we say - encouraged her to go to America. He said it was because of the war, but I'm not so sure!"

"You mean Lady Elizabeth could be a little difficult?"

"That's a polite way of putting it, Mrs Heywood."

"So there must have been many more servants before the war?"

"Oh yes! At one time there were twenty-three servants inside and outside, now we only have twelve including the gardeners. Some of them now are not much more than children. Look at Mary, Florence, and Albert; we've lost a lot of experience. Some positions like His Lordship's valet no longer exist now. The only other experienced household staff we have left are Mr Jennings, Cook, and Mr and Mrs Evans."

"Mrs Evans, she's Her Ladyship's maid?"

"Yes, that's right, Joyce has been with Her Ladyship for over twenty years now."

I could see Mrs Morgan hankered for the past when Middlebourne Manor ran like a well-oiled machine. I could so easily visualise the banquets and weekend guests, the shooting parties and visiting dignitaries. It was a world away from my own, but strangely I mourned its departure nearly as much as they did. I realised more than anyone that my very presence there represented the wind of change. The war had to end one day, but I was equally sure the wind of change would keep blowing. Mrs Morgan and Jennings were probably the last of their kind, and I had an enormous respect for both of them.

The next person on my list to deal with was the Estate Manager, Phillips. He held sway over much of His Lordship's estate and from what I had been told and seen for myself, he was definitely up to no good, so I asked Jennings in a private moment what he thought about him.

"Strictly between you and me, Mrs Heywood, I don't like him and I hear stories from many people. He seems to have interests in too many things that should not concern him. I couldn't prove it, but I'm sure the man is dishonest."

"Thank you, Mr Jennings, I value your opinion. I shall need to see him and his books as soon as possible."

"He's out of his office most of the time, but that's where you need to see him, where he keeps all his affairs."

"How do I know when he will be there, without telling him I'm coming?"

"Yes, I see. Leave it to me, Mrs Heywood, I will send young Albert to tell you when Phillips is there."

I was grateful for Jennings' help, but it was clear from his manner that his attitude had not changed. He was prepared to be professional in his dealings with me. He was even being helpful, but Jennings was not yet prepared to accept me as his superior. I could see this was a situation I needed to resolve.

However, I had plenty else which needed doing, so I set about my day and waited to hear from him. I was slowly accumulating a list of useful contacts, people from whom I could purchase goods and services. Some items were urgent, like a mirror and coat stand, but others, like new curtains for my office window, were less so.

My office needed to be impressive. I always used to notice that, when I walked into the office of a shipowner, if it was very impressive, it would make me feel inferior, even intimidated. I reasoned that this was working to the advantage of the shipowner, putting me at a disadvantage when I negotiated a price. If I was to be Personal Assistant, I needed to impress everyone who entered *my* office. I intuitively didn't want to intimidate people, but realised I probably needed to, so I drew up plans to redecorate and properly equip my office.

All my information told me that Phillips was a bully who was feathering his own nest. I was also told to be careful how I dealt with him; that was an ominous warning which stayed with me. I was sure he was mismanaging estate affairs, and so I had to decide in advance how to deal with him. This would be a significant test of my authority, so I couldn't afford to get it wrong. I decided to consult Lady Caroline, and on finding her in the Drawing Room, I asked if she could spare me a moment.

"I need some advice, Lady Caroline. You told me before that you don't trust your Estate Manager, Phillips. Well, I've been asking around and many people say the same thing."

"Personally, I don't like the man, but my husband always relied on him. Why do you ask?"

"When I worked on the farm, I heard a lot of stories about Phillips. Now that I have made enquiries here, I'm afraid there seems to be little doubt that he is dishonest. He uses His Lordship's estate as if he owned the place. I'm sure he profits from the farmers' produce and worst of all, he intimidates them into cooperating with him."

"This is dreadful, does my son know about this?"

"I'm not sure he does, Lady Caroline. Phillips has made sure everyone is in fear of saying anything about him."

"Well, if you're right about him, what do you propose to do?"

"This is my reason for coming to see you; I need your advice."

"I think we need to know what Edward would have to say."

"I thought you might say that Lady Caroline. But he gave me authority over the whole of the estate, so I can't afford to be seen as lacking that authority."

"I see what you mean. Do you propose to dismiss Phillips?"

"I do. I think anything else undermines my position."

"You're quite right, Mrs Heywood, but that would be such an unpleasant thing for you to do. Are you sure you want to go ahead with it?"

"I'm terrified at the prospect, but now that I know about him, I just *have* to do it."

"This is obviously why my son values you so highly, my dear. I dislike Phillips, he is aggressive and unpleasant and I really do admire your spirit. My only advice is that if you are sure about him, then he must go, and he will have to go immediately. You mustn't allow him the time to cover his tracks."

Just at that moment, the young footman Albert appeared and entered the room very politely.

"Excuse me, My Lady. Ma'am, I've just seen Mr Phillips go into his office. Mr Jennings asked me to tell you."

"Thank you for the message, Albert. Just one thing, I am not Ma'am, I'm Mrs Heywood."

"Sorry, Mrs Heywood."

"Thank you, Reynolds, that will be all," Lady Caroline said.

I smiled at her, and she gave me a reassuring smile back. I could see I had her support, and that meant a lot to me. It was approaching lunchtime, so I needed to see Phillips soon in case he went anywhere for lunch. I set out that morning to look attractive, not intimidating. I was wearing a pretty knee-length dress with the usual shoulder pads. It was often to my advantage to look attractive when dealing with men, but this would not be one of those occasions. I would have to confess I felt incredibly nervous, particularly about my appearance, so I rushed down to the kitchen to see Mrs Morgan.

"Do I look intimidating, Mrs Morgan?"

"Not at all, Mrs Heywood, you look lovely if I may say so. Why do you ask?"

"I'm on my way to see someone and it will probably not be an amenable meeting, so I don't want to look too feminine. Do you understand what I mean?"

"I've got an idea," she said, turning towards the scullery maid. "Fetch me a coat and a hat that will fit Mrs Heywood, would you; the older, the better."

The scullery maid, Caitlin, came back with a drab old coat and a rather battered hat. As I put them on, Jennings smiled, albeit reluctantly.

"Not exactly intimidating, Mrs Heywood," Caitlin said, "but you frighten the life out of me!"

Everyone laughed. I hadn't mentioned why I needed to look less feminine, but they all realised it was Phillips.

As I left, Mrs Morgan whispered, "He has a very quick temper, watch out for it, and you can use it against him."

I put my hand on her arm, thanked her, and set off towards the Estate Office. Evans, the footman, opened the door for me, looking at me in some astonishment.

"What do you think of my new look, William?"

"If I might be permitted to say, Mrs Heywood, I doubt that coat would look as good on anyone else."

"Careful, William, you're getting close to that line we discussed!"

I stepped through the door and took a few paces before I turned back to face him. "But that was a kind thing to say, William, thank you."

As I walked down the steps leading from the Main Entrance, the military guard stood to attention. It was the corporal I had reprimanded on my second day.

"Bring your rifle and follow me, Corporal."

He did as I asked without question. We both walked to the Estate Office, which was in a group of outbuildings close to the house. It was a converted stable, and the building looked charming from the outside. It would have made an idyllic cottage with its own courtyard had it not been set in the grounds of the Manor among other buildings. It was only the Estate Office sign which gave any indication of its use.

"I want you to stand out of sight, Corporal, and keep your

ears open; I need you to witness what's said. You might also need you to rescue me, so stay alert."

"Rescue you, Mrs Heywood?"

"Yes, Corporal. I have reason to think you may have to escort this man, Phillips, off the estate. In fact, you might well have to arrest him."

"I can't arrest a civilian, Mrs Heywood?"

"Actually, Corporal, if I say so, you can. I'm told he has a very quick temper; he can be a violent man."

"If this man thinks he can threaten you, Mrs Heywood, then as long as I'm around he would be making a terrible mistake."

"That's very reassuring, Corporal."

I had never set eyes on Phillips before, so at least I had no preconceptions. The corporal stood to one side of the door while I knocked nervously. A gruff voice shouted, "Come." His office was cluttered with paperwork - I had never seen a more disorganised mess. The clutter was long-standing, the cobwebs bore testament to that. The room and its contents would have been at home in a Dickensian novel. As for Phillips, he was a man of about fifty, wearing a tweed jacket, twill trousers, with a dark red waistcoat and a check shirt. His tie was loosened, and his collar undone, revealing a filthy line around the inside.

It might have been his intention to look stylish in a country way, but in reality, it didn't work. The crumpled jacket and stained tie spoke more of a man with no social graces. To add to my disapproval, his office stank of cigarettes and that unpleasant smell of decaying books and files. He looked up at me with some bewilderment, the cigarette in his mouth drooping a long section of ash from the end.

"Who are you, what do you want?" he said, in an overly aggressive manner.

The ash fell from his cigarette, dropping partially down his front and onto the desk, but he just ignored it. As he tapped what was left of his cigarette ash against an already full ashtray, I noticed his nicotine-stained fingers.

"I'm Mrs Heywood."

"Oh, I see. His Lordship warned me about you."

"No, he didn't, he would have informed you, no more."

"Well, what do you want?"

"I need to get to know all my staff, Mr Phillips. I need to know the workings of the estate."

"You wouldn't understand the workings of your own kitchen, let alone an estate! Best leave it to people who do."

"I would like us not to get off on the wrong foot, Phillips. I would like you to show me around the estate and give me the benefit of your experience. The object is that we work together."

"Huh! That isn't going to happen, is it. Why don't you just sling your hook and let me get on?"

"One last time, Phillips, will you cooperate with me? We could start by going through the books together."

"Not a chance, there's no bleeding way an upstart girl like you is going through my books!"

"Don't make the mistake of thinking you can foul-mouth me, Phillips. I worked in the London Docks; I can hold my own against any foul-mouth. I'm calmly asking you to cooperate with me."

"And I'm telling you - you can bugger off and do whatever it is you do in the house."

I tried desperately hard not to lose my temper. It was important that I remained in control of the situation. I concluded from his reaction that his books were a sensitive issue. He certainly acted as if he had something to hide, but I needed to be sure.

"I'm not intimidated by a loud-mouth like you, Phillips. I'm not leaving this office until I've had a look at your books."

He jumped to his feet, hastily stamping the butt of his cigarette into the overflowing ashtray. Aggressively stepping around his cluttered desk, he came towards me, trying to intimidate me into submission.

"I'm not telling you again, girl, clear off. Get out of my office, go back to London where you belong."

He was obviously nervous about me seeing his books, doing all he could to frighten me off. Standing with his face inches from mine he lit another cigarette. He blew the smoke in my face and pointed his grubby nicotine-stained finger towards the door. I just needed him to go that extra inch.

"And what's a grubby little man like you going to do if I refuse?" I said, staring right back at him.

He almost touched his nose to mine as he snarled at me, his vile breath making me recoil. He really was the most objectionable character. Then, finally, he crossed the line. He grabbed me by the lapels of the old coat I was wearing and pushed me violently against the wall. I let out a scream to alert the corporal. My soldier's timing was impeccable, kicking open the door and pointed his rifle squarely at Phillips.

"Stand aside please, Mr Phillips, sir, or I will be obliged to shoot you."

The look on Phillips' face was priceless! The silly man had predictably overstepped the mark, just as I had invited him to.

"Are you all right, Mrs Heywood?" the corporal asked calmly.

"Only thanks to your intervention, Corporal. This man attacked me; you witnessed the assault. Arrest him, take him into custody, and call the Civil Police."

"You'll never get away with this, Heywood, you can't pin anything on me," Phillips snarled.

"I think you're in for a rude awakening, Phillips. How about demanding money with menaces, embezzlement, and now assault?"

Phillips panicked and tried to move towards the door. My overzealous soldier swung the butt of his rifle into Phillips' stomach. He gasped and bent over double, falling against his desk. The corporal then thumped Phillips' head down onto the desk, leaving his nose bleeding.

"I saw that, Corporal, he assaulted you as well."

"He certainly did, it's not your day, is it, Mr Phillips?"

The corporal led Phillips out of the office at gunpoint as I removed the old coat and hat. I followed on behind, feeling rather triumphant. Even as he was being escorted away, he tried to foul-mouth me. He really was an odious character.

"Oh, just fuck off, Phillips," I said, "you tried to intimidate the wrong person this time; your days here are over."

The corporal smiled approvingly and gave Phillips another shove, locking him in the storeroom without further ado.

"I'm sorry, Corporal, there was no need for the kind of language I just used."

"What language was that Mrs Heywood?"

"You're a good man, Corporal, I won't forget this."

"He didn't stand a chance, did he - Phillips, I mean. I'm not sure you needed me at all Mrs Heywood."

"What's your name, soldier?"

"Harris, Mrs Heywood, Corporal Harris."

"Next time I need help, I'll ask for you, Corporal Harris."

The Police arrived and took Phillips away, and his demise was immediately common knowledge. It was a turning point for me. I needed to stamp my authority on the house but had not anticipated for a moment I could achieve it within my first week. Phillips would never know the service he provided me.

It subsequently came to light that his record-keeping was good. The estate books were untidy, but properly set out. No wonder the previous Earl kept faith with him. Fortunately, however, his personal records were equally well set out. There were details of every dealing; he kept receipts for all the produce he sold on behalf of the farmers. Phillips intimidated Reg and all the other farmers into allowing him to act as an agent between them and the purchaser. He obviously didn't reveal to them or to His Lordship that he was taking his own 'commission'.

It was much the same kind of intimidation which often

existed in the Docks. Things went missing regularly, and all too often it was the honest docker who found himself with little option but to be complicit. I despised the bully boys; their gain was always the honest man's loss. I'm sure this was why I despised Phillips so much, and why I made it my priority to get rid of him. Eventually he was convicted of embezzlement, serving a lengthy term of imprisonment.

My satisfaction with a job well done was short-lived, however, as I quickly realised that I had to replace Phillips. Jennings had told me about the assistant, Mr Norton, but I had to assume he was at least in part complicit with Phillips.

I asked the young footman Albert to find him and send him to my office. I even thought about asking for Corporal Harris. Albert was away a long time, and my next appointment arrived, the local builder and decorator.

I wanted my office completely redecorated. The wallpaper was peeling off the walls, and the decorative plaster cornice was a filthy grey colour. I explained what I wanted and left him to look around my office while I continued with some paperwork. The builder walked around the room tapping the walls, muttering about the damp, and all the problems he had to overcome. I was far more concerned about confronting Norton.

"I'm sorry," I said, "I don't mean to be rude, but I'm not interested in the problems you have to overcome; just quote me a price to do what I've asked of you. And I have been looking at some of the maintenance work you have carried out here over the years. His Lordship must be your biggest client by some margin. The problem is that there's no indication in your prices that you value His Lordship's patronage.

We both know you have been systematically overcharging. Your association with the estate has been a long one, but that is finished now, we are starting again. Let me give you a word of advice - if you wish to exploit your customers you would be better advised to do that with your less important accounts.

It's very foolish to exploit your best customer, Mr......I'm sorry I didn't catch your name?"

"It's Fuller, Mrs Heywood."

"Okay Mr Fuller, I think we understand each other. I look forward to receiving your estimate for the work, and I would advise you to think carefully about it. Thank you for your time. Now I have another appointment."

He was quite elderly; his brown jacket frayed at the cuffs, his shirt frayed at the collar, and he just seemed to deflate before my eyes. My impression was of an autumn leaf fluttering down into the long grass. I didn't enjoy treating people like that, but Fuller was unworthy of respect after the way he had constantly exploited the estate.

"Just one thing, Mrs Heywood," he said, "I can tell there was a door in this wall at some time, so it might be better if we fill it in properly."

"Show me exactly where you mean, Mr Fuller."

The hidden door was between my office and His Lordship's. They were obviously originally adjoining rooms, so I made a snap decision.

"Restore it back to its original condition, Mr Fuller. Provide me with a nice door, and will you get this old servant bell working for me? Oh, and one last thing, Mr Fuller. Did I mention my acceptance of your estimate will depend on you finishing this work by the end of next week?"

It left me wondering why on earth I was even considering using this man. Just as he was leaving with his tail between his legs, a lovely-looking man almost bumped into him. This was obviously Norton, and not what I expected in any way, shape, or form. In his middle thirties, and wearing a very smart three-piece tweed suit, he had wavy brown hair and beautiful eyes. I would have to confess that I was a little taken aback; he did not look remotely intimidating.

"Come in, Mr Norton, I understand you were Phillips' assistant."

"That's right, Mrs Heywood, I was appointed two months ago."

"Oh, I didn't realise, I assumed you had been with us for some time."

"No, as I understood it, the previous assistant fell out with Mr Phillips and left suddenly. I was pleased to be offered the job."

"What did you do before, Mr Norton?"

He explained that he had been an Estate Factor for a large estate in Scotland. He wanted to move back to England where he came from and when he heard about this job, he applied for it. When I asked him if he could provide references from the Highland estate, he reached into his inside pocket and produced them. He immediately impressed me, but I needed to know if he had been party to Phillips' shenanigans.

"Tell me honestly, Mr Norton, did you know what Phillips was up to?"

"I had an idea, but what you're really asking me is, was I a part of it. No, I wasn't, and I don't think I could have gone on much longer, knowing about it."

I was hoping he would say that, wanting to believe he was an honest man. I think it was his eyes; he had such lovely eyes. I just couldn't believe he could possibly be a crook like Phillips.

"I'm more than satisfied Mr Norton, so you're no longer assistant to the Estate Manager." He looked a little shocked. "No, I'm sorry, I mean you are now the Estate Manager. I assume that you are both capable and willing to take over from Phillips?"

"I am Mrs Heywood, I'm more than capable."

"Good, that's settled then. I will come over to your office tomorrow morning at 10.30. I need you to show me around the whole estate. I need to know how everything works, and I want you to tell me how you can improve the sale of the farm produce. I want an alternative system which is both good for the farmers, and good for the estate."

"That's a tall order, Mrs Heywood, with less than a day's notice."

"Don't tell me you haven't thought about it, Mr Norton. You're a smart man, you haven't seen what's been going on here without thinking how you could improve it. I'll be disappointed if you haven't."

"10.30 it is then," he replied, his brown eyes creasing towards their outer edges as he smiled. "You do realise it's Sunday tomorrow, Mrs Heywood?"

"Is it? I hadn't realised. Is that a problem, Mr Norton, do you have to go to church?"

"No, I'm not a religious man, Mrs Heywood."

"And is there a Mrs Norton you might have made plans with?"

"No, I can't say there is."

"I don't understand then, what's the problem with tomorrow?"

"There isn't a problem, Mrs Heywood. I'll be in the Estate Office from 8.30 onwards, should you decide to come earlier."

Chapter Eleven
Greg Norton's Early Morning Tea

I walked home that evening feeling more than a little pleased with myself. My first week had gone so much better than I could have imagined. I remembered my first morning when I felt completely out of my depth in a strange environment. What little self-confidence I possessed had drained away at the steps of the Grand Entrance. The responsibility His Lordship had placed upon me was weighing heavily on my mind, and above all, Phillips was a dreadful worry for me. I knew he had to go - it was essential for the estate - but it was also an essential test of character for me.

As I approached the cottage, I felt an unaccustomed spring in my step. Spencer Tracy greeted me with more than his usual enthusiasm; I wondered if dogs could sense your mood. Dotty was just coming out of the scullery wrapped in a towel. Steam was bellowing into the kitchen, together with the smell of coal smoke from the copper.

"You look chirpa, Lily, let me guess. You haven't been shovelling pig shit today?"

"No, I've had a splendid day; in fact, I've had a great week."

She rubbed her hair with another towel, and each time she lifted it like a veil from her face, she had a smile. When she put the towel down, her next reaction was, as always, to look at her hands and inspect her nail polish, then a glance down at the polish on her toes.

"How on earth do you keep your nail polish intact, Dotty?"

"Gloves, and constant attention. One of my little obsessions, you see."

She breezed out of the kitchen, leaving her wet footprints on the quarry-tiled floor. She paused at the door.

"I told you, Lily, I *knew* you could do it! I've left the bath for you."

"How kind, Dotty, but maybe I'll just have a quick wash."

Spencer Tracy continued in his playful mood, and pursued Dotty up the stairs. I smiled even before I heard Dotty's comment.

"For Christ's sake, bugger off, Spencer!"

We all helped with the preparations for our evening meal. Gran had acquired some lamb chops, obviously not ration issue. I suspected Reg might have had something to do with it; we all looked at them with joyful anticipation.

I noticed that Gran struggled a little now to peel potatoes with her arthritic hands. She was slow and methodical, but above all, she would never give in. Her pride would not allow her to admit she needed help, so we needed to be subtle about it. Whatever her problems, she remained the commanding officer, while we were her subalterns.

For all her brash manner, Dotty had a heart the size of Reg's hay barn. She would always notice when Gran was struggling, and that evening was no exception. Dotty worked harder than all of us, but she was always alert to Gran's needs.

"Come on, Gran," Dotty said, "I need you to sit down and darn that sock of mine. I need it for tomorrow - I'll do the spuds."

We all willingly helped Gran, but in a way, it made me sad to watch her decline, I just wanted her to go on forever. She was such a source of inspiration in my life; I treasured her above all else. She had a wonderful photograph of her wedding day; I find it uncanny, because I look exactly like her. I was always conscious of the fact that she was a part of me.

As soon as we finally sat down to eat, they didn't stop asking me questions. I told them about Phillips, and how I got rid of him, knowing they would find out from Reg, anyway.

"*You dismissed Phillips!*" Gran said. "I thought only His Lordship could do that!"

"Actually, no, Gran, he's vested those powers in me."

"I don't understand how you could dismiss him, Lily, but I'll tell you what, though, that horrid man had it coming."

I could see it delighted Gran; she loathed him. When I told them about the soldier arresting him, and what happened to Phillips' nose, they all thought he got exactly what he deserved.

"What I don't understand, Lily," Dotty said, "is why do you have soldiers there?"

"It's just a formality."

"Oh my goodness, Winston Churchill lives there, doesn't he?"

"Don't be silly Dotty, it's just a Government department, it's the Joint Technical Board. Really, it's just His Lordship in his office. The guard is just regulation for any government department."

Dotty entertained us as she always did. She carried a bucket of hot water from the copper into the kitchen for the washing up. Pretending she couldn't lift it, she struggled across the room, protesting that we all worked her too hard. She was indomitable until the moment came when her eyes closed involuntarily. We all knew then it was time for bed. By the time I arrived in the bedroom, Dotty was in a deep sleep. This always gave Fiona and me some time to talk in whispers.

"I got a letter today from Johnny," she said excitedly.

"You've really got a thing going with your flyer, haven't you?"

"I know, I can't believe it! I can't stop thinking about him."

"Does he feel the same?"

"He does! The moment we meet, he kisses me and we just stand there locked in each other's arms. I don't want it to stop!"

"How many times have you seen him now?"

"Twice. Well, three times including that first day."

"The way you talk, Fi, I would think you had known him for months, not just met him on three occasions."

"I know, it feels like I *have* known him for months! I'm seeing him tomorrow and I'm counting the minutes."

"Take none of it for granted, Fi, enjoy every second."

"Don't worry about that, Lily. I know it's all happened so fast, but the way I feel, I think I must be in love with him."

"Fi, you're so lucky, I so much hope it works out for you. You haven't ..."

"No, not yet, but oh God, I want to."

"*Oh my goodness, Fiona Robinson*, I'm actually a little shocked! I never for one moment thought I would hear you say a thing like that. But I think you're right, you really *are* in love, aren't you?"

"I know, I can't believe I just said a thing like that, but it's true, I really want to. I'm just so excited!"

"I can tell it's not advice you'll listen to but really, Fi, please try not to rush things. This is different, isn't it, you're committing your heart."

"I know you're right, but everything's different now. We don't talk about it, I can't even bring myself to think about it, but we all know Johnny's a fighter pilot. Don't make me say it, Lily, please. We just have to love each other while we can."

"Oh Fi, you're right, what was I thinking?"

"Thinking of you and Gerry, weren't you?"

"I suppose I was, is it that obvious?"

"Did you really not feel like I do when you and Gerry got married?"

"I've never felt like you feel, Fi, I wish I had."

"But you slept with Gerry before you got married."

"I enjoyed every minute, but I'd trade it all if I could feel like you do right now."

"Oh Lily, that's such a sad thing to say. You can start all over again; look at you, you're still young. You're so lovely, men fall over themselves to be near you."

"That's not the same though, is it. Maybe one day I'll find someone like your Johnny."

"You will, Lily, and Dotty and I will be bridesmaids."

"Go to sleep, Fi, or you'll have me in tears! Who else would I have as bridesmaids, anyway?"

-oOo-

The following morning I woke early, so I took Norton at his word. The girls liked to lie in on a Sunday morning, and I crept downstairs as quietly as I could, trying not to wake Spencer. I made myself a cup of tea and a slice of toast. I had learned some valuable lessons that week, particularly about how I looked. I wore trousers, with a plain blouse tucked into them. I also put on a pair of Oxford shoes with a low stacked heel, not my usual high heels. I just wanted to look a little less feminine, which was strange and difficult at first, because I usually tried to look my best.

I set off at 10 past 8, wanting my arrival at the Estate Office to coincide with the stroke of 8.30. Everywhere was quiet that Sunday morning, the sun was shining and the air was still. Perhaps ten minutes into my walk, I suddenly realised I was not only noticing the flowers in the hedgerow, and the cooing of the early morning wood pigeons, I was enjoying it. I consciously breathed in the scented air, looking for the different flowers. There was the spicy aroma of yarrow, the alluring smell of musk mallow, and a lovely yellow corn marigold which seemed to shine in the morning sun. I realised I wasn't dragging my shadow behind me and was not climbing an impossible slope. Somewhere behind me I had discarded death's cold clammy cloak of misery.

Norton was an intriguing character. I confess I took a liking to him immediately, though he was a little too sure of himself. When he said he would be in his office by 8.30 just in case I came early, I thought it was probably bravado. This was why I set off early with the deliberate intention of catching him out. I waited until the stroke of 8.30 before I knocked on the door.

"Good morning, Mrs Heywood, come in."

"You're a man of your word, Mr Norton."

"Of course. I've made us both a cup of tea, I hope that's all right."

There were two cups of tea standing on the corner of his desk, a gentle waft of steam rising from the freshly poured cups. Norton had completely surprised me.

"How did you know I would be here at precisely 8.30, Mr Norton, when I said I intended to come at 10.30?"

"Your reputation goes before you, Mrs Heywood. I guessed you would want to impress me with your work ethic."

"Why would I want to impress you, Mr Norton?"

"I think you want to inspire your staff. You'd like everyone to work with the same dedication and enthusiasm that you do."

"So why were *you* here at 8.30 with two cups of tea at the ready?"

"Isn't that obvious, Mrs Heywood? I wanted to impress you with *my* enthusiasm and work ethic."

"You've succeeded, I'm impressed!"

"So am I, Mrs Heywood, you're everything people said you were, and more besides."

"I'm flattered, Mr Norton, but please don't make the fundamental mistake of thinking flattery will sway my judgment in any way; it doesn't."

"I'm not trying to flatter you, Mrs Heywood, I'm trying to establish grounds for mutual respect. You said I had impressed you, so you should know that you impress me. I think that's a good basis for mutual respect, and for our future professional relationship."

Wow, I really *was* impressed! Norton was a sharp talker, and I suspected he had the intellect to back it up. Trouble was, I didn't believe that he was not trying to flatter me - he was! A bit of flattery always goes a long way, but I had to resist indulging him. Then again, I had allowed myself to play along with his game; so why did I do that?

"Okay, Mr Norton, enough of this. Let's have your cup of tea and then you can get on with showing me around the estate."

We drank our tea, and I asked him some pertinent questions to which he had all the answers. In fact, he seemed almost too good to be true. The job of estate manager was second only to my own. It was a critical position. I needed someone with flair and imagination, someone who could drag the estate into the twentieth century. I had doubted I would find someone with all the talents required. My assumption had been that I would have to constantly oversee the position myself and yet, sitting there in front of me, appeared to be the perfect solution!

We drank our tea, and he placed the cups in his kitchen sink in preparation for our departure, appearing to be well-domesticated. I followed him out of his office towards a very muddy Bedford van. The back was full of things which might relate to the management of the estate. There was a bale of straw and a milk churn; I didn't ask why but could see that he was a hands-on manager. He brushed some mud off the seats, and I immediately realised why he wore an old pair of plus fours with a pair of boots behind the seat.

"Will I require boots, Mr Norton?"

"It might be a good idea."

"In that case, I'll direct you to my Grandmother's house; it's not far."

A short drive later and we stopped outside Gran's cottage. He waited in the van while I went in. I rushed upstairs and quickly changed into my WLA uniform and boots; if he was trying to intimidate me with a bit of mud, he'd made a mistake. When I came back downstairs, the girls had their faces pressed against the front window.

"Who is he, Lily?" asked Fiona.

"He's the new estate manager, he's showing me round."

"He looks lovely, I'm coming too, Lily," said Dotty with a beaming face.

"Don't you dare set foot outside that door, Dotty!"

That was exactly what Dotty *would* do, so I asked Fi to hold her down if necessary. I quickly left them and stepped back into the van, much to the surprise of Norton.

"You were a Land Girl, Mrs Heywood!"

"Indeed I was, I've shovelled pig shit with the best of them!"

I could see he was itching to say something, but perhaps he was conscious of overstepping the mark, and just smiled at me. What followed was a complete tour of the estate - the woodland, the tenanted houses, and the farms.

The last tenant on the list was Reg. We parked the van in Reg's yard and stepped out into the cow muck. Changing my clothes had been the right thing to do. Reg was pleased to see me, and I was happy to see him. I put my arms around him and kissed his cheek while he pretended to push me away.

"I don't know, what is it with you girls?"

"You know you love me really, Reg, and I've got rid of Phillips for you."

"I know, I couldn't believe it when Mr Norton here told me. He was up to no good, Lily, there's not a farmer on the estate who doesn't want to thank you."

"I know, Reg, but he's gone now. Tell me something, Reg, forget that he's standing next to me. Tell me what you think of Mr Norton."

"You mean pretend he's not there?"

"That's it, you won't be offended will you, Mr Norton?"

Norton obviously felt awkward, but I knew I could trust Reg.

"He's a good man, Lily, he'll be okay."

"Thank you, Reg. Mr Norton here will get you a better price for your produce, and things will improve a lot for you from now on."

"I don't know how you do it, Lily, everything's changed since you've been here."

"For the better, I hope, Reg."

"Bless you, Lily."

We left Reg with an enormous grin on his face, only surpassed by the grin on Norton's face.

"What are you smiling at, Mr Norton?"

"It's you, Mrs Heywood, Reg is usually a miserable sod, now look at him."

"I can't take all the credit, there's three of us, and nobody can be a miserable sod around my friend Dotty."

We drove the short drive back to the Estate Office. Every time he looked at me, he smiled, but I did my best not to show any recognition. The Bedford van rattled and bumped along the country lanes, every pothole becoming a test of my ability to stay in the seat. At one particularly deep rut, the empty milk churn fell over, making me jump out of my skin.

I had immediately liked Norton. There was an undeniable chemistry between us which I enjoyed, while knowing equally well that I had to compartmentalise any such feelings. Anything else would be a disaster, and if Norton were not aware of that, it would be a problem. I didn't want to say anything, because that would only draw attention to it.

I was somewhat relieved when we arrived back in his office, not having realised just how bad some of the estate roads were. We went into his office and I sat down as he produced a notebook from the desk drawer, handing it to me.

"Take a look at this, Mrs Heywood, I'll be making us another cup of tea."

Norton's small kitchen was next to the office, and his private rooms were above. After handing me the notebook, he walked away into the kitchen. I watched him until he disappeared out of view before opening the notebook to see page after page of all the things he had listed which needed improving, all the inefficiency and waste.

At the back, I found he had produced a line drawing connecting all the points he had noted, with various lines crossed out and many corrections. I turned the page over, and there was another such line drawing, this time neat and tidy. As Norton returned with two cups of tea, I realised it was a flowchart, and I followed various aspects of the chart, thinking aloud.

"This is excellent, Mr Norton. So you are suggesting all the dairy farmers have their milk collected each day by the same tanker. We can pay them a higher price by selling to a single dairy?"

I studied the flow chart again. "And I see you propose a similar arrangement for the cereal and livestock producers. Do you intend to negotiate a collective price with the merchants in future?"

"Yes, but there is much more to this, Mrs Heywood. Some tenants currently pay a nominal ground rent, which bears no resemblance to their profitability at all. Some maintain their boundary fences properly and others do not. As you've seen, some estate roads are barely passable, and some land is productive and some of it is not. They even compete by producing too much of the same crop! It's a mess, Mrs Heywood, there's no collective organisation and with the possible exception of Home Farm, the farms are too small to be efficient."

"You paint a sorry picture, Mr Norton, but I have to say it fits in with what I've seen while working in the Land Army. Do you see a solution?"

"Short of evicting the tenants, no! I realise that is not an option so all I can suggest is that the estate runs a central cooperative which not only buys and sells the produce but also organises who produces what. It could also centrally purchase fertiliser, materials, hire equipment, grain storage, even labour. I think the estate needs to take back control of roads and boundary fences, and all of that needs to reflect in the leases and rents. There is also the problem that, as long as the war lasts, there will be shortages of everything, so little of this is likely to happen."

"What do you think we can feasibly achieve in the short term?"

"I can set up a purchasing cooperative for most of the produce, and I should be able to pay the farmers a better price and show a return for the estate. The lease agreements will need bringing up to date."

"I want the tenants to be consistently better off than they are now. Can you ensure that?"

"Of course."

"Can you consult with a suitable dairy, and grain merchants, and produce some hard and fast figures?"

"Yes, I can."

"Your purchasing collective will have to operate like a separate company, it might even be better if it *were* separate. I'll speak to the estate lawyers about it, and about the lease agreements."

"What about His Lordship, do you not need his say-so?"

"No, I don't, the entire estate is my responsibility."

He sipped his tea, while looking at me over his cup, a wide grin on his face.

"What?" I asked.

"I started working on these figures weeks ago, assuming it was a waste of time. I didn't think for a moment anyone here would understand it, much less act upon it! You've quite taken my breath away, Mrs Heywood."

I was hoping he didn't realise to what extent he'd taken *my* breath away! He was just everything the estate needed and was also everything I needed. I didn't understand the farming business, nor did I have time to find out. Here was a man with flair and imagination who really knew his job. I really needed him.

"Mr Norton, it's Greg, isn't it? I don't have time to beat around the bush. I have important work to do here so I will tell you something I would never normally want to admit, but these are not normal times, are they? You're a wonderfully capable man, not to put too fine a point on it - I need you. You will have my absolute support, but can I rely upon you? I mean, for the duration of the war, can I completely and utterly rely on you?"

"I see what you're saying, effectively you're asking me to swear allegiance to you."

"I'm not talking about anointing you in holy oil, Mr Norton."

"Don't short-change yourself, Mrs Heywood. I'll be honest with you as well; this is not something I intended to say either. I've left some domestic issues behind in Scotland and came down here just looking for - well - anything, really. I wouldn't want to commit to this or anything else for the long term, but for the duration of the war, I would be happy to swear allegiance to you."

He sat smiling at me, while I sat smiling at him. I offered him my hand in the time-honoured custom of shaking hands on the deal, but he took my hand in his and just held it. Only after considerable delay did we shake hands. I could tell he was a natural-born womaniser; I doubt he could even be otherwise. I didn't mind, he was immensely likable. I guessed he knew it, but I also knew I couldn't allow myself to see him in that light.

"It's reassuring to have you on my team, Mr Norton, I think together we can achieve great things here. You won't do anything to spoil that, will you?"

I didn't allow him the time to respond, but he knew exactly what I meant. I stood up and turned towards the door. He immediately stepped forward and opened it for me. I thanked him and as I walked away, I realised it was undeniable that there was a chemistry between us.

Then I suddenly realised it was nearly 2 o'clock. I knew the girls were going to the pub for lunch, so I thought I would see if I could get there in time to join them. I thought about Norton all the way, couldn't get his face out of my mind. It was only the sight of the pub which finally turned my thoughts to other things.

-oOo-

As soon as I stepped through the pub door, there was Dotty, the Queen Bee, surrounded by her loyal 'worker bees' dressed in blue. Johnny and Fiona were there together, immersed in each other's eyes. Neither Dotty nor Fi noticed me, they both had too much else to occupy them. Suddenly realising I didn't feel like the company of the airmen, I quietly turned around with nobody seeing me, and headed home. I had too much on my mind and doubted they would find me enjoyable company.

Gran was out. I guessed she was with Aunty Mavis, so I made myself a sandwich and sat in the armchair, contemplating what just happened with Norton. Not in my wildest dreams could I have imagined things falling into place so well. It was not just him. Mrs Morgan was a real ally; I could rely on her.

I felt I could rely on many of the household staff. Jennings was the one resisting me, always polite and professional in his dealings with me, but I was aware of a hidden resentment and decided I would have to work on him. I was fighting to keep my eyes open and must have fallen asleep, because I woke with a start to find Fiona and Johnny standing over me.

"Oh, how embarrassing, I must have fallen asleep."

"Don't be silly, Lily, I'm not surprised you're asleep. I'll just show Johnny to the kitchen, he can make us a cup of tea."

They left the room with their arms around each other and Fiona returned a few minutes later, by which time I was waking up.

"Sorry, Lily, I didn't think you would be here. This is really awkward, you see…….."

I interrupted her. "Yes, I can see, Fi, don't worry. I was going out for a walk, anyway, just let me go upstairs for a moment."

I felt excited for her, for both of them. I only had to look at Fi to see what this moment meant to her. She was talking to me, but she was not really there; her passion had taken over all of her senses. I realised theirs was an incredibly special relationship, and they were about to make love together in a way they would never forget. It would be one of the most memorable moments in Fiona's life.

I quickly changed the bedclothes and pillowcases and put a drip of 4711 Eau De Cologne on the pillow. Then I tidied up Dotty's clothes and made the bedroom look as presentable as possible.

Only when satisfied I had done as much as possible, did I go back downstairs to find them so tightly bound in each other's arms, I could hardly see a space anywhere between them. Putting my arms around them, I kissed them both on the cheek, and left without saying a word. They hardly seemed to notice me. Three cups sat on the table, full to the brim with tepid tea.

I spent a couple of hours with Gran and Mavis; at least then I could ensure Gran didn't go home. The two sisters were inseparable; I always enjoyed their reminiscing. On that occasion, the conversation was about when Mavis first met her husband-to-be. Gran was prompting her as they fed off each other. Mavis was a few years younger than Gran, but altogether frailer, the only exception being when she talked about her Ted. It was difficult to visualise either of them as young, spirited women, much less being in the arms of a young, vibrant man.

Mavis pushed her head back into the armchair and took a long, deep breath. She could do nothing to change the deep furrows that were the signature of her face, but mention Ted, and her eyes changed. Perhaps it was the image of Fiona's face, so fresh in my mind, but when Mavis followed her mind back sixty-five years, it shone through her eyes as clearly as if she were nineteen years old again! I realised her age might be a great physical barrier, but Mavis' moment of reliving the past was as tangible as Fiona's present was for her. I sat smiling at her, at the pair of them.

"What are you smiling at, Lily?" asked Gran.

"I'm smiling at you two; look at you, you both think you're still nineteen years old."

"We are luv, we're everything we've always been. When I'm gone, it won't be this old bag of bones you bury in the ground, it's everything I've ever done and experienced that goes with me."

She was right, I just needed them to remind me. We drank tea and enjoyed Mavis' cake, while the conversation jumped over a period of sixty or more years. They wanted to talk about me, and I enjoyed them talking about themselves. It was a lovely afternoon.

"Good heavens, look at the time!" Gran said. "We'd better go home and prepare something for the girls, Lily."

The two of them made their plans for seeing each other the next day, worrying about exactly where and at what time would be best. It was always the same, despite them only living two doors apart. Eventually we got away, and I approached the cottage cautiously. I really didn't want to interrupt anything. As we came closer, I could see Dotty through the window, and hoped she had not been there long. We found Fiona and Johnny sitting on the sofa. They were both rosy cheeked and looking like the cat that got the cream.

"Gran, this is Johnny," Fiona said.

Johnny was very polite, and he looked dashing in his uniform, though his tie was not as perfectly knotted as when he arrived, and he had missed a button on his shirt. Otherwise he conducted himself with his usual self-assurance. Dotty had obviously only just arrived, full of her afternoon with the airmen, which only provoked a disapproving look from Gran.

Then Gran said, "And what have you and Johnny been doing this afternoon?"

Fiona turned bright red, and Johnny stuttered, "We had a lovely time together, I mean, we…um, well it's just been nice hasn't it, Fi?"

"Yes, very nice, it's been really nice."

Dotty might have been out all afternoon but could sense their obvious discomfort. This was too much mischief for her to resist.

"Just how nice has it been, I mean has it been really, *really* nice?"

"Yes, it has been. Nice, I mean," Fiona replied, her face becoming even redder.

"I had a nice afternoon," Dotty said, "but I'm not sure it was as nice as *your* afternoon."

Thank heavens, Gran was oblivious to this banter! For all that she felt she was still only nineteen, she was of an age which would strongly disapprove. I ushered her away into the kitchen where she put on her pinny, and when I went back into the front room, Fiona was giving Dotty what-for. She was exploding with joy and happiness and telling Dotty off was as good an outlet as any. It was an intensely private moment between Fiona and Johnny, but the fact that we knew, and they knew that we knew, meant they had no option but to share their happiness with us.

Johnny didn't take any persuading to stay for tea. What followed was an evening full of great joy, and perhaps just the occasional innuendo. I had never seen Fiona looking so radiant as they both hung on each other's every word and lived in each other's eyes. Even Dotty smiled contentedly at them.

The three of us never forget that evening together. When we reminisce now, just as Gran and Mavis did then, we think of that night, and we smile.

Chapter Twelve
The Second Week

The following morning I woke before my alarm clock rang and pulled back the thin curtain to see the countryside glowing in the early morning light. I glanced over to see Dotty and Fiona still fast asleep. Perhaps it was just my imagination, but I was sure Fiona had that same smile on her face! I was up, dressed, and had breakfast started before they both came downstairs. I felt a fresh energy, a new confidence. I was wearing the two-piece suit I bought in Tunbridge Wells before they rationed clothes on the 1st of June.

"You look smart," Dotty said, as she sat down at the table, pushing aside the ever-excited Spencer Tracy.

"Yes, this is my new look for work, what do you think? I need to look smart, business-like."

Fiona looked at me over her bowl of porridge.

"Have you thought of having your hair up?"

"Not for a long time; do you think I should?"

"I'm not sure you can look business-like with that shock of red hair."

"It's not red, it's auburn."

"Let me try it for you, I think it would really suit you."

It turned out that Fiona was good with hair; she had a talent that none of us suspected. The moment we had cleared away our breakfast things, she fetched a little bag of hair brushes, combs and ribbons. She pulled my hair back and started experimenting with various options. I trusted Fiona, so just sat back, allowing her to do whatever she wanted. Gran and Dotty sat at the table spellbound but saying nothing. Even Spencer was unusually content, his head on Gran's lap, being made a fuss of.

Finally, Fiona stepped back with her arms folded, looking rather pleased with herself.

"Well, what do you think?" she asked.

"I think that's bloody amazing, Fi, when did you learn to do that?" Dotty asked, obviously impressed with Fiona's skills.

Fiona went into the front room and removed the mirror from the wall, saying she had always enjoyed hairdressing, even helped out at a hairdresser for a brief time. She held the mirror up in front of me, and what I saw was an altogether different woman. I looked so much more sophisticated, understated, but elegant and confident.

"Fi, you're a genius, thank you."

"You look great, Lily, go and knock 'em dead," said Dotty, "what do you think, Spencer?"

As soon as she mentioned his name, the stupid dog rushed around to Fi and jumped up at the mirror. She held the mirror up high out of his reach and returned it to the front room. Inevitably, Spencer followed on behind with his head firmly between Fi's legs. As I left for work, all three of them were in fits of laughter, which only added to Spencer Tracy's over-excitement.

I enjoyed my morning walk to the Manor; it was a time to breathe in the fresh country air and prepare my mind for the day ahead. When I worked for George, I had complete confidence in my ability to do the job, but this time it was different, I had everything still to learn about this one. My old demons were still there, but I took some comfort from the fact that the people of Middlebourne seemed to think more highly of me than I did of myself. In my world of self-loathing and anxiety, this was a definite step forward.

Gerry was still there, as was Ian, sitting somewhere in the back of my mind, always waiting to torment me. My tactic was to make an agreement with them. I would allow them to loom large and fill my existence, but only at a time of *my* choosing. In return, they would remain in the shadows until I invited them out. Perhaps it was getting rid of Phillips or maybe my new suit and hair. Whatever the reason, I was walking down the road smiling, something I had not done for a long time. I could see from a distance that it was Corporal Harris on guard at the barrier. He noticed me as I approached, and stepped out of his little hut, smiling at me.

"Morning, Corporal, lovely morning."

"It certainly is Mrs Heywood. I don't mean to overstep the mark, but may I say you look really good this morning."

"If I was a male officer, you wouldn't say that, would you, Corporal?"

"I'm sorry, Mrs Heywood, you're right, I've overstepped the mark, haven't I? Trouble is, none of my officers look as good as you."

I had to smile at the cheek of the man. I shouldn't exchange pleasantries with a corporal of the guard, but he was a delightful chap, and he didn't mean any disrespect. In fact, his past conduct showed the exact opposite. I decided I couldn't change who I was, but if I could win respect and still be me, then maybe that might be to my advantage.

"Behave yourself, Corporal Harris, but I'll take that as a compliment."

I walked on, feeling good about myself. If I had ignored him, or worse, reprimanded him, I would not have had such a pleasant start to my day. I walked on towards the Manor. The long drive was designed to impress and intimidate the visitor, with the Manor House looming large in the distance, growing ever larger as you approach. I noticed a thrush wrestling with a worm near the edge of the drive. It was wary of me, but not sufficiently intimidated to let go its prize. I smiled at the lovely bird as I passed, thinking I too was not intimidated, and wasn't about to let go of my own prize, either! My confidence grew with every stride as the Manor filled my vision in all directions. William straightened his back as I approached the entrance.

"Morning, William, how are you this morning?"

"Just fine, thank you, Mrs Heywood."

"And Mrs Evans?"

"Yes, fine, thank you for asking, Mrs Heywood."

Florence was running down the staircase, stopping the moment she saw me, straightening her uniform.

"Don't fall down the stairs, Florence, we can't do without you."

"Sorry, Mrs Heywood, can I do anything for you?"

"I don't think so; just enjoy your day."

"I will, thank you, Mrs Heywood. May I say I like your hair like that?"

"Do you think it suits me?"

"It really does."

"Talking of hair Florence, I've got you some extra shampoo; Mrs Morgan has put it to one side for you."

"Oh Mrs Heywood, thank you."

"My pleasure, Florence."

I was a little early entering my office; I had become used to finding my tea and biscuits already on my desk. Ten minutes later, Mary knocked on the door with my tea.

"I'm not late, am I, Mrs Heywood?"

"I think you're two minutes early, Mary!"

"I'm sorry, Mrs Heywood."

"I'm joking with you, Mary. Just put it down on my desk."

"Can I say, I so admire what you did with Mr Phillips the other day. Nobody below-stairs liked him; he was a horrible bully. You were so brave, Mrs Heywood, you being an attractive woman and all."

"Sit down for a moment, Mary, let me talk to you."

Mary sat down timidly. "I'm sorry, Mrs Heywood, I shouldn't have spoken out of turn."

"No, not at all, it's not that, I just want to talk to you. I can tell you're an intelligent young woman. I assume you have had a good basic education, probably not a lot different to mine. You're a maid, a house servant, but that's *what* you are, that's not *who* you are. I dismissed Phillips in my capacity as His Lordship's Personal Assistant, not as a woman. That has nothing to do with it. As for being attractive, you seem to think being feminine somehow prevents you from having authority. That's nonsense, Mary, you can be whatever you want to be. Never think of yourself as being anything other than a capable person with potential."

"I wish I was, Mrs Heywood, but we're not all like you. You only have to walk into a room and everyone pays attention."

"Tell me, Mary, what were you good at when you were at school?"

"I didn't take any exams or anything, but I was good at numbers, you know, maths. I even came top of the class once or twice, and I liked English lessons."

"Maybe that's one of your talents; mathematics can open doors into many things. I've got some books, you can borrow them if you like, you might find them interesting."

"I'm a maid, Mrs Heywood, it's not my place to be thinking about things like that."

"Nonsense, Mary! Remember what I told you, that's *what* you are, not *who* you are; there's nothing stopping you from improving yourself."

"Well, if you say so, I mean, thank you, Mrs Heywood. You're so kind to us all."

"It's my pleasure, Mary, I'll bring those books with me tomorrow."

Mary was a sweet girl. She got as far as the door, and I could see she was hesitating. She reached for the handle, not quite opening the door.

"What is it, Mary?"

"I hope I'm not saying the wrong thing, Mrs Heywood, but nobody has ever noticed me and Florence before. Nobody above-stairs really talks to the servants and I can't help but wonder, why are you so kind to us?"

"When I was about your age, Mary, we had a family friend who saw something in me, something that no-one else saw. He offered me a job in his business and over the years, he taught me everything he knew about that business. He took a chance on me, and in the process, he changed my life forever. I would not be here today if it weren't for him, I owe that man everything. And do you know what started it all - a simple act of kindness. I vowed I would never forget that."

Mary self-consciously straightened her pinny.

"Will that be all, Mrs Heywood?"

"Yes, Mary, but remember what I said - you can be whatever you *want* to be."

She stood at the door thinking about what I had told her, and finally looked back at me with a wonderful smile, her eyes sparkling. She reached again for the door handle without looking away from me until she slowly opened it and went out of the room. I couldn't help but smile, thinking of myself when George asked if I would like to work for him; I was really not so different to Mary. I drank my tea, thinking my day really had got off to an excellent start.

Mrs Morgan was the first to come and see me, wanting to discuss her food ration purchases. When we had dealt with the matter, she mentioned a conversation she had with Jennings. He was apparently concerned about his father, who could no longer get about very well, and she said Jennings was worried.

"Where does his father live?" I asked.

"They moved to Sevenoaks several years ago to be nearer to Mr Jennings," Mrs Morgan replied.

We said no more about the matter, but it occurred to me that if I could assist in any way, it might help me break down the barrier Jennings had created between us. I was winning hearts and minds, but not Jennings'. He was far too polite to tell me to my face, but I knew he felt I was acting above my station. The butler was central to the running of the household, so I needed to have him on side.

Later that morning, I received a telephone call from Fuller, the builder.

"I'm working on my estimate for the work to your office, Mrs Heywood. In view of the rather brief time you have allowed me, I'm wondering if it will be possible for you to view some wallpaper samples, and we need some decisions regarding light fittings. I'm sorry to be pressing you, Mrs Heywood, but I really need this done today if we are to have any chance of meeting your deadline."

I sensed he was trying hard to placate me, so I offered to go to his office to look at his samples.

"Where is your office exactly, Mr Fuller?"

He gave me his address in Sevenoaks, and it occurred to me that I could also see Mr Jennings' father. My next problem was how to get there? I wouldn't have time to catch the bus to Tunbridge Wells, and then a train to Sevenoaks, but as good luck would have it, I bumped into Lady Caroline.

"Good morning, Mrs Heywood, how are you this morning?" she asked in that elegant way of hers.

"Oh, I'm fine, Lady Caroline, thank you."

"You look very smart, my dear. I like your hairstyle too; in fact, you look very authoritative."

"This is how I should look, isn't it? I'm sorry, I didn't realise last week."

"Well, it certainly befits your position."

"I wish you had told me, Lady Caroline. You know I value your advice."

"I didn't want to interfere, but maybe we know each other well enough now. If I have anything to say in the future, then I will."

"Thank you, I really do value your advice. In fact, you could help me now, I need to get to Sevenoaks. Is there a car that can take me to Tunbridge Wells? I can get the train from there."

"Of course, can you drive?"

"Yes, I can, but what with the petrol rationing and everything, I've not driven very much since I learned to drive. In fact, I've not driven very much at all."

"There are two cars in the garage. Take one of those and ask Evans to drive you."

"Evans, the footman?"

"Yes, he was my late husband's chauffeur, but my son often insists upon driving himself now."

"That would be so helpful, Lady Caroline, it would save me a lot of time. By the way, I was talking to Mary this morning. She's a bright girl and it would be a shame if we ever lost her. If at some time you needed help with your bookkeeping, I think Mary has the potential to step up."

"Are you implying that I *need* help, Mrs Heywood?"

"Oh my goodness no, I didn't mean that at all, please don't think that. No, actually I mean the complete opposite; the manner in which you keep your books and accounts is exemplary. Should the occasion ever arise, your accounts are the perfect example of how it *should* be done. I know that Mary would like to learn, and I can't think of a better tutor."

"It would never have occurred to me to even consider such a thing. It has never been the role of a Countess of Middlebourne to teach a member of staff anything."

"Of course it isn't, Lady Caroline, please forgive me, what was I thinking? I didn't mean to suggest anything improper. I act without thinking sometimes. I tend to approach things head-on without sufficient thought for the consequences."

"I'm not sure that is the case, Mrs Heywood. I find you to be very thoughtful in your actions. When you suggest I should show Mary how to do the accounts, I suspect you have given that suggestion considerable thought. So tell me why you think I should break with hundreds of years of protocol and tradition."

"May I ask if any of your predecessors has ever undertaken the house accounts?"

"Not to my knowledge, no."

"Would it be presumptuous of me to assume that you broke with precedent because, unlike your predecessors, you had an existing expertise to apply to the situation."

"Yes precisely so, and I can see the comparison you are making, Mrs Heywood. No wonder everyone speaks so kindly of you, I think you could talk me into anything! Leave it to me, I'll see what I can do."

I thanked her and went directly to William to inform him of Lady Caroline's suggestion. His face lit up at the prospect; it was immediately apparent to me why he always looked rather bored in his role as footman.

"Just let me change my uniform, Mrs Heywood, and check the petrol situation. I'll bring one of the cars round to the front."

"That's fine, William, I've got to see Mrs Morgan first."

I made my way to the kitchen where I found Mrs Morgan in her office hunched over a pile of invoices. When I asked if she had the address of Mr Jennings' parents, I could tell that she was rushed for time. While she was looking for the address, Mary approached me.

"Anything I can do for you, Mrs Heywood?"

"No, actually I've got to pop out for a while, but I'm hoping to be back by lunchtime. Perhaps you could ask Cook to make me a sandwich and bring it to my office when I get back?"

"I'll make you a sandwich myself, Mrs Heywood. I'll keep an eye open for when you return."

"Thank you, Mary."

"Here we are, Mrs Heywood," said Elsie Morgan, "I knew Mr Jennings had written it down somewhere."

"Thank you, Mrs Morgan. I'm going into Sevenoaks to see Fuller the builder, so if I can do anything for Mr Jennings' father, it's a convenient time for me to do so. Not a word, mind; this is just between us. By the way, I can see you're struggling to find time for this paperwork. It's only a suggestion, but I think Mary is quite capable of helping you with that."

"I wonder if she could. I'm not sure Mr Jennings would approve, but I'll think about it."

I smiled in agreement and left via the Servants' Entrance because it was the shortest route from the kitchen to the front entrance. I noticed the expression on their faces; even this simple act of social defiance made an impression on them.

Chapter Thirteen
The Drive to Sevenoaks

The moment I stepped outside, I saw the Rolls-Royce parked in front of the Manor. It had never occurred to me that William would take the family limousine! He stood to attention by the car door, looking splendid in his chauffeur's uniform. He looked like a different person and the car was gleaming, as were his eyes. As I approached him, I was aware of the garden and kitchen staff watching me.

"This is really not suitable, William. I *can't* be noticed being driven in the family Rolls-Royce."

"Why not, Mrs Heywood, I thought you'd enjoy it?"

"I would, William, oh believe me, I really would. That's the point though, isn't it, I can't be seen to be taking advantage of a car like this."

"Well, it's this or the Rover-16."

"Whatever that is, it will be fine. Are we okay for petrol?"

"Strictly between you and me, Mrs Heywood, I've managed to get a drum from the military."

"I didn't hear that, William."

William duly returned with the Rover which was far more suitable, and we were soon on our way. I made one concession as we were driving.

"You were right about the Rolls-Royce, William, I'd love

173

you to drive me in it. Maybe one day there will be a suitable occasion."

He nodded back with a cheery smile. We didn't go to Tunbridge Wells. William was determined to drive me directly to Sevenoaks and before I knew it, I was standing in Mr Fuller's office. It was a small property, set back from London Road, overlooking his builders' yard with all the usual piles of wood, bricks, and equipment. As a promotion for the business, his office was decidedly unimpressive. The wind of change had not blown through that building for many a year. There were shelves everywhere, each one sagging under the weight of decades of old files and documents.

There was obviously another room attached to the office, a kind of inner office. I could see a very senior lady through the glass of the door. The poor woman was painstakingly pressing the keys on an old Royal typewriter. It must have been over twenty years old. He did at least have the wallpaper samples laid out ready for me to look at, and brochures of light fittings, but any confidence I might have had in Fuller was becoming lost in the dust of his office. I kept feeling that he was trying hard to please me, but other than that I had little reason to have confidence in the man. I was wondering if I had made a mistake going there, but the situation was rescued when a much younger man came into the room.

"This is my son, Robert, Mrs Heywood, he will be personally in charge of the work."

This was an altogether different prospect; the young Mr Fuller was sharp-eyed and confident.

"Delighted to meet you, Mr Fuller. Please give me your opinion regarding these wallpapers."

"I've had a look at them, Mrs Heywood, after my father told me of your requirements. You want your office to be in keeping with the grandeur of the Manor, but you also want it to reflect the status of its purpose, and of your own position."

"I don't recall explaining my requirements in quite those

terms at all, Mr Fuller, but if I had, then I think you have expressed it very well."

"Let me show you what I have in mind, Mrs Heywood."

He produced some detailed drawings which showed some additional decorative plasterwork, various mouldings and his choice of wall coverings, and wall lights. The drawings comprised each wall of my office on a continuous run of paper. When I had studied the details, he stood the paper on edge and folded the sections so that I was looking at a three-dimensional representation of my office. He finished his presentation with a perfectly fitting square of carpet. I was extremely impressed and told him so, in no uncertain terms.

"Mr Fuller, you've given both time and attention to my project, not to mention your considerable talent, I'm impressed! I need people with talent that I can trust, and I have confidence in your judgment on this project. However, we all know this business has abused the reliance which the Earl placed in it, and I shall require you to price this work very much with that in mind. It would be a shame if the estate had to lose a man of your ability, Mr Fuller; your business has considerable ground to make up."

Mr Fuller senior skulked away from the desk, giving me the distinct feeling his day had come and gone. Robert Fuller escorted me to the door.

"I'm not my father, Mrs Heywood. Things will change around here; you need not concern yourself in that regard."

"I'm not concerned, Mr Fuller, this isn't my future at stake here, it's yours. I'll promise you one thing - if you win my trust and never abuse it - then I'll put myself out to support your business."

"You're very direct, Mrs Heywood. I'm not concerned either, because I *know* I shall win your trust, and I will not abuse it - those days are over. If you will pay for the materials for your office, I'll provide all the labour free of charge, and I'll meet your deadline."

"Why are you offering to do that when I think you realise that I want you to do the work?"

"I know you do, but I'm genuinely ashamed of the way my father has treated his most valued client. It's taken someone like you, Mrs Heywood, to shake my father out of his seat. I just want to make a gesture, to show appreciation for this second chance. You didn't *have* to do that."

He was right; I didn't have to give them a second chance but was very pleased I had. When I left, we had a mutual understanding. He promised to telephone me that same afternoon as soon as he had worked out his estimate. I walked out onto the road, unable to suppress the smile on my face. As I approached the car, William jumped out and opened the door for me.

"Thank you, William, that went a lot better than I expected."

"That's good, then. Where would you like to go next, Mrs Heywood?"

I handed him the piece of paper with the address on it.

"Do you have any idea where this is, William?"

"No, I'm sorry, but I'm sure we can find it; we'll just need to find a postman to ask."

We found the address without too much trouble, and William could park right outside the terraced row of houses. I would admit to being slightly apprehensive as I approached the house. That soon passed, however, as the lady who answered the door could almost have been my Mother. A little older, she looked rather like her, and spoke with that same London accent.

"Hello, my name's Lily Heywood, I'm Lord Middlebourne's Personal Assistant."

"Oh yes, what can I do for you, dear?"

"I just called on the off-chance. Charles mentioned that his father was poorly, I just wondered if there was anything I could do to help."

"That's very kind, dear, come in."

She immediately introduced me to Mr Jennings senior. We talked for some time, finding quickly that we had a lot in common, as they both came from the East End of London. As soon as they realised that I was also from the East End, their attitude changed immediately. The best china came out, together with a fruit cake exactly like my Mum always made. Betty fussed about arranging the cups and saucers, which was the whole point of having 'best china'! These simple things were a matter of great pride in the East End.

We sat with our tea and cake, chatting like old friends. Betty and Tom were a delightful couple, and immensely proud of their son Charles. One should never underestimate the status afforded to the butler of a stately house. They told me that Tom had a nasty abscess on his leg which apparently refused to heal. The problem was that they couldn't afford the regular visits from the doctor or nurse required to improve his situation. I felt so sorry for them; here was a veteran from the First War, unable to get around simply because he couldn't afford proper treatment. He might have been my own Father!

"Do you not pay into the local Provident scheme?" I asked them.

"We couldn't afford it," Betty said.

"But if you told the District Nurse Association that you really can't afford it, I expect they would have sent you someone free of charge."

"We can't ask for charity, dear, oh no, we can't do that."

This was so typical of people from my part of London. Fiercely independent, they would never ask for what they considered 'charity'. The social bond between friends and neighbours meant that help was always freely given, but never expected nor asked for.

"This won't do, will it," I said, "I won't stand by while our butler's father is suffering like this. Leave it to me, Tom, expect a visit from the District Nurse tomorrow."

"We can't accept charity, Mrs Heywood," Betty said adamantly.

"This isn't charity, Betty, this is His Lordship paying for it. I think it's the least he can do for his butler. Do you not agree?"

"Well, I suppose, if you put it like that. It's really kind of you to do this for us."

"My pleasure, Betty, I look forward to getting a progress report."

They were so grateful and reluctant to let me go. When I finally left, they both enthusiastically waved me goodbye as I walked towards the car. William was wondering why we had stopped there, but I saw no reason for him to know. I was about to step into the back of the Rover when I changed my mind.

"Move over, William, let me drive, but I warn you I haven't driven for some time. Will you keep an eye on me?"

George had taught me to drive, but I was rusty as I nervously sat behind the wheel. There was a certain amount of gear crunching, and when finally I pulled away, I threw William back in his seat rather more forcibly than intended. He smiled and didn't appear to be too nervous, although I noticed he gripped the door handle at some junctions. Considering I hadn't driven for a long time, I thought I did rather well, and by the time we were back at the Manor I was feeling quite confident.

"That was fun, William, I really enjoyed that."

"I hope you didn't enjoy it too much, Mrs Heywood. I'd like to drive you again if I can."

"Don't worry, William, you will."

I thanked him again as I rushed back to my office. As soon as I got to my desk, I contacted the Association and asked them to send a private nurse right away, with the invoice to be sent to the Manor. I was pleased with my morning's work.

There was a knock on my door - it was Mary.

"I saw you come back, Mrs Heywood. I've made you a nice egg sandwich, and a fresh cup of tea, I hope that's all right?"

"Bless you, Mary, that's very much all right, thank you."

"Oh good, I'll come back for the plate later. Mrs Morgan said she would show me how she records the invoices in her book. She thought perhaps I could do it, and Mr Jennings said it would be all right. You wouldn't mind, would you, Mrs Heywood?"

"No, not at all, I think Mrs Morgan has had an excellent idea, I wish I'd thought of it."

Mary smiled. "I can't believe it, Mrs Heywood. You were only just saying I could do anything I wanted, and then an opportunity has come along."

"There you are then, Mary, what did I tell you? You never know - in the fullness of time you might even end up helping Lady Middlebourne with her accounts."

"I really can't see that happening!"

"Trust me, Mary, if you believe in yourself, and you try hard enough, you could do anything. Let me give you a small piece of advice, Mary. If you enjoy doing this kind of work, ask Mrs Morgan what else you can do to help her, and don't be afraid to work extra hours if it means you can take on more. Above all, Mary, enjoy whatever you do, always take pride in even your smallest achievements."

"You mean I should even enjoy cleaning the grates?"

"Absolutely, you should, that's exactly what I mean! Do it as well as you possibly can and then smile at a job really well done. You see, everything you do is a reflection on you, Mary. Your sense of achievement comes from within, so make yourself indispensable, be proud of yourself."

"Do you really believe that Mrs Heywood?"

"As you build your confidence, you'll come to believe it as well. Also, Mary, I have confidence in you; don't let me down, and above all, don't let yourself down."

"I won't let you down, Mrs Heywood, I can promise you that."

She was a bright girl; she had a spark about her, and above all, was eager to learn. When I spoke to her, she listened, and when she understood my advice, I could see the reaction in her eyes. Trying to further her career gave me an extraordinary amount of pleasure. When she had left my office, my mind returned to more mundane things, but the smile remained on my face. I had to contact the estate lawyers, and in between bites of my sandwich, I telephoned them, and a rather grouchy secretary answered my call. When I asked to speak to Mr Roberts, she told me it was lunchtime.

"Well?" I said.

"Well, Mr Roberts is just going out to lunch," came the reply, "you will have to phone back. Who did you say you are?"

"This is Mrs Heywood, I'm Lord Middlebourne's Personal Assistant. I understood that Mr Roberts acted for the estate; has he ceased to fulfil that role?"

"No, we deal with the estate affairs, but not at lunchtime."

The woman's condescending tone was infuriating, but I had dealt with many secretaries like her in the shipping industry.

"I see. Well, the thing is, I *do* work at lunchtime, so if Mr Roberts cannot fit in with my schedule, then it will be difficult for him to represent the estate. Would you be kind enough to thank him for his past attention? I require a more flexible approach from now on - goodbye."

I waited for the phone to ring back. This approach had always worked in the past, but not always as quickly as it did that day. When I answered, it was Roberts himself.

"Mrs Heywood?"

"Yes."

"Mrs Heywood, Lord Middlebourne informed me about your appointment, how can I help you?"

I explained Norton's proposals for the farm tenants, and he listened with interest.

"If you are asking me if the leases can easily be overturned, then the answer, Mrs Heywood, is technically yes. They all contain land husbandry clauses, and innumerable clauses relating to maintenance, and upkeep of fences, roads, watercourses, and buildings. The point is - the way they wrote the leases - each tenant will be in long-standing violation of dozens of clauses."

"I get the picture, Mr Roberts, and what about Mr Norton's idea for the purchasing cooperative?"

"Splendid idea; I can easily build the terms and conditions of the cooperative into a new lease agreement."

We discussed a few more things; he was extremely helpful, and I thanked him for his advice. I had no doubt that a disproportionately large invoice would follow, but the lunch incident was not mentioned. My next port of call was to see Norton again. It was 1.50pm. Wondering if I would still find him in the Estate Office having his lunch, I quickly made my way over there. I noticed the Bedford van parked next to the office, so assumed he must be there as I knocked on the door.

"Mrs Heywood, what a delightful surprise, come in, can I make you a cup of tea?"

"Actually, Mr Norton, yes, thank you."

I followed him in to find that what had been Phillips' office now looked refreshed and tidy. As he continued on into his kitchen he momentarily paused. He reached over to the only book lying on its side on the bookshelf, flipping it upright to match the rest. He was a methodical man.

His office smelled of wood polish, and something else that I didn't recognise. The wood panelling had previously been an amalgam of dust and cobwebs but the grain of the wood now reached out with a warm glow. The filthy carpet was gone, replaced by a beautiful rug in shades of rust and green. I sat thinking this was exactly how an estate manager's office should look - an accounts ledger in its place on the desk, with a small neat pile of correspondence.

As Norton came back into the room, he looked exactly

how an estate manager should look. He had obviously been wearing an autumn coloured three-piece tweed suit with knee breeches. Now the jacket was placed neatly on the back of a chair. His brown leather brogue shoes were shiny, and the knot in his tie sat perfectly in the collar of his check shirt. His brown wavy hair had been cut immaculately, as befitted a man of his station.

He was carrying a small tray with a pot of tea, cups, saucers, milk jug and plates. The remains of a once much larger Madeira cake were on a separate plate. Tray in hand, he leaned forward and placed a cup and saucer on a small table next to me. He was close enough that momentarily his aftershave overpowered the smell of wood polish. I felt he used the time arranging my cup and saucer in order to remain in close proximity; I could have easily moved aside a little but I didn't. Then he sat opposite me and crossed his legs, placing the tray next to him.

"I have to know, Mr Norton, what is that smell, apart from the wood polish, I mean?"

"Yes, I know what you mean, it's linseed oil. I treated the panelling with it, hoping the beeswax would mask it a bit more, but it will disappear soon enough."

"What you've done here is transformative, I can hardly recognise it."

"Apart from the filth, there was the dreadful smell of old books and paper that Phillips lived with, not to mention the cigarettes. I couldn't live here with that smell."

"I don't blame you, but really this is wonderful."

We continued to exchange pleasantries until he reached for the teapot. I quickly stood up and approached the tray.

"Let me do that, you made the tea so the least I can do is pour it." He watched my every move as I poured the tea. "By the way, I've had a conversation with the estate lawyers, and I wanted to bring you up to date. The leases can be overturned, though I wouldn't want a confrontational situation. I want the farmers on-side, but we know they will be resistant to change. I think the answer, therefore, is a gradual approach. Also, I suspect there might be some alterations here at the Manor, though I'm not sure yet how it will affect the farms."

"How do you mean, what alterations?" he asked.

"You know we have a military presence here. That seems to be an unfortunate regulation but perhaps you've noticed, they have no proper accommodation. There will also be more administration done here. I can't help but wonder if we might even end up with some more outbuildings. The problem is that there's nowhere suitable, as far as I can see."

"I would imagine you're looking at Nissen huts or similar buildings."

"Exactly my thoughts, but they might demand more land."

"The tenants won't give up their land voluntarily, so His Lordship might have to give up some of the Home Farm." It was the only moment when Norton's rather lovely smile wavered a little, as he ran his fingers around his chin.

I could almost see his mind working, as he continued. "You don't think they might compulsorily purchase any of the farms, do you?"

"I have no idea, but if they wanted to, are there any tenants who would go voluntarily?"

"Two of them have no obvious heirs, so you never know."

"So such a thing might be helpful to them?"

"At the right price, it might be possible. You're thinking beyond the war, aren't you, Mrs Heywood?" he queried, as his disarming smile returned.

"I share your vision for the estate, Mr Norton. A centrally managed cooperative of tenants makes economic sense to me, and we need to be thinking long term. Will you have a quiet word with the tenants you mentioned? We must leave them with no idea that they have even talked to you about it. Do you understand what I mean? And would you put some of your ideas in place - things like the bulk milk buying?"

"I already have things in place for the milk. I'm still working on the other produce; that's a lot more difficult. Would you like some more tea?"

"Yes, thank you, and this wonderful cake, where did you get this from?"

"Oh, this is Cook's special Madeira cake, I was telling her about Dundee cake and she took pity on me."

"Did you enjoy your time in Scotland? I've never been there."

"It's a beautiful country, especially the Highlands, where I was. You feel the landscape is so much bigger than you are. To stand on the top of a Munro on a cloudless day is to breathe the same air as the angels. The heather moors and streams, the snow-capped mountains - it gets into your blood just like the malt whisky. The Highlands have a singular identity, and the moment you recognise it, that's the moment you've become a part of it."

"You make it sound wonderful, Mr Norton. I can hear it in your voice, a part of you is still there, isn't it?"

"I suppose it is. Maybe that's part of the deal, it becomes a part of you, and you give a piece of yourself in exchange."

"That left-behind piece of you - has that got anything to do with the domestic situation that you mentioned?" The moment I asked, I realised it was a completely improper thing for me to say. It was telling him more about myself than I was asking about him. I tried to back-pedal.

"I'm sorry, Mr Norton, I don't know why I said that. Your private life is exactly that, private."

"Don't worry, Mrs Heywood, none of us can walk through life without disturbing the grass. When we look back, we can all see our well-trodden path."

He had a lovely way of expressing things. I hadn't changed my view - he was an incorrigible womaniser - but he was not superficial. He had a depth of character which intrigued me; he was an impressive man. One thing was certain, I just knew instinctively he was in complete control of his remit. It was the man rather than the estate manager who was troubling me. His wonderful good looks and charm, combined with his obvious attraction towards me, was proving difficult to deal with.

I wasn't made of stone; of course I was attracted to him - what woman wouldn't be! There was an undeniable spark between us, which only required the close proximity of the other for that spark to jump the gap. Obviously, we both felt it, and I prayed he wouldn't cross the line. Perhaps more to the point, I knew if I allowed myself to cross that line, my position would be in jeopardy. We talked some more until it was time for me to leave. As we stood up together and walked towards the door, he opened it and stood in such a way that I had to move close to him to get past. He was not being remotely intimidating, just being Greg Norton, and I moved past while avoiding his eyes.

"Keep me up to date with your progress, Mr Norton. As soon as I know anything about that other matter, I'll let you know immediately."

When I returned to my office, I realised I had been with Norton for over two hours. I would have sworn it was only half an hour! There were several matters demanding my attention which concentrated my mind, and among them was a telephone call from Robert Fuller. True to his word, he presented me with an estimate for materials only, and assured me that he and his men would start work first thing the next morning. I closed my office door that evening with a contented smile - it had been an excellent beginning to my second week.

As I headed towards the Great Hall, I could hear excited chatter in the distance. Moments later, I heard Jennings interrupt that chatter with what amounted to a stern reprimand.

"Stop that noise at once," he shouted, "what do you girls think you're doing? Where is your uniform, Florence, what on earth is going on here?"

I rounded the corner to see Mary and Florence standing to attention with their hands clasped in front of them, staring down at their shoes. Jennings was standing there in all his magnificence, appearing to be apoplectic.

"It's my night off, Mr Jennings," Florence said, not daring to look at him. "Mrs Morgan said I could."

Jennings raised his chest up, placing his fists on his hips.

"Did she indeed, and the reason for all the noise?"

Florence glanced momentarily at Mary before looking down again at her shoes.

"We were just excited, Mr Jennings. I'm sorry, Mr Jennings."

"You don't have a night off during the week, Florence. What on earth is Mrs Morgan thinking of? I think you both need to stop this nonsense and get back to work, immediately."

As I approached them, I could see Florence had spent a long time with her hair and was dressed to go out somewhere important.

"Good evening," I said, as if I had heard none of the conversation.

"Oh good evening, Mrs Heywood," replied Jennings. "I hope these stupid girls were not disturbing you."

"Disturbing me, no – why - what have you two been up to?" I turned and looked at Florence. "You look nice, Florence, are you off out somewhere?"

"Well, Mrs Morgan said it would be all right. You see, it's my friend, he's signed up to join the army, he has to go tomorrow and this is the last chance I will have to see him."

"You didn't tell me you had a boyfriend, Florence."

Florence rapidly flushed all the way from her neck to her mascara. I could almost feel the glow of her embarrassment. Her accomplice Mary stood in silence.

"Well, I've not really told anyone else about him, but I suppose he is. He's special to me."

"That's wonderfully romantic, Florence, what's this lucky boy's name?"

"Harold, Mrs Heywood, well, he's Harry really. He's lovely, I mean he's really nice, Mrs Heywood."

"I can see you like him, he's a lucky young man, isn't he, Mr Jennings?"

Jennings stood impassively, looking as stern as he could manage.

"Come on, Mr Jennings, don't tell me there hasn't been an occasion when you were excited about meeting a young lady."

"Well, I suppose, when I was younger," he said begrudgingly.

I detected a slight narrowing of his eyes, and maybe a hint of movement coming from the corner of his mouth.

"*Mr Jennings!* Do I detect the memory of a past flame bringing a smile to your face - I believe I do!"

"Well, possibly, we were all young once, Mrs Heywood."

"Just so, Mr Jennings, but what has this got to do with you, Mary? Has Mrs Morgan given you the night off as well?"

"No, Mrs Heywood."

"I didn't think so. Why is this girl standing around, Mr Jennings, do you not have some work for her?"

"I do indeed!" he replied with great relish.

"I'll leave that situation in your capable hands then, Mr Jennings, and if you're going out Florence, I suggest you stop delaying Mary and allow her to get on with her work."

"Yes, Mrs Heywood, I'm sorry, Mr Jennings," Florence could barely disguise the glee in her voice.

"I'll walk out with you, Florence, I was just leaving."

"Oh no, I'll go out the Servants' Entrance, Mrs Heywood," she replied with a smile.

"Yes, of course. Well, we mustn't delay Mr Jennings any longer."

Jennings barked his orders at Mary as if trying to compensate for losing his command over Florence. I hurriedly walked away towards the Main Entrance.

"Good night, William, thank you again for driving me this morning."

"My pleasure, Mrs Heywood."

As I walked on toward the barrier, I could hear Florence's footsteps behind me, as she hastened her stride to catch up with me.

"I'm so grateful, Mrs Heywood, what you just did, I mean, it was wonderful. I don't know what I would have done if I couldn't see Harry tonight."

"How well do you know Harry, Florence?"

"I've known him for two or three months now."

"Yes, but how *well* do you know him?"

"I don't know what you mean, Mrs Heywood?"

"Yes, you do!"

"Well, if it's what I think you mean, then not that well."

"Listen to me, Florence. Harry will be posted somewhere, and you will not see each other again for many weeks, it could be months. You know that, so emotions between you will run high this evening. Enjoy each other, make your promises, but tonight is definitely not the time to get to know him even more. You know what I'm saying, Florence?"

"I think so, yes."

"It's the war, it changes us all. There are an awful lot of young women, and some of the men for that matter, who ruin their lives for a moment's passion. I don't want to see that happen to you, Florence, promise me."

"I won't, and thank you for being concerned about me, Mrs Heywood. I'm not used to people being concerned about me. It's …. well, thank you for thinking about me."

"What about your family, Florence, they must be concerned about you?"

"Not really. My Mum had nine children, and would you believe it, my Dad walked out on us."

"I didn't realise, that's really hard on you. How does your Mum manage?"

"My Dad never did anything to help anyway, so Mum said it was good riddance. I'm the second oldest, and all I've ever done is run around after everyone. My Mum didn't seem to notice me, I wonder now if she even notices I've gone."

"Oh Florence, that's so sad, I'm really sorry. Does it make you feel rejected?"

"Well, I'm not sure she wanted any of us."

"Do you feel it's your fault, do you blame yourself?"

"Well, it must be my fault, why else would she reject me?"

"So do you think everyone has a low opinion of you?"

"I'm just a housemaid, everyone has a low opinion of me."

"What do *you* think though Florence, do you have a poor opinion of yourself?"

"You're asking me a lot of questions, Mrs Heywood."

"I know, you're right, it's none of my business, I'm just concerned about you."

"You understand, don't you Mrs Heywood, but how could you know how I feel?"

"I recognise it in you, Florence, and let me tell you something. I know it's hard to overcome these feelings, but trust me, you're *not* worthless. You should be proud of yourself; you've come from a deprived and obviously difficult background and yet - look at you - you're a fine young woman."

"Do you think so, really? Mrs Morgan has been kind to me, and now I've got you as well. No, I didn't mean I've *got* you, oh I'm sorry Mrs Heywood, I don't know what I'm trying to say."

"I know what you're trying to say, Florence, and it's sweet of you. Now, you run along and have a lovely evening with your Harry. And remember, he obviously thinks you're a fine young lady, and so should you."

"Good night, Mrs Heywood, thank you."

She waved to the guard on duty and then waved back at me again as she skipped her way towards her young man.

"Teenagers," I said to the guard, "what it is not to have a care in the world!"

"I can't remember, Mrs Heywood, it seems we have all the cares of the world on our shoulders these days."

"One day, Private, this war will be over and we'll all skip down the road again."

I waved him a cheery goodbye and made my way home. I was thinking about Florence most of the while, my concentration elsewhere. As I approached Gran's cottage, Spencer Tracy confronted me, bounding down the road towards me, but I didn't see him until it was too late.

"No, no, no, no! Don't jump up at me, Spencer, *no, get down!*"

He was a lovely dog, but so unruly. His enthusiasm to greet me knew no bounds, and it was impossible not to make a fuss of him. Mavis stood in her front garden laughing at my attempts to stop him jumping up.

"I think he understands every word you say, Lily, and ignores every one of them."

"You're right, Aunty Mavis, but I can't have my clothes ruined."

"Spencer," a loud voice called from the cottage. It was Dotty coming to my rescue. Spencer's ears immediately flattened, and he skulked back, met by Dotty's wagging finger.

"How do you do it, Dotty, when he just ignores me?"

"Well, he's a boy dog, isn't he, you know the effect I have on the fellas."

Chapter Fourteen
The New Office

The following morning, I arrived at the Manor earlier than usual, and was pleased to see that Corporal Harris was on guard at the barrier.

"Good morning, Mrs Heywood, may I say ...."

I quickly interrupted him. "Don't say it, Corporal, or you'll have to apologise again! Now listen, there will be builders arriving this morning. They're here to do some work for me, so don't give them a hard time, okay?"

"Don't worry, Mrs Heywood, I'll send them right through."

"I wasn't *worrying*, Corporal, not with you in charge."

"That's not a compliment, is it, Mrs Heywood?"

"Whatever gave you that idea? Just get this damned barrier open."

I really enjoyed my morning banter with Corporal Harris. It was wrong, and no doubt his military superiors would have taken a dim view of it, but he was one of my trusted people, and I always liked to keep my trusted people close to me. Besides, he always put a spring in my step.

"Morning, William, when some builders arrive, will you direct them to my office?"

"Of course, Mrs Heywood."

My first task was to remove the desk and all my office bits

and pieces, and it occurred to me that logically I should use His Lordship's office. His desk was very tidy, but I put all of his things away in the cupboard and locked the door, making sure the builders would see nothing they shouldn't. Mary arrived with my tea just as I had cleared everything.

She looked bewildered. "Where should I put your tea, Mrs Heywood?"

"Put it in His Lordship's office, would you? And then would you help me carry my desk and filing cabinet?"

My desk was very heavy, and we struggled to carry it between us. The young footman Albert noticed us struggling and rushed to help.

"You shouldn't be doing that, Mrs Heywood," he said, "I'll find Mr Evans, and we'll move it for you."

"Nonsense, Albert, just get on the other end of this desk."

Between us we managed to move it, then we moved my various bits and pieces, including the three books I had brought in for Mary.

"Where would you like these?" she asked.

"Those are for you to borrow, Mary, and keep them for as long as you need them."

"I wondered if you would remember, thank you. What you did to help Florence last night, that was brilliant, Mrs Heywood, she would have been so upset if she couldn't go."

"How is she this morning?"

"She's very quiet, I think she's upset that he's going away."

"That's the thing about this wretched war, it affects everyone's lives."

There was a loud knock on the open door. It was Robert Fuller and his team of builders. And so began a period of chaos which would continue right through to the end of the week. It all became worse when they removed the plasterwork covering up the concealed door. Suddenly I could no longer escape the builders, even in His Lordship's office. I dealt with everything as best I could, but it was exceedingly difficult, and so I used any excuse to go and see people. Towards the end of the week, Norton put his head around His Lordship's door.

"Morning, Mrs Heywood, is there a convenient time today when I could see you to discuss the leases?"

"Convenient, Mr Norton, it would be a godsend! If we make it at lunchtime in your office, I'll bring my sandwich."

"I'll have the kettle on."

Robert Fuller had got to the stage of the work where the dust and distraction was just too much to bear, so I decided to ask Mrs Morgan if I could use her little office. When I went to see her, she was sitting at the table with Mary, in front of a pile of invoices.

"Morning, Mrs Morgan. This was such a good idea of yours to show Mary how she can help you, how is she doing?"

"She's a sharp girl, is our Mary, I only have to show her once."

"I never doubted it," I said, smiling at Mary.

Rather than disturb them, I made some excuse and moved on, beginning to feel like a second-hand piece of furniture in search of a home. I glanced at my watch to see it was already nearly lunchtime. The lure of Greg Norton and his clean office was too much for me, so I made my way over to the Estate Office. I was early, but his greeting was no less welcoming. He made some tea, and offered me cake again. This time it was a sponge; he obviously had Cook wrapped around his little finger. He had a way with women, or at least he had a way with me.

The difference between being extremely personable and being over-attentive or intimidating can be a fine line for a man. Greg Norton was a skilled practitioner of the art and we had a wonderful lunch together. It may only have been a sandwich, but he had a way of making it seem like so much more. Eventually, when we had finished our last cup of tea, he mentioned what it was he wanted to tell me.

"I've spoken to those tenants, as we said, and I think two of them may sell their lease if the price is right. The best thing is that their farms are adjacent, so His Lordship could combine them into a more economic size."

"That could be useful. I would hate farmers like Reg to be disrupted by all this. How is Reg, is he happy with the new milk collection?"

"You know Reg, he's being paid substantially more than he was before, but all he does is grumble about the collection time not suiting his cows."

"That's Reg! Do you need me to talk to him?"

"I know you could charm Reg, Mrs Heywood, but I can cope with him."

"Take care of him, Mr Norton, I've got a soft spot for the old sod."

"You're very genuine with your affections, Mrs Heywood, I really admire that about you."

"What do you mean?"

"I mean people like Reg - and most of the staff here, for that matter - they speak so warmly of you. I can assure you that's not normal for an authority figure."

"Perhaps I should take that as a compliment."

"I meant it as one."

He was looking at me more intently than he needed to, and our proximity was just close enough for one of those sparks to jump the gap, so I decided I should go.

"I've really got to go, Mr Norton, I can't leave those builders alone too long with access to His Lordship's office."

"Would you have dinner with me one night, Mrs Heywood?"

My heart jumped in my chest! It was the sheer surprise of his invitation; I just didn't see it coming. I looked at him, trying not to be too expressive, while I gathered my thoughts.

"I don't think that would be appropriate, do you?"

"I didn't intend to suggest anything inappropriate, Mrs Heywood, I can assure you. You're such wonderful company, and I just thought ... no, I'm sorry, I wasn't thinking, was I, it was a silly idea."

"It wasn't a silly idea, Greg, it was a lovely idea, it's just that for the foreseeable future it mustn't happen."

It would have been better if I had said nothing. It was the 'foreseeable future' part which opened the door. I created an implied assumption that when the war was over, things between us might be different.

"That's a lovely way of putting me in my place, Mrs Heywood."

"That's not my intention, Greg. It is His Lordship's Personal Assistant you're talking to; none of this is me. I don't find it easy to separate the two, so please don't make it any harder for me."

He reached out and took hold of my hand, just holding my fingers gently in his.

"It was the Personal Assistant who made me pledge allegiance, and nothing has changed."

I momentarily squeezed his fingers before letting go. I felt we had both said quite enough, it was time for me to leave. He opened the door for me very politely, and I left without looking back, which took considerable willpower.

As I sauntered back to my office, my mind was full of what had just happened - what *had* just happened? Greg the Estate Manager was perfect, I needed him. Greg the man sparked something in me I didn't even recognise in myself; I needed him as well. I struggled to reconcile the two needs in my mind. I hardly knew the man on a personal level, but the connection I felt was something I hadn't known before; it shook the very foundation of my inner belief in myself.

"Everything all right, Mrs Heywood?" asked the guard on duty at the Manor entrance.

"Sorry, Private, I was miles away there."

"Too much to worry about, Mrs Heywood?"

"Actually, Private, you're dead right. It *is* too much; there are some things I just don't have the time to worry about."

He had no idea what I was talking about, but by the time I reached my office, I had made up my mind that whatever I was feeling for Greg Norton, it would have to wait. Robert Fuller and his men were tidying up the finishing touches to my office, and the transformation was breath-taking. I stood at the door, looking in with my mouth gaping open.

"Not a problem, is there, Mrs Heywood?" asked a slightly nervous Robert Fuller.

"No, Robert, I couldn't be more pleased, what you've achieved here is outstanding."

"Can we move your furniture back in for you?"

"Oh yes, that would be wonderful, thank you."

By the end of the day, I couldn't possibly have been happier. Robert Fuller came back from loading his van for a last inspection, and we stood together in the middle of the room.

"I know I'm biased, Mrs Heywood, but I think we've achieved exactly what you wanted. When a person enters this room for the first time, it is still obviously a part of Middlebourne Manor, but it has an impressive style of its own, with a feeling of authority. Those little feminine touches that you wanted - I think this magnificent room is a perfect reflection of you, Mrs Heywood."

"You don't have to give me the sales promotion, Robert, I can see the results of your flair for myself. You have a rare talent, you need to promote that side of your business, you're so much more than a builder."

"You're very kind, Mrs Heywood."

When he offered me his hand, I drew him towards me and kissed his cheek.

"I don't normally kiss the builders, Robert, but you're one of my trusted people now. I know I can rely on you."

He left with a wonderful smile on his face, and lipstick on his cheek. I knew the Manor needed people like him, and I could tell he wouldn't be a disappointment.

It seemed to be the perfect end to the week. As I sat at my

desk in the middle of this huge and impressive room, I felt I had truly arrived. It was late, and the business of the day was over.

There was a loud knock on my door, which took me by surprise.

"Come in."

It was Jennings, who opened the door and stood there in all his finery. His expression was stern but unfathomable, though I suspected he was not best pleased.

"What do you think about my new office, Mr Jennings?"

"I haven't come to discuss your office, Mrs Heywood. I deeply resent your interference in my family affairs. What business was that of yours?"

"I'm not sure I follow you, Mr Jennings, I don't feel that I have interfered."

"You have been to my parent's house; they are people of modest means, but we have our pride."

"I think what you mean is that you have *your* pride, but how have I offended you; I thought I was being helpful?"

"My family affairs are exactly that, they are not your concern. It's my privacy that you have ignored."

"Oh Mr Jennings, I am so sorry, I was only thinking of your father. I can see that I have caused offence, and that was never my intention. As you say, your parents are of modest means, but if you think my knowledge of their situation in any way affects my opinion of you, then I can assure you that is not the case. My parents are exactly like yours, the house I grew up in is exactly like theirs, our backgrounds are remarkably similar. You even come from the East End of London the same as me, although for some reason you've chosen not to mention that."

"What is your point, Mrs Heywood?"

"I should have spoken to you first, I realise that now, but my point Mr Jennings, is that we're the same, you and me. Why can't we both be proud of our background and families?"

"I don't need a lecture about my family."

"Are you sure this is really about your family, are you sure this is not about your attitude towards me? Why do you resent me having this position?"

"Well, as you mention it, yes it rankles to have a woman your age acting as my superior, and a woman from my class."

"Let me tell you something, Charles, I'm in this position out of merit. Do you seriously think His Lordship would place me in this position otherwise? It's not your position to judge me on anything other than my ability to do my job, just as I wouldn't presume to judge your private life. I'm fed-up with your attitude towards me. As one East Ender to another, you need to stick your old-fashioned prejudices where the sun doesn't shine; you need to move into the twentieth century."

He was visibly shaken. An immensely proud man, he would never have been spoken to in such terms by a woman before. He looked bewildered, but I was determined not to soften my approach. This was a critical moment in our working relationship because he *had* to accept me; the alternative was unthinkable. He stood in silence for what felt like an eternity, but gradually his wide eyes narrowed into a slight smile.

"Well, as one East Ender to another, Lily, perhaps I should be big enough to admit that my Dad thinks you're wonderful, so maybe that should be good enough for me."

"I'm touched, Charles, that wasn't easy for a proud man like you to admit; I admire and respect you for saying that. Neither of us created the hierarchical system we have here, but this is where we are. I'll extend you every courtesy befitting your office, I only ask that you treat me the same. I will stand by and support you in everything you do, but above all you have your place, and I have mine. Can we work together on that basis?"

"It seems I have little option, Mrs Heywood."

When he left my office, I wondered if I might have handled the situation better, but all I could do was to wait and see. It was a slightly unsatisfactory conclusion, but I tried to push it from my mind. It had been another long day, so I finished a few things, and I was finally looking forward to going home. On my way across the magnificent hall I caught sight of Mr Jennings, and he drew my attention.

"Have you got a moment, Mrs Heywood?"

"Of course, Mr Jennings."

He led me to his private office and invited me in.

"Would you have a glass of whisky with me, or would you prefer a gin and tonic?" he asked.

"A glass of gin and tonic would be lovely, thank you."

He poured the drinks, and I wondered why he had invited me. He looked cheerful enough, so I hoped this was to be something pleasant.

"I've been thinking Mrs Heywood; to be honest, you gave me a lot to think about. I'm not unaware of the fact that I'm set in my ways, Mrs Morgan regularly reminds me of it. When your name is mentioned below-stairs, Mrs Morgan won't hear a word against you, and all I hear from Florence and Mary are kind words. I think, therefore, that perhaps ... well, what I'm trying to say, Mrs Heywood, is that I'm not too proud to reconsider my opinion.

I've watched you these past two weeks and seen how you deal with people. I also admire how you dealt with Phillips, and what you have achieved in such a brief time. The fact of the matter is that I've gained an enormous respect for you. I admit, it's been a grudging respect. I'm afraid my pride initially wouldn't allow me to admit it. You spoke to me earlier as one East Ender to another, and so may I say, I think you're a class act, Mrs Heywood."

"*Mr Jennings,* you've taken me completely by surprise! Would it also surprise you to know that I hold you in precisely the same regard?"

He raised his glass to me, and we drank a toast to the East End. The air was cleared, and we talked for more than half an hour about our childhood memories of London. When he realised that I was born in Stockwell, he poured scorn on my East End credibility.

"Looks like you found me out, Mr Jennings, but my father *is* a real East Ender, my husband was, and I did end up living in Stepney."

"Nevertheless," he beamed, "Stockwell isn't the same."

"Perhaps we could keep this between ourselves, Mr Jennings."

We both laughed. I had finally completed my list of crucial allies. Jennings had just become another of my trusted people. He was a proud man; I realised that the way he had now accepted my authority was not in any way an act of weakness on his behalf. Quite the contrary, I felt he had displayed great dignity and strength of character. I thought about our encounter all the way home.

It was 7.45pm before I opened the front door. Gran and Dotty were still sitting at the dinner table waiting for me.

"We'd almost given up on you, Lily," said Dotty, "it's Saturday night, for goodness' sake!" The exasperation in Dotty's voice was self-evident.

"I'm sorry, really I am, it's just been such a day."

"Fi couldn't wait. It was a choice between you or Johnny."

"No contest then!"

"Nope, none at all."

I told them about my day and must have mentioned Greg Norton.

"He's that lovely looking man we saw in the van, right?"

"Yes, he is lovely, isn't he?"

"You've got a thing for this bloke, Lily, haven't you?"

I changed the subject, but I wasn't hiding it very well. By the time I finished the washing up, there was very little of the evening left. Dotty had been out with the flyers for the afternoon and had clearly drunk a few pints with them, and we were all tired. Gran was dropping off in her armchair and Dotty was just reaching the same point, struggling against the weight of her eyelids.

When I suggested an early night, we all agreed. As soon as I was in bed, Dotty was keen to question me about Greg Norton. But as she was asking, her eyes were closing, so she didn't even notice that I hadn't answered.

Chapter Fifteen
His Lordship Returns

On Sunday morning I woke to see that Fiona had not returned. Smiling to myself, I wasn't at all alarmed; I realised exactly what that meant. Dotty was still sound asleep; she never looked dishevelled in her sleep, her short dark hair rarely out of place. Awake, she was always so full of energy, so the only time her face was expressionless was when she was like that, fast asleep. I looked at her lying there like a china doll, looking quite beautiful in an unconventional way. This alone could not explain her magnetic attraction for the opposite sex. She possessed a charismatic charm that seemed to fill any room instantly upon her arrival but lying there, she was just like anyone else.

With my clothes under my arm, I tiptoed out of the bedroom, determined not to wake her. Waking Dotty was like fully opening the window on a windy day! I did, however, disturb Spencer, but he merely stretched his back and shook his head, as if to say, 'why have you woken me so early?'

"Go back to sleep, Spencer, that's a good boy."

I made a fuss of him and for the moment at least he slumped back next to the range, enjoying the residual heat left over from the previous night. I made myself a cup of tea and a slice of toast. I had already decided to go back to the Manor that day, just to be sure everything was prepared before His Lordship's return.

Having had a quick wash in the scullery in chilly water, I put on a skirt and blouse, and brushed out my hair. I always felt I had to make some effort to look nice but spent less time than usual that morning.

Somehow, I tricked Spencer into thinking I was just going into the other room and closed the front door as quietly as I could, standing for a moment to be sure I got away with it. There was no sound from Spencer, so I turned to face the day.

Nobody was about. We had only recently passed the mid-summer equinox, so the night had been short and the early morning air was still. There was just the hint of a mist rising in the low sunshine. The only sound was the call of innumerable birds singing their hearts out with a single black-bird sitting high on the cottage thatch, determined to be heard above all the rest.

For all my London heritage, I felt a part of this country scene. As I walked towards the Manor, I soaked up every detail like blotting paper and – like blotting paper - everything around me left an indelible image on my mind.

As I approached the barrier, I felt awake, fresh, and in-vigorated. For some silly reason, I was hoping it would be Corporal Harris on duty. I really enjoyed our morning banter; it always made for a pleasant start to my day. He was half asleep, crumpled up on the little bench in his hut, but as he heard my footsteps, he jumped to attention.

"Good heavens, Mrs Heywood! I didn't expect you this morning, and not at this early hour!"

"I like to keep you on your toes, Corporal, you weren't asleep, were you?"

"I think I must have been. I dreamed a beautiful woman was walking along the road towards me."

"Well, I hope you weren't disappointed when you realised it was only me."

"The one thing you never do, Mrs Heywood, is disappoint."

"This isn't another of your inappropriate compliments, is it, Corporal?"

"Do I look like the kind of man who would be influenced by a pretty face?"

I smiled at him. "Get this barrier open, Corporal, before you find yourself in trouble!"

"You have a wonderful day, Mrs Heywood," he said, as I went on my way.

I walked on a dozen paces, stopped, and turned around.

"You *are* that kind of man, Corporal, but you're a lovely start to my day."

The private on guard by the door *was* fast asleep, and I toyed with the idea of giving him a prod and a good telling-off, but I just crept past him. The Great Hall was silent; nobody was about as I walked towards my office.

As I rounded the last corner, I had the shock of my life, coming face to face with His Lordship! I felt like a naughty schoolgirl who had run helter-skelter into the headmistress. I stopped dead in my tracks with my mouth open.

"*Oh, good heavens! Mrs Heywood!* I didn't expect to see anyone," he said, appearing to be equally shocked.

He looked completely different to all the other occasions I had seen him, with his hair dishevelled, wearing an open-necked check shirt and a V-neck knitted waistcoat over a pair of very crumpled corduroy trousers. What I noticed most of all was that he was wearing slippers; of all things, those baggy old slippers appeared the most incongruous part of his outfit.

"I didn't mean to startle you, My Lord. I just thought I would come in and prepare for tomorrow."

I had caught him totally off guard; he stood motionless for a moment, trying to formulate a suitable response.

"I must apologise, Mrs Heywood, I can't possibly be seen dressed so inappropriately. This is inexcusable; you must forgive me. I will go and dress in a manner appropriate to receive you."

"Please don't, My Lord, you are not at all inappropriate, I assure you."

He really didn't know how to respond. It was the first time I realised how formulaic his life was, but he obviously felt uncomfortable, so I tried to put him at ease.

"What's inappropriate for you, My Lord, is what everyone else regards as normal," I said, smiling. "But may I just suggest you discard the slippers; they really are a step too far?"

I reached down and removed my shoes. "There we are, My Lord, that places our sartorial inappropriateness on an equal footing."

He was hesitant, but eventually he kicked off the dreadful old slippers and smiled the most beguiling smile.

"You really do have a solution to everything, Mrs Heywood. Do you realise how disarming that is?"

I smiled in response. "Have you seen the improvements I've made to my office?"

"I've seen nothing, Mrs Heywood."

I opened the door, and he stood open-mouthed, staring into the room.

"I am quite without suitable words. I did not anticipate this, and if I had, I could not possibly have envisaged what I see before me. This is incredible; how on earth have you achieved all this, and may I ask at what cost?"

"I have achieved all this because I put my trust in a young and talented designer, and furthermore he carried out the work at the cost of the materials only."

"How, Mrs Heywood, how *do* you achieve these things?"

"Your father always used Fuller the builder for estate repairs and maintenance. I looked into the accounts, My Lord. Mr Fuller has been abusing the trust your father placed in him and was systematically overcharging you. I dealt with that situation, my Lord, and suspect you will find that Mr Fuller senior will retire shortly, to be replaced by his son, Robert Fuller. I now consider Robert Fuller to be one of my trusted people. Doing this work for me at cost price is a gesture of his goodwill."

"You amaze me!" he said, gently shaking his head.

I suggested we should sit down, but just at that moment he noticed the adjoining door. He smiled at me, walked over to the door, and opened it. For a moment I wasn't sure whether he was pleased or annoyed, so was worried in case he disapproved.

"Excellent, I wondered if you would find this door; well done."

I breathed a sigh of relief. "Shall I get us some tea, My Lord?"

"Splendid idea," he replied, as he moved one of the chairs into an appropriate position.

Robert Fuller had restored the bell-pull in my office, so I casually pulled it as if accustomed to doing this. Obviously, below-stairs were not anticipating anyone, as there was a long delay, but eventually Florence appeared, straightening her uniform.

"Good morning, Florence. Can we have some tea, and I expect His Lordship would like some biscuits."

"Of course, Mrs Heywood, and good morning, My Lord."

"Oh yes, good morning, Florence," he replied.

"Has Harry written to you yet?" I asked her.

"He must have written the same day, Mrs Heywood. Oh, it was lovely; he can write so nicely." She was clearly besotted with her young man and was about to tell me something else. "Oh, I'm sorry, My Lord, I'll fetch the tea for you."

She smiled at me as she scurried out of my office.

"What have you done to my staff, Mrs Heywood?" he asked, with a reassuring smile on his face.

"I like them, My Lord, and they seem to have accepted me."

"I assume that does not apply to Jennings; he is not re-nowned for his adaptability."

"Quite the opposite, My Lord. Mr Jennings and I found we have a lot in common; he's also one of my trusted people."

"Wonders will never cease, but what about Phillips? That was an interesting test I left you with."

"When you say test, My Lord, did you really see Phillips in that light?"

"I did indeed, so tell me, what is your opinion of him?"

"I no longer need to have an opinion of him, My Lord. I dismissed him."

"*What!* You dismissed my estate manager; you mean, he has gone?"

"Not just gone, My Lord, he's in prison awaiting trial for embezzlement."

He sat back in the chair, crossing his legs, and folding his arms, with a look of astonishment on his face.

"My test, Mrs Heywood, was for you to discover that he was using the estate for his own enrichment. I assumed you would discover that, but it didn't occur to me you would tackle him yourself."

"I took one of the soldiers with me, just in case, which proved to be a prudent decision."

"Don't tell me, Mrs Heywood, another of your trusted people?"

"Well yes, I do trust Corporal Harris. He is - as you say - trusted."

Florence arrived back with the tea and biscuits and arranged it all neatly on my desk.

"Will that be all, My Lord?" she said.

"Yes, thank you," he replied.

"Thank you, Florence, that was kind of you," I said, "and do you know if Cook will be baking any of her scones today?"

"I don't know, Mrs Heywood, but if I tell her you asked, I know she'll bake some for you. Oh, and for you, My Lord, of course."

"Yes Florence, thank you," he said with an enormous grin on his face.

Florence was unable to suppress her own smile as she left.

"I've been absent for two weeks and you seem to have taken over my household, Mrs Heywood. Oh, and by the way, have you dismissed any more of my staff?"

"I haven't found that necessary, My Lord, but I have promoted the assistant estate manager; he is now your estate manager. Are you familiar with Mr Norton, My Lord?"

"Yes, I was introduced to him, seemed like an agreeable man. Is he up to the task?"

"He is more than up to it, My Lord, he's an exceptional man in my opinion. Mr Phillips would not have told you that."

"If your opinion is that Norton is an exceptional man, then I know that to be the case. You realise, of course, that I left you alone intentionally?"

"You forced me to assume responsibility, I realise that. I hope I haven't disappointed you."

"I'm not sure you are capable of disappointing me, Mrs Heywood. But tell me honestly, did you expect to sweep all before you, as you appear to have done?"

His Lordship's authority was such that when he asked for my honest answer, I felt a compulsion to bare my soul to him. He just had that effect on me.

"No, My Lord, I expected nothing. I'm just a working-class woman thrust into a position of absolute power; it terrified me! If the staff had realised how much I was shaking inside, I'm sure I wouldn't have got away with any of it. I just decided to be myself, and if it worked, then it worked. If it didn't, I was prepared to admit it to you and walk away."

"Did you think for one moment, I would leave my estate in the hands of someone in whom I didn't have total confidence?"

"No, I didn't, but that's the problem. I'm not sure that you appreciate the heavy burden your expectations imposed on me."

How could he know that I did everything to hide my insecurity? I never wanted anyone to see my inner struggle; my confidence was only real as long as I pretended it was.

"I'm sorry if I seemed heartless, Mrs Heywood, but I did indeed fully appreciate the magnitude of the challenge I set you. I knew you would have sleepless nights, and that you would agonise over decisions. I knew you would have to question your entire character. You have learned more about yourself in this past fortnight than I could have taught you in six months. Congratulations, Mrs Heywood!"

As always, he left me speechless. I had been a puppet, and he was pulling the strings even in his absence. And yet he was right about me in every respect, seeming to know me better than I knew myself. I hated his smug attitude, but I so admired his confidence and self-assurance. I had become my own contradiction in terms. If I was his puppet, then he was in complete control of me. A part of me just wanted to submit to that control, but another part of me wanted to rebel.

"Would you like another cup of tea, My Lord?"

"Yes, thank you, I would."

I poured the tea, and he sat watching me intently. He still intimidated me, even as he sat there in his socks. Having poured the cups, I picked up a biscuit and dipped it into my tea without a second thought. He sat looking at me, and when I displayed an enjoyable expression as I lifted the biscuit to my mouth, he proceeded to dunk his own biscuit. I watched him as he had watched me, except that he left the biscuit too long in the cup. As he lifted it up, part of it broke away and dropped onto his chest. He looked down at the soggy biscuit on his woollen waistcoat like a little boy whose Beano comic had been confiscated!

I instinctively pulled the handkerchief from my sleeve, stood up and went over to him. I bent over and wiped away the biscuit without thinking about it, and my hair must have brushed against his face. He raised his hand to brush my hair aside, but the effect was to brush the side of my face. I instantly felt awkward when I realised what I was doing.

"Oh, I'm sorry, My Lord, what was I thinking?"

He looked up at me with a strange expression; it was some form of displeasure, so I was convinced I had done the wrong thing.

"I need to make something abundantly clear, Mrs Heywood."

My heart sank. I must have overstepped the mark and was about to be put firmly in my place.

"We will be working extremely closely together, and I need a level of trust and understanding which circumvents the usual sensitivities. I am afraid worries about causing each other offence are a luxury we cannot afford. Do you understand what I am saying, Mrs Heywood? Nothing you do or say will ever offend me; I can assure you of that. Whilst I appreciate that I can be insensitive, I need you to overlook that fact. We must allow nothing to distract from our work; do you think you can do that, Mrs Heywood?"

"I think so, but it will be rather difficult, I do feel intimidated in your company."

"And I am in awe of you, Mrs Heywood, so perhaps we can make a pact!"

"Why would you be in awe of me, My Lord?"

"Oh, my dear Mrs Heywood, ask one of your trusted people like Jennings, or your man Robert Fuller. You are a force of nature, and have you looked in the mirror recently?"

I was not prone to blushing, but I could suddenly feel the warmth spreading over my face. In one sentence, he had dragged my self-esteem off the floor and placed me on a pedestal. And moreover, he found me attractive. His Lordship *was* human; he liked me! I finished wiping away the soggy biscuit without further apology and sat back down.

"Tell me," he asked, "what is the secret to this strange activity of immersing one's biscuit in tea?"

It was probably just my nervous reaction, I burst out laughing almost uncontrollably. He looked at the biscuit quizzically before he too burst into laughter. It was a defining moment in our relationship. The laughter didn't last, however. His expression changed, as suddenly he looked serious.

"I have a confession to make Mrs Heywood. Of necessity, I have not been entirely straightforward with you."

"That sounds ominous, My Lord."

"You will shortly fully appreciate the reasons for my subterfuge; I would just ask you to bear with me for a moment. Your appointment has not been exactly what you think it is. I placed you in complete control of my estate, intending to watch your progress."

"I don't understand, My Lord; are you saying I have been on trial here?"

"Yes, I am afraid so, and you have been on trial for a position that I could not tell you about before. You see, Middlebourne is about to become a department of the War Office, but it has nothing whatever to do with 'the Joint Technical Board'."

"I think you need to explain, My Lord?"

"First Mrs Heywood, I must remind you of the terms and conditions of the Official Secrets Act which you have signed. What I am about to tell you is a state secret that only a handful of people have clearance to access. Your situation has potential repercussions; if you decided not to continue in your position, then your future becomes uncertain. So by granting you that access, I will be taking a giant leap of faith, so I must ask if you are prepared to take that giant leap with me."

"You're asking me to take a leap into the unknown; how can I agree to the unknown?"

"I chose my words precisely Mrs Heywood; it is a leap of faith. I have formed my opinion of you, and I am prepared to take that leap."

"In that case, My Lord, so am I."

"Excellent! Throughout my career Mrs Heywood, I have been involved with military intelligence, the Secret Intelligence Service. It is a complex organisation with various sections, and some might argue not sufficiently focused. We tried combining various departments but still had considerable overlap; we were not sufficiently coordinated.

Then, after the outbreak of war, the Prime Minister instigated a new organisation by combining some sections of SIS. This new organisation is extremely focused. We call it the Special Operations Executive. The Prime Minister has charged me with creating a section of SOE here at Middlebourne. We have just one specific objective.

You see, Mrs Heywood, we have been losing this war. We almost lost our Expeditionary Force in France - it was little more than a miracle that 338,000 British and Allied troops were evacuated from Dunkirk.

Then came the battle for air supremacy, where we prevailed by the narrowest of margins. Had the Nazis continued to attack our airfields, I can tell you, Mrs Heywood, it would have been a different story. Hitler made a mistake when he directed the Luftwaffe to bomb London and our great cities. Intelligence tells us he is about to make a second mistake. We are sure that he is about to open an eastern front - that he will attack Russia."

"Does this mean we're no longer under the threat of invasion?" I asked.

"It does, Mrs Heywood; the tide of this war is showing signs of turning. The outcome of the Battle of Britain means that we are no longer losing the war, but neither are we winning. We cannot defeat Hitler while we stand on this green and pleasant land; we have to defeat the Nazis *in* Europe. In short, Mrs Heywood, we have to invade mainland Europe, there is no alternative. The strategy and planning for that invasion will be years, rather than months, in the making. It will have to be the largest military operation in history, but it will also have to be the most secret."

I sat frozen to my chair. He was telling me things of such national importance it made my head spin. One moment, I was concerned with how many ounces of fat my ration card would allow, and the next moment I was trying to visualise the logistics of an invasion of Europe. I was in no rush to respond, concentrating on my breathing, trying to think clearly. Just the prospect that the war was turning had invigorated me.

As I thought through the details of what His Lordship had told me, it made perfect sense. Throughout all that had gone before, I felt I was cowering from the Nazis. They took the two men closest to me, and I felt powerless to do anything, but now I realised why we had to take the fight to them. It was a revelation, and my heart soared.

"Are you telling me, my Lord, that the specific objective you mentioned is the invasion of Europe?"

"Precisely Mrs Heywood, this is the task before us."

"But how My Lord, how do we do that from here in Middlebourne?"

He jumped to his feet. One moment he was relaxed and smiling, the next moment he radiated energy into every corner of my office. He strode across the room to retrieve his slippers and without knowing what I was doing, I put my shoes back on.

"Follow me," he said, invoking all his authority.

We went straight through the adjoining door into his office. There was a momentary pause as he glanced at the new door.

"Excellent idea, Mrs Heywood, very convenient."

His office was relatively bright that morning, the sun at just the right angle to allow a shaft of light to shine through the window. He marched me over to the far side of the room, where an enormous map of Europe was pinned to the wall. He stopped abruptly in front of it, hands on his hips, as I stood next to him.

"Look at this map, Mrs Heywood," he said as he reached for a cane and pointed to Britain, tapping it forcibly against the south coast.

"Fortress Britain here and everywhere else German-occupied

Europe. An invasion force will have to be assembled, the scale of which will be unprecedented. It will have to be the greatest amphibious invasion force the world has ever seen. Aircraft, ships, landing craft and above all, men, hundreds of thousands of men. So my question to you, Mrs Heywood, is: where would you land the invasion?"

"I have no idea, My Lord."

The tempo of his voice was increasing with every word he spoke. His facial expression, his hands, his arms, he was becoming more and more animated; I could almost feel the energy crackling from his fingertips.

"Think, Mrs Heywood, think aloud, let me share your thought process. Think two, maybe even three years from now. The Germans will anticipate an invasion, they will have turned occupied Europe into a fortress. Think, Mrs Heywood, the largest invasion force which the world has ever seen, where do you land it?"

Fifteen minutes earlier I would have been totally intimidated by him, unable to think on the spot for fear of ridiculing myself. Somehow, he had changed that, his energy just sweeping over me, infusing, and energising me. My mind was racing in all directions, I knew I wasn't about to make a fool of myself, whatever I said.

"Well, we have to put men ashore, so I'm thinking not rocky coastline, I'm thinking of shelving beaches. The longer the crossing, the more warning we give the enemy, so I'm thinking about the shortest, fastest route across the Channel, here, Calais." I pointed my finger at the map. He said nothing, so I continued.

"So now I am thinking the Germans will have defences, probably formidable defences. They will assume Calais would be our obvious target because it's the closest, so maybe they concentrate their defences there. The advantage must be with the well-prepared defender, and I'm thinking a protracted battle to gain a foothold on the beach would be disastrous for us. So, I've changed my mind; forget Calais, forget any coastline that is really well defended."

"Excellent, Mrs Heywood! You can assume when the time comes that they will defend all of this coastline," he pointed along the coast of France.

"I can't believe all that coastline will be equally well defended, there's too much of it, there must be weaknesses. The Germans will have to prioritise their efforts, so we need to know where that weakness is. I would also assume they will have to prioritise their land forces behind the coastal defences, so we need to know where."

If I thought his enthusiasm couldn't reach a higher pitch, I was wrong. His smile was infectious, his eyes darting back and forth from the map to me, as he shifted his weight from one foot to the other, with one hand behind his head, and one clasping his chin. He was speaking faster and faster.

"Correct, Mrs Heywood. Keep going, keep going!"

"Well, isn't it superficially obvious, My Lord? We have to land where the Germans don't expect us to land; it would be impossible otherwise. We have to take the least obvious crossing, to the least defended landing site."

"Yes, yes, absolutely right, now follow that reasoning; how do we do that?"

His energy was so infectious, I became as animated as he was. I was thinking fast and speaking quickly.

"The Germans must never know our intentions. We have to keep our plans a secret - hundreds of thousands of people involved - and yet somehow, we have to maintain complete secrecy. We need a second strategy, to ensure they don't discover our chosen crossing, so we should make the enemy think we intend to land somewhere else."

I thought for just one second that he would actually hug me! I think it even crossed his mind.

"This is why I need you, Mrs Heywood! Do you realise how rare this kind of clear rational thinking is? And so continue your hypothesis; see it through to a conclusion."

"Okay, well, in order for an amphibious landing to be successful, we have to know exactly where the best landing site is, relative to the changing defences. The Germans must never know where we plan to land, so we have to deflect attention away by convincing them that the invasion will be somewhere else. It all boils down to intelligence, My Lord. This is our role, isn't it? We have to gather it, disseminate it, and above all keep everything secret."

He finally stood still, just looking at me, but saying nothing, with a pleasant yet indefinable expression on his face.

"Well, say something, My Lord, have I got it all wrong?"

"I'm trying not to be surprised by you, Mrs Heywood. I am trying my best to expect this kind of response, but frankly you continue to amaze me. I will adjust, I can assure you; just promise me one thing."

"Anything, My Lord."

"Promise me, if I ever take you for granted, you will divest me of that presumption."

"What a wonderful thing to say, My Lord, I really appreciate it, but you no longer have to worry about my sensitivities. You can take me for granted, and I'll still not let you down."

"I have always worked alone, Mrs Heywood, never relied on anyone, probably because I found no-one I could depend upon. This is an unfamiliar experience for me, just as it is for you. I have been working and preparing for this operation since Dunkirk. The scale and complexity of this task is beyond the ability of one person; I cannot do it alone. I need you, so knowing I can completely rely upon you, Mrs Heywood, well, it's a tremendous weight off my shoulders!"

"I need to understand the structure of the organisation you envisage My Lord. I need to know not just what your objective is, I also need to know how you intend to go about it."

"The first thing to realise is that secrecy is paramount, and this is the basis for our operation. We must restrict the number of people who know what our aim is. We will need analysts and support personnel, but we can remain small and self-contained. You must view secrecy like a pyramid, from base to apex, from personnel to the Prime Minister. This is our great strength, I only report to the PM, you will only report to me. I no longer have military rank, the War Office has not requisitioned my estate, they are here at my invitation. Military command does not apply to you either, Mrs Heywood, you will outrank everyone here, regardless of who they are."

"I don't understand, My Lord, how can I as a civilian outrank everyone else?"

"Perhaps I failed to mention Mrs Heywood, you were never going to be my Personal Assistant, you are my Chief of Staff. Your authority comes directly from the Prime Minister."

I was momentarily speechless. The magnitude of what he was telling me made my head spin even more. He spoke with such authority and sincerity that I didn't doubt a word of what he had told me.

"I need to ask you, My Lord, how is all this possible, where does your authority come from?"

"You're right to ask that question, Mrs Heywood, this is the key to our success. Mr Churchill is a close family friend. I have known him since I was a child. It was he who suggested that I should establish a new section of SOE, and when I suggested we use my estate as cover for that operation, he agreed immediately. This is the Prime Minister's initiative; he is standing firmly behind us and this is the source of our authority Mrs Heywood. We are a part of what some are calling Churchill's secret army."

"Where do we start, My Lord?"

"We have already taken the first step, Mrs Heywood."

"In that case, can I make a suggestion? I think it will be much better if you call me Lily."

"I am what I am, Mrs Heywood, I'm sorry, I mean Lily. I am cast in the mould of the Ninth Earl; do you realise what that implies for me? Certain protocols are difficult for me to overcome."

"How can I *not* realise, we are from such different worlds, My Lord. But now that I understand what lies ahead of us, it's perfectly clear to me that we do need to work closely together. I'm afraid your protocols represent a barrier between us, do you not see that? We need to remove those barriers. Edward, please, you need to let me in."

"Of course, I am sorry, Lily, forgive me. You're the wind of change, and I'm the sturdy oak resisting the gale, but even I know that the gale will always prevail!"

"Good, I'm pleased we've dispensed with the formalities. Now tell me again, Edward, where do we begin?"

As difficult as this was for me, I realised only too well that the uncharted ground between the Ninth Earl and a woman from Stepney was a giant chasm for Edward. Credit to him, he took that step without hesitation.

"Infrastructure, Lily, we start with infrastructure."

"Explain."

"We need to have Intelligence personnel, and we need accommodation for them."

"You mean Nissen huts or temporary buildings?"

"Yes, but the problem is where do we put them?"

"We could put them on the land where the tenants are prepared to sell their leases; there are two of them. Do you think the Ministry would buy the leases from you, with some form of buy-back option after the war?"

Edward was silent for a moment, looking right into my eyes.

"Brilliant!"

"Okay, what else do we need, Edward?" I asked, gaining in confidence with every second.

"Communications, I've already arranged that; there will be a team of Engineers from the Post Office here tomorrow. We need secure lines to the Prime Minister, the War Office, Bletchley Park and the rest of Military Intelligence."

"Why do we need to communicate with a park?"

"Bletchley Park is just about the most secret place in Britain, Lily. It's our centre for code- breaking and the collection of intelligence."

"Can we do it, I mean, do we as a nation have the capacity to launch such a massive invasion?"

"No, we don't." My heart stopped - so what had been the point of our discussion, but he continued. "We need support. We can rely on the Commonwealth, but you are right to see our weakness, Lily. The fact is that we need the Americans."

"But they aren't *in* the war, they're not fighting with us."

"You're right again, Lily, and yes, somehow that must change."

"This is an enormous problem, isn't it, this is your Achilles' heel?"

"I know, trust me, I know, and the Prime Minister knows it only too well. If there is one person who might change that situation, then it's him."

"Is he as wonderful as I think he is, Edward?"

"I'm not sure I would use the term 'wonderful' to describe Winston, but he too is a force of nature. His ability to influence events through the sheer power of oratory is unparalleled. You have seen how he can lift an entire nation, so if anyone can draw in the Americans, it's Winston Churchill."

"I will confess, Edward, I've adopted him as my hero. I've read all his speeches. I can even quote some of them."

He smiled in approval, and I sensed we both shared the same hero figure. We talked non-stop until lunch time, when my suggestion of some sandwiches was met with instant approval. The world of Secret Intelligence was as foreign to me as any faraway land; I was stepping into it with more apprehension than it is possible to describe.

The magnitude of our undertaking, the responsibility for my part in it, all weighed heavily on me. I knew I was standing at the crossroads of a monumental moment in history. Part of me was overwhelmed and terrified, another part was exhilarated. The rest of the day just vanished, somehow it was 6 o'clock in the evening! Fatigue flooded over me like an incoming tide. I could physically feel my brain ache.

"I am so tired, Edward, perhaps I should go home?"

"Home - are you not staying here?" He looked quite shocked.

"No, I haven't been. It's terribly kind of you to offer me a room, but I haven't used it."

"As you wish, my dear, but I think you will change your mind as our days lengthen."

I sensed he was probably right, but for now at least I needed the comfort of Gran and the girls. I didn't feel I could truly relax yet in the Manor. The barriers were certainly coming down, but the divide between Middlebourne and Stepney still felt like an obstacle to me. I thanked him for everything, and no doubt was over-effusive. I might be calling him Edward, but I was still very much in awe of the man. The fact that he had such a high opinion of me, and even liked me, was an enormous boost to my confidence. My demons still tormented me, but I held them at bay.

"So it all begins tomorrow, Edward? The first step on a long march."

"It does, and we *will* succeed, you and I, Lily, never doubt it. I'll see you in the morning."

"Good night, Edward."

"Good night, Lily.

Chapter Sixteen
The Long March Begins

I made my way home without really seeing or hearing anything around me. When I was halfway, I was even unable to remember who had been on guard at the barrier. The girls had everything ready for dinner when I arrived, and nobody complained that I had not been there to help. Even Spencer seemed to sense that I wasn't in the mood to fuss over him that night.

"You're really preoccupied, Lily, are you sure you're okay?" asked an obviously concerned Fiona.

"Bless you, Fi, I've had such a day, my brain feels like custard."

"Tell us about it, Lily, a trouble shared and all that," Dotty said, trying to cheer me up.

I told them His Lordship was there, and how we had spent the day together talking about what we would be doing at Middlebourne. I told them as much as I could, which was very little.

"So what's going on then, Lily?"

"I can't, Dotty, I just *can't*. Maybe that's why my brain has turned to custard."

They laughed and joked and did everything to raise my spirits and slowly but surely, they nearly succeeded. Dotty looked as if her efforts to cheer me up had exhausted her, as she sat at the table fighting against the weight of her eyelids. Fiona and I smiled at each other as we both placed an arm under hers.

"Come on, Dotty, it's bedtime."

She offered no resistance as we helped her to the door. Nobody else I knew worked as hard as Dotty; she would push herself until she dropped. They both put themselves to bed, as I washed and changed in the scullery. By the time I arrived upstairs, Dotty was fast asleep. I said goodnight to Fi, but just couldn't drop off. Tired as I was, I just lay there.

"Are you still awake, Lily?" asked Fiona.

We talked for a while, as far as I could, without telling her anything. I hadn't realised I was referring to His Lordship as Edward.

"You like him, don't you?" Fiona said, casually.

"Do you know, Fi, I didn't even realise, but I do. I used to loathe him; he can be so smug, he used to infuriate me. I've met nobody like him, he's incredible."

"I told you that the first time you met him; you were all gooey-eyed."

"It's not like that, Fi, really, he's an Earl and I'm from Stepney. I like him very much, and I know he likes me, but it can never be like that."

"I suppose you're right, it's a shame though, isn't it?"

"How is it with Johnny?"

"It's wonderful, Lily, I love him."

"I'm so happy for you, Fi, I really am."

"It will happen to you, Lily, you just wait and see."

"I hope so, I want it to. What about Dotty, does she still not have anyone?"

"She's got dozens of them, you know Dotty, but then again she's got no-one."

"Why is that Fi, do you know?"

"I really don't know. She's all over them until one of them

wants to take it a bit more seriously, then she drops them like a stone. I can only think she's had a nasty experience at some time, I worry about her, Lily."

We talked some more until the silences grew longer; finally Fiona didn't answer at all. It felt like only moments later when my alarm clock rang. For a few seconds my conscious brain had to catch up with the subconscious part which had turned the alarm off.

Suddenly I was awake, my heart rate was quickening, and I felt a sense of urgency, knowing what lay ahead of me. I hurried downstairs to make a start on our breakfast, wanting to leave as soon as possible. The first I heard of the girls was Dotty as she came down the stairs with Fiona.

"Piss off, Spencer, you stupid dog."

"Oh, my goodness me, your language, Dorothy!" said an appalled Fiona.

"Morning, I've got breakfast ready," I called.

No sooner had they joined me than I was finished. Apologising for my haste, I excused myself from the table and rushed back upstairs. A final five minutes in front of the mirror and I was ready. The girls looked at me in some amazement as I rushed down the stairs and out of the door.

Corporal Harris was on duty at the barrier, looking puzzled as I approached him.

"Morning, Mrs Heywood, what's going on? The place is full of Post Office people."

"Oh, it's nothing, Corporal, they're laying some extra telephone lines, that's all. When did they arrive?"

"At 6 o'clock, an hour and a half ago."

"Crickey, they start early, I'd better get on. I don't even have time for one of your inappropriate compliments, Corporal."

"That's a shame, Mrs Heywood, because I must have dropped off, and I was dreaming......"

"Goodbye, Corporal, and stay awake!"

I arrived at the Manor to find three large Post Office vans

with engineers carrying all kinds of equipment. I rushed straight to my office to find it occupied by various people, together with Lord Middlebourne. He was his usual immaculate self, with his three-piece double-breasted suit.

"If I'd realised, My Lord, I would have been here much earlier."

"It's all in hand, Mrs Heywood, don't worry."

I glanced through the adjoining door to Edward's office to see a similar commotion going on there. Two men were installing a contraption in the corner of the room, comprising two enormous metal boxes.

"What's that, Edward?" I whispered.

"That is the frequency changer, Lily."

"What's that?"

"It enables the scrambler phone, an essential piece of equipment. Those boxes house the frequency changers. It is all very straightforward; the audio signal is first attenuated to reduce the dynamic range. The next process is to pass it through a low-pass filter, which only allows the 20-2000 Hz part of the frequency to be fed to a ring mixer."

"Of course, yes, very straightforward!" I said smiling.

"Well, it is, you see. That frequency is then added to the 2500Hz signal from an oscillator. It's all to do with the sum of the difference between the two signals."

"How do you know all this, Edward?"

"We need secure communications, and I need to be absolutely sure it *is* secure. I can't just take a man's word for it; therefore, I need to understand it. Never allow a so-called expert to baffle you with complexity, Lily, it places the expert in control. You need to be in command of the detail."

"Show me again how it works, Edward."

When I finally understood the basics of the frequency changer, I asked him an even more basic question.

"Why do you need to have these big ugly boxes in your office?"

"They have to go somewhere secure; it was either your office or mine. I looked at your new designer office, and I looked at my old-fashioned and somewhat antiquated office - and here they are."

"That was an excellent decision, Edward, if I may say so."

He smiled a beautiful smile. It didn't happen very often, but somewhere inside that aristocratic exterior, there was a lovely man. I smiled back, but the moment only lasted a second. Then the men from the GPO surrounded us with cable. One man appeared to be in charge, so I approached him.

"Can you provide me with an internal connection to the estate manager's office, as well as to Lord Middlebourne's office?"

"Yes, Mrs Heywood. You'll need a different voice terminal. I only have a 328 in the van, but I could convert it to an SA5030."

Edward was right, I was agreeing to something about which I hadn't the faintest idea.

"Lord Middlebourne," I called across the room, "will a 328 converted into a SA5030 be fit for purpose?"

"Oh yes, perfectly satisfactory."

An hour later, there were two new telephones on my desk, and the same on Edward's. Both the scrambler phones had a green handset. I assumed the work was over, but in fact they were there for another four days digging trenches and erecting poles, including a radio mast. The moment they left my office, I spoke to Edward about another matter.

"When do you expect we will need to provide temporary buildings for the additional personnel?"

"As soon as possible, Lily. I was assuming we would have to sacrifice a large part of the Home Farm, with all the subsequent loss of food production. I hadn't considered that any of the tenants might relinquish their leases."

"It might just be a question of price; shall I go and see them?"

"Yes, you do that, and I will look into your idea about the Ministry paying for it."

I needed Greg Norton in on this. This was when direct communication with him would have been useful, but this time I just set off, hoping to find him in his office. As luck would have it, he arrived there just as I did. I watched him park the Bedford van at the side of the Estate Office.

He opened the van door and unfolded his body with athletic ease then, having stepped out, he swung the door shut. He straightened his back, pulled his waistcoat down, and adjusted his tie, looking as smartly dressed as ever. As he turned towards his office, he saw me. There wasn't a moment's hesitation, an instant smile spread across his face.

"Mrs Heywood, please, come in, make yourself at home while I put the kettle on. Will you share my lunch with me?"

"Is it lunchtime? I hadn't realised."

"It's a bit early, but it's a convenient time for me."

"I can't deprive you of your lunch, Mr Norton."

"You most certainly can! Given the option of all my lunch by myself, or half of my lunch with you, there's absolutely no question which I would prefer."

I reluctantly agreed, so we sat in his little kitchen, and he fussed around, providing me with a cup, saucer and plate. All the while, he rarely took his eyes off me. I had just come directly from being with Edward, and however foolish, but I suppose inevitably, I made comparisons.

They were both in their middle thirties; Edward was a good-looking man, but Greg more so. They were both always very smartly dressed, but Edward more so. Greg radiated a sensual presence; Edward didn't.

Greg seemed to be incapable of even pouring a cup of tea without that sensual part of him being present. I was always conscious of his face, or his hands, or the way he moved his body. Edward didn't do that - he wouldn't even know how to do that. Intellectually, Greg was an intelligent man, his conversation was always engaging.

Edward, however, was on a different level entirely. Conversation with him was not just engaging, it was challenging and stimulating. I wanted to get to know and understand Edward more. I saw a glimpse of a different man earlier that day; I felt that the more I knew about him, the more there would be to find out. I wanted to know more about Greg, but I already realised that would mean going to bed with him. Perhaps that was the essential difference between them.

He finished pouring my tea and brushed my arm as he moved away. It was seemingly unintentional, but it was just his way of reinforcing his physical presence.

"I'm sorry, I didn't ask you what you wanted to see me about," he asked courteously.

"Our discussion about the tenants, the two who might sell their leases. Lord Middlebourne agrees, so we need to approach them."

"Now?"

"Yes, as soon as we've finished lunch."

"Okay, that's fine. I've already worked out a fair price for both of them, based on the length of lease left and how productive their farm is."

"You're sure it's a fair figure?"

"Quite sure."

"Good; so you barter the offer with them, offering £250 less, then I'll override you and offer your fair price."

"Remind me not to barter with *you,* Mrs Heywood!" Once again, his smile was disarming.

We finished our lunch together. I enjoyed our conversation, but this matter was pressing, and I reminded him that we needed to get on. Fortunately, it was only a quick drive to the first of the tenants. I recognised it immediately; it was the farm next to Reg's, I had spoken once or twice to the farmer.

We pulled up in the yard next to the farmhouse; everything spoke of neglect. Doors and gates were hanging on one hinge if they had a hinge at all; some were propped up with old timbers. The barn roof sagged dramatically in the middle, and weeds were growing among the roof tiles. The fence we parked next to was little more than a line of joined repairs, literally held together with string.

I watched with interest to see how Greg would deal with the situation. I wanted these people handled sympathetically; they had been tenants for a long time. The tenant Mr Golding greeted us warmly enough, and we were immediately invited into his kitchen.

Greg was very understanding, having already paved the way during their first meeting. Golding would soon come to know the reason for the purchase, so I told him the military needed the land. I added that a compulsory purchase may not be so generous, which was probably true.

After another cup of tea, Greg suggested an offer and Golding had obviously already decided. He was well past retirement age, and this opportunity was coming at a convenient time for him, but like all farmers, negotiating a better deal was a way of life.

"I told you, Mr Norton, I want this matter dealt with generously. Offer Mr Golding another £250; he deserves to retire in comfort."

It was a momentous decision for Stan Golding and his wife; this was his life's work. It was perfectly clear to me he should have retired several years ago, and I felt sure this was not a decision he would regret.

"We will have to find somewhere else to live," Stan said, "we'll need time to find somewhere."

"Do you think Lord Middlebourne would allow Mr and Mrs Golding to live here for a month or two while they find somewhere?" Greg asked.

"Yes, he would, I'll make sure of it."

Stan thought about the offer and smiled at his wife before looking back at me.

"Reg is right about you, Mrs Heywood."

"I wouldn't believe all that Reg tells you, but if I were you, Stan, I'd get this sale signed the moment Mr Norton has the paperwork. Don't allow the War Office to dictate the price."

"I will, Lily, bless you."

Greg and I left, smiling at each other.

"I don't know what magic you have over these farmers; I just wish I had it."

"Oh you have enough magic of your own, Mr Norton, trust me."

I can't imagine why I said that; it was a silly admission about something I didn't need to mention. The other tenant was equally cooperative and a couple of hours later, we drove back to Greg's office, feeling quite pleased with ourselves. The moment we arrived, I reached for his telephone, remembering the number for the estate lawyers. The operator had to connect me, but eventually I got through to the same grouchy secretary that I fell out with before.

"Good afternoon, this is Mrs Heywood, Middlebourne Manor."

"Yes, Mrs Heywood, I'm afraid Mr Roberts is out of the office. Can I help you?"

This was much better; Roberts must have spoken to her.

"Yes you can, I will hand you over to Mr Norton, the Estate Manager. He will tell you exactly what he requires you to do, and please make sure Mr Roberts has the paperwork on Mr Norton's desk tomorrow evening latest. This is an urgent matter. If there are any complications, neither Mr Norton nor I have the time to hear about it, do you understand?"

Greg was grinning from ear to ear as I passed him the telephone with my hand over the mouthpiece.

"Forgot to mention, Greg, I'm having a direct line installed between our offices."

As I left and hurried back to my office, it was a moment before I realised - I was calling him Greg. I stopped only briefly for a quick word with the guard at the door, and then with William. Florence caught sight of me as I hurried across the Hall.

"You look as if you're in a rush, Mrs Heywood."

"I can't stop Florence, just tell me quickly, another letter from Harry?"

"Oh yes, he writes nearly every day."

"He's a lucky boy, your Harry," I said as I hurried away.

I found Edward in his office, studiously studying some files.

"It's done," I said, "both the tenants will sell for a fair price. I think we can rush it through in a few days, and I've agreed they can stay on in their houses until they find somewhere else."

"Excellent, Lily, well done, I assumed you would - just as well - the sappers will be here by the end of the week. I am not sure if we will have buildings or Nissen huts, but I am told they will do it within a week or ten days. And you were right about the funding - the War Office is covering all the costs."

"It's begun, Edward, hasn't it? We've started the long march into Europe."

We looked at each other. I had not intended to say something quite that profound, but neither of us said anything for several seconds.

"Well-chosen words, Lily, well-chosen indeed." He hesitated for a moment, obviously deep in thought.

"Next task is to select the people we march with, our trusted people, the best of the best. We need creative thinkers and analysts. We need some of the best brains in Britain, and I want our own aerial reconnaissance analysis, and I want our own reconnaissance pilot."

"Where do we find them?"

"Aerial reconnaissance is based at RAF Medmenham. We will work with them a lot, but for our most sensitive activities, I want our own trusted analyst. These are the files on the best analysts at Medmenham; go through them and select the one who most impresses you. The same applies to a pilot. There will be times when we will need our own trusted pilot, and we need a special kind of person for a role like this. I'll go straight to the top; I'll ask Air Chief Marshal Dowding to talk to the appropriate people."

"Is that a dangerous job?"

"Good lord no, they just take photographs."

I didn't understand at that moment that Edward was being facetious. It was much later that I realised reconnaissance pilots flew unarmed planes into the most dangerous situations imaginable. My first misguided thought was that this was surely safer than being a fighter pilot, and I knew the ideal person - a man I desperately wanted to survive the war.

"I think I can save us a lot of time, Edward; I know a Battle of Britain ace who flies Spitfires. He's Wing Commander Johnny Albright, and he's based not far from here at Biggin Hill."

Edward made a note of the name. "Leave it to me," he said.

"And where do we find these other incredibly clever people?"

"Oh, we've already found them; they are at Bletchley Park." He handed me a pile of files. "Go through these, Lily, and remember that these are not ordinary people, each of them has been selected for extraordinary ability. We will need a geologist, plus a military expert with detailed knowledge about military hardware. Also, someone with local knowledge of France especially; someone who can speak European languages. He must also be well-versed with coded communications. Then we will need someone who can pull all those skills together and combine it into report form. You are also looking for something else. We need them to be creative thinkers, people who can look at things from a fresh perspective."

I picked up the files and headed quickly towards my office.

"No, no, first rule of secrecy, Lily, never let it out of your sight. Those files must never leave my office. You read them, then they go back into my safe."

"Of course, I'll sit over here."

We read files and compared notes all afternoon. I realised I was affecting people's destinies but did it without a second thought. Come the evening, we had five files put to one side.

"Are you sure this is enough, Edward, it's a very small team for such an enormous task?"

"There will be many more support personnel to add to it, and I've not even mentioned field agents yet."

"You mean spies – we'll operate spies?"

"Field agents, yes. We will initially share SOE operations, but the time will come when we shall need our own agents. The fewer people we can operate with, the more secure we remain."

Edward's confidence in his ability to set up this operation knew no bounds. For my part, I felt I was placing pieces of the jigsaw into the puzzle as directed, but I was not yet seeing the bigger picture. At times it was overwhelming, and I would draw strength from him as I needed it, but the pressure was weighing down on me. I kept going for as long as Edward worked, and he showed no signs of tiredness. Just at the point where the rising tide of fatigue was lapping against my chin, he suggested we should stop.

"I can see you're tired, Lily, come and have a drink with me."

I seized upon the suggestion like a drowning woman clasping at a straw. We both locked our office doors, and I followed him obediently, almost struggling to place one foot in front of another. As we walked towards the Drawing Room, he half turned, until we were walking together.

"Did I mention, Lily, we have a designation within SOE, we are to be known as Station M."

"Is that M for Middlebourne?"

"All SOE stations are designated with a Roman numeral, Bletchley Park is Station X, and M is 1000. I'm sure there aren't 1000 stations, so yes I think 'M' is just very convenient."

"It really *is* happening, isn't it, Edward?"

"Of course! Did you ever doubt me?"

"Actually no, I have an almost messianic belief in you! It's kind of frightening and comforting at the same time."

"Interesting choice of words, Lily, I think this could be the basis for a philosophical discussion."

"Actually, Edward, I can think of nothing I would like more, but tonight I'm afraid I might fall asleep, and that would embarrass us both."

"Then let us just sit quietly and draw energy from each other."

We did exactly that. We sat in the Drawing Room, Jennings brought us two very large glasses of whisky, and I just sat there, trying to take it all in. There was not a shred of energy Edward could draw from me, but he seemed to have enough for both of us.

"Would you tell me about your sister, Edward, Lady Elizabeth?"

"She is in America. I'm afraid the life here before the war was a little too subdued for her. She is a moth-like creature, drawn inexorably towards a bright light."

"You speak as if there is animosity between you."

"I regret to say that there is a little. There are obligations when one is born into this family, my sister enjoys the privileges, but derides those obligations."

"That's important to you, isn't it, duty to your family and its history?"

"It's what I am, Lily, I'm proud to be the Ninth Earl of Middlebourne. If I did not take that responsibility seriously, this institution would crumble, and along with it, all the commitment of my forebears would have been for nothing."

"I admire that, I can't believe your sister doesn't."

"It's not all privilege, Lily, we have to exist within a rigid structure. I had to go to the right schools, I have to belong to the right clubs, I have to be patron of the right charities. I have to attend the right events. I even have to marry the right woman. My sister would not submit to those conformities. Some might say she is a free spirit; I would say she has debased the very institution that she now flaunts to her American friends."

"What does she do in America?"

"I think she is what they call a 'socialite,' she also claims to be a singer, some kind of occasional cabaret artist. I suspect she would stand in whatever spotlight illuminated her the brightest."

"I didn't know you felt so strongly about her, Edward. I apologise for asking you."

"Apart from my Mother, and my late Father, I have never mentioned this to anyone. This kind of thing could be scandalous, I would have to be careful who I mentioned it to. It's good to talk to someone about it, Lily."

"I'm honoured, Edward. I confess I can't understand your sister. Not to value your heritage, be it this, or as humble as mine; well, it's unthinkable to me."

"Thank you for your understanding, Lily; my sister could learn a lot from you."

"May I also ask who it is that you intend to marry?"

"It's an intricate process of status, family position and helpful connection."

"Goodness, does love not even come into it?"

"Historically no, provided it's a suitable match, one would just hope love might follow."

"And is there a candidate who you regard as the front runner?"

I suddenly realised that I was becoming far too intrusive, especially because I realised that I was asking for my own personal reasons. To my surprise, he didn't take offence, and didn't tell me to mind my own business.

"The Strattons' daughter, Lady Beatrice. I've not even discussed it with her; it's just one of those unspoken understandings."

I desperately wanted to know everything about this woman but did my best to resist.

"I wish you happiness, Edward," I said, hoping it sounded sincere, which it was not.

"At least that is something I don't have to think about until after the war."

Edward was an immensely reserved and disciplined man; it was significant that he had confided in me. He asked me about my family and told me a little more about his. We were edging closer together with each revelation; these were giant steps for Edward.

I intuitively took a dislike to Lady Beatrice, a lady of whom I knew nothing, but of whom I was insanely jealous! My mind was diverted from one Lady to another, however, when Lady Caroline came into the Drawing Room.

"Good evening, Edward, Mrs Heywood," she said as she sat down with us.

"Good evening, Lady Caroline, have you had a pleasant day?"

"I have, Mrs Heywood. Edward tells me you are his Chief of Staff, which is not a position I am familiar with. This is presumably something from within the lexicon of my son's military jargon. However, he assures me that you outrank everyone. How do you feel about that, Mrs Heywood?"

"I've never felt that I outranked anyone, so this is difficult for me to comprehend. I have to be honest - I'm overwhelmed by His Lordship's confidence in me."

"I'm sure you will cope admirably Mrs Heywood, and if you outrank me, it is my place to help and advise you as you see fit."

"My Lady, I think we both know I have neither the wish nor the prospect of outranking you! It's obvious to me that I need you."

"I am always here if you need me. I have noticed that between yourselves you have dropped the protocol of surnames;

may I say I rather approve of that. I feel I know you now, Mrs Heywood, and I share Edward's opinion of you, so may I call you Lily? And I would be pleased if you would refer to me in private as Caroline."

"I'm deeply touched, Caroline; I would be delighted."

Chapter Seventeen
The Boffins Arrive

B y the beginning of July 1941, the German invasion of Soviet Russia, 'Operation Barbarossa', was well underway. This was significant for us at Station M, as it confirmed that the potential for an invasion of Britain no longer existed, and so the war entered a new phase. Station M quickly took shape during the year. The buildings erected by the sappers comprised single-storey brick construction with corrugated roofs and green-painted metal-framed windows. Known ubiquitously as Huts, each one had a designated number. Hut 1 was the living quarters, Hut 2 was the canteen, Hut 3 was the boffins' domain, while one end of Hut 4 was the photographic reconnaissance and film processing hut, and the other end was the radio communications room.

The sappers had built the huts in no time at all. It amazed me how quickly they appeared, but it soon became apparent that the word 'basic' actually meant minimal. They provided each hut with a stove, but this was more a necessity to stop the huts from freezing during the winter, rather than for providing any creature comfort. There was mains electricity, and water from the Manor's own supply. The boys from the GPO came back again to install telephones.

Basic furnishings included beds in the living quarters, and

reasonable cooking facilities in the canteen. The boffins only had tables and chairs, together with some tall cupboards. I quickly requested a lot of office equipment, and several other items I was sure we would need. It was basic, but I could see it was sufficient to get us started; we could improve things as we went along. All we then needed was our boffins, and within days of the huts being completed, they arrived.

The first person to arrive was our photographic reconnaissance expert, Margaret Hawksworth, known as Maggie. She had a big personality, and her irrepressible smile disguised an even bigger intellect. She came complete with an assistant, Shirley, who seemed quiet in comparison. Maggie was one of the top photo reconnaissance analysts at Medmenham, aged 28 and married to a Medical Officer.

"Hello, Maggie, I'm Lily Heywood, Chief of Staff. Probably easier if you call me Lily."

"Pleased to meet you, Lily. Can you explain why I'm here, and what exactly is this place?"

"I'm afraid you're here because I selected you, I wanted the best!"

"Well, I'm flattered, do I assume this is something top secret?"

"You assume right, Maggie. I'll show you both to your quarters and will explain everything later."

Maggie had an easy-going nature, and I knew instantly that we would get on well together. Our other boffins all arrived together from Bletchley Park, sitting uncomfortably in the back of an army lorry. I was there to greet them as they stepped out into the daylight. They jumped down from the back of the lorry one at a time, each one stretching and complaining about the uncomfortable journey.

I had not known what to expect. Perhaps if I was honest, maybe I was expecting a strange-looking bunch of mad scientists. With only one exception, they had scant regard for their appearance, and some of the customary social graces seemed to elude them. There was, however, something about them, and I warmed to them immediately.

The youngest was Roland, they called him Rolo, he was the cypher expert. He spoke every language you could imagine and had been a part of the Bletchley inner circle with Alan Turing. Out of them all, Rolo best fitted my stereotypical image of the mad scientist. He had long frizzy hair, round thick-lensed glasses, his jacket collar was sticking up on one side, while his shirt collar reciprocated on the other side. His thick glasses were a little unnerving, making it difficult to see if he was looking at you. Perhaps that was for the best, because he had a way of staring right through you, as if you weren't there.

Corky introduced himself with a confident, affable manner. He was actually Nigel McCorkindale, but 'Corky' suited him. He was partial to a drink, so I always wondered if Corky came from his surname or the cork in a whisky bottle. He had a short stubble beard, and a weathered smile. He carried his jacket slung over his shoulder, with his shirt sleeves rolled up. Unlike Rolo, it was immediately apparent that he was an extrovert fun character. It turned out that Corky had many talents, as they all did, but first and foremost he was a geologist.

The next one I shook hands with approached me with an endearing smile, looking me up and down very much as a woman, rather than as the Chief of Staff. Patrick O'Connell was a delightful Irishman with a wonderful sense of humour. He looked the least professorial with his open-necked shirt, woollen waistcoat, and green corduroy trousers. His soft Irish lilt, combined with his wonderful use of language, gave him an instant charm. He was our Intelligence coordinator, among many other things.

Last, but definitely not least, was 'Woody', actual name Ronald Woodford. He stood out from the rest, being the oldest at 48. He was a smart and flamboyant character, with his brightly coloured bow tie and two-tone shoes. He greeted me with extraordinary charm and graciousness, kissing the back of my hand. He spoke with a crystal-clear upper-class English accent. Somehow, he just looked like a history professor from Oxford University, which indeed he was before being recruited by Bletchley Park. He was our military historian and all-round military expert. Unlike the rest, when he jumped down from the back of the lorry, his first concern was to brush the dust from his blazer while straightening his brightly coloured bow tie and running his hands over his neat haircut.

The four men had been together at Bletchley, so they arrived as a team, which was immensely helpful. They obviously got on well together, with a level of camaraderie and banter between them which flowed back and forth like the ripples on a pond. It was mostly above my head; they seemed to exist on a different level - especially Rolo - I think he had a level all of his own. He could not have been more different to the extrovert Corky, while Woody with his refined accent and smart clothes was the exact opposite of Patrick's casual dress and Irish charm. And yet somehow these obviously diverse characters gelled together beautifully.

When I introduced Edward to them, the fact that he was Lord Middlebourne didn't seem to register with them at all.

"Ladies and Gentlemen, may I introduce Lord Middlebourne?" I said.

He happened to shake Corky's hand first.

"Lord Middlebourne, delighted to meet you, that's a bit of a mouthful, probably best if we work on first names, I'm Corky."

"Yes, of course, please .... call me Edward."

"If that's your name, what else would we call you then?" asked Patrick.

"Well indeed," Edward replied, "and welcome to Middlebourne Manor, or more correctly Station M."

I was amazed - it took ages for Edward to call me Lily, and for me to call him Edward; the boffins dismissed that barrier before it even existed. We all stood in a huddle in the middle of the hut, looking at each other.

"I know," I said, "it doesn't look like much, does it?"

"That's an understatement, Lily," replied Patrick, "my bank account has more in it."

"This is just the start," Edward said, "and if everyone will take a seat, I shall explain our purpose here."

Edward gave them the same speech he gave me, about Britain having no other option but to defeat the Nazi regime in Europe. It was stirring stuff; then he elaborated.

"Europe has found to its cost that the Nazi concept of all-out war means the mass indiscriminate annihilation of anyone, or anything, which stands in the way of its deviant ideology. For as long as the Nazi regime exists, everything we hold dear will remain in peril. We cannot maintain our British way of life in isolation while a cancer grows ever stronger just twenty miles from our southern border, and neither can we negotiate with a morally bankrupt ideology.

Let me be clear: what is at stake here is nothing less than the British way of life, our cultural heritage, our customs, even our language. We have no alternative, we *have* to destroy the Nazi regime, and there is only one way we can do that. We have to invade German-occupied Europe."

"We don't have that capability, old boy," said Woody, authoritatively.

"Quite right, Woody, but you're assuming we are alone. Hitler is a threat to anyone who does not share his ideology, and like all tyrant dictators, he will grow ever more depraved with time. He is not just a threat to us, he is a threat to the Free World, and the Free World will soon come to realise that. The Russians realise it now, and more significantly, so will the Americans. Combined with our Commonwealth allies, to-gether we could assemble an invasion force the likes of which the world has never seen."

"Oh bejesus!" uttered Patrick, "I guessed it was something big, but not this feckin' big."

"Well indeed, Patrick, I might not have expressed it quite like that, but an invasion of Europe will as you say, be big. In fact, it will have to be the largest amphibious invasion force ever seen."

"And what's our part in all this, Edward?" asked Corky.

"Let me ask Woody that question," replied Edward. "As a military historian, Woody, where and how would you mount the world's largest amphibious invasion?"

"Come along now, old man. Such an invasion would be unprecedented. I couldn't tell you where, or how; I would need a vast amount of information before I could even consider it."

"Welcome to Station M. This is the task the Prime Minister has charged us with. Our responsibility is to decide where *and* how we can do this."

"We would have to analyse every yard of the Channel and Atlantic coasts," said Corky. "We will need a detailed understanding of the geology, topography, local infrastructure, German defences and likely response. And what's more, many of those parameters will evolve; this will take years!"

"I agree, Corky," replied Edward, "all we can do is hope the Battle of Britain has given us that time."

"We know Hitler is moving against Russia now," Woody said, "and the thing is, old boy, history has not been kind to armies following that route. This *will* give us more time."

"Can we do all that with a team this size?" asked Rolo dispassionately.

"We have the whole of the Intelligence community and SOE at our disposal, should we need it," replied Edward, "and most importantly, the Prime Minister is with us. But in answer to your question, Rolo, we may only be a small group, but we are not just any group, are we? We have selected you from the best. Look at the expertise we have sitting here in this room, and the resources we can call upon. If *we* cannot do this, then who can, and so if we just trust in our ability, we *will* get the job done."

"For some reason, Edward, I believe you," Maggie said, "we *can* do this."

"Actually, old man, history is littered with unprecedented military victories," Woody said. "The fact that such an invasion would be unprecedented is reason enough for us to *make* it happen."

"Well said, Woody, we can do it. So when do we start?"

"You just did, Corky," I replied.

I thought Edward was at his inspirational best; he'd motivated our team of boffins. He continued with his usual talk about secrecy, and his concluding remark was sobering.

"Should our German enemy, for whatever reason, have advance knowledge of where and when we will invade, then the largest invasion force which the world has ever seen will fail catastrophically. History would not look kindly upon those who planned for such a disaster."

"Not look kindly!" exclaimed Patrick. "Bejesus, we'd be burned at the stake!"

"Exactly so, I couldn't have expressed it better myself," said Edward.

There was a tangible crackle of excitement; I was standing in a room with some of the sharpest minds in Britain. I was not remotely in the same intellectual league as those people, but rather than feeling excluded, they positively infused me with energy and enthusiasm.

As I left them to settle into their unfamiliar environment, I was thinking we had just created something extraordinary. The combined intellect of Hut 3 was surely an unstoppable force which we would soon unleash upon Hitler. After all that had gone before, with Dunkirk and the Blitz, it was the most invigorating feeling.

The last member of our inner circle joined us a week later. Wing Commander Johnny Albright turned up in an RAF vehicle, looking rather bewildered. I arranged to meet him.

"What the hell is all this about, Lily? I've been told to report here for special reconnaissance."

"That's right Johnny, welcome to Station M."

"What are you talking about, Lily, what's going on here? I've not been told anything."

It was all something of a shock for Johnny, so I sat him down in Hut 3 with the boys and explained why we needed a pilot of his experience.

"An invasion....an invasion of Europe, are you serious?" he said incredulously.

Patrick came to my rescue. "Oh yes, to be sure we're serious all right, my boy, and you better bring us back some damned fine pictures or this lovely lady here will have your guts for garters."

"I'm easily pleased," said Maggie, "as long as all your photographs are perfect, I'll be happy!"

We all explained more about Station M, and the task ahead of us, and Johnny gradually realised what we had recruited him for. He was bewildered, but I sensed he felt the same feeling of invigoration that I felt.

"It's an enormous privilege, old man," said Woody, "you've just become a member of the most exclusive club in Britain."

"We will write our own history, Johnny," I said, "and you're part of it now."

Johnny left us that day still a little bewildered, but he immediately became a vital cog in our machine and so with our first tentative steps, Station M became operational. There were many support staff to settle in, such as the canteen crew and radio communications. The military guard needed to increase, which required another separate hut to act as barracks, and they also needed feeding. Much to the relief of Cook, the army provided a small mess hall. It all involved the sappers returning and erecting even more buildings, but things were really falling into place. We were a small team, but part of what was becoming a much larger operation.

Edward fitted into the group seamlessly. Intellectually he was one of them, but more importantly, they instantly accepted him as one of them. He felt completely at ease with these like-minded people, and as the work of Station M progressed, Edward spent more and more time in Hut 3, which was really his natural environment.

In Edward's absence, my job escalated week by week. I developed my contacts at Station X, and one or two other sections of SOE, but the function of each section of SOE remained autonomous. This made my initiation into the world of Secret Intelligence difficult at best. It made my task even more complicated during those first weeks while all the formalities had to be dealt with.

Initially, the visiting Generals and War Office officials intimidated me enormously. However, with virtually no exception, these people knew nothing about our specific purpose. Most of them thought we were the 'Joint Technical Board.' Gradually I learned not to be intimidated by this constant stream of officialdom, developing various clever tricks to get rid of them.

One junior War Office official was particularly obnoxious, intent upon treating me as if I were the scullery maid. He was demanding to see all the paperwork relating to the sale of the tenanted farm leases.

I had a favourite ruse for obnoxious people like him. Just at the point where he was becoming intolerable, my telephone conveniently rang while he was standing in my office. I could disconnect the incoming call and pick up the green phone at the same time.

"Good morning, Prime Minister .... yes I'm very well, thank you, sir .... no I'm sorry sir, I can't speak freely, I have one of your officials in my office .....what did you say your name was?"

I had caught the dreadful man's attention. "Guthrie," he said, sheepishly, placing his hands by his side as if he was standing to attention.

"Guthrie, sir....... yes, he's taking up a lot of my time

unnecessarily......yes, he is being very tedious .... in those actual words Prime Minister? ...... very well." I placed my hand over the receiver. "Mr Guthrie, the Prime Minister would like you to stop wasting my time, tick your damned boxes and sling your hook."

I often wondered if that little ruse might come back to haunt me, but it never did! The only reliable connection between SOE sections was through the head of SOE and the Prime Minister. We weren't known as Churchill's Secret Army for nothing, and so my connection to the Prime Minister's Office became a vital link.

I spoke regularly to Mr Churchill's secretary, Elizabeth Layton, and we formed a close working relationship. Strangely, I never actually met Elizabeth, but I felt that we were friends. I did meet Winston Churchill, several times, but I will never forget the very first occasion when I spoke to Mr Churchill. Elizabeth telephoned me on the scrambler phone.

"Morning, Lily, he wants to talk to Lord Middlebourne. He says it's urgent."

"I'm sorry, Elizabeth, he's out of the office. Can I deal with it, or shall I ask him to telephone back?"

"Hang on, he's here. I warn you, he's in a terrible mood."

The next thing I knew, Winston Churchill himself was on the other end of the telephone! I froze in my chair.

"Who is this?" he bellowed. "Where's Middlebourne?"

"I'm sorry, sir, he's out of his office, this is Mrs Heywood."

His loud voice and intimidating tone abated almost immediately.

"Ah, so finally I get to speak to the infamous Mrs Heywood. This is the Prime Minister."

"Yes sir, I know who it is, how can I help you, sir?"

"You're very calm, Mrs Heywood, I can usually manage to put the fear of God into people."

"You have done exactly that, sir, I can assure you, but it's my job not to show it."

"I've heard a lot about you, Mrs Heywood, not least from Lord Middlebourne. I am looking forward to meeting you."

"That would be a great honour, sir, and a pleasure."

"Which is it, Mrs Heywood, would it be an honour, or a pleasure?"

"I am sure it would be both, sir. I'm sure I would be mindful of the one and intoxicated by the other."

"In that case, I must be mindful when I meet you, Mrs Heywood, I fear that I too will be intoxicated!"

"How can I help you this morning, Prime Minister?"

"You have already helped me, Mrs Heywood. You have lifted my spirits, but I also want to know when I will receive your latest assessment of the Nazi coastal defences."

I dealt with all the Prime Minister's questions, and when he finally ended the call, I felt myself physically crumple into my chair. I sat staring at the wall until a loud ringing sound in my head jolted me back to reality. It took me several seconds to realise it was my telephone ringing.

-oOo-

It quickly became apparent during the latter part of 1941 that my workload was constantly expanding. With Edward spending an increasing amount of time in Hut 3, I desperately needed an assistant. I discussed it with Edward, who agreed with me, and said we should instigate the recruitment process immediately.

I had a better idea - I asked Fiona to come to the Manor. I wanted her to see first-hand what I was about to offer her. Fiona was a highly intelligent woman and realising that I was unable to discuss the matter at home, she never questioned it for a moment. We were on the same wavelength; I knew we would get on working together. Above all, I knew I could trust her implicitly; and she was more than capable of doing the job.

A few days later, she duly arrived at the barrier. I had instructed Corporal Harris to escort her up to the Manor steps, where William was waiting to escort her to my office. She was a little overwhelmed, and this was compounded when she saw my office.

"Miss Robinson to see you, Mrs Heywood," William announced.

"Come in, Fi, thank you, William."

"Oh my goodness will you look at this; is this all *your* office? Wow, you really are important, aren't you, Lily?"

"Come in and sit down, Fi, I've got something interesting to talk to you about."

"Does this mean you'll tell me what's going on here, Lily?"

"Not yet, Fi, first I need to know if in principle you would like to work as my assistant?"

"Do you think I'm capable of doing whatever the job entails?"

"I have absolutely no doubt."

"Then in that case, yes, so now you can tell me what this is all about."

I produced the Official Secrets Act and gave her the lecture just as Edward had presented it to me. I even laboured over the point about the capital punishment. Fiona didn't seem that surprised, signing it and taking it all in her stride, until I explained the full significance of our work at Middlebourne.

"As far as I know, Fi, the only people in Great Britain outside of this place who really know what goes on here are the Prime Minister, his secretary, and his Chief of Staff. Here, it's Lord Middlebourne, the handful of boffins in Hut 3 and me, and now you. You must protect that secret with your life, Fi; the security of the country depends upon it."

Fiona turned pale. "I guessed it was some kind of Military Intelligence establishment, but not this! It's daunting, and a bit frightening, but I won't let you down, Lily."

"I already know that Fi, it's why you're here."

I gave her a tour of the establishment, which bewildered her just as it had amazed Johnny. The team had gelled together well by that time, and Fiona could see she was joining a very well-organised professional group. I think we impressed her, and finally I introduced her to Edward.

"Edward, I would like you to meet my new assistant and dearest friend, Fiona Roberts. I should say immediately Fiona's fiancé is Wing Commander Johnny Albright."

Fiona was aghast. "Why is that relevant, Lily?"

Edward answered, "You were correct to declare the interest, Lily. It's only relevant, Fiona, because your fiancé is seconded to Station M."

Fiona stood in silence. Her introduction to the tangled web we wove was necessarily brutal. Nevertheless, she had the wherewithal to learn fast and fitted easily into the organisation. Within next to no time, she was indispensable and effectively my deputy. Using her natural poise and elegance to great advantage, in my absence her authority was never questioned, which allowed her to fit in seamlessly.

The key to success was our close friendship; we instinctively worked hand in glove. I believe the bond between us was a key component to the success of Station M. There were other changes during that first year. Edward was right when he said it would be easier if I lived in the Manor. As my hours grew longer, it was perhaps inevitable, but I had been reluctant for several reasons. I wanted Gran and Dotty in my life, and it also meant that I was imposing myself upon Edward's family.

Edward and I could not have been closer in the work environment, but I felt strangely uncomfortable being a part of his personal and family life. They treated me very much as one of the family, but I never forgot the fact that I was not. Perhaps it was just my inner demons, but I needed to ease myself into the new situation, starting by only staying the occasional night. I think it spoke volumes for Edward's generosity of character that gradually I became one of the family.

We would work increasingly late into the evenings, feeding off each other's energy. When we finally locked our office doors, we would slump into comfy chairs in the Drawing Room, and Jennings would bring us generous glasses of whisky. Sometimes I would kick off my shoes, stretch my toes and feel the tension draining from my head through my body, spreading out into the deep pile of the carpet.

Edward would sit opposite me, though he would rarely abandon his elegant dress code; even loosening his tie was inappropriate. It was customary for Edward to dress for dinner, but even he at the end of a tiring day did not always have sufficient strength to comply with the ritual. We would sit, glass in hand, still discussing the day's events, too tired to move, content just to smile at each other.

Lady Caroline, however, had no intention of breaking with tradition, and so every evening she would appear for dinner looking every bit like the countess she was. Just occasionally, we would all dress for dinner. Edward would look resplendent in his formal evening wear, and I confess sometimes it made me feel momentarily as if I were the Lady of the Manor, but then like Cinderella returning from the ball, I would feel like an imposter.

My professional relationship with Greg Norton inevitably changed during 1941. I completely dropped the title Mr Norton, he was always 'Greg'. He tried to maintain the etiquette of referring to me as Mrs Heywood, but one day he just called me Lily. I didn't object, and that was that. I enjoyed being with him; he was so different to Edward, energising me totally differently.

I imposed more and more upon him because he was so good at his job, and I admired him even more. I felt it was probably only a matter of time before his magnetic attraction eclipsed my better judgment. Heaven knows I wanted to but somehow, I held him at arm's length throughout 1941.

Station M flourished during that time, the boffins applying

their combined genius to great effect. Johnny Albright flew many reconnaissance missions out of Biggin Hill, and Maggie interpreted every detail. I was pleased with how quickly we gelled as a team, and how effectively our intelligence was building up an ever-clearer picture of the entire European coast. We had some idea about the primary German defences and some infrastructure away from the coast. We were making progress, but there was one thing holding us back - we didn't have the Americans on-side.

-oOo-

Everything changed on December 7th when the Japanese attacked Pearl Harbour. We heard it first directly from Station X. Initially, we couldn't believe it. Edward and I rushed into the radio communications room where everyone gathered around us. All we knew was that Pearl Harbour was under attack.

Gradually the full magnitude of it emerged, and there was a stunned silence in the room. The boys produced maps and classified documents relating to Pearl Harbour, and we quickly realised the potential impact such a raid might have had. It soon emerged that the home of the American Pacific Fleet suffered serious damage.

This was dreadful news, the only saving grace being that the American aircraft carriers were out at sea, escaping the raid. The following day, Congress approved Roosevelt's declaration of war against Japan. Three days later, Japan's allies - Germany and Italy - declared war on America. Suddenly, everything had changed. The war had broadened to include Japan and the Pacific region. Now the entire world was at war.

"Do you realise," Woody said, "this means every region of the world is at war."

"Mankind's gone stark-staring feckin' mad!" Patrick proclaimed, with a look of disbelief in his eyes.

"You're right, Patrick," Rolo said, "how else can you explain the desire to destroy thousands of years of civilisation?"

"Civilisation comes down to people, Rolo," I said. "Total war means lying beneath the rubble of your home, not knowing if you're dead or alive. It means seeing a little boy crushed beyond recognition and having your loved ones killed without even a grave to weep over."

"I'm sorry, Lily, I didn't realise," replied Rolo.

"It's not your fault, Rolo," I said. "Patrick's right, the entire world's gone mad."

"You're the voice of reason, Lily, in a world where reason has become a scarce commodity," said Edward. "However, the fact is the Americans are now *in* the war, and we are no longer fighting alone."

"You were right about the Americans, old boy," replied Woody, "with the United States standing alongside us, we can finally put an end to the madness."

"The end justifies the means, Lily," said Patrick, "a lot more people will lie beneath the rubble of their houses before this is over; that will be the price of freedom."

They were right, and quickly the atmosphere in Station M changed irrevocably as an unfamiliar sense of urgency pervaded every hut. However difficult, an invasion of Europe had now become a practical possibility, and it depended to a large degree upon us.

Just days later, on December 10th, the battleship Prince of Wales and the battlecruiser Repulse were both sunk by Japanese land-based bombers and torpedo bombers. It was a tragic day for the Royal Navy. I felt that loss personally; Prince of Wales had engaged the Bismarck alongside my husband's ship, the Hood. The news left me feeling low. I needed something to lift my spirits, and it was Elizabeth Layton who unexpectedly came to my rescue.

Chapter Eighteen
Winston Churchill
comes to Station M

Just two days after the sinking of the Prince of Wales, Elizabeth telephoned me to say that the Prime Minister intended to come to Middlebourne the following week, and would I make the arrangements. My jaw dropped and Elizabeth sensed my apprehension.

"Don't worry, Lily, it's good news! Station M has suddenly become the key to the invasion, so he wants to come and give you all a pep talk."

"A pep talk from the Prime Minister! That's wonderful, Elizabeth, I can't wait to tell the boys."

The moment I put the phone down, I told Fiona and her reaction was the same as mine. I rushed over to Hut 3, where Edward and the boys were standing in a huddle, looking down onto an enormous map. It was particularly cold in there and they looked slightly ridiculous, dressed in scarves and winter clothes. Woody even had gloves on; they looked more like a group of carol singers. The stove was burning in the corner to little effect, but I rushed over to stand next to it, blowing into my cupped hands.

"We have a visitor coming next week," I said, unable to conceal my excitement.

"Not another bod with an expenditure form?" Edward enquired.

"No, you will not believe who it is."

"Oh, God! It's General Allington again, isn't it?"

I couldn't contain the smile on my face any longer. "The Prime Minister is coming to see us. He wants to give us a pep talk - I think it means one of his rousing speeches."

There was uproar - the prospect excited everyone in Hut 3. Edward tried to calm the situation, saying it was just a routine visit, but it wasn't. This was an incredibly significant moment, and we all knew it. They were full of questions, none of which I could answer, other than to say he was coming in just three days' time.

I hurried back to my office to get warm again, and together with Fiona and Elizabeth we started completing the details. We scheduled him to arrive late in the morning, talk to us all, have lunch with the family and leave by 2 o'clock, just three hours in all. Jennings and Mrs Morgan went into a tailspin, while Fiona and I panicked to make available every conceivable report or document he might want to see. Edward was the only one of us to remain calm. On the evening before the visit, we sat in the Drawing Room, drinking whisky.

"You're very calm about this, Edward."

"Well Winston is a close friend of the family; he's spent many joyful days here in the past."

"But this is about Station M, this must be to do with the Americans entering the war."

"That would be my assessment, yes."

"This changes the entire course of the war, Edward. Our work here depended upon it."

"It was only a matter of time, Lily, I was confident about that; I am surprised that you doubted it."

He could infuriate at times, and that was one of them! Meeting the Prime Minister might not have been a momentous occasion for Edward, but it was for me and for Fiona; we couldn't have been more excited.

When the big day finally came, two cars and two military vehicles drove up to Middlebourne Manor. I was trying to imagine Corporal Harris at the barrier. Fiona had forewarned the guard that we had some top brass visiting, but she couldn't say it was the Prime Minister. I don't suppose for a second Corporal Harris asked to see the PM's identity, but I would love to have seen Brian Harris's face!

I excitedly watched as the vehicles came to a halt outside the Manor, and Edward rushed forward to stand by the Prime Minister's car to greet him. As he stepped out of the car, Edward quietly addressed him by his Christian name and Mr Churchill called him Edward. I stood by, feeling insignificant and sure I would do or say the wrong thing. Having warmly shaken Edward's hand, he then turned towards me. My heart was thumping!

"Ah, and this must be Mrs Heywood," he said in that unmistakable voice of his.

"It is a great honour, Prime Minister."

He stood for a moment looking at me while he reached into his inside jacket pocket for a cigar which he rolled between his fingers. He said nothing for what felt like an eternity, his attention concentrated upon the cigar. I was unsure if I should step back or just stand there; perhaps he didn't intend to say anything else to me. He didn't light the cigar; he just ran it under his nose. I assumed his smile showed the pleasure he was anticipating from the cigar, but all the while he was smiling at me.

"Now tell me, Mrs Heywood, which is it, do you find our meeting to be an honour, or a pleasure?"

I was taken aback. He obviously remembered our telephone conversation. I returned his smile as I considered how to reply.

"At this moment sir, it feels very much like an honour, but I can easily see how it might become intoxicating."

He looked at me approvingly, then at Edward, who must have been wondering what on earth was going on.

"Just a little private conversation between Mrs Heywood and myself," he said, smiling all the while, "and talking about intoxication Edward, get your people together in the Great Hall, and have them each bring a glass."

One of the Prime Minister's aides produced some bottles of whisky, Johnny Walker Red Label, apparently from his own supply, and we all quickly assembled in the Great Hall as he had instructed. Everyone below Level One Clearance was excluded, and all the doors were closed.

Glasses were filled and Mr Churchill stood in the middle of the Hall. He pierced the end of his cigar with a matchstick, and his Romeo y Julieta was ceremonially lit. We gathered closer around him, nervously holding our glasses. We all knew this would be a significant moment; the room was crackling with anticipation. There was a long silence as he stood there puffing on the cigar, all the while looking around at us.

"We assemble here in the Great Hall of this magnificent house thanks to the hospitality of Lord Middlebourne. So first I must thank you, Lord Middlebourne, for making possible the vital work you undertake here. It is impossible for me to overstate the importance of that undertaking.

We stand here together at the crossroads of history; the Nazi tyranny has lain waste to the historic nations of Europe. We alone in these great British Isles have stood defiant in the face of the onslaught. Undefeated, we are the last remaining beacon of hope, the last outpost of the civilised European nations.

Today we no longer stand alone. The great industrial might of the United States of America is now mobilised and will be brought to bear against our common Nazi enemy. Together, we will build an invasion force, the likes of which the world has never seen. A mighty and irresistible force, which will free the civilised world of the aberration which has befallen it. You alone in this Great Hall understand the enormity of the task ahead, and you alone can ensure that we succeed.

When victory is finally ours, the peoples of the Free World will come together, united in homage to the brave and the fallen. You will receive no such recognition; I will not pin medals to your chest. The great British people may never know the part you will play, nor the debt they will owe. However, come that glorious day of celebration, I can assure you all of one thing, no-one will stand taller than those gathered here today. Victory in Europe!"

The room momentarily stood in silence, then we raised our glasses, and a tremendous roar erupted: "Victory in Europe." The atmosphere was indescribable; I looked at Fiona, she had tears running down her face the same as I did, and Edward was so moved he seemed unable to raise a cheer. I did something quite out of character, I put my arm around him and briefly hugged him tightly. He didn't know how to respond, but he managed a smile.

Mr Churchill shook the hand of everyone in the Hall; it felt like an age before the atmosphere settled down. Fiona rightly wanted to shake his hand, and so she joined the others. I felt awkward that so many deserving people like Fiona were not joining us for lunch, but apparently the PM was insistent - he wanted a quiet intimate lunch. When the time came, I led him into the Family Dining Room, where it was just the four of us sitting together at the dining table. Mr Churchill sat at the head of the table. Edward would normally have been at the other end, but we decided he would be too far away, ridiculous in the circumstances. So Edward, Caroline, and I sat around Mr Churchill. Jennings and the staff attended us with beaming pride.

"Ah, Jennings," the Prime Minister said, "do you still have any of that wonderful Cognac?"

"I do indeed, sir, I have it standing at room temperature for you."

"You have anticipated me well, Jennings, thank you."

I smiled at Jennings, a mixture of approval and admiration. The Prime Minister then addressed Caroline.

"I have such wonderful memories of our times together sitting around this table; wonderful days, Caroline."

"Yes, I miss them, Winston, promise me you will bring Clemmie just as soon as this awful war is over."

"That is what the nation is fighting for, Caroline. We demand the right to share food and conversation with our friends, nothing more. And what say you, Mrs Heywood, will you be enjoying food and conversation sitting around this table after the war?"

He left me momentarily speechless, and I had no idea what to say.

Finally I said, "I'm not thinking that far ahead, sir. Maybe we should win the war first."

"Oh, we *will* win the war! How can we not, with people like you and Edward working for the war effort?"

"That's a kind thing to say, sir, and after that rousing speech you gave us today, I believe we *can* do anything."

"Do you think it did the trick?"

"I was moved to tears, Prime Minister, I've never been so inspired by the English language. I've read all your speeches, sir, but today you directed your words to us personally. You spoke to each and every person in the Hall. Yes, sir, I think it did the trick."

"That is extremely gratifying to hear, Mrs Heywood, I had no time to prepare the speech as I would normally, so yes I'm pleased to hear you say that. And so tell me, Mrs Heywood, have you finally decided, is our meeting an honour, or a pleasure?"

"It's a tough decision, sir, but I would say it's an enormous pleasure."

"And I will confess to intoxication, Mrs Heywood, and we all know I do not mean as a result of too much alcohol."

"I'm sure I don't know what you mean, sir!"

"Spare an old man his delusion, Mrs Heywood! And it will help if you would call me Winston."

"Lily, please call me Lily."

"Nothing will give me greater pleasure, Lily. You're from London, I believe, which part?"

"Stockwell, and then Stepney, within the sound of St Mary-Le-Bow bells."

"And proud of it, I would wager, and so you should be! Nobody has suffered more at the hands of the Luftwaffe than the magnificent people of East London. So many have lost homes and loved ones, but their spirit is unbreakable. They are an inspiration to the entire country. Have you lost anyone, Lily?"

"I lost my house in Stepney, and I lost my best friend and her two young boys. They killed my brother at Dunkirk, and my husband was on board HMS Hood. So yes, I've had my share of heartache."

"I am truly sorry, my dear, you have suffered more than your share, but I can see it has not broken your spirit."

"It's been hard, sir, believe me. I have my difficult days, but it just makes me want to fight back; how dare that monster destroy my home and my friends and family? Hitler made a terrible mistake when he thought he could break the British people. We didn't give up in the East End during the Blitz, it just made us more determined to fight back. The more they destroyed our homes, and killed our loved ones, the more determined we became. I saw it every night during the Blitz; they'll never break the spirit of the British people."

I hesitated then, realising I had allowed myself to get carried away, not appropriate at the dining table.

"I apologise, Caroline, I shouldn't let my emotions get the better of me like that."

Winston put his knife and fork down forcibly against his plate, the sudden noise making us all look up with a start.

"*Never* apologise for the pain that monster has inflicted upon you, Lily!" he said, in a raised voice. "Hitler has unleashed a mighty spirit; I can see it sitting here before me now.

We *will* be victorious, I promise you, and it will be because of people like you, Lily. They will never defeat a nation whose spirit is unbreakable! If I were you, Edward, I wouldn't let this woman out of my sight!"

I looked at Edward, who was as embarrassed as I was, and Winston could see our embarrassment; he was toying with us. Caroline helpfully changed the subject, and our lunch continued. I'll never forget a single word of that conversation with Winston Churchill; it was the most memorable meal of my life.

When the time came for him to go, I really didn't want it to end, but his brief time with us was over. He warmly hugged Caroline and shook Edward's hand with his other hand on Edward's shoulder. The occasion completely overwhelmed me, and I couldn't help putting my arms around him, and I kissed his cheek. The moment I did so, I realised it wasn't appropriate.

However, he smiled happily so perhaps I hadn't overstepped the mark, after all! I finally plucked up the courage to call him Winston.

"I'm sorry, Winston, I seem to have left some lipstick on your cheek."

I reached for a handkerchief, but he stepped back with a beaming smile.

"Good Lord, are you mad, Lily? I'll wear this with pride for the rest of the day!"

As he left, one of his entourage diplomatically commented on the lipstick.

"Do you have a handkerchief handy, sir, looks like lipstick on your cheek?"

Winston smiled at the man, and I heard his reply. "Just remember, behind every lipstick there are a woman's lips. I notice you haven't any lipstick on your cheek!"

He visited Hut 3 and shook everyone's hand again. There was a genuine warmth as he wished us all well with our task.

Having stayed half an hour longer than his schedule, his aides were becoming agitated, and he was ushered away towards the cars. As the cars drove away, he raised his hand out of the car window in his customary two finger victory sign. We all stood waving like children at a carnival.

The anti-climax when he had gone left us feeling drained; it was as if a great storm had blown through Middlebourne, leaving us standing amongst the wreckage! We made our way back to Hut 3, where we all sat together with one of the bottles of whisky. No useful work was done for the rest of that day, but the lift in morale was immeasurable.

Chapter Nineteen
1941 Christmas

The work rate stepped up during the remaining weeks of 1941, with the certainty of an invasion of Europe invigorating everyone. Few people celebrated Christmas in the East End of London in 1940 during the Blitz, but this year was different, especially for us. We had the Americans in the war with us, so we had another reason to celebrate. Edward invited me to join them for Christmas, which was exceedingly kind, but I explained that my parents were coming down from London to stay with Gran, so it was obviously a time for me to be with my family. I was looking forward to it, not having seen my parents since I moved to Gran's, and I was desperate to be with them again.

It was a relief in some respects. I loved being with Edward in the work environment - we were perfect together - sometimes I felt as if we were two halves of the same person. But when we tried to continue that closeness outside of Station M, it didn't always work. There would be occasional awkward silences, which I knew were my fault, and I felt that Christmas might have been such an occasion.

Our plans for the festivities at Gran's were going well. It would be much the same as so many Christmases had been before. We had always gone to Gran's for Christmas; it was one of those inviolable family traditions. The only year when we hadn't gone was in 1940 during the Blitz, so this year would be extra special. Fiona and I were discussing it when Greg came into the office. He was not being his usual flirtatious self because Fiona was sitting at her desk on the other side of the room. The three of us talked about Christmas.

"What are your plans, Greg?" Fiona asked.

"Oh, I'm not sure. I half thought about going back to Scotland for a few days, but it's a lot of travelling."

"Do you not have family somewhere around here?" I asked, hoping he would say yes.

"Well, kind of. I don't get on with my stepfather at all. You know - can't be in the same room - that kind of not getting on."

"Yes, that's the worst kind of not getting on, isn't it," I said light-heartedly.

"Actually, it is, because it means I don't often get to see my mother."

"I'm sorry, Greg. I didn't mean to make light of it."

"Oh no, don't worry, I'm used to it."

"You're not by yourself, are you, not on Christmas Day?" asked a concerned Fiona.

"Probably, but that's okay."

"It's not okay at all!" exclaimed Fiona. "Why don't you come and have Christmas lunch with us? I feel sure Gran wouldn't mind. You'd be welcome, wouldn't he, Lily?"

"I couldn't do that, I'd only be in the way," he said.

I don't know why I said it - it just came out before I had time to think.

"Of course you wouldn't be in the way, looks like that's settled then."

And so it was that Gran had a full house for Christmas lunch. She momentarily panicked, not able to see how she could find enough food for nine people, and where they would all sit. However, Aunty Mavis said she would bring all manner of food, and Greg surprised us all by offering to bring as many pheasants as we could eat. As for seating, Mavis would contribute her kitchen table and chairs.

We sat at the kitchen table the evening before Christmas Eve, gluing together paper chains with flour and water paste, while Gran decorated an enormous Christmas tree which Jim had produced from somewhere. I had been so preoccupied with Station M, the festive season seemed to just creep up on me. When it finally arrived, it burst into my life full of colourful decorations, candles, mince pies, and smiling faces. It all started on the morning of Christmas Eve with the shock of my life when I saw William pull up outside the cottage in the Rolls-Royce.

"What on earth are you doing here, William?" I asked.

"I hope you don't mind, Mrs Heywood. Mr Jennings told me your parents will arrive at the station at 11 o'clock this morning and suggested it would be nice if I picked them up for you."

"But you can't just steal the family car, William!"

"Oh no, I asked Lord Middlebourne if it would be all right, and he thought it was a splendid idea."

I just didn't know what to say; it overwhelmed me. As always in those situations, I reacted without thinking, putting my arms around William; it was inappropriate and very embarrassing for all concerned. However, the look on my Mum and Dad's faces was worth every moment of my embarrassment. As I stood on the platform waiting for them, it so reminded me of the last time I saw them except, on that occasion, they were on the platform and I was on the train. As their train pulled into the station, there they were, waving frantically from the window, while I was jumping up and down waving my hands above my head as the train came to a halt.

We had our differences over the years, but I was so pleased to see them. We just stood for an age, arms around each other, and couldn't stop talking; it seemed to take ages for us to leave the platform. The porter took their luggage on a trolley, and we slowly made our way to the car park. I said nothing, just walked towards William who was standing next to the Rolls-Royce, looking rather splendid in his uniform. The look on my parents' faces was something to behold! As Dad reached for one of their cases, William quickly stepped forward.

"No, sir, allow me," he said.

Then, as William opened the door for Mum, she looked at Dad, and then at me. I just grinned like a Cheshire Cat - it was priceless! They sat in the back of the Rolls-Royce feeling like the King and Queen of England, enjoying every second of the journey to Gran's. If I'd suggested we turn around to do it all again, it would have delighted them.

I thanked William again, and I hadn't forgotten Jennings' part in it either. Then Gran appeared, walking down the path, and the hugging started all over again, despite Spencer Tracy trying to come between them. I introduced them both to Fiona and Dotty.

"This is Fiona and Dorothy. They are not just my best friends, they're also part of the family now. This is my Mum and Dad, Pam and Jack."

"Hello," Fiona said, hugging them both warmly, "I've been so looking forward to meeting you both, I feel as if I already know you."

"Hello, Lily's Mum and Dad," said Dotty. "What should I call you, Pam and Jack, or shall I call you Mum and Dad?"

"Oh, that makes us feel old Dotty, it's Pam and Jack."

"Give me a hug then, Pam, you'll get your turn, Jack, don't worry."

Dotty overwhelmed my parents; I can't think of a moment when they were not smiling. She became instantly attached to them, which was lovely for me to see, but it made me wonder. Was it just Dotty's effusive warm nature, or was it a need she had? It was just a transient thought in what was otherwise a wonderful family day of fun and reminiscence. I'm sure Mum and Dad were thinking of Ian and Gerry, just as I was, but they weren't mentioned.

"Your friends are lovely, Lily," Mum said, "and Fiona is so elegant and sophisticated; she really is charming, isn't she?"

"She is, and she's such a wonderful friend to me."

"They're just as you described them in your letters; I thought you were exaggerating about Dorothy, she really is a live-wire, I can see what you meant now."

"Trust me, Mum, you've seen nothing yet!"

Christmas morning was chaotic. Dotty woke us up early, with a child-like excitement that could not be contained. I looked at Fiona as we both glanced at the clock and smiled.

"Merry Christmas!" Dotty said, with a beaming smile.

"Merry Christmas, Dotty," we said in unison.

"I'll get breakfast started," she said, "come along, you two."

As Dotty left the bedroom, we could hear Spencer Tracy bounding up the stairs to greet her. I looked at Fiona, waiting for the inevitable.

"For Christ's sake, bugger off, Spencer, get down, you stupid dog! Get *down!*"

We both burst out laughing. By the time Fiona and I appeared, Dotty had boiled eggs and toast ready on the table. Gran appeared with Mum and Dad, and to Dotty's obvious delight, Christmas Day was well and truly underway.

"Morning Pam, morning Jack, Merry Christmas!"

"Merry Christmas to you, Dotty," Mum replied.

"Are you all right in that loft room, it must be freezing!" asked Dotty.

"It is a bit cold, but we'll be okay."

"We can swap if you like, Pam, can't we, Lily? I don't feel the cold anyway, no sense, no feeling you see!"

"No, we're fine, really," my Dad said.

As soon as we finished our breakfast, everyone became involved preparing Christmas lunch. Gran was in her element, directing and shouting at us all; I don't think the smile dropped from her face for a second. Then there was a bang and a clatter as Jim struggled in with Mavis's kitchen table. Spencer immediately ran to help by jumping up at Jim and to my surprise, Greg was struggling with the other end of the table.

"Merry Christmas, Greg, how did you get roped into this?"

"I turned up at precisely the wrong moment," he said, with a broad smile.

He went back and forth with Jim, cheerfully carrying chairs and crockery, ably assisted by the increasingly excited Spencer. Slightly red-faced, Greg removed his tweed jacket, and hung it over the back of a chair, rolling up his sleeves. He looked smart in his tweed suit, but he also looked attractive in his waistcoat, with the sleeves rolled up. They were gone for some time, until finally they came back with cheeks puffed up, each taking tiny steps, shuffling their feet along. Jim was a big man, and Greg wasn't so far behind him, but they were really struggling to carry Mavis's upright piano.

"What on earth are you doing, Jim?" Gran asked, as we all looked on in amazement.

"It's Christmas, Margaret," Mavis said, "don't you complain now! You know you like Lily to sing for us at Christmas."

"I'll never be the same again," joked Greg, rubbing his back.

"Neither will I," said Jim, "this damned silly dog will be the death of me. Can't you control him, Dotty?"

"*Spencer!*" Dotty shouted.

Spencer ran to her, and immediately sat down, looking up with his doleful eyes.

"I don't know what you mean, Jim, look at him, he's perfectly well-behaved!"

Christmas Day was soon in full swing, with the lunch table beautifully arranged, and everyone wanting to help. Finally, Gran insisted everyone else should sit in the front room while she directed Fiona, Dotty and me towards the kitchen. We obediently followed her, and all Dotty could talk about was how gorgeous Greg was.

"He's lovely! You work with him all the time, and you're telling me you haven't.... you know?" She chose her words carefully around Gran, fearful of a slap around the ear.

"We're work colleagues, Dotty, I told you."

"Well, in that case he's fair game then."

Inexplicably I said, "Please don't, Dotty, I know you could, but please don't. It would spoil everything."

"Not for me, it wouldn't, he's too good to waste."

Fiona and I hadn't discussed Greg at all, but she intervened, taking me by surprise.

"I agree, Dotty, he's lovely, and I know you find him irresistible, but Lily's right. Please don't, would you promise me?"

Dotty looked at us both. "What's going on here .... oh I see ... I suppose I'll just have to not notice him ..... oh shit!"

"How many times have I told you about that language, Dotty!" shouted Gran, as Dotty ducked away from a slap.

I created an awkward moment, but Gran had reduced us all to laughter. We didn't mention the matter again, not openly anyway. Our Christmas lunch was a wonderful if overcrowded success. We'd never had pheasant for Christmas before, and now we had four of them! Gran placed them on two large plates and summoned Dad to come and carve them. This was Dad's moment when he would receive all the praise that was rightly Gran's. Fiona lifted the stuffing from the oven while Gran stirred the gravy, and I produced a bottle of French champagne - also a first.

"Don't ask me how I got this," I said, as I popped the cork.

The cork shot across the kitchen and into the scullery. Boris the cat was keeping away from all the hubbub, nestling next to the warmth of the copper. Alarmed by the flying cork, he took flight and Spencer went after him, causing pandemonium. The champagne overflowed the bottle, and everyone fell about laughing.

Eventually, we all raised an assortment of different-shaped glasses. Some were overflowing, some were just bubbles, but each was full of Christmas cheer. I doubt any of us thought about the war that day, which was perhaps why we were all so happy. I was surrounded by everyone I loved, and perhaps one that I might come to love. I couldn't think when I last felt that happy. Dotty was the Queen of the Ball, just seeming to explode with joy. Mum and Dad were besotted with her.

"Did you have Christmases like this with your family, Dotty, before the war?" Mum asked.

"Not really, not like this. Is this how you always celebrate it, Pam?"

"Before the war we did, it was always like this, wasn't it, Mum?"

Gran smiled in agreement. "Best times are always when the family's together."

Dotty momentarily dropped her smile, as her big eyes just narrowed slightly, but then, in an instant, the mercurial Dotty was back, although she was gone just long enough for me to notice.

"What about you, Greg, do you have wonderful Christmas memories?" Fiona asked.

"When I was a kid, I had wonderful times, but I have to confess not for some years now."

"What about you, Fi?" Mum asked.

"Yes, not so different to this, really. All the family used to come to our house in Chelsea, wonderful memories. Maybe after the war things will be the same. Mum and Dad are in Devon now, with my sister."

"It's such a shame Johnny can't be here today, Fi," I said.

"It is, but I'll see him soon, and I really feel like this is my family now."

"I know what you mean, Fi," said Dotty, "this is *my* family now. You see, I don't ..... well, you know, you're not such a bad family to have, are you?"

"And you don't make a bad granddaughter either, Dorothy," said Gran, "just watch your language in my kitchen!"

Finally, it was Christmas pudding with custard - what could be better? Even big Jim couldn't manage a second helping. Everyone sat there content and replete. I'd thought eating too much had been consigned to peacetime, but that Christmas was traditional in every sense. Eventually we had to find the strength to do the washing up, and who was the one who always had a reserve of energy?

"Come along, galley slaves, the washing up calls," pronounced Dotty. "Not you, Gran, you sit down and make eyes at Greg."

Dotty washed up almost single-handedly, while a line of us stood with tea towels. It all formed a scene of ordinary domestication, which would have been perfectly normal during peacetime, but that Christmas, it was a welcome reminder. Greg sat laughing and chatting to my Dad, while Mum referred to me and Greg as 'you two.' It was an unsettling situation. I really enjoyed being with Greg, but I had not intended for us to be thrust together like that.

We all settled back in the front room to open presents, and that was the only moment when I thought about the absence of any young children, perhaps even my own child. Christmas wrapping paper was scarce; anything would do. Delightful gifts were even scarcer, but it didn't matter; home-made things were the order of the day. I was sure people all over the country were sitting just like us, looking at hand-knitted socks and jumpers. Dotty's eyes looked fit to burst when she saw several presents were for her.

In amongst the presents, there was a small box wrapped in proper Christmas paper. It was for me, from Edward. When he gave it to me, he said it was not to be opened until Christmas Day. I had given him a small present of a Cuban cigar; it was actually awfully expensive.

I opened my present carefully, pulling back the lovely

wrapping paper to find a small jewellery box. Mum and Fiona both looked over my shoulder as I opened the box to reveal a pair of exquisite pearl and ruby earrings. My heart stopped; I was completely overwhelmed. I had no idea what to think; I expected nothing remotely like that from Edward. Mum and Fiona were as amazed as I was, and inevitably Mum couldn't understand why my employer would buy me such an extravagant and beautiful gift.

"Can we not say anything about this?" I said, trying not to look as if I had a secret lover.

Mum didn't understand, but Fiona as always could read my mind. She smiled at me knowingly and drew Mum's attention onto something else.

I whispered into Fi's ear, "I don't know what this means, either."

For some strange reason, I didn't want Greg to see the earrings, and so I put them away. Beer was the only alcohol easily available during the war so, trying not to dwell on the earrings, I eagerly reached for another glass. As I did so, Greg came over and stood close to me.

"I'm sorry I don't have any presents," he said.

"Don't be silly, we don't need to buy each other presents."

He looked at me with those lovely eyes. "Thank you for asking me to come, Lily, your family are wonderful."

He was about to say something else, and part of me wanted him to say it, but just at that moment, the sound of the piano filled the room. Gran was still a wonderful pianist, despite the arthritis in her fingers. She taught me to play when I was just a child. I could play from memory but I wasn't very proficient at reading music. Gran and I were inseparable when I was little, and it was always the music that bonded us together. She used to get so cross with me when I couldn't read a sheet of music, but then she would play it for me, and I'd copy her almost note for note.

Now she played a few favourites and soon we were all

singing along. The party atmosphere was wonderful, and the house was full of merriment. Then Gran played something different, looking at me all the while. The contrast with her sing-along was stark, and everyone stopped singing to listen.

"What's she playing?" asked Dotty.

"Un Bel di Vedremo."

"What does that mean?"

"It means 'One fine day we shall see'. It's the famous aria from Madame Butterfly."

This was Gran's favourite aria, which she taught me to sing right from childhood, or so she used to say.

"I'll know when you've become a woman, Lily, because that's the day you'll be able to sing this properly."

I think they were wise words. I practised it hundreds of times, struggling at first with the language, but quickly memorised it. Now Gran sat at the piano smiling at me, and I knew I had to sing it for her.

Gran was always in tears when I sang 'Un Bel di Vedremo'. Knowing this day would be no exception, I faced away from her; I would be unable to finish it otherwise. Despite a lot of classical training, I didn't regard myself as an opera singer. Gran insisted that I could have been, but within the confines of a small room, I could certainly sound like one.

I just enjoyed singing, and thanks to Gran, this was also one of my favourite pieces. Every time I sang the aria, it transported to another place, another time. It was an exhilarating experience.

Gran was always fine while Madam Butterfly waits for Lieutenant Pinkerton's ship to arrive in the harbour. Gran could even cope with her speculating about the Lieutenant appearing. However, as soon as the moment of realisation comes for Cio-Cio-San, Gran's tears well up and if I'm facing her, then I'm the same! That's when I struggle to hold the crescendo.

Gran composed herself and started playing, I stood up

straight and filled my lungs. The aria starts gently enough and gradually builds in tension till the moment of realisation finally comes for Cio-Cio-San.

At that moment, if not before, I *am* Madam Butterfly; I fully inhabit the part. The crescendo is the most challenging, but also the most thrilling part of the aria. I really want my audience to feel Madam Butterfly's anguish in my voice. When I succeeded, as I did that day, it was a wonderfully exhilarating experience.

The moment I finished, everyone was clapping me, but it always takes me several seconds to come back from wherever the aria has transported me. I turned and put my arms around Gran, who was in tears as usual. What really surprised me was the sight of Dorothy with tears streaming down her face, so I went straight over to her, putting my arms around her. She was sobbing her heart out.

"What's wrong, Dotty, what is it?"

"I've heard nothing like that before! I don't even know what the words mean, but it was just wonderful - and all this - and you - and Gran! It's all too much for me, I'm sorry."

"Let's go upstairs, Dotty, come along."

I gestured to Fiona, and she quickly came over to us, and we went upstairs together where we could be alone.

"I'm sorry," Dotty said, "I really don't know what came over me. I had no idea you could sing like that, Lily. *Christ*, I had no idea anyone could sing like that!"

"That was *such* a surprise!" Fiona said, as she held Dotty's hand. "You've got the most amazing voice, Lily, it was wonderful. I think everyone had tears in their eyes, I know I did."

"Gran always cries. It makes it difficult for me to sing. If I look at her, my voice cracks."

"It's not just me, then?" Dotty said, trying to smile.

"No, that's the whole point of opera," I explained, "it's telling a story through the emotion of music."

Dotty dried her tears, spreading makeup all over her face,

and though she attempted to smile, her lovely eyes told a different story.

"What is it really, Dotty, we're your best friends, can you tell us?" Fiona said, trying to reassure her.

"I just didn't expect that voice. Lily, it was so moving, it just did something to me. And it's all this family thing, seeing everyone so happy, I've never had that. When I was a girl, I was treated so badly, but I just thought that was normal. Then, when you realise it wasn't normal, it just all seems so much worse."

"What happened to you, Dotty?" I asked.

"I can't talk about it. I'll never talk about it."

"Well, you don't have to," Fiona said, "you've got us and we're your family now."

We talked for a few more minutes and amazingly, the effervescent Dorothy quickly returned, leaving not a trace of the frightened little girl from moments earlier. Whatever her past trauma was, she could step into the other Dorothy seamlessly. Perhaps the real Dorothy would always remain a mystery, but the Dotty that we knew and loved is the most amazing woman I have ever known.

Dotty insisted we go back downstairs while she sat in front of the mirror. Fiona and I were making light of the entire affair, when Mum mentioned that we were just in time to listen to the King's Christmas speech, so I shouted upstairs to Dotty.

"Hurry, Dotty, it's the King's Christmas speech in five minutes."

When Dotty reappeared, she filled the room with her presence as if nothing had happened, and we all stood in a huddle around the wireless. We smiled at Dotty as the King referred to "Our one great family." He spoke of "The men who in every part of the world are serving the Empire" and he spoke about the women "Who, at the call of duty, have left their homes to join the services, or to work in factories, hospitals or fields." We all felt as if the King was talking directly to us; it was very moving.

No sooner was the King's speech over than we settled down to tea and Gran's home-made mince pies. It was just the most wonderful day. They all wanted me to sing some more arias, but there are only a handful I feel confident to sing. I sang some of the most popular ones, "Vissi d'arte," "O mio babbino caro," and one of my favourites "Ebben! Ne andro lontana," from the opera La Wally.

Gran's sheer delight as she accompanied me is my enduring memory of that Christmas. George introduced me to the opera, it was his passion. He encouraged me and paid for my lessons, but I wouldn't be a singer without Gran. Even the voice I was born with, I owe to her. Being able to repay her with such joy, simply by giving back some of what she had given me, that was the greatest gift of all.

Later on, we found some swing music on the wireless, and despite there not being enough room, we somehow managed one or two dances. I can't imagine a happier day. We repeated the entire thing on Boxing Day. The food might have been cold leftovers, and no-one had the energy to dance, but it was another wonderful day.

Christmas 1941 was incredibly special for many reasons. For years afterwards, at Christmas time, someone would inevitably say, "Do you remember Christmas '41?"

-oOo-

It was back to work the day after Boxing Day, back to reality. I carried my things back to my bedroom at Middlebourne, and the contrast with my other life could not have felt wider. As I sat on the bed gazing at my beautiful room, which was larger than all of Gran's bedrooms combined, there was a knock on the door.

"Come in."

It was Florence, smiling cheerfully.

"Morning, Mrs Heywood, I saw you carrying your clothes with you. Can I help you with tidying up and putting away?"

This was neither Florence's job, nor my place to accept such help, but I could see she wanted to, so I said yes. She was really pleased to be helping me.

"Did you have a lovely Christmas, Mrs Heywood?"

"I did, Florence, thank you; it was wonderful. And what about you?"

"We were busy with His Lordship's guests, but we had a wonderful lunch below-stairs in the evening. Albert drank too much; he was funny."

"Tell me about young Albert. He doesn't say very much, does he?"

"He's a lovely boy, very shy, and you might think he's a bit slow, but he isn't, not a bit of it; he's just quiet."

"I'll remember that, Florence, thank you for telling me. How were the Christmas guests, anyone interesting?"

"Not really. Lord and Lady Hollingworth, and the local MP. Oh, and Lord and Lady Stratton and their daughter."

"Oh, I've heard of her, that's Lady Beatrice. What's she like?"

"She's nice, I like her."

Foolishly I wanted to know about Beatrice and Edward, but hesitated about asking Florence, until eventually I could put it off no longer.

"Is she pretty, Lady Beatrice?"

"Oh yes, very."

"And did Lord Middlebourne seem, you know, attentive towards her?"

"I know what you're asking me, Mrs Heywood, and no, I don't believe he was."

Florence smiled at me knowingly. Then we had a lovely chat about other things as she rearranged my wardrobe and put my things away. I suddenly realised this was what having a lady's maid must be like.

"Leave your clothes on the bed next time, Mrs Heywood, I'll put them away for you."

Having thanked Florence, my next job was to thank Jennings for organising William to pick up my parents in the Rolls-Royce; that had really touched me. Later on, I found him in the kitchen with Mrs Morgan and the rest.

"Mr Jennings, I need to talk to you," I said, trying to look stern faced.

"Yes, Mrs Heywood, what can I do for you?"

"It's what you've already done, Mr Jennings. You altered the arrangements for my parents' arrival."

"Well, I'm sorry, Mrs Heywood, I thought it was a nice thing to do."

I was thinking about our little contretemps after I helped Jennings' father, but couldn't keep up the pretence any longer. I let the smile appear on my face which I'd been trying so hard to conceal.

"It wasn't just a nice thing to do, Mr Jennings, it was a really lovely thing you did." I stepped outside of all protocol and kissed him on the cheek. "Thank you."

Jennings appeared to be genuinely embarrassed but really, I think I pleasantly surprised him. Mrs Morgan and Joyce Evans laughed, and the girls were both giggling.

"Nothing wrong with kissing a handsome man like Mr Jennings," I said, as I left the kitchen.

I then went directly over to Hut 3 where, I assumed, I would find Edward. Sure enough, I could see him through the window. They were all standing together, staring at something. They must have recently made up the stove because smoke was billowing out of the chimney and filling the air with the sweet smell of burning hardwood. I hurried into the hut to get out of the cold, rubbing my hands together.

"There are some new gun emplacements being built, Lily, come and look at this," Edward said.

"Did you have a nice Christmas, Lily?" Patrick asked.

"I did, Patrick, thank you."

"Oh, I'm sorry!" said Edward. "That was thoughtless of me, I'm pleased you have had an enjoyable Christmas, Lily."

"Yes, I did, thank you. Has everybody else had a lovely time?" I asked them.

"We only took a few hours off for a Christmas lunch," Woody said, "we've hardly left this place."

"You're making it sound as though I've been away for weeks, it's only been three days!"

"It's nice to have you back, though," said Corky, waving at me from the other end of the hut.

I screwed up a piece of paper and threw it at him in jest.

"You know that piece of paper was top secret? It contained Hitler's collar size," he retorted.

I wanted to thank Edward for the wonderful earrings, but the hut was not the right place. After studying the reconnaissance photographs of the new gun emplacements, I headed off back to my office, scurrying out of the door as they showered me with balls of screwed-up paper. It was not until lunchtime that I had the chance to talk to Edward privately.

"Edward, I've been desperate to thank you for my earrings. They are wonderful. I don't know what to say, I'm totally overwhelmed."

"This sounds rather as if you like them."

"Like them, Edward, I love them! I have never dreamed that I would wear earrings like that - they are just exquisite."

Every fibre of my body wanted to take him in my arms and kiss him. It's what you do when a man buys you a present like that. I was having to restrain my arms from reaching out, but I had to do something, so I leaned forward and took his hand in mine.

"Thank you, Edward, but above all, thank you for wanting to give me such a gift." I squeezed his hand and quickly kissed his cheek.

"Thank you for my cigar, Lily, where on earth did you find it?"

"Best if you don't ask me, but you might notice it's the same brand the PM smokes!"

As we smiled at each other, I would have given anything to know if deep inside he was desperate to hold me. I wanted to believe he did, but he wasn't about to let his defences drop. The days between Christmas and New Year went quickly; we were so busy. New Year's Eve seemed to creep up on me just as Christmas had. Edward was having a few of the local dignitaries coming to stay the night. He invited me, but I declined in favour of a simple night at the pub with the girls.

Not knowing what to expect, I hadn't really thought about it. When we arrived at The Forge on New Year's Eve, the pub was full, and Middlebourne Manor was well represented. Two of the guards were there, including Corporal Harris. Florence and Mary were off duty and it delighted me to see all of our boffins had taken a night off, including Maggie.

Johnny Albright and two other flyers were there. I just had time to give Johnny an enormous hug before Fiona threw herself into his arms. I was still trying to adjust to seeing Fiona behave like that. Normally so dignified and middle class, her apparent abandonment with Johnny continued to amaze me. I used to joke that it was all Dotty's corrupt influence. I knew Greg would be there, but there was no sign of him just yet. Dotty launched herself at the other flyers, and I naturally gravitated toward my boffins.

The beer was flowing freely, and I decided my boffins were adorable. We had a wonderful rapport; their minds were so sharp and their clever humour beguiling. Woody looked fetching with his flamboyant bow tie, plus a pair of brown and white two-tone shoes. Maggie was another lovely character. Although she was married, she spent a lot of time with Patrick. I noticed that night how they looked at each other.

Greg arrived and headed straight toward me. We were all squeezed together around a table, but he *would* sit next to me, regardless. To be fair, he had no option but to put his arm around me, as he pushed his way onto the high-back bench seat. Being Greg, he left his arm there!

We drank a lot of beer, but as we counted down the seconds to 1942, we all raised yet another full glass with varying amounts of froth running down the sides. There was an enormous cheer, and cries of 'Victory'. I think every man in the pub kissed every woman, and every woman kissed every man. Maggie spent an awfully long time kissing Patrick, and Fiona hadn't stopped kissing Johnny all evening.

I don't think I missed anyone, and Corporal Harris made sure I didn't miss him. He hugged me tightly and really kissed me, and I damned well kissed him back. It was perhaps typical of Greg that he avoided me until last. He would have reasoned that, in those circumstances, he who kisses last, kisses longest. I was too drunk to think about it, much less avoid it. I turned, and he was there.

"Happy New Year," he said, and kissed me.

I just closed my eyes and enjoyed every second. It was not a New Year's Eve kind of kiss; it was something far more passionate. We broke apart and even 'in our cups', I think we were both a little surprised about what had just happened.

Everybody sang 'Auld Lang Syne' while trying our best to hold hands all around the room. All the while, though, it was Greg I was thinking about. It was just a kiss, but our relationship had become irrevocably closer.

Chapter Twenty
1942, Dieppe And the Field Agents

The new year marked a ratcheting up of our efforts. Having the Americans in the war had changed everything, and we now thought in terms of a timetable for the invasion. The logistics of assembling such an enormous invasion force was daunting, but the military planners concluded they could do it within a two-year time frame, so 1944 became our target date. When I was first told about the timetable, I immediately felt a crushing sense of responsibility. We knew it was coming, it was what we were planning for, but by putting a date on it, those plans became a stark reality.

I went immediately to Hut 3 to tell the boys. The stove was burning as usual - the smell of wood smoke will forever remind me of Station M. The boys all sat with their winter clothes on, thick woollies, gloves, and scarves as usual. They were all sitting at their different tables, each one surrounded by varying amounts of paperwork. Some like Woody were well organised, with everything in its place. Others like Patrick peered over a mountain of apparent chaos. The floor was covered with the usual balls of screwed-up paper. All were obviously deep in thought, mostly leaning on their elbows or gazing up at their own rising cloud of cigarette smoke.

"Summer of 1944," I said, with little or no emotion.

"Do you mean the invasion, is that confirmed?" asked Edward.

"That's the target date. They have called it D-Day. That's D-for-day!"

I expected a cheer, perhaps even a celebration, but they just looked up at me. Patrick loosened his scarf and drew heavily on his cigarette.

"We need to get it right then, don't we," he said, blowing the smoke away.

We all knew what 'getting it right' meant. If we got it wrong, the consequences were unimaginable - the lives of thousands of men were in our hands. That only a handful of people would ever know if we failed did nothing to ease the burden of responsibility that we all felt. Corky walked over to the stove and placed another log in it.

"I think I detect a chill wind blowing," he said.

The real meaning of his comment was not lost on any of us.

"Okay," said Edward. It was all he had to say to gain the undivided attention of everyone. "We've got our Channel coast map established, now we need to fill in the details. We need to understand everything about the beaches, and inland as far as there is anything significant which we would need to know about."

Patrick sat tapping his pencil on the table.

"It's feckin' impossible, Edward. We have nothing like enough personnel; we need to reduce the amount of coast we analyse."

"Patrick's right, Edward," I said, "we need to eliminate as much of the coast as possible. We need to concentrate on what we *can* do, not what we can't do."

Corky was doodling with his pencil but pressed too hard and the lead broke. He looked at it in disbelief, as if it couldn't have happened.

"What if," he said, "we concentrate our efforts on a

favourable stretch of coast, and next year the Germans fortify that section? We wouldn't have a well-researched 'Plan B'."

"That's right," replied Edward, "we still have to extend our potential landing sites as far as we can."

"There's only so much I can gather from aerial reconnaissance," Maggie said, "and our field agent intel is always second-hand, we need our own agents on the ground."

"We do, you're right, Maggie," agreed Edward. "The French Resistance is brilliant but we can't always rely on the FR. It's been fine using SOE's Section F agents, but as we refine our intelligence, we shall need our own people."

In the space of just twenty minutes, we had adopted a new strategy. Half the team would work quickly to eliminate the coastal stretches considered definitely impossible. The other half would work to establish the most favourable areas. We had a traffic light system - green was the most favourable, amber was 'maybe', red was to be avoided at all costs. We had been sharing intelligence from field agents in other sections of the SOE, but Edward decided it was now time for us to operate our own agents.

The nearest training school to us was STS 5, which was at Wanborough Manor, Puttenham, near Guilford. After initial training at Wanborough, our agents would advance to special training, including parachute training at Ringway, Manchester. We selected our agents from Wanborough, and they came to us after advanced training. We also recruited a specialist training instructor, so that our agents could further their training with us.

Working directly with the Prime Minister and the head of SOE, it was amazing how quickly Edward made all of this happen. We had a new hut built by the Spring of 1942. It was exactly the same as our existing huts, and although it was some distance away from huts 1-4, the sappers put a number 5 on it. Hut 1 had an extension built on the end, giving us more living quarters. Station M was steadily growing, and our trainer and agents arrived soon after.

Just as the boffins were selected for special abilities, so were the field agents, but unlike the rest of Station M, these people were putting their lives directly on the line. I was totally in awe of them. They volunteered to be dropped into an enemy-occupied country, knowing full well that capture meant certain death. The enormity of their courage was difficult for someone like me to understand. Talking to them, getting to know them, did not increase my understanding at all.

We started initially with four agents, three men and a woman. The woman was charming. Twenty-five years old, single, her name was Rosemary, and she had been working in a munitions factory. When I asked her why she volunteered to do this, she just said she wanted 'to do her bit'. I couldn't see those special qualities which made her so well suited to this role. She just seemed like a genuinely nice young woman. However, when I looked again at her file, a different Rosemary came to light.

She had an almost unique ability to stay calm in the face of adversity - the normal adrenalin rush which applies to the rest of us seemed not to apply to her. Her coordination under stress was, therefore, extremely good. She had also been an athlete, and so her physical abilities were second to none. What made her particularly suitable for Station M was her exceptional observation and memory skills. The instructor assured me she could also take care of herself in a tough situation. They trained her in using a range of weapons, and as a last resort, she could break my neck in less than a second. I said it reassured me to hear that!

-oOo-

The Japanese War had no direct bearing on our work, but we had to know everything that happened anywhere in the world. Anything which might affect the outcome of the war was important for us to know. The Japanese War consumed British resources and lives, so we needed to know every detail.

We had already lost our capital ships, Prince of Wales, and Repulse and then, in February, the Japanese captured Singapore, taking 60,000 prisoners. It was a serious defeat and a grave blow to morale. A backdrop of defeat and humiliation was not conducive to thinking positively about an invasion plan. However, we had no option but to forge ahead against the menacing situation of a world at war.

During the night of 31st May, the sound of aircraft woke us flying overhead, hundreds of them. It terrified me and I rushed outside, but it was too dark to see. It quickly became apparent, however, that these were RAF bombers, and it happened over three nights in May and June. It was the first of the so-called 1000 bomber raids. On that night, it was Cologne, and was followed by Essen and Bremen. I had mixed feelings the next day when I went into Hut 3.

Corky was jubilant. "At last, Hitler's got a taste of his own medicine."

"I thought I wanted them to suffer, just as we did," I said, "but when you've been on the receiving end, well, I'm suddenly thinking of people like me cowering under a staircase."

Patrick looked up over his reading glasses. "This is the madness of war, Lily," he said in his usual considered way. "Hitler has made this *total* war. Under his rules of engagement, the country which kills the most men, women and children, wins."

"Oh Patrick, is that true?"

Edward sat back in his chair and drew a deep breath.

"It's true, Lily. Had we not won the battle for air supremacy, Hitler's aim was to bomb us into submission, killing so many innocent men, women, and children that we would lose the will to resist. They have sown the wind, Lily, and now they must reap the whirlwind. This is the task which lies before us; we need to ensure the whirlwind gets off the beaches."

As always, Edward had a way of expressing things; he was an incomparable motivator of people. The whirlwind didn't just blow over Germany - it blew through my office one day in early August. I knew Edward was on the green phone to the Prime Minister and I could hear raised voices coming from his office. I looked at Fiona, curling my lower lip down and raising my shoulders. Sure enough, Edward stormed into my office, incandescent with rage.

"I can't believe it! I just can't believe it!"

"Calm down, Edward, tell us what's happening," said Fiona.

"The PM has sanctioned a raid against Dieppe. It's supposed to be a rehearsal for the invasion, and they have not consulted us."

"I don't understand; we put Dieppe into the red category," I said.

"For God's sake, I know we have!"

"Why would the PM do that, why are we not advising on this?"

"I'll tell you why, it's the damned Russians. Stalin has put pressure on the PM to open a second front, and Mountbatten wants a trial beach landing. A practice for the invasion, and he doesn't even know we bloody well exist!"

I had never seen Edward so furious, and never heard him say a word like 'bloody' before.

"Why hasn't the PM told him about us?" asked Fiona.

"Because we don't exist. It's not just us, it's SOE, he will never admit that we exist."

"We need to look again at our Dieppe assessment, and we need to do it now," I said.

Edward agreed with me and we all rushed over to Hut 3, where everyone looked up at us with a startled look as we burst into the hut. They were deep in their own concentration and took a moment to adjust.

"Everything we have on Dieppe," I snapped.

I created a sense of urgency, and there was a certain amount of rushing about. Maggie produced the aerial reconnaissance, Corky found his geology report, Woody produced the fortification assessment, and Patrick eventually slammed his overall assessment on top of the pile.

"What the hell is this for?" asked Patrick sharply.

Edward looked at the paperwork, as we all stood around him, watching his eyes rapidly moving over the documents, scanning the information.

"You designated Dieppe as red; why Patrick?" he asked.

"I can answer that in one word, Edward," Corky replied, "shingle."

"Why are you asking?" said Patrick.

"I'll tell you why," replied Edward, still looking angry, "the silly buggers are just about to land an amphibious assault on the beach there."

"Oh bejesus, you're not feckin' serious, who are the idiots organising it?"

"No less a person than Rear Admiral Louis Mountbatten, ably assisted by Montgomery, and the Joint Chiefs of Staff. To be fair, I am told Montgomery eventually wanted to cancel the entire thing after a rehearsal went wrong. Trouble is, he's ended up in Egypt, along with General Alan Brooke, so they have no meaningful input. It's just about to go ahead, and there is nothing we can do."

"What do you think the outcome will be then, Edward?" I asked.

"Well, who knows, it's heavily fortified, there are coastal batteries, and there is the shingle."

"What's the problem with the shingle?"

"Only the fairies can dance over a shingle beach, Lily," replied Patrick. "It's tough going, right? You land a vehicle or a tank on a shingle beach and it doesn't move far, if at all."

We all looked at each other in despair. "Maybe they've taken these factors into account," said a hopeful Maggie, "maybe there will be a heavy bombardment of the gun batteries. Perhaps it's also an airborne assault?"

"I hope you're right, Maggie, we'll know in a few days' time," answered a resigned Edward.

It was a few days later when the news broke - just about everything had gone wrong. There was no heavy bombardment. Men and vehicles became stuck on the shingle beach, being cut to shreds. On the 19th August 1942, there were 3367 Canadians killed, wounded, or captured, as well as 275 British commandos. We lost a destroyer, 33 landing craft, and 106 aircraft, and another 550 men.

Dieppe had been an unmitigated disaster. Hut 3 analysed exactly what had gone wrong. It amounted to inadequate intelligence concerning German defences and local geology, combined with disastrous judgment from the Chiefs of Staff for the Army, Air Force and Navy in advising the Prime Minister. If we planned the invasion of Europe like Dieppe, we would fail!

It left me thinking about all those wives, sweethearts, mothers, fathers, sisters, and brothers - all that combined grief. If there was any good at all to come out of Dieppe, it was a lesson in how *not* to carry out an amphibious landing. Lessons were learned, and for Station M, it reinforced the onerous sense of responsibility we already felt.

We stepped up our efforts to define our 'green zones' and for the first time, we sent in two of our agents. It was a straightforward mission to reconnoitre several locations identified by Maggie as 'places of interest,' which meant she was unable to identify them from the reconnaissance photographs.

Rosemary's code name was Kestrel, and Phillip was Merlin; we called it 'Operation Puffin'. They were to cross the Channel at night, in a small fishing boat, being dropped off at two separate locations along a remote part of the French coast. The weather forecast was good, it was a simple in-and-out operation, no radio transmission required. They had two days ashore, and the same boat would come back for them at a set time - what could go wrong?

Maggie specified the mission, and we all had some input, but I had to sanction it and select the agents. The night they were crossing the Channel, I was unable to sleep at all, and Edward could see how concerned I was the next morning.

"You've made one mistake, Lily, you've made it a personal issue by getting to know the field agents."

"I know, I realise that now."

All I could do was to wait until they returned, which felt like an eternity. The 'suitcase radio,' was the mainstay for SOE field agents. It was also one of the principal reasons for agents being detected. The Germans would track unidentified trans-missions from separate locations, allowing them to triangulate a position. 'Operation Puffin' was a low risk, quick in-and-out mission, no radio transmissions required.

Kestrel and Merlin duly returned as planned. I could breathe again, but it was clear I needed to distance myself from the agents. I just did not have the steely courage they had. I made a point of not being involved during the debriefing.

Chapter Twenty-One
A Spy in The Grounds

As 1942 progressed, Johnny Albright's reconnaissance flights were stepped up, as was the use of our own agents, often in liaison with the FR. Johnny would personally remove the film from the onboard cameras on his reconnaissance Spitfire. Then he would drive directly from Biggin Hill to Station M, where Maggie and her assistant would develop and analyse the film. Intelligence from other SOE agents and additional photo reconnaissance from RAF Medmenham was also sometimes available. All the while, our veil of secrecy made working with other Sections very restricting.

With a view to the timetable, it became imperative that we concentrate our reconnaissance efforts in a more defined area - we needed to decide upon a general location. Our analysis gradually narrowed down the green zones and although we couldn't predict the Germans' next move, the Normandy coast of France was looking increasingly favourable. Edward asked the Prime Minister to sound out the opinions of the Chiefs of Staff regarding a longer sea crossing, and the answer came back that yes, it was possible.

Things were going well; confidence at Station M was growing. Then, in the summer of 1942, something happened that I shall never forget. The guard raised the alarm; they had discovered an intruder. The soldiers gave chase, but the intruder evaded them, and I instantly demanded a full report. There was a paranoia at the time about German spies, and it was easy to assume the worst. The incident occurred in the field agent training section; the guard spotted someone covertly observing the activities. When challenged, the person managed to escape and although the soldiers gave chase, they were easily out-manoeuvred and out-run. The result was that the intruder got clean away.

This was potentially serious; it could even mean that the whole operation at Station M was compromised. I thumbed through the report frantically, until I got to the description of the person - 5 ft 7 inches tall, short dark hair, wearing dungarees - but most telling of all was the observation that the person was possibly female! I just knew it was Dotty. Reg's farm was right next to the training section - Dotty would have no trouble finding a vantage point from where she could observe the training sessions. As for out-running and out-manoeuvring the soldiers, nobody was fitter and knew the terrain better than Dotty. She would not have had the slightest trouble shaking off the soldiers.

I asked Corporal Harris to drive me to Reg's farm in one of the military vehicles.

"Will I need my rifle, Mrs Heywood?"

"Definitely not, Corporal, but take it anyway, I just need you to look authoritative."

"Oh, I can do that all right, Mrs Heywood."

We bounced along the country lane as if it were an emergency, which the intrusion was, but I assured the corporal that this was whatever the opposite of emergency was - he *could* slow down. However, it was all to no avail; we finally skidded to a halt in Reg's yard. We stepped out of the vehicle, the corporal with rifle in hand. We must have looked like an improbable pair, standing there in the cow muck, him in his uniform, me in my smart suit and heels. I knew our arrival would gain Dotty's attention, and sure enough, I could see her peering at us from within the pig shed. I gestured for her to come over. She stepped out of the shed and I'd never seen Dotty looking so deflated.

"I'm in trouble, aren't I, Lily?"

"Do you realise how close you were to being shot, Dotty? So yes, you bloody fool, you *are* in trouble, big trouble."

"Oh shit! I thought I was. I've been watching them for a day or two, they fascinated me. I know what's going on, Lily, they're spies, aren't they? And this is a training camp."

"You didn't hear that, Corporal Harris, did you?"

"Hear what, Mrs Heywood?"

"How do you know that?" I asked her.

"I've overheard them, and all the physical training stuff, I'd be so good at that."

"This really is a problem, Dotty." I knew her so well; she was not about to let this drop. "You must come with me to the office."

"I'll do better than that, I'm going to join you! I want to do what they're doing. I just know I'd be good at it. You can organise it for me, Lily, can't you?"

I had no idea what to say. I couldn't have anyone, not even my best friend, running around with the knowledge Dotty now had; she created a real problem. I looked at Corporal Harris.

"I find myself in a difficult position, Corporal. This woman has been incredibly stupid; I have no option but to take the matter further. The trouble is, she also happens to be my dearest friend. Do you see my problem?"

"I'm not sure that I do, Mrs Heywood. We interviewed this witness, and she says she's seen nothing. Bit of a wasted trip if you ask me."

"I'm looking forward to our next New Year's kiss, Corporal."

"No need to wait that long, Mrs Heywood."

"Watch it, Corporal!"

Dotty finally realised the gravity of her situation, and the risk Harris was taking for her. She reacted as Dotty always does, throwing her arms around him. They already knew each other from meetings in the pub.

"Thanks mate, you're a bloody star, that's what you are, Brian!"

We drove her back to the Manor, and I marched her into the office.

"Dotty, what are you doing here?" asked an incredibly surprised Fiona.

"The intruder - you're looking at her," I said.

"Oh, my goodness! You *are* in trouble, Dotty."

"Get me the Official Secrets Act, will you, Fi? At least that's a start."

We sat Dotty down and explained the significance of the Act. I laid it on as heavily as I could, especially the part about capital punishment. Finally she was taking it all seriously. Despite or perhaps as a consequence of events, we could see Dotty was deadly serious about wanting to train to become a field agent. This was not one of her impetuous ideas; she had obviously thought this through. We both tried to discourage her. It was not that I thought that she was incapable. Quite the opposite, she had already demonstrated her capabilities. No, it was not that. I just couldn't bear the prospect of her being in harm's way, and Fiona felt the same.

"I really want this, Lily, if you won't organise it for me, I'll just apply, anyway."

I knew Dotty would do exactly as she said and reluctantly, I made it happen for her. I used my contact at Wanborough Manor to get Dotty enrolled for the basic SOE training course. I also tried to ensure she would not go on to higher training. I asked that her training should be particularly rigorous, especially in the foreign language section, thinking it might be Dotty's weakness. Fiona agreed with me; the possibility of our best friend being put into harm's way was a prospect neither of us could contemplate.

-o0o-

Inevitably our focus at Station M concentrated upon the invasion, but we remained acutely aware of the progress of the war, of anything which might have a bearing on D-Day. Not least of our worries was the battle for the North Atlantic. The build-up of the American war effort in Britain depended upon the Atlantic crossing. Edward told me that during one of his conversations with the Prime Minister, the PM admitted that he had more sleepless nights over the North Atlantic than anything else.

Probably the best-kept secret in Britain was the fact that Station X had broken the secret U-boat codes. Designated 'Ultra', it was this breakthrough which changed the course of the war. The battle for the North Atlantic was the longest campaign of the war. By the end of summer 1942, the battle of measure and countermeasure was swinging in favour of the Allies, but the PM was desperate for a victory, a decisive shift in the war. He saw both the need and the possibility of such a shift in North Africa. The Suez Canal, together with the North Atlantic, was vital to British interests. We had successfully defended the Canal, but the Axis forces remained poised to break through to the Canal and beyond. Winston Churchill seized the moment, dismissing General Auchinleck and replacing him with Montgomery.

We were well aware of the significance of the war in North Africa, where an intelligence advantage was gifted to Montgomery from Ultra. The final battle started on October 23rd, and by November 4th, Field Marshal Rommel was in full retreat. El Alamein was a decisive victory for the British and Commonwealth forces. It was the victory Winston Churchill needed, and the news was well received everywhere. Corporal Harris punched the air when I approached the Manor, and even Jennings let protocol slip, quoting from a newspaper headline.

"Complete victory. Bloody marvellous, Mrs Heywood!"

There was unanimous agreement; it *was* bloody marvellous. When I opened the door into Hut 3, spirits were high; there were screwed up balls of paper everywhere. El Alamein was a significant victory in its own right, but there were wider issues. We had safeguarded the Suez Canal, and opened up the possibility of advancing into what Winston Churchill called the enemy's 'soft underbelly.' It was by any measure a turning point in the war, and not least for Station M - it confirmed that D-Day was firmly on track.

As the days of 1942 grew shorter and the nights grew colder, we worked harder than ever, and finally we made the momentous decision that Normandy should be our priority. All our analyses indicated a Normandy landing between Cherbourg and Le Havre. We had to weigh the strategic advantage which we felt Normandy offered against the longer sea crossing; we felt the advantages far outweighed the disadvantages.

Edward discussed the basic principle of a Normandy landing with the Prime Minister, the implication being that Station M would concentrate its resources there, at the expense of other areas. It was a gamble. If the Americans disagreed, or if the situation on the ground changed, we would not have a well-researched alternative to offer. The Prime Minister agreed with us, giving us the go-ahead to work on the assumption of a Normandy landing.

Edward made the announcement in Hut 3. "Okay, listen up everyone, I've just spoken with the PM, it's Normandy. We have the go-ahead."

We expected the news, but it immediately raised spirits. It didn't mean we could forget about the rest of the Channel and Atlantic coast, but it meant we could focus our efforts.

"At last, now we can really get down to business," said a relieved Patrick.

"That's right," said Edward, "now the proper work begins, but I have to remind everyone, Normandy has to be the best-kept secret in Britain. From now on, secrecy is our priority. Nobody outside this room must ever hear the word mentioned. I need not explain what is at stake."

Edward's words were greeted with silence. They all well understood the importance of our work, but understanding is one thing, bearing the burden of such a responsibility was quite another. The moment passed, and everyone got back to work, but there remained a palpable sense of urgency.

-oOo-

Following the victory of El Alamein, Montgomery had control of the Suez Canal and its vital oil interests. Although the Axis Forces were in retreat, an enormous part of North Africa was still under their control. The colonies of Morocco and Algeria were dominated by the Vichy French, which complicated the situation. Against this backdrop, the Allies decided to launch an invasion of North Africa to consolidate the Allied Forces in Egypt, and to open up the possibility of an invasion of Southern Europe.

'Operation Torch' began on 8th November 1942. British and American forces, under the command of General Eisenhower, launched a three-pronged attack on Casablanca, Oran, and Algiers. In some respects, 'Torch' was a valuable rehearsal for D-Day while, in other respects, such as the involvement of the Vichy French, it was quite different. It was a huge operation comprising 120,000 men, 500 aircraft, and several warships, and included all the elements being planned for D-Day.

The North Africa invasion was to have a profound influence upon the progress of the war. It paved the way for the subsequent fall of Tunis following 'Operation Vulcan' on 6th May 1943. The Axis forces finally surrendered in Tunisia on 13th May that year. This opened the way for the invasion of Sicily in July, and the 'soft underbelly' of German-occupied Europe.

For the military and logistics planners, North Africa was a significant success, but it provided us with only limited useful intelligence. The Vichy French were a confounding issue, and also the topography and geology of North Africa was not comparable to Normandy. The victory was a tremendous boost to our confidence - we had confirmation that a large-scale amphibious landing was practical, and the possibility of a southern invasion would divide the German war effort.

1942 ended on a high note for us, with just one exception. I received a report from Wanborough Manor. Dotty had sailed through initial SOE training, and not just sailed through; they commended her as the outstanding female trainee. She would go on to higher training. My heart sank and when I told Fiona, she had the same reaction.

"Do you know, I'm really not surprised, Lily. When you look at Dotty, she has all the attributes, plus she's got the heart of a lion."

"You're right, Fi, she has, and look how she can walk into a pub and have everyone eating out of her palm within five minutes! How many people can do that?"

"Imagine what she'll be like if she finishes advanced training; can you imagine an even more confident Dotty?"

"Not really, it's a daunting prospect, isn't it! What if something happens to her though? I couldn't live with myself."

"Oh don't, Lily, I can't even think about such a thing."

"It's something I do have to think about, Fi. I send our agents over the Channel, not knowing what awaits them on the other side. It's a terrible responsibility, Fi! It really weighs heavily on me; I'm not sure I'm strong enough."

"Don't worry, Lily, you *are*."

"I hope so! If I am, then it's only because of you and Edward, I couldn't do it without you both."

"Couldn't do what without me?" asked Edward.

"I didn't see you come in, Edward. We were just talking about Dorothy; she's passed initial training with a commendation!"

"I'm not surprised, your friend Dorothy is a very exceptional woman. I don't think I've ever met anyone like her before."

"That makes three of us, Edward," replied Fiona with a smile.

"It has been an inordinately long day," he said. "It would revitalise my spirit enormously if both of you fine ladies would grace my Drawing Room with your presence and share a glass with me."

Edward was normally a stickler for his version of protocol. He had never asked Fiona to join us for a drink, because she was my assistant and technically lower rank in his eyes. I was surprised but delighted at his suggestion. I didn't regard Fiona as lower rank in any way, shape or form; we just worked together. She could step in as my deputy at any time. Above all, as my friend, I wanted her to share the close relationship I had with Edward. Her response, while entirely understandable, was disappointing.

"That's really kind of you, Edward." There was a hint of surprise in Fiona's voice as she continued. "But the thing is, I'm seeing Johnny tonight, in fact he's picking me up in less than half an hour. So if I have to choose, well - as enticing as your offer is - I'm afraid Johnny wins hands down!"

"I quite understand, Fiona, I would be a poor substitute for a dashing Wing Commander."

"Oh no, I didn't mean it like that."

Edward was smiling unreservedly. "I was talking to Wing Commander Albright only the other day, and I asked him if he appreciated how lucky he was having you for his fiancé."

"What did he say?" I asked him.

"He said he was entirely cognisant of the fact. I think his actual words were, 'I knew I was the luckiest man on earth the moment our eyes met.' However distressing it may be for me to forgo your company, Fiona, I wouldn't attempt to compete with your Wing Commander!"

Fiona blushed and was at a loss what to say.

"I think you'd better be off, Fi," I said, "I don't want Johnny blaming us for keeping you late."

She collected her things and made her way towards the door.

"Did he really say that Edward?" she asked.

"Yes he did, the man's besotted, so you'd better not keep him waiting."

Fiona left, trying to look as composed as possible, which was not usually a problem for someone so elegant. She walked sedately towards the door, but then the moment she was out of sight, we could hear her footsteps quicken along the Hall. Edward and I grinned at each other.

"Come along then, Lily, let's have that drink."

We locked our office doors and made our way to the Drawing Room. I eagerly surrendered to my fatigue, slumping into one of the leather Chesterfield chairs. Jennings soon followed. I always marvelled at his immaculate appearance, and his impeccable conduct. It was obviously a matter of great pride that his collar was always starched, with his bow tie sitting perfectly; I really admired that about him. At the end of a long day, when I was feeling tired and dishevelled, he was a reassuring reminder of calm and order.

"What can I get for you, My Lord?"

"The usual, Jennings, please."

"Mrs Heywood?"

"I'll have whatever His Lordship is having, thank you, Mr Jennings."

"That will be two large single malt whiskies, then."

I kicked off my shoes and stretched my legs, letting my arms drop either side of the chair. I just sat there, feeling the tension draining out through my toes. Then it suddenly occurred to me: I was dishevelled, my mascara probably smudged over my face, and yet I was sitting there in front of Edward, without the slightest concern for my appearance. Even he had undone his collar and loosened his tie.

"What are you thinking, Lily?"

"I'm thinking we are becoming very relaxed in each other's company, Edward. Tell me, is my makeup smudged?"

"I suppose we are, and yes, it is."

"Do you mind?"

"Do I mind that my Chief of Staff is entirely human like the rest of us? No, it's very reassuring."

"Is that the only way you see me, Edward, as your Chief of Staff?"

"I am a very disciplined person, Lily, I *have* to see you as my Chief of Staff." We sat silently for a moment, and then he added "Not that you make it easy for me. You test my discipline at times, especially when your eye makeup is smudged, and you stretch your toes like that."

I smiled and stretched my toes some more - perhaps I smiled too much. Edward never ever dropped his guard, and yet I had the distinct feeling that he just had. I wanted to pursue it further, but sitting there, in the opulence of the Drawing Room, with the Earl of Middlebourne sitting opposite me, it just felt inappropriate. So I sat quietly repeating his words in my mind, wanting to believe that I was more to Edward than just his Chief of Staff. Jennings came back with two exceptionally large single malt whiskies and placed one in front of each of us.

"Is everything all right below-stairs, Mr Jennings, nothing I need to worry about?"

"Everything is fine, Mrs Heywood. Miss Robinson deals with most things."

"You make me feel redundant, Mr Jennings."

"Not in the slightest, I would regard that as a sure sign of a well-run household."

"I quite agree, Jennings," said Edward. "I became redundant the day Mrs Heywood arrived."

"How is your father now, has his leg properly healed?" I asked Jennings.

"It has indeed, he asks after you every time I see him."

"Give him my best wishes, will you, Mr Jennings?"

"It will be a pleasure, Mrs Heywood."

Jennings left us with our whisky, and Edward sat smiling, looking very content.

"What are you smiling at, Edward?"

"Not only do you know my butler better than I do, now I find you even have some kind of relationship with his father."

"It's only because I take an interest in them, Edward. You should try talking to them......Oh, I'm sorry, I didn't mean it to sound like that."

"No, you're quite right. The wind of change has not blown through this house for several hundred years. Now that it has, I think perhaps I need to change with it."

I had a momentary glimpse that evening of the other Edward, the one behind the aristocratic exterior. He remained his usual reserved self for the rest of the evening, and during dinner, but I felt closer to him. Each time I glimpsed the inner Edward, it was like another piece of a jigsaw puzzle. It was only ever fragmentary pieces, but I liked the picture which was forming. On each of those rare occasions when he let his defence drop, he seemed not to rebuild it.

I realised only too well that my job came first, but I don't think I would have been a woman if I hadn't found him attractive. I wanted him to feel the same about me. I held no delusions about the future. I just felt the need to be with the man rather than the Earl.

-oOo-

Christmas and the New Year were rapidly approaching, and I barely had time to think about it, but fortunately Gran had it all in hand. Christmas was to be a rerun of the year before, a reassuring reminder of my childhood Christmases. Mum and Dad were coming to stay again, so when I eventually had time to think, I really looked forward to it. There were two big differences this year. Dotty did not have leave from her training to come home, and I felt obliged to accept Edward's invitation to join him for New Year.

Christmas Day and Boxing Day were the same as the previous year - Greg joined us again - we ate too much - we drank too much - Gran played the piano and I made her cry by singing for her! It was even more enjoyable for being familiar. During the war, we would cling to familiar things, those things which made us feel normal, something in our lives that was dependable. Everyone enjoyed themselves, but I missed Dotty. I knew she would have been the bubbles in the champagne.

Edward bought me a lovely watch which, like the earrings the previous year, really took my breath away. I bought him a pair of cufflinks, actually they were the most expensive present I had ever bought. Once again, I wasn't sure what we were trying to say to one another. And oh yes, Greg kissed me again, for the third time that year! I was accepting the possibility that it might involve us in a relationship, even though I was trying not to.

Outside of Station M, this was a strange time for me; Greg had kissed me three times, and I spent a fortune having a dress made especially for New Year's Eve. I kidded myself that I needed it for the dinner party, though the reality was that I wanted to impress Edward. I really didn't know what I was doing.

Caroline insisted I use her dressmaker for all my clothes. Restrictions and rationing made buying nice clothes almost impossible, so I was not about to refuse. I had several suits made, and some lovely skirts and blouses, but nothing as glamorous yet as an evening gown. When I suggested it to Caroline, she was more enthusiastic than I was. Before I knew it, I had two lovely ladies fussing around me with measuring tapes and design books. There had been little need for evening dresses in Stepney, so I just placed myself in their hands.

It was quickly decided that the colour I needed to go with my auburn hair was green, and because I had a good figure, it should be flattering rather than concealing. They showed me various ideas and assured me this was just the starting point. Caroline had complete confidence in these two ladies. They previously worked as seamstresses in a London fashion house, and then entered the world of haute couture on their own account. Looking at the wonderful dresses they produced for Caroline, I could see why.

I felt fortunate that they were prepared to apply the same attention to mundane garments such as my dress suits, but it all showed how difficult it was for them during the war. Only when they arrived for the fitting did I fully appreciate the full extent of their talent.

The dress was magnificent in a glorious jade green, which was perfect with my auburn hair. I just loved the slinky feel of the satin-backed heavy crepe fabric, cut on the bias, but the style was something else entirely. A cowl neckline with a dramatic plunge V back, ruched down the back of the skirt and ending in a tiny elegant train. I was speechless. I had become used to wearing suits during the day, and simple casual clothes in the evening. When I finally looked at myself in the mirror, wearing their creation, I could hardly believe the image staring back at me.

"Let me look at you," Caroline said, as she walked excitedly around me.

"It's wonderful, isn't it, I've worn nothing like it - ever!" I said.

"It really is, but I have to tell you, it's also *you*, my dear. You're a beautiful woman, you were made to wear a dress like this."

"Do you really think so? This is a long way from being Chief of Staff, isn't it! This is not a part I'm used to playing, not at all."

"Don't worry, Lily, nobody can look as lovely as you and not enjoy it, trust me. You are my son's Chief of Staff, and he never stops singing your praises, but actually I think *this* is the real you."

I stood in silence for a moment; she made me look at myself in another light. I enjoyed being feminine, and wasn't past exploiting the fact, but I had always placed my career and achievements first. Caroline could see she had made me think.

"Forgive me if I am speaking out of turn, Lily, but you don't have to be afraid to be seen as an attractive woman. You have not become successful *because* you are attractive. I think it's just all part of who you are; it's a part of your inner strength and confidence. You should celebrate it, not seek to deny it."

I didn't know what to say; Caroline was very insightful, so perhaps she was right. I would always go to so much trouble with my appearance, but then, when people found me attractive, I would often resent it, in case it diminished their opinion of me. Maybe I had done enough to prove myself; perhaps I could be successful and yet still enjoy being a woman. As Caroline suggested, maybe I could have it all.

ooOoo

Florence came to my room on New Year's Eve to help me dress and get ready. I mostly submitted to her role as my lady's maid, but never more so than that evening. It was very unnatural for me to accept someone helping me with such things, but Florence enjoyed it so I didn't feel I was imposing on her. She was exceptionally good with my hair; she had a real talent for it.

Considering her background, her natural flair for makeup and for what coordinates with what was amazing. It was both a sign of the times and of her deprived background that she had homemade recipes for creating all kinds of makeup. She mixed charred cork and Vaseline to make a great mascara, so effective that I had adopted it for my own.

I hadn't told her about the dress, so when she asked what I would wear, I couldn't wait to see her reaction. The moment she opened my wardrobe, she was unable to contain her excitement.

"Oh, my goodness, why didn't you tell me, it's beautiful, Lily! Oh I'm sorry, Mrs Heywood, I didn't mean to say that - I'm sorry."

"Don't be daft, Florence, I'm not Her Ladyship and besides, when it's just the two of us like now, I rather like you calling me by my name."

"I'm not sure about that, Mrs Heywood. Mary told me what you said about taking pride in your work, about always doing the best you can. Well, I am, Mrs Heywood, I want to be your lady's maid, and I want to do it properly, and as well as I can."

"That's really commendable, Florence, but you do appreciate that I'm not a 'Lady'?"

"You are to me, Mrs Heywood. I can't believe a title would make you a finer lady than you are already."

"Florence, you really are sweet. I think that's the nicest compliment I've ever had, thank you. I'll do my absolute best to live up to your expectations. If you would like to call me Lily in private, I think it will be fine."

"Could I really? I'd like that," she said, looking very timid but pleased.

She helped me into the dress and her excitement was contagious, making me feel confident in myself. When I was ready to go downstairs, she was still fussing around me like an old mother hen. I knew Edward had invited other guests. I met Lord and Lady Hollingworth briefly once before, but none of the other guests, so was feeling rather nervous. Here I was, a girl from Stepney sharing New Year's Eve with a room full of titled and distinguished people; my heart was pounding! I was not frightened about letting myself down; my greatest fear was letting down either Edward or Caroline.

I made my entrance into the Drawing Room with all the elegance and poise I could muster. Wearing my hair up allowed my pearl and ruby earrings to shine to their full effect. My evening gown was stunning, there was no other word for it - I felt positively glamorous. Edward was visibly taken aback, rendered totally speechless - that was very reassuring! We momentarily stood smiling at each other; I was enjoying the moment, knowing I had completely taken his breath away. It was Caroline who stepped in to introduce me to the guests. And so the evening began.

None of those people knew anything about Station M. They did know something was going on at Middlebourne and that I had some kind of function there; undoubtedly, I was something of a curiosity to them. These were the type of people, however, who wouldn't dream of asking, which all conspired to place me in a rather difficult position. I wasn't one of them, but neither did they have a convenient pigeonhole in which to place me.

I felt ill at ease, and it also placed the guests in a similarly strange situation. Societal position was an integral aspect of their lives. I suspect being unsure where I belonged in the order of things was probably very disquieting for them. They were all superficially very polite to me, but that was tempered as it so often is with comments such as the one from Lady Hilton.

"I can tell from your accent, my dear, that you come from London. What brings you to Kent, and to Middlebourne?"

"I have family ties here."

"Oh, did your family work on the land?"

"Yes, they did. My Grandfather's family can trace their history back for generations in this area."

"I think that is so important; at least you know where your family came from. Even a connection with the soil is better than having no connection at all. So many people today do not understand about their heritage, I find it quite appalling. My own family extends back as far as Magna Carta."

"Yes, of course it does. I can tell from your objectionable manner that you're suffering the mental and physical effects of generations of inbreeding."

No, I didn't say that! I wanted to, but remained very polite, smiling sweetly. With Caroline's help, I think I held my own with most of the women. Even the ghastly Lady Hilton ended up being pleasant enough, despite so nearly being on the receiving end of a piece of my mind.

The men were a different prospect, falling over themselves around me but not graciously. If for one moment they thought they were impressing me, they singularly failed. This was not a role I was remotely used to. I tried to think how Dotty would have dealt with the situation. However, with Caroline's encouraging smiles, I played along with them.

We eventually went through into the Dining Room, where the full splendour of Middlebourne Manor imposes itself upon you. Jennings and the staff conducted themselves magnificently. I was treated kindly enough but was not a natural fit in that rarefied environment. These were the kind of circumstances which allowed my demons freedom to torment me. I so much wanted to be a part of Edward's world, but soon realised that Stepney had not prepared me for it, and neither were the guests prepared for this woman from Stepney.

When the clock struck twelve, I found myself pleased

that the evening was nearing its conclusion. We all stood up and welcomed in 1943 with the usual toasts and well wishes. The men kissed their wives, and that was it! I suspect they were afraid to kiss me for fear of what their wives would say. Caroline hugged me and kissed me on the cheek. I turned to Edward who was standing next to me, looking awkward as only Edward can. I put my arms loosely around him and he kissed my cheek, smiling at me, while I smiled back up at him.

"Happy New Year, Lily."

"Happy New Year, Edward."

I stood there thinking, *'Why doesn't he take me in his arms and do this properly?'* But he didn't! The guests were staying overnight, which meant I would have to endure them again at breakfast. Happily, they all retired at 12.30, and I was about to do the same when Caroline and Edward sat back down, so I joined them. Jennings asked if we wanted anything.

"Do you know, Mr Jennings, I would love a cup of cocoa."

"What a delightful idea, Lily," said Caroline. "I'll have the same."

"And for you, My Lord?"

"If the women in my life are having cocoa, then so shall I," Edward replied.

"I thought you handled Lady Hilton admirably, Lily," said Caroline, "what an insufferable woman she is."

"I agree," said Edward, "I apologise on her behalf. I almost felt sorry for her. She has a diminutive intellect, and you were casting a long shadow over her, Lily. She did not know how to deal with a woman of your stature. I hope I would not offend you, Mother, if I choose not to invite her or Lord Hilton again."

"Oh, please don't do that on my behalf, Edward."

"No, actually, Lily, none of our guests this evening did themselves any credit, and that woman *tried* to offend you. She may not have succeeded, but anyone who even tries to offend you, offends me."

"Edward, that's sweet, but I've already told you - you don't have to worry about my sensibilities. As soon as I open my mouth, people know I come from the East End of London, and they can make of that what they will. Lady Hilton would turn her nose up at a Birmingham or Liverpudlian accent! It's not my problem, Edward, it's hers."

"I'm sure you're right, but I will not tolerate her in this house again."

"You're my knight in shining armour, aren't you, Edward?"

"I'm not at all sure I fit such a dashing profile, Lily, but yes, I suppose I am. If you ever needed me to come to your rescue - well, that would be something you could implicitly rely upon."

"Edward, do you realise what, in a roundabout way, you have just said? That was really lovely!"

I smiled at Caroline, and she smiled back. She knew her son better than I did - Edward had dropped his guard again, and I think she enjoyed the moment nearly as much as I did.

Chapter Twenty-Two
1943 Operation Skua

February 1943 saw what remained of the German Sixth and Fourth armies surrender to the Soviets at Stalingrad, and 90,000 Germans went into captivity. This defeat, combined with their retreat in North Africa, was a significant setback for Hitler's regime and a boost for our invasion plans.

Spirits were high in Station M during the opening months of 1943, our task now focused, with everyone rising to the occasion. Our field agents were regularly crossing the Channel with quick in-and-out missions. We might almost have been excused for thinking it was just routine, our agents even starting to refer to our regular fishing boat as the ferry. Our complacency, however, was misguided, and about to be cruelly dashed. In the process, I was to learn one of my hardest lessons of the war.

'Operation Skua' set off from Portsmouth on the night of 2nd March. The fishing boat was to offload three agents, one each close to Vierville-sur-Mer, Arromanches-les-Bains, and Villers-sur-Mer, all on the coast of Normandy. When the fishing boat failed to return to Portsmouth the following morning, the alarm was immediately raised.

We alerted all assets in the area to look for the little boat. We were so concerned, Edward scrambled Johnny Albright to fly over the route that we knew the boat would have taken. It quickly became apparent that it was not adrift without power, nor was there any trace of wreckage. Johnny didn't return to Biggin Hill until his fuel tanks were empty, the Merlin engine of his Spitfire sputtering as he approached the runway; he could have done no more.

Reluctantly, we contacted FR. We really didn't want to broadcast the fact that we had lost a small fishing boat. The implications, should our message be intercepted and decoded, were obvious. We waited for two days, two agonising days, until we received the worst possible news. They had sighted a German E-boat off the coast at Vierville, the only reason they noticed being a small explosion drawing attention to it in the dark. These fast-attack boats operated along the coast, but we hadn't considered them a serious risk. I regarded a small fishing boat to be inconspicuous, as French fishermen continued to operate during the war, albeit with restrictions.

Later that same day, Edward received a message from Station X confirming that wreckage had been found on the beach. He came straight over to Hut 3, appearing calm and composed as he broke the news to us. I knew him well enough, however, to know it was just a charade. The news confirmed our worst nightmare. Our boat had been sunk, and with no contact from any of our agents, it was clear we had lost them with the boat.

I was absolutely devastated - I knew them all. For me, once again, the war had suddenly become very personal. The boys only knew their codenames, and the other field agents in Hut 5 had no idea they were missing. The only two people who knew the identity of the missing agents were Maggie and me. I had selected them, and Maggie had briefed them on the mission.

Having told us the terrible news, Edward went over to Patrick to discuss something or other, but I could see he was struggling with his emotions. The boys were all silent, while

I tried desperately hard not to show any emotion. It was a struggle that we would all inevitably lose.

Everything came to a head when Maggie entered the hut. The terrible news shouldn't have been a shock to any of us - I think we were all expecting it. But it was just that moment of realisation when your worst fears and expectations become reality.

"They've found some wreckage, Maggie. It's confirmed, we've lost them," I said.

Poor Maggie, she broke down in tears, which was the excuse we all needed. The outpouring of grief was spontaneous. It was a cathartic moment, and the reality of war stalked Station M from that day on. With so many lives depending upon us, we had to continue, but the evil spectre of death was always there to remind us it was never far away.

Somehow, we had to put this dreadful event behind us. Nobody knew that better than I did, but it affected me deeply. I stared death in the face once before; I knew what that cold grey hand feels like as it draws you away from this world. I knew it was never more than an inch away, inviting you to cross that boundary. Here it was again, tugging at my sleeve, reminding me that every decision I made could affect someone's life. Death makes for an unwelcome work companion.

Our only information about the incident came from FR. We knew our boat was lost, but what we didn't know was how they had been discovered. Maybe it was just a chance encounter which would have resulted in an inspection of the vessel. We knew our agents would never allow themselves to be captured, and so they couldn't allow the boat to be boarded. Everything I knew about Kestrel told me she would have remained calm. She would have assessed the situation, realising their only chance of escape was to open fire on the heavily armed E-boat.

There was little doubt in my mind that this is exactly what happened. Her bravery, and that of her comrades, was beyond doubt. She would have died fighting. Winston Churchill told us that come the day of celebration, no-one would stand taller than the intelligence community of Station M. For once, I think he got that wrong. I shall never forget the people like Rosemary who in my opinion stood head and shoulders above the rest of us.

The circumstances of this disaster left us with a serious dilemma. If the E-boat had been a chance encounter, that was one thing. If they discovered us because of German intelligence, that was another matter entirely. We only had two options for getting our agents into Europe. It had to be a boat or an airplane, but a parachute drop was not without its dangers.

Though many SOE agents lived among the local French, such integration carried high risk. Agents rarely stayed in the same house for more than one night; it all meant a continuous chain of deception. It also required agents or the French Resistance to use radio communications, which itself was an inherent risk. Our tactic of using the quick in-and-out missions had much to commend it and in so many ways, a fishing boat was ideal for coastal reconnaissance.

Edward and I spent much of the afternoon discussing the issues, and I made the point that I didn't feel qualified to make life and death decisions concerning the agents. Unless he felt that he was, I suggested we appoint a Head of Field Operations to plan and organise the reconnaissance missions. He agreed immediately, and in fact he already had someone in mind, a Major serving with the SAS.

This was how things worked at Station M, decisions being made almost on the hoof. We had no time for committee meetings or for the production of reports. With the decision made, and a phone call to the Prime Minister's office, they sequestered the Major to Station M.

Writing to the agents' next of kin fell to Edward, but I told him I wanted to do it. Not only did I feel responsible, I felt a personal connection with Rosemary, with all of them. I felt it was my duty. I sat at my desk that evening trying to compose a suitable form of words to send to Rosemary's parents. What could I say which would offer them even a crumb of comfort? I couldn't even tell them the nature of their daughter's deployment. I had to tell them she died serving her country, but that national security prevented me from giving them any details. I expressed the hope that after the war, perhaps they might be allowed to know more.

I was not supposed to make any such comment, but if it ever became possible, I thought they had a right to know. I finished by saying, 'Rosemary was a remarkably capable young woman. She stood head and shoulders above her peers, and I deem it a great honour that I knew her. Please believe me when I say you can forever be immensely proud of your daughter.'

I couldn't write on Middlebourne headed paper. This was supposed to be sent via the War Office; I could not even explain who I was. I made the decision to collaborate with Elizabeth Layton and have the letters sent from the Prime Minister's office. When I explained the situation next morning to Elizabeth, she agreed immediately. Finally, with tears rolling down my face, I sat thinking about what a remarkable woman Rosemary was. Then there was a knock at my door; it was Greg.

"What is it, Lily, what's happened?"

Greg had signed the Official Secrets Act as a formality, but I couldn't tell him what had happened.

"I can't tell you, Greg, I wish I could, but you know I can't."

"You've lost someone close to you, haven't you, can you at least tell me that?"

"Yes, I have, it's not family or anything, but ......" I buried my face in my handkerchief.

"I'm taking you out for a drink," he said, "just for once, Lily, do as someone else tells you."

His voice was firm. He walked round behind me, and

holding my arms, he helped me up onto my feet. I felt if I had resisted, he might have just lifted me up, anyway. No doubt I must have looked awful, but I didn't care as he put his arms around me and I cried into his shoulder. I couldn't remember the last time I stood in the arms of a man. It was a comfort I had so long denied myself, and one that I needed now more than ever. We just stood there holding each other for ages. It was the comfort I needed; no doubt for Greg it was something else. As I composed myself, I realised he smelled nice, and that I was nuzzling into his neck.

"I'm sorry, Greg," I said as I pulled away, "I needed that."

"I think we both needed that, I feel a lot better for it!" he replied with a smile on his face.

I think the loss of our agents had combined with the intensity of my workload; I had reached my limit. For the moment at least, I had given in. I just wanted to stop thinking about D-Day, Station M, and Rosemary.

"Just take me out, Greg, and put a glass in front of me."

I locked my office door and put my head around Edward's door to say goodnight. He was so deeply engrossed in something, I'm sure he didn't notice Greg. He shouted after me as we walked away.

"Will you be joining us for dinner?"

"No, not tonight, thank you, I'll be eating out."

I was so distressed I did something I hadn't done before. Without even thinking about it, I placed my arm in Greg's as we walked out of the Manor. Inevitably the ever-attentive Florence heard my footsteps, rushing over to see if I needed anything. I'm not sure if it was her shoes, or just Florence, but she made a distinctive sound when she walked, so I knew it was her without looking. As she approached, I immediately realised what I was doing, and instinctively withdrew my arm from Greg's, probably looking rather silly as I gave him an apologetic smile.

"Good evening, Mrs Heywood, Mr Norton. Can I do anything for you, Mrs Heywood?"

"No, Florence, thank you, I'm fine. I'm just going out."

"I hope you and Mr Norton have a nice evening together, Mrs Heywood," she said, with a wonderful smile on her face.

"Be off with you, Florence, I'm just going out for a drink."

"Of course, Mrs Heywood, I understand," she replied, as she scurried off.

Greg smiled - he could see the funny side of it.

"It's not funny, Greg. I can't be seen to do anything that undermines my position."

"You mean you can't be seen to be a woman! Have you looked at yourself in the mirror lately, how exactly do you hope to achieve that?"

"That's not what I mean, and you know it. It was hard enough being accepted here because I *am* a woman. Now that I'm accepted for the position which I hold, I can't lose that authority."

"I know, I often wish it were different, but actually, your strength of character is the thing I admire most about you."

"Really, do you mean I'm not just a pain in the arse?"

"I wouldn't go that far!"

I laughed as I glanced around to see if anyone else was watching. I put my arm back in his as we continued on our way. He drove me to the Kings Arms, which was a pub in a nearby village. It was a nice enough pub, we went there occasionally, but for me it didn't have the atmosphere of our local. I knew why Greg decided to go there, and I appreciated it. We sat in the corner, but I still found I was looking around to be sure there was nobody there to see me out with Greg.

"Don't worry, nobody will notice I've got the Chief of Staff to go out on a date with me!"

"Is that what this is, Greg?"

"Absolutely it is! You'll wreck my sense of achievement if you say otherwise."

I couldn't help but smile - he was such an incorrigible womaniser. If he had any idea how much I wanted him, I knew he would have been all over me like a rash. It was difficult to resist him, but I was not about to let anything distract me from what I had to do.

That evening was exactly what I needed - a couple of pints, a bite to eat, and Greg's handsome face sat opposite me. He did much to help relieve my tension, as did the beer. We just chatted freely; I felt very relaxed in his company. I don't know why I mentioned it, but something he had said about his past came into my mind.

"Is that 'domestic issue' you mentioned all resolved yet, Greg?"

He looked a little taken aback that I had mentioned it.

"Well not entirely, but I can deal with it."

"I assume 'it' is a woman, a woman you left behind in Scotland?"

"Yes, there was a woman in Scotland, but it's over now, we've all moved on."

"If you had moved on, it wouldn't still be an 'issue' would it?"

"You're interrogating me, Lily, and I'm not sure I want to talk about it right now."

"You're right, forgive me, it's none of my business."

"You could easily make it your business, Lily, but in the meantime, you're right. I think it's best if we leave it at that."

He'd put me firmly in my place, and I immediately realised two things. I was jealous of a woman I knew nothing about, and Greg had not moved on. Both revelations played on my mind, but neither of us allowed it to spoil our evening and we changed the subject.

Rosemary was always there to haunt me; sometimes it felt as though she was sitting right next to me. I knew she would have approved of Greg - who wouldn't? Despite it all, we had a lovely time together, the evening ending all too quickly. On our way back to the Manor, I thanked him for taking me out of myself.

"You were right, Greg, I've had such a terrible day, you were exactly what I needed. Thank you."

"Well, I'm pleased, but you know it was Lily, the woman, who needed cheering up, not the Chief of Staff."

"You're right, I admit it, and so it's Lily, the woman, who is thanking you."

"Do you mean it wasn't the Chief of Staff I just took out on a date?"

We smiled all the way back to the Manor. I really enjoyed being with him. We gently came to a halt outside the Manor entrance, and he said what he invariably said at such moments.

"Would you like a nightcap at my place?"

"I don't think so, Greg, but thank you."

Greg acknowledged the guard on duty as he ran round to open my door. As I climbed out of the vehicle, he made sure I stepped into his face, and he kissed me. It was not a passionate embrace or even a lingering kiss, but it was a kiss, all right. Did that finally mean we had a relationship? I wasn't sure, but I knew if I was going to my own room, then I needed to go immediately.

"Good night, Greg, and thanks, that really was lovely."

"Goodnight, Chief, see you tomorrow," he replied with his wonderful smile.

I gave him a wave as I stepped inside the entrance. It was fairly late, but Florence had been watching out for me.

"Have you had a good evening, Mrs Heywood?"

"I have, Florence. It's been a hard day for me, and he was just what I needed."

I asked nothing of her, but she followed me as I walked towards my room.

"He's nice, isn't he? Mr Norton."

"He is, but you won't talk about it to anyone, will you, Florence?"

"Of course not! I'm surprised you feel the need to say that Mrs Heywood. I would never repeat anything about you to anyone, not in any circumstances."

"Yes, I'm sorry, Florence, I know you wouldn't, I'm just tired."

"Can I put your clothes away for you, and maybe a cup of cocoa?"

"Why are you so good to me, Florence? It's not your job to take care of me. I bet Mr Jennings would be cross with you if he knew how much time you spend looking after me."

"I don't think so. I asked him if I could, and he specifically told me to make sure you wanted for nothing."

"Really, Mr Jennings said that?"

"He did, so everyone's happy."

"Why are *you* so happy though, Florence?"

"Nobody has ever been as nice to me as you are, Mrs Heywood, so it's just something I can do in return. And what with you being so important and all, well, when I go below-stairs and say I need something for you, everyone jumps to, so that makes me kind of important as well!"

I couldn't think of anything less appropriate for a woman from Stepney than to have a lady's maid, and yet I had acquired one that I didn't have the heart to turn away. Florence was a delightful girl, I really liked her - little did I realise then how long our relationship would last.

Finally, I sat in bed enjoying my cup of cocoa. I was absolutely exhausted, expecting to drop off immediately, but my memory of Rosemary tormented me well into the night.

Florence finally woke me, knocking on my door. She had decided that she should wake me up each morning with a cup of tea, and while I drank my tea, she laid out my clothes for the day. I really *did* have a lady's maid!

Chapter Twenty-Three
Enter Major McBride

Following the loss of our agents, the ensuing days were very difficult. I was relieved when our new Head of Field Operations arrived, Major Antony McBride. Initially I thought he was just another 'Hooray Henry' from Sandhurst, but quickly changed my mind. He was about 35, tall with broad shoulders, and very impressive in his uniform. His smart appearance belied the fact that he was an SAS officer with considerable experience behind enemy lines. He came to us from North Africa, where he was one of the SAS raiding parties blowing up German airplanes! His experience gave him an unmistakable air of confidence which he used to wonderful effect, while not displaying a hint of arrogance.

All this was despite the fact that he walked with a limp, caused by an injury received while on active duty. The cruel fact was that his injury was our gain; without it, he would still be on active duty. The SAS in those days in North Africa were totally informal; they didn't operate like a conventional regiment. We at Station M had evolved into an informal organisation, and I think Major McBride appreciated that. Edward formally introduced me to the Major.

"This is my Chief of Staff, Lily Heywood. Lily has no

military rank other than that she outranks everyone else here. You will soon come to realise why."

"Mrs Heywood, your reputation precedes you. It's a pleasure to meet you."

"Welcome to Station M, Major. The first thing you'll notice here is that we dispense with all formalities, so please call me Lily, and we all refer to Lord Middlebourne as Edward. Do you prefer Antony or Tony?"

"Well, everyone calls me Mac, so I've just kind of adopted it."

Once Mac had settled in, I could see why Edward had selected him. He was exactly what we needed, my only concern being that he was very much a man of action. I just hoped he would be content directing operations rather than taking part. It was never easy for a man like him to adjust to his injury.

We soon replaced our agents, almost as if they were a commodity we had ordered from the local supplier. It made me feel slightly uneasy, but this time there was a difference - Mac selected them. I discussed it with him and explained my experience of losing Rosemary and the others, and he told me what I already knew; I had to remain detached from operations.

Edward was very experienced in the intelligence world, but he had never operated as an active field agent. There had been occasional talk in the intelligence world that some sections of SOE were undisciplined, and at times unprofessional. I had heard those rumours. It was a sobering thought when I considered my part in 'Operation Skua'.

Mac immediately became an invaluable asset, making his first job the analysis of our failure. First, he looked at every factor we had taken into consideration, including tide, weather, and phase of the moon. Then he looked at all the intelligence I gathered about the German E-boats known to be operating in the area.

Although I took advice on each one of the factors, I had been the one who approved and gave the go-ahead for the operation, so I felt to some extent that I was on trial. Mac was a no-nonsense soldier, quickly coming to his conclusion, and asked for a meeting with me, which I arranged for the following morning. He was exactly on time and announced his presence with a loud knock on my door.

"Come in, Mac, sit down."

"Good morning, Lily, is it okay if I discuss this in front of Fiona?"

"When I'm not here, Fiona is Chief of Staff, so do carry on."

"I'll get straight to the point then. I have looked at every aspect of the mission. You had all the parameters correct, including your selection of Kestrel."

"That *is* a relief, Mac! This entire thing has been really worrying me."

"I'm afraid you made one fundamental error. Who made the decision to have the boat run along the coast dropping off the agents?"

"I did; Edward and I discussed it, but it was my decision."

"That won't happen again. On that occasion they must have discovered your boat on its first drop-off at Vierville, because we lost everyone on board, so your planning was not to blame. From the intelligence we have, my guess is that it was down to bad luck."

"So you think we should continue to use fishing boats?"

"That's my opinion, yes, but we'll only go to one destination at a time. If I'm honest, Lily, I think you and Edward have been lucky. You've become complacent. All this nonsense about calling the boat a ferry, and treating it like a joy ride, that's finished. There's nothing more effective in ending complacency than getting people killed."

"You don't mince your words, do you, Mac!"

"I figure that's why I'm here."

"That's exactly why you're here! Never be afraid to tell me straight whatever you think I need to know. You're in charge of Field Operations now, so just tell me how you want me to organise it for you."

"No problem. If it's reconnaissance, I want a report on the target. I need to be briefed by each of the analysts who have selected that target. I also want to know everything we know, and what we don't know about that target. I need to make up my own mind on how important the target is, and how much risk we are prepared to accept. The same will apply later to sabotage, and to disrupting the enemy, but I must always have the final word as far as risk assessment is concerned."

"Welcome to Station M, Mac, we've just got a lot better at what we do!"

He looked a little taken aback. "I'll be honest, Lily, I came in here this morning expecting you and Edward to be defensive and disagree with me. I was prepared to walk away from the entire thing. Edward said I would soon find out why you're his Chief of Staff, and I can see he was right."

"I can only do what I do, Mac, because of Edward and people like you and Fiona. Our mission is far bigger than any individual, we're a team."

Just at that moment, Edward came into my office, looking incredibly pleased. "Sorry! I was held up with the PM, what's the verdict, Mac?"

"I'll tell you later, Edward," I said, "I've been all through it with Mac. It wasn't exactly our fault, but only because we were lucky; we'll do things a lot better in the future."

"That's a relief, and has Lily dealt with any concerns you might have, Mac?"

"She has, and I can see how this works. Your Chief of Staff runs a tight ship."

Edward continued to look incredibly pleased with himself as Mac left my office.

"You look like the cat that got the cream, Edward," Fiona said.

"So will you when I tell you what the PM just told me. Our gamble has paid off. It's Normandy; that's official."

"Oh, thank God it's settled. Who made the eventual decision?" I asked.

"Eisenhower's Chief of Staff, Lieutenant-General Fredrick Morgan. He's gone with all of our recommendations; we just have to double-check precisely which and how many beaches."

"This means we change up a gear, doesn't it?" Fiona said.

"It does, it means D-Day will probably happen in less than a year, and there's still a lot of the fine detail to get right."

We were all elated that our decision to concentrate our resources on Normandy had been vindicated. Anything else would have been a terrible setback. Edward and I went over to Hut 3 to share the news, which they greeted with a cheer. I think we all knew our cheers were more relief than celebration, and we all knew these high spirits would be short-lived. Sure enough, Edward soon brought us all back down to earth.

"This is it, ladies and gentlemen, D-Day will be on the Normandy beaches in maybe less than a year's time. Only a dozen or so people know this, and half of them are in this room. The responsibility for the choice of landing site is ours, and the lives of countless people depend upon our decision-making. This is the final phase; this is what we have been working towards.

For the selection of beaches, we need to know every detail of geology and topography, including the seaward approach to the beach - Corky, that is your department. We must know every single gun emplacement, every beach defence, and where their troops are located - Woody, that's your department, and you will have to brief Mac on this; sabotage might be an option.

Establishing a beachhead is our prime objective, but we must also be sure about the route inland. We need geology and topography - that's you again, Corky. We need to consider the best strategic route with consideration to the probable German reinforcements and defences. All the strategic places such as bridges, railway crossings, easily defended locations.

The military planners will need our input - that's you, Patrick.

We need to think about misinformation and misdirection to convince the Germans we are landing somewhere else - that's me, and Rolo, and you Patrick. We all work with Mac; whatever we need on the other side, he's your man. We need all the help we can get from FR, but we must be so careful with our information - that's you, Rolo. You need to maintain and develop your contacts at Bletchley and always work with Mac if his agents are involved. Maggie, you are going to work double-time. You're our eyes, we must see everything and miss nothing. Rolo, you're our ears, and the same applies to you - hear everything and miss nothing."

"What do I do, Edward?" I asked.

"We shall each concentrate on our own area, but we all overlap. We must keep a constant perspective, an overview of the entire operation. We must not overlook anything, and we must coordinate everything, that's you, Lily. Finally, you and Fiona: you are the glue which holds us all together. You're the ones who make all of this work, Lily."

There was total silence in the room. You could have heard a pin drop.

Eventually Patrick said, "Plenty of time for a beer then."

I ventured a question, "How far inland does our remit extend?"

"Good question, Lily, I don't know precisely. Corky and Woody will work that out for us. We need a map showing how far our analysis extends, I suggest we only go as far as special considerations dictate. We're basically only concerned with establishing a beachhead and the initial advance inland away from the beach. Keep it within five to ten miles if you can. Beyond that, it's up to the military planners to do their own analysis."

Gradually the silence became replaced by an ever-increasing buzz of activity. I could physically feel the intensity of the room moving up to another level. We were in the countdown stage to the greatest invasion the world has ever seen; we were all excited and terrified at the same time. The intellectual challenge was what these people thrived on; it was the sheer burden of responsibility which caused the sweat to form on their brows.

Our operation grew in intensity during the spring and summer of '43. Everyone knew what they were doing, and we worked together like a well-oiled machine.

Mac fitted in perfectly; our field agent operation had attained an additional level of professionalism. He worked closely with Rolo, so he was kept constantly up to date with intercepts relating to German coastal activities. Little did Mac know it, but his field agent operation was also one of the beneficiaries of Ultra. I took Mac's advice and tried to keep my distance on a personal level.

Chapter Twenty-Four
Dotty's Back

One morning in July, I was standing in Hut 3 talking with the boys. I had my back to the door, so I didn't see it open; I just heard a familiar voice.

"Hello, you lucky boys, my name's Dotty."

I spun round in total surprise!

"Dotty, what the hell are you doing here?"

"I've come to see *you*, Lily, give me a hug."

The boys instantly stopped what they were doing. They pushed their papers, maps, and files to one side. Sitting with their mouths open, they gazed at the tornado which had just burst in through the door. She threw her arms around me and for the moment I was just elated to see her.

"Introduce me to these lovely men, Lily."

"You're not supposed to *be* here, Dotty! You must leave immediately!" I said.

"I thought this was Station M, where I'm *supposed* to be! I've dropped all my kit off in Hut 5, so I came to look for you."

"Do you mean you've been stationed here, *with us*?"

"I know, you can't believe your good luck, can you? I told you I'd be good at this; they reckon I'm the best. You ask Mac, he wanted me and no-one else."

I knew Mac was concerned that he had no female agent,

but it just hadn't occurred to me for a moment that Dotty would be the one. It was my worst nightmare come true - Dotty putting herself in harm's way because of me. There was no point in me not being pleased to see her; it was far too late for that. She was such a character, and it was wonderful to have that light shining in my life again. Maggie came into the hut at that point, so I introduced her to Dotty.

"Which one of these lovely men do you have your eye on, Maggie?" asked Dotty.

To my complete astonishment, Maggie said, "That one," pointing towards Patrick.

"Fair enough, he's yours!" Dotty said, with her usual air of mischief.

I introduced Dotty to the boys. She was on top of her form, and none of them would have met anyone quite like her; she was all over them. I knew it was just a show, this wasn't the real Dorothy, but I'm not at all sure the boys realised that. As soon as it seemed appropriate, I suggested we go over to my office to see Fiona. Dotty reluctantly prised herself away from the boys, and we prepared to head over to the main building.

"Bye-bye, boys, I know you'll miss me, but I promise I'll be back."

She talked excitedly all the way over to the Manor where it was Corporal Harris on guard by the door. When Dotty was caught spying on Hut 5, Corporal Harris had let her off the hook, and neither of us had forgotten that. He was a lovely chap, grinning as we approached.

"Dotty, what have you been up to now?" he said.

"Thanks to you, Brian, I'm an indispensable part of this outfit now!"

"Blimey! Is this true, Mrs Heywood?"

"I'm afraid so, Corporal, it's all your fault."

"Yes, it's your fault, Brian," Dotty said, "but don't worry, I haven't forgotten I owe you one."

He smiled approvingly as we went inside, where I then

had to explain to William, and then to Albert, that Dotty was likely to be a regular visitor. I just put my head around the office door.

"Guess who's here, Fi?"

With that, Dotty made her grand entrance. "Ta-dah! It's me! Hello, Fi."

"Dotty, what the hell are you doing here?" exclaimed Fiona. She got up from her chair and rushed towards Dotty with her arms open. We three had so much to talk about, and so little time available. It had been months and it was a wonderful reunion.

"Look at this office! Wow, you two must be *so* important, and look at you, Fi, you're really posh now, aren't you?"

"Where are you staying, Dotty? Are you in Hut 1, or are you going home to Gran's?"

"They told me Hut 1, but if I can, I'll go to Gran's with you, Fi."

"Oh, Gran will be so pleased! It's not the same without you and Lily there."

"Look, you two, I'd better go, I don't want to get into trouble again, not on my first day. What about the pub tonight?"

"Perfect," said Fiona, "I'm meeting Johnny there tonight. What about you, Lily?"

I was just about to answer when my telephone rang. It was Biggin Hill.

"I'm sorry, Mrs Heywood," said a woman's voice that I didn't recognise, "it's Wing Commander Albright. I'm afraid he's been shot down over the coast of France."

I froze on the spot, my heart nearly jumping out of my chest, unavoidably looking over at Fiona. Whenever she knew Johnny was flying, Fi would instinctively look in fear at the telephone every time it rang. She intuitively knew from my expression that something was wrong. I was in a terrible position. What could I say, with Fiona listening? There were questions I just had to ask.

"Do you have any details; did he bail out?"

I had to ask that, we had to know, but immediately Fiona became hysterical.

"I'm so sorry, Mrs Heywood," the voice said, "that's all we know. If we hear anything, I will call you straight back."

I was not even able to thank the woman for calling me, I was unable to speak. Dotty clung on to Fiona who was screaming '*no*' repeatedly, but all I could tell them was what I had just been told.

"He's most likely bailed out okay, Fi. I'm sure he'll be all right."

I wasn't sure about anything; I could feel myself trembling. For a moment, I had no idea what to do or say; Fiona's reaction froze me to the spot. Hearing Fiona scream, Edward came rushing into the room, looking at us in horror.

"What's happened?"

"It's Johnny. He's been shot down, that's all we know."

Edward immediately went to comfort Fiona; I knew she was in excellent hands with the two of them. Her screams had so wrenched at my heart that I just had to get out of my office so I could think. I stood there in the hallway with my head in my hands. Then I realised there were things we could do. I ran as fast as I could over to Hut 3, burst through the door, slamming it against the wall, making everyone look up with a start.

"Johnny's been shot down!" I shouted, with tears streaming down my face. "Everyone, use all your contacts in FR. *Please,* do everything you can; we need to know if he bailed out. Rolo, use your contacts at Bletchley, open message, ask them to listen out. Use every contact we have, MI6, and SOE. See if there's anyone with eyes and ears anywhere near St-Mere Eglise."

Rolo jumped up from his chair so quickly that it fell to the floor behind him. He dashed towards the door, briefly putting his hand on my shoulder. He didn't say a word, rushing on his way to the communications hut.

"Oh, my God," said Corky, "does Fi know?"

"She knows and is in a terrible state. For God's sake, find him alive! I can't tell her he's gone, I just can't."

Within moments, messages were being sent to every contact we had. I'd done all I could, so I hurried straight back to Fiona. She was desperately trying to cling to the hope that Johnny had safely bailed out, while I tried to convince her that was most likely what had happened. Edward and Dotty were brilliant. Nobody could have done more. Edward especially was more compassionate and understanding than I had ever seen him; he had discarded another piece of his defensive armour.

It was the most desperate time; one by one the boys from Hut 3 came over to my office, each hugging Fiona, trying to reassure her as best they could. It was devastating enough when we lost our agents, but this was family. Station M was united in anguish.

Edward, Dotty, and I sat with her all afternoon. I knew that the longer we went without news, the less likely it was that Johnny was in the hands of the Resistance. The hours went by agonisingly slowly. Seeing Fiona in such anguish brought back all the pain from that dreadful day when HMS Hood sank. I knew exactly how she felt, or perhaps not? I never shared the kind of love with Gerry that Johnny and Fiona had. Her pain was unbearable to see.

I went back over to Hut 3, knowing the boys were doing everything humanly possible, but I just had to do something. Rolo was still in the Radio Room, and the others were pacing the boards.

"What are the chances he bailed out? Okay, Woody, tell me the truth."

"We don't know how he has been shot down. If it was ground fire, that's maybe not so good, but if it was a German fighter plane, there is a chance."

"Why is that Woody? I need to know."

"A fighter usually attacks from behind. Johnny's reconnaissance Spitfire is the low altitude variant. It's unarmed, but it retains the armoured panel behind the seat, so he has a chance."

"Do you mean they don't all have that protection?"

"That's right. They design many of the PR variants for maximum speed and altitude; armour is heavy."

"Even if he bailed out safely, Lily, he *could* be in the hands of the Germans," said Patrick.

"I know, but at least he would be *alive!*"

They reassured me as much as they could, and at least Woody had given me a straw I could cling on to. I thanked them for all their efforts and dashed back to my office, deciding not to mention the armour plate to Fiona.

We spent the rest of the day in a state of suspended animation as the hands on the office clock seemed not to be moving; it was a dreadful torment. Not until 8 o'clock in the evening did my green phone ring. It was Station X, so I just knew it was about Johnny. My heart raced as I picked up the receiver. Filled with dread in case it was terrible news, I could hardly speak to the woman on the other end.

"Mrs Heywood?" a woman asked.

"Yes, do you have any news for me?"

"Rolo has asked me to look out for FR messages, anything to do with a pilot. I don't know if this is what you need, but we have a coded message which says, '*reconnaissance pilot safe, repeat reconnaissance pilot safe.*' No names, Mrs Heywood. Is this the message you wanted?"

I couldn't speak, barely managing to acknowledge the woman. I looked at Fiona, and all I could say was, "He's safe!" The room erupted; I thought Fi would explode with joy! She kissed Edward like I'd never kissed him, she hugged me and Dotty, and then she screamed at the top of her voice, "*He's alive.*"

The word spread to Hut 3 almost immediately. Those who

weren't already in the office came running over. Florence and Mary stood at the door wondering what was going on, so I beckoned them to come in and celebrate with us. Jennings offered his good wishes and Fi launched herself at him, giving him an enormous hug.

"Will that be all, My Lord?" he said.

"No, Jennings, would you get some bottles of champagne from the cellar with enough glasses for everyone."

"It will be a pleasure, My Lord."

Fi couldn't stop crying, but they were tears of joy. Everyone wanted to hug her, and she tried to thank each one, but could hardly speak. When the champagne arrived, it was a party atmosphere like no other I have experienced. We had all been plunged into the depths of despair, only to be elevated to the very peak of euphoria. Florence and Mary poured the glasses and handed them to us, both receiving a hug from Fiona. Everyone raised their glasses in a toast to Johnny's speedy return.

Patrick whispered into my ear, "If this is what love does to you, I'm not sure I can risk it!"

"I thought you and Maggie *were* risking it, Patrick?"

He replied in his soft Irish lilt. "Ah, well now, this might just be the cause of my concern!"

"You're having a bad effect on this man, Maggie," I said.

Their relationship was supposed to be clandestine. Maggie had tried hard to keep it under wraps, but in that heady atmosphere, she put her arms around Patrick and kissed him. There was another cheer for them, which they acknowledged with slightly embarrassed smiles. Dotty was standing with Mac, so I walked over to them.

"Bring him home, Mac, send Dotty. It could be your first operation, Dot, and when you find him, tell him he's never to do this to us again."

We had difficulty communicating with FR. We were not exactly sure where Johnny was being held, and it was several days before conditions were right for Mac to send a boat over.

Fiona struggled with the waiting. When conditions finally fell into place, Dotty came over to the office first thing in the morning, where I was sitting with Fiona.

"I'm going down to Portsmouth now. I'll get your boy back for you, Fi, don't you worry. Can you imagine the look on his face when he sees me!"

We laughed. It was true; the very last person Johnny would expect was Dotty. As Dotty told us the details of the operation, her absolute calm and professionalism struck me. I looked at Fiona and smiled.

"Is this really you, Dotty, where has the old Dotty gone?"

"Yes, I know, I'm no longer Dotty by nature. I realised something on the training course. I've never been the best at anything, so I took myself seriously for once. The thing is when you *are* good at something, it gives you confidence, doesn't it? I've not had that before, not really, so whenever you send me over there, whatever it is, you know I'll get the job done."

"Please don't get complacent, Dotty, we need you to always come back to us."

"I've learned that one; complacency is the word Mac hates most of all. Seriously, that will never happen."

We wished her well as she went back to Hut 5. A little later, as I was walking over to Hut 3, I saw her climbing into the back of an army vehicle carrying a Sten gun over her shoulder. I thought I knew Dotty, but this really was another person. The adorable Dotty I knew was still in there somewhere, but I had read her file - she was formidable, and woe betide anyone who stepped in her way.

Three days later, I was on my way over to the Estate Office when an army lorry rumbled to a halt outside the Manor. A soldier jumped out of the cab and walked round to the back to unfasten the tarpaulin. A very welcome face appeared with a beaming smile, as she blinked into the unaccustomed sunshine. Dotty didn't wait for the driver to open up the back of the lorry. She leapt out over the tailgate with the Sten gun still in place over her shoulder. A moment later the tailgate dropped with a loud clunk. There was Johnny, still in his flying suit, looking a little forlorn, but all in one piece. He needed help to get down from the lorry, so I rushed over to them, and helped Dotty get him down.

"Don't you ever do that again, Johnny Albright!" I said, as I hugged and kissed him. "Are you okay?"

"Sprained ankle, and a couple of bruised ribs, but apart from that only damaged pride," he said with a grimace on his face.

"Come on, Dotty, let's get him to the office. There's some-one over there who might just want to see him."

We helped him towards the office with his arms over our shoulders. He was obviously in more discomfort from his injuries than he was letting on, but Fiona was the only thought on his mind. Both the guard on duty and Albert the footman offered to help, but Dotty dismissed their good intentions out of hand, positively affronted by the offer. I had made it a rule that there should be no weapons inside the Manor, so I insisted the guard take care of Dotty's Sten gun. It was then I realised that she also carried a handgun. Eventually we arrived at the office, where we stood outside the door.

"Can you take your weight if you lean against the door surround?" I asked Johnny.

"I expect so; why?"

"Because this is as far as Dotty and I go. This is a moment for you and Fi."

I opened the door, and Dotty and I left them alone. As we turned our backs, we heard Fiona's cry of "*Johnny!*" I looked at Dotty and we both smiled as we headed off to Hut 5 where Dotty would be debriefed.

"I've never seen two people so in love, have you, Dotty?"

"No, I haven't, it's kind of wonderful, isn't it?"

"It is, I'm envious, I'd like some of what Fi's got."

"Wouldn't we all, Lily! Maybe one day."

"Did you find him okay?"

"Eventually," she said, swinging the Sten gun back over her shoulder. "FR only communicate when they have to. My contact knew someone, who knew someone else, who knew where he was."

"Promise me, Dotty. When you go back, please take no more risk than you have to. I've overcome a lot in this war. I just can't face the prospect of losing you as well."

"Don't worry, I've found the first real home I've ever had here in Middlebourne. I'll drag myself back here by my fingertips if I have to."

She put her arm in mine, her confident smile as indomitable as ever. When Dotty said she would drag herself back by her fingertips, she really meant it. Being near Dotty filled me with energy, but now that she was an operational field agent, I would live in constant fear of losing her.

-oOo-

The invasion of Sicily on the 10th July was another significant turning point in the war. We eagerly absorbed every item of information received about 'Operation Husky'. It involved 150,000 troops, 3,000 ships, and 4,000 aircraft. As a combined air and amphibious landing, 'Operation Husky' was second only to D-day itself. Just as with the North African invasion, Station M played no direct part in the operation, but we tracked every detail, trying to tease out any lessons which might apply to D-Day. Since the war, the Italian campaign has been overshadowed by D-Day, but it remains a great tactical and logistical success.

By August, the Axis forces were in full retreat, evacuating the island. It was a tremendous success for the Allies; for the first time it brought the Mediterranean Sea lanes within the Allied sphere. They removed Mussolini from office, the Italian army surrendered and later, with Mussolini removed, the Italians joined forces with the Allies. The planned German offensive at Kursk was abandoned, and 20% of the German army was diverted to protect Southern Europe.

The invasion of the Italian mainland began on the 3rd September 1943, with the main invasion force landing at Salerno on the 9th September. Incredibly, German commandos rescued Mussolini from captivity, and Hitler set him up as a puppet ruler in Northern Italy, but by October the Italian government had declared war on its old ally Germany. The Allied advance towards Rome proved to be a slow and costly affair; it would not be until April 1945 that a new offensive finally brought the Italian war to an end.

Part of the reason for the slow advance in Italy was that attention was being drawn towards preparations for D-Day. The logistics planning for the invasion was now well under way. An ever-increasing number of Allied troops were being stationed all over Southern England.

Winston Churchill met with President Roosevelt at a secret meeting in Quebec, code-named 'Quadrant,' where a provisional date for the invasion had been decided - it was to be May 1944.

At that meeting, 'Operation Overlord' finally became a reality. They also decided to appoint a Supreme Commander for all Allied forces. Probably against Churchill's wishes, the President's proposal was accepted, and later in the year General Dwight D Eisenhower was approved.

Chapter Twenty-Five
Over the Rainbow

The events in Sicily were momentous for Station M. The more our position in Europe became consolidated, the more certain D-Day became. It was like a ratchet which, a click at a time, increased the pressure on us. It intensified all of our activities, and each of us felt the ever-increasing burden of responsibility. The atmosphere had changed in Hut 3; the rolled-up balls of paper were now fewer. Now I would often leave the Hut without having them hurled at me.

The visible signs of tension were everywhere to be seen - cups of tea not drunk and the cigarette smoke thicker than ever. The overflowing ashtrays which they seldom emptied. They were now often scruffy and unshaven, the drumming of fingers on table-tops and the tapping of pencils only adding to everyone's tension. Tempers were sometimes frayed.

Our attention was now being drawn towards a more pro-active approach to the invasion. We now considered sabotage and other countermeasures which might disrupt German communications, defences, and troop movements. Our detailed analysis of the Normandy coast gave us an unparalleled insight into German infrastructure. Principal targets would be eliminated by bombing or by Naval bombardment, but there was also plenty of scope for us to disrupt communications and transport.

This was where Mac came into his element. His experience behind enemy lines with the SAS, combined with our team of highly trained field agents, gave us a formidable capability. This all required its own reconnaissance and intelligence.

None of this was without internal friction, as there was still coastal reconnaissance and analysis to be done. As his remit expanded, Mac was being put under constantly increasing pressure to send agents over the Channel, though he remained resolute about not putting his agents at undue risk. It all rather came to a head one day in Hut 3 during the early autumn of 1943.

"When can you get me that reconnaissance I need at Saint Laurent, Mac?" asked Patrick, the tone of his voice abrasive.

"Oh for Christ's sake, Patrick! I told you, I'd have to pull someone away from elsewhere. It's an unacceptable risk."

"To hell with the risk, move your feckin' agent, Mac, I *need* that intel!"

The conversation grew ever more heated between them; as they raised their voices, they lost all rationality; they just ended up shouting at each other. I couldn't contain myself any longer.

"Enough, Patrick!" I shouted. "I'm putting a stop to this right now. Don't you ever put Mac under pressure to compromise one of our agents, how dare you! You're sitting here nice and safe, while they risk their lives for you. Mac knows what he's doing, never question his judgment again. Do you hear me? Never let me hear you question a risk assessment again. Have I made myself clear, Patrick?"

There was a deathly silence, as Patrick just sat there at his table, looking like a deflating barrage balloon. His bad-tempered outburst was totally out of character for this mild-mannered Irishman. My outburst was equally out of character for me. I realised only too well I was thinking of Dotty being placed at risk.

"I've been an eejit, haven't I?" he said, fidgeting with his matchbox.

"You've been more than an eejit, Patrick. But it's not just you, I've badly overreacted as well, I'm really sorry."

We had all overreacted, tensions were high, we were all feeling the pressure. It was my job to hold Station M together, and I should have realised the big-hearted Patrick would do my job for me.

"Me Mammy used to say that you grow in stature every time you make a mistake, so I thought that meant I was growing taller every day. Then she tells me I've just made another mistake, because you only grow in stature if you admit your mistake and learn something from it. Well, okay Mammy, if you can hear me, I made a mistake, and I've learned not to be such a bad-tempered eejit. Give me your hand, Mac."

Mac shook Patrick's hand warmly and slapped him on the back.

"Wise woman, your Mammy, I'd like to meet her one day."

"Oh, to be sure you will, we'll all meet her soon enough. As for you, Lily, me Mammy would have been proud of that bollocking you gave me, but she always gave me a hug after a telling-off."

I stepped forward and put my arms around him, hugging him tightly. The tension in Hut 3 just seemed to flow across the floor and seep out under the door.

"Thank you, Patrick," I said as I hugged him.

"Thank me for being an eejit?"

"No, you fool, thank you for having a wise Mammy."

"Actually, I contrived the entire thing to get you in my arms."

"I wouldn't put it past you, but I've got another idea. Why don't we all stop work early tonight? You boys make yourself presentable, and then we'll all go down to the pub and get pie-eyed. You have a shave, Woody, and for God's sake, Rolo, wear another shirt."

"Lily, my dear, that's the most sensible thing I've heard in weeks," replied Corky.

"Yes, it sounds good to me," I said. "I want you all looking smart, mind. I can't be seen in the pub with a bunch of scruffs."

As I prepared to leave the Hut to return to the office, I noticed them screwing up old sheets of paper. Knowing what was coming, I made a dash for the door, only to be bombarded with balls of paper. I slammed the door shut behind me, and leaned back against it, smiling. This was more how Hut 3 should be. As soon as I told Fiona, she said it was a brilliant idea. She would go with us. And just then Edward came into the office.

"What would be a brilliant idea?" he asked.

"Lily's taking Hut 3 to the pub tonight," replied Fiona.

"What would be the purpose of such an event?"

"The purpose, Edward," I said, "is to relieve a bit of the tension in Hut 3. The boys are all stressed and getting bad-tempered. They haven't had a break for ages."

"Well, in that case, perhaps I should attend this function as well?"

"It's not a function, Edward, it's just us having a few pints, unwinding a bit, and letting off steam. It would be lovely if you would come with us."

"As you know, I am not accustomed to frequenting the Public House, but perhaps I could make an exception in this instance."

"That would be great, Edward, the boys would appreciate you going as well; it will be a good boost to morale."

We all met up that evening outside the Manor entrance. Dotty got to hear about it from Mac, and she had to be there. The boys had obviously taken to heart my comments about their unruly appearance. They turned up looking smart and apart from Corky, all were clean shaven, with freshly ironed shirts and smelling of aftershave. Woody was sporting one of his flamboyant bow ties. Dotty and Maggie were arm in arm with the boys, and to my profound surprise, Edward offered an arm each to me and Fiona.

This was how we set off for the pub, all of us marching triumphantly down the road. It might sound like an inconsequential thing, but I very much doubt that Edward had ever walked arm in arm with two women in his entire life. That evening turned out to be quite extraordinary, not just because Edward experienced things he had never imagined before; it was to be especially memorable for me.

I never did become a professional singer - I might have dreamed about it on the odd occasion, but it was never to be. I still have a tinge of regret about it because that night in the pub, I think perhaps for the first time, I discovered exactly what my voice was capable of. It was to change my attitude to singing forever.

We drank a lot of beer that night. There was a lot of fun and a lot of banter, and to my surprise and delight, Edward was a part of it all. We entered that stage early in the evening, where it felt perfectly appropriate for us all to sing together. However, the problem was that we were not all singing the same words! Other people in the pub registered their annoyance with some disapproving looks.

"We need you to sing for us, Lily," said Dotty, "then we can try to sing along in time."

I had little say in the matter. A path was quickly cleared towards the piano. Rolo rushed forward to open the piano lid, while Woody brushed off the seat. Having drunk just enough to lose any inhibitions I might otherwise have, I didn't need a lot of encouragement. As I sat at the piano, the pub was full of the noise of people talking, laughing, and enjoying themselves. Behind the bar, there was the sound of glasses clunking, and people shouting their orders.

My crowd gathered around me, and I started with a wonderful song popularised by Vera Lynn, 'A Nightingale Sang in Berkeley Square'. The song started gently, and gradually I became aware that the pub had fallen silent. Having people listening to me boosted my confidence enormously, because it was unusual in a pub for people to stop talking and listen to the singer.

When I finished the song, there was loud applause, and cries of '*more, more*', not least from my crowd. Then a lovely man stepped forward with a harmonica. He had some difficulty walking. Slowly but surely, he came over and stood next to me, and spoke with an American accent.

"That was wonderful, my dear. My name's Cole, and I would deem it a real honour if you would allow me to accompany you on my harmonica."

I was apprehensive about it. He might have been hopeless, which would have caused a lot of embarrassment for all concerned, but I made what proved to be one of the best decisions of my life.

"My name's Lily, and the honour would be entirely mine, Cole."

"Wonderful; you just play, Lily, I'll come in behind you."

Edward offered him a chair which he readily accepted, and I sang 'Stormy Weather'. He took a little time to start playing, but when he did, he was good. I mean, he didn't just play a tune on a mouth organ; he was a proper harmonica player. He made that thing sing in its own right, and I found myself trying ever harder to be worthy of his accompaniment. I sang, 'As Time Goes By', and 'You'd Be So Nice to Come Home To'.

After each song, the crowd were shouting out requests. Vera Lynn was extremely popular, so I had to sing 'There'll Be Bluebirds Over the White Cliffs of Dover', and 'We'll Meet Again'. The crowd went wild. I hadn't sung in front of an audience for a long time, so it was immensely gratifying to hear the response.

When we stopped for a short break, Edward placed two glasses of beer on top of the piano, one each for me and Cole.

"Lily, that was wonderful," Edward said, "I had no idea! You really are a wonderful singer."

"Why thank you, kind sir," I replied, "and what about Cole here! I've never heard the harmonica played like that before. You must be a professional musician, Cole?"

"I've been a musician all my life. I'm kind of retired now, after a riding accident did this to my leg. I always carry this harmonica in my pocket though; you never know when it might be useful. And what about you, Lily, you're not the average singer, what's your singing background?"

"I don't really have one, Cole. I used to sing in the Tunbridge Wells Choral Society, and I've had classical training, but for many years it's just been the occasional night in the local pub, like tonight."

"I can hardly believe that Lily, I thought you were a professional singer. Your range and your musical interpretation are both wonderful. Where does it all come from?"

"Oh, I know exactly where it comes from! It's just an accident of birth really. My Grandmother is wonderfully talented, she had a beautiful voice. It seems that she has passed some of her ability on to me."

"Was she a professional singer?"

"No, not at all. She's largely self-taught, but she performed with the local Choral Society. Then I followed in her footsteps, so for a while we sang together. She never stops encouraging me."

"Extraordinary!" he said, looking quite mystified. "You've got a rare talent, young lady."

Just at that moment someone in the pub asked if I would sing 'Over the Rainbow'.

"Have you sung that song before?" asked Cole.

"Not in public, no, but it's a lovely song."

"I worked on an arrangement of that song which I think works really well, but I've yet to find a singer with the voice to do it justice. Do you know, I think *you* could do it. Will you try it for me?"

"If you think I could, I'd love to try."

344

Cole jotted down the lyrics for me, grouping the words into phrases, and making notes under each phrase. Then he started playing some chords to give me the feel of his arrangement.

"Forget how Judy Garland sings it; everybody's heard that. Think about the words, Lily, I want you to live every emotion in each word. Think of a future after the war, think of a place where you would like to be, and who you'd like to be with. This is *your* dream you're singing about and keep your grandmother in your mind. You're singing it for her."

"I'll burst into tears if I do that!"

"Don't worry, we can stop, and then you can start again. I want you to use the full range of that beautiful voice of yours. Use all your classical training but keep all that emotion."

It seemed like the whole pub was in on the conversation. You could have heard a pin drop as Cole played the melody in total silence. He could play his harmonica in the most extraordinary way; sometimes it sounded almost like a voice singing. His arrangement of 'Over the Rainbow' was slower than the Judy Garland original, requiring a much wider vocal range. He held on to certain words to emphasise the lyrics, and then he raised the third chorus to a really high crescendo, before slowing it right back down again. Each word became individually important. He played the melody as I mentally rehearsed the lyrics, conducting every word with exaggerated movements and gestures. I became completely immersed in his interpretation of the song, then he asked me to hum along with his accompaniment, modulating my voice accordingly.

"I think you have it. You see, if you practise singing the words, you'll lose the emotion. I want you to sing it for the very first time. You have the voice to do this, Lily, you can hold that crescendo, I want you to *live* those words. So let's do it, Lily. The war's over, you're where you always dreamed you would be, you're with the one you love. This is your dream, Lily, it's a dream that really can come true! Are you ready?"

I concentrated so hard on the image he gave me, and

already had tears in my eyes, but said I was ready. He began the melody, and I followed, singing the first line, and slowly building into the song. I don't know how Cole did it, but I was there in that faraway place of my dreams. I was with Edward; Gran was there with us, and all the troubles of the war seemed a long way away. I wanted that dream so badly. I'd never inhabited a song so completely, nor sung with such emotion. It added an extra dimension to my voice that I'd never experienced before.

Just at the point where the third chorus crescendo began, I totally believed it really could come true. Somehow, even with tears rolling down my face, I still held the top note perfectly. I just sang my heart out, like I'd never sung before; nothing else seemed to exist. When I got to the last note, there was a deafening period of silence, and then everyone went absolutely mad, though for a moment I was oblivious to it. When I finally registered the applause, I couldn't believe my singing could ever generate such a response from an audience. I was overcome with emotion and the boys gathered round to comfort me.

Cole just sat there with tears in his eyes, as I did.

"You did it, Lily, that's what I was looking for! That was remarkable."

"This was you, Cole. *You* did this, who are you, you're not just a retired musician, are you?"

"Well, I've composed a few things of my own, but this was your night, Lily. Look at this crowd; *you* did that. Hey look, I've got to go, but promise me one thing, Lily, that you'll keep singing, and if you ever come over to the States, you be sure to come and see me."

With that, the people he was with helped him towards the door, apologising for the rush, saying they were already late for an engagement. I shouted after them.

"How would I find you in America, Cole?"

"I'm in the book - Porter," he shouted back.

I have no idea why I was so slow on the uptake that night, but it was some time before I realised who that man was, and to this day I have no idea why he was there. Although everyone wanted me to, I couldn't follow that song - I was emotionally drained. It would be fair to say that, towards the end of the evening, we were all more than a little drunk. Some, like Woody and Corky, more than the others. We had reached that stage of the evening where we put our arms around whoever was near, and we all sang along together, albeit out of tune. Edward sang with us, and he put his arm around me.

It was lovely to see him letting his hair down, just like the rest of us. He enjoyed the evening, as we all did, and it drew us even closer together. Eventually, when 'last orders' had been called, we walked back to the Manor. We were all singing 'Over the Rainbow', while swaying in unison with each other. Dotty entertained us, making sure the air was full of laughter and merriment. What the inhabitants of Middlebourne must have thought, I cannot imagine! We arrived outside Gran's cottage to drop off Dotty and Fiona, and inevitably Gran came out to see what all the noise was about.

"This is my lovely Gran," I said, bracing myself against the fence.

Patrick was the first to step forward. "Gran-mammy give me a hug!" he said, throwing his arms around her.

Everyone else followed his lead, with Gran protesting vociferously, while the smile on her face said something else entirely. I suspect the fresh air had helped in part to bring Edward back a little nearer towards his normal reserved self, because he offered to shake Gran's hand.

"I didn't expect to find you amongst this drunken rabble, My Lord," said Gran with some surprise.

"Madam, I can assure you, my part in this merriment has been solely one of maintaining order and decorum amongst my colleagues."

Dotty leaned on Edward's shoulder, saying, "Where do you think it went wrong, My Lord?"

"I suspect it was that third pint of beer, or perhaps the fifth, it was certainly *one* of them."

Gran laughed and then pretended to be cross as she clipped Dotty behind the ear.

"Get yourselves inside, you two girls. You're a disgrace, all of you, fifth pint indeed!"

"You are perfectly correct in your observation, madam," Edward said, "my colleagues are an absolute disgrace, especially Dorothy! I can only apologise on their behalf."

I can't remember when I laughed so much, we all fell about laughing; Edward was being so funny. Gran waved us all goodbye, before scolding Dotty and Fiona again.

"Me Mammy will enjoy meeting your Gran, when the time comes, Lily. What a fine woman."

"She is, Patrick, but I don't want her meeting your Mammy just yet."

"Mammy's got all the time in the world, Lily."

We finally made our way back to the Manor, much to the amusement of the guard on duty. We stood in front of the Manor hugging each other and commending ourselves on such a good evening. They eventually made their way towards Hut 1, still singing 'Over the Rainbow', leaving me with Edward, and we walked into the Manor together. I tripped on the step and nearly fell over, only saved by Edward's timely intervention. I made a joke of it, and he smiled as I righted myself, pulling against his outstretched hand.

It was some moments later that I realised we were still holding hands, and we continued to hold hands as we made our way into the Great Hall together. Florence appeared on the other side, walking directly towards us. The moment she saw Edward, she hesitated and turned as if she had forgotten something, promptly walking away. I was walking hand in hand towards my bedroom with the Ninth Earl of Middlebourne. Though I hadn't quite grasped the situation, Florence obviously had. We were walking up the stairs together, talking and laughing as if this was a perfectly normal occurrence. It was Florence's reaction that made me realise - this was anything but a normal situation!

My heart jumped in my chest. Was I reading too much into it, was I just imagining things? He escorted me to my bedroom door, which was something he had never done before. We were still holding hands. Perhaps we were just steadying each other, but eventually we both finally stood there, looking at one another, and I suddenly felt as sober as a judge.

"I'm sure tomorrow I will regret imbibing so much alcohol," he said, "but I must confess, Lily, that was good fun tonight."

"You sound surprised, Edward."

"I suppose I am. It's not an activity I would normally indulge in, but there's a first time for everything. The most memorable thing was your singing. You really are magnificent, you know."

"That's very kind, Edward, thank you."

Then there was a period of silence. It was an agonising moment of indecision. I felt intensely awkward, not knowing what to say, and realised he felt the same. Finally, he put his arms loosely around me and kissed my cheek. It was not exactly how he would kiss his mother's cheek, but nevertheless, it was still my cheek.

"Good night, Lily, sleep well."

"Good night, Edward."

We stepped back from each other, pushing against the unseen force that was pulling in the opposite direction. I was intoxicated both by the beer and by Edward, both had robbed me of my free will. I wanted to throw myself back into his arms, but it felt as if we were both puppets being controlled by an unseen puppeteer.

"Good night, Edward," I said again, as I opened my bedroom door.

Even as I stepped into the room and turned to close the

door, I was hoping he would follow me. He stood there as if he too was being restrained by the same puppet master.

"Good night, Lily."

I sat on the bed with my head spinning, and all I could think about was Edward. I slowly got out of my clothes, and one by one they just fell to the floor. Florence had laid out my nightdress, which I put on, just in time to fall into bed.

I fell instantly asleep, only to be quickly woken with the inevitable call of nature that so much beer ensured. Having struggled back from the bathroom still half asleep, I vaguely remember getting back into bed, and then hearing a knock on my door. There was just a brief moment while I was still half asleep that I thought it was Edward, a silly thought which evaporated as quickly as a raindrop on a hot summer day.

"Shall I leave your tea outside the door, Mrs Heywood?"

"No, you can come in, Florence," I called back.

"Sorry, Mrs Heywood, I thought perhaps... well, you know, sorry."

She glanced at the other side of the bed, and at my clothes.

"Looks like you had a good night."

"We had a fantastic night, Florence. I'm sorry about my clothes."

"Don't you worry, I'll take care of it. Which suit would you like to wear today?"

"Did you really think I was in bed with His Lordship, Florence?"

"Oh, I couldn't say!"

"Yes, you can."

"Well, you *did* look like you were enjoying each other's company."

"I suppose we were. Would I have shocked you?"

"No, not at all."

"You amaze me, Florence, tell me what you're thinking."

"Oh no, it's not my place to make such comments, I'm sure."

"You might as well say it, as think it. Besides, I would like to know."

"Well, if the truth be told, I know you like Mr Norton, and he is lovely isn't he, but I think you and His Lordship were made for each other. That's what I think."

"Oh my, you do surprise me! But surely you realise a woman from Stepney could never become a countess."

"I suppose you're right, but we can dream, can't we?"

"We certainly can, Florence. Talking of which, how is your young man?"

"He's wonderful, his letters are amazing. I told him - after the war he really must become a writer. I can't wait for him to come home."

"You really love him, don't you?"

"He's all I can think about, so I suppose I must do. I just want him back."

She suddenly looked sad and turned away from me. I had seen that look so often when people described their loved one who was serving in the forces. The anxiety was only ever just beneath the surface. It only took a single word, or a stray thought, for a happy feeling to be quickly vanquished. The sense of dread which replaced it was an unbearable burden.

Florence soon picked herself up, but I knew so well how she felt. Eventually I joined Edward and Caroline for a slice of toast, though I was not quite sure I could manage even that. Edward looked decidedly jaded, despite being his usual immaculate self.

"Good morning, Lily, how do you feel this morning?"

"Morning Edward, morning Caroline. I confess I have, occasionally, felt better!"

"Yes. I think I know what you mean. I was just telling Mother about your remarkable performance last night. Do you know, Lily, I have heard nothing like that before, I don't think there was a dry eye in the building. You have such a beautiful voice, but to use that voice as you did last night, well, it was such a privilege to be a part of it!"

"Edward, what a wonderful thing to say, but I think you will find that Cole had an awful lot to do with it. He didn't just build me up for the performance; he built up the audience. He knew exactly what he was doing, but it worked for me; I've never sung like that before."

"I don't think anyone there last night will ever forget it," Edward said.

"Do you know, Lily, he hasn't stopped talking about it this morning," Caroline said. "I so wish I had been there."

"It was a rowdy evening, Caroline. I'm sure you would have found Edward's behaviour deplorable!" I said, smiling. "But I'll be pleased to sing the song for you one evening."

We both managed a cup of tea and a slice of toast, and with the memory of our night out fresh in our minds, it all felt more like a slice of peacetime normality.

Inevitably, it couldn't last. As Edward glanced at his watch, I gulped my last mouthful of tea, and we both stood up from the table.

-o0o-

Come the Autumn of 1943, military planners confirmed our landing beaches between Cherbourg and Caen. Originally three, they expanded the number to five, and now we had our five code names - Utah, Omaha, Gold, Juno, and Sword. We continued reconnaissance, because we needed to know every grain of sand and blade of grass on those beaches. Above all, we needed to pinpoint every German position and gun emplacement. And now we were also concerned with German infrastructure, and how to sabotage it.

SOE, with all its Sections, had far-reaching capabilities, but all the while the secrecy limited what we could share. We were the only Section which knew where and when D-Day would take place, and this made centralised planning difficult.

F section (France) was the largest SOE Section by far, but crucially most of the networks relied upon the FR. The risk was considerable that captured Resistance fighters might talk which, together with the fear of infiltrators, meant the SOE had to plan its D-Day tactics without knowing where or when that might be.

Although our remit only extended a maximum of ten miles beyond the beachhead, we alone knew where the Germans would have to respond following D-Day. Woody now devoted considerable time on planning various scenarios following the invasion. What would the German response be and critically, where would it come from, and how could we disrupt it?

There was only so much that we could do with our limited resources, so decisions had to be made. We needed to have the full capability of SOE, and especially F Section, brought to bear on the invasion, but we could not tell them where or when.

Edward and I set up a meeting with the head of SOE, Major General Colin Gubbins, and between us we planned the way forward. We would designate an area around the landing sites as our most secret and critical. Then, going further out within areas of ever-increasing radius, we would gradually reduce that critical designation. We had to ensure that RAF or SOE operations did not inadvertently draw disproportionate attention to the Normandy beaches.

Finally, there were time-critical operations which had to be actioned just moments before, or else during the landings. We had to work on the worst-case scenario that all operations with the French Resistance might be compromised, and so no operation must of itself be capable of giving the Germans vital knowledge about D-Day.

Edward had difficulty putting his full trust in FR. He was aware of intelligence reports detailing the full extent of the Vichy Government's collaboration with the Germans. Petain's dictatorship was not just subjugated to the Nazi ideology;

intelligence showed that Petain's regime *shared* that ideology.

Almost immediately, his Government had decided of its own volition to round up those it considered undesirable, such as Jews, Romanies and Communists. They held these people in internment camps which would eventually become transit camps for the Nazi extermination programme.

SOE couldn't operate without the brave and loyal support of the French Resistance movement, who were themselves bitterly opposed to the Vichy Government. The problem, as Edward explained, was the fragmented nature of the FR in a country where loyalties were divided.

We decided that our own agents alone would carry out operations in the critical zone. While the FR's involvement would be essential, they would not be told about the invasion details until it was almost in motion. Our job was now to orchestrate clandestine operations through Gubbins, so that they could put the full weight of SOE behind the invasion effort.

The scale of our operation was such that we all agreed we should completely step away from active involvement in the misinformation and deception effort. We had no option but to leave it entirely to the London Controlling Section (LCS) which was the secret body set up to operate the Allied deception strategy.

Edward was slightly disappointed. Our team of 'boffins' had been chosen because of their ability to think 'outside the box', but the scale of the deception operation was beyond our limited capability. Our strong links with the LCS remained in place, and we continued in an advisory capacity.

Both Edward and General Gubbins agreed that we should designate the Pas de Calais as the English Channel landing site for deception purposes, as well as Norway. 'Operation Fortitude' as they codenamed it, was divided into two deception strategies - north and south. 'Fortitude' would be another of the great successes of the war.

Our autonomy within SOE had worked well up to that point, but now that operations were to become more proactive, we both realised that we needed the full reach of SOE and Bomber Command. I had not met General Gubbins in person before, but Edward knew him and had nothing but praise, saying he was the right man, in the right job, at exactly the right time.

I came away from that meeting with Gubbins finally believing that an end to the war really was in sight. Edward and I had never once spoken about the war ending. Neither of us had thought beyond our own task, but as Edward drove us back from the meeting, I mentioned it.

"Do you ever think about life after the war, Edward?"

"I don't think I have thought about anything *but* the war since it started. I can't imagine things will ever be the same again."

"I agree, I don't see how it could be, except we'll not be trying to kill one another!"

"You're right, that's the very definition of peace. I just hope the Nation can redirect all that collective spirit and energy towards peace. The road to recovery will be a long one."

"I'm not sure everyone will be able to. Where I used to live has been completely destroyed in places, and so many have died. I'm afraid the community has died with them, never to return."

"I fear that may well be the case, but never underestimate the power of the human spirit. Just look at what we have achieved at Middlebourne."

"What do you think you'll do, Edward, when Station M is finally wound up?"

"I've not thought about it, but logically, I will have to bring the estate into a sustainable condition for the future. What about you, Lily, have you given the future any thought?"

"Not until this moment, no, I have no idea what the future holds for me. I no longer have a past, so my future will be something new."

He didn't answer, so I sat thinking about what I'd just said. I really had no idea what the future held for me, but in my heart of hearts, I couldn't imagine a life without Edward. I had unintentionally given him the opportunity to comment upon the future, or perhaps even of *our* future, but he chose not to respond.

I tried to convince myself that I was overreacting, but I so wanted him to tell me that my future was at Middlebourne. When he didn't, I felt rejected and miserable. There was so much Station M business to discuss and it was foolish of me to have let such thoughts enter my mind, but once I had, it was difficult to dismiss them.

Chapter Twenty-Six
Girls' Night Out

The last few weeks of 1943 seemed to race by. We were all in a state of heightened anticipation, with a distinct feeling that the sand in the hourglass was running out. Military planners were busy completing every detail of the invasion, and since all of it hinged upon our intelligence, there was not a person in Station M who did not feel the heavy burden of that responsibility. Our response was to check and recheck every detail, so our agents were spending ever-increasing time across the Channel. I worried continually about Dotty. For all that she thought she was invincible, I knew she was not.

One evening, not long before Christmas, Dotty had two days before she was going back across the Channel. The missions were becoming longer and longer. She had no idea when she would be back and suggested a girls' night out. It had been such a long time since any of us had found time to just talk together by ourselves, all four of us agreed immediately.

As the only place in the village where people could relax and socialise, the pub was very much an oasis. Stepping through the door was like entering another era, where the war, if it existed at all, was in another place and time. We walked in together with the feeling that here, at least, we could forget the build-up towards D-Day. It was still early, and the pub was quiet, so we acknowledged the one or two people we recognised and headed for the bar.

"Evening ladies, what's all this then, a girls' night out?" asked Roger the landlord.

"It certainly is, Rog," replied Dotty, "let's have four of your finest."

"Coming up, ladies. You sit down and I'll bring them over to you."

We sat at one of the round tables near to the fire. We were just close enough to enjoy the warmth, but far enough away to avoid the occasional downdraft which would send a waft of smoke into the room. Roger came over with a tray of beers and placed them in front of us, signalling the start of our evening. He put another log on the fire, which momentarily crackled and sent sparks in search of the chimney. We all smiled; everything was as it should be.

"It's just another world, isn't it?" Dotty said. "No-one here could even imagine what we do."

"I know," replied Fiona, "but you don't have to be so happy about it, Dotty."

"Well, why not, someone has to do what we do, so why not be cheerful about it?"

"It's the gravity of it all. Does it never worry you, Dotty?" asked Maggie.

"No, never, I've never felt more alive."

"Well, there are days when it gets on top of me, I can tell you," replied Maggie, "and I'm not the one taking the risk."

"Maggie's right, Dotty," said Fiona, "you take all the risks, we don't."

"I only risk my *own* life, and I'm damned careful about it. You girls risk other people's lives, so don't tell me I've got more to worry about; I couldn't shoulder your kind of responsibility."

"Be that as it may, Dotty, please be careful," I said. "You act as if you have nothing to lose, and that's not the case, is it?"

"You're always worrying about me, Lily, but you shouldn't. If I had someone like Johnny, maybe I'd lose my edge, but I've only got myself to worry about. When I'm over there, I'm really alive, I seem to be able to think and act twice as fast."

"You talk as if you miss it when you're not over there," Maggie said.

"Maybe I do. You're not complete without Johnny, are you Fi, and look at you and Patrick, Maggie, you come alive when you're together."

"I suppose that's right," Maggie said.

"Well, it's the same for me, I need the adrenalin."

"But we're not taking such a risk, Dotty," Fiona said.

"I'm not so sure about that. What about when Johnny was shot down, Fi? I've never seen anyone suffer as much pain as you did that day. We all take a risk, one way or another."

"That's very philosophical, Dotty," I said.

"Crikey, that's another of your long words, Lily, I must remember that one, what does it mean?"

"You know full well what it means! We've caught you out being serious about something for once."

"Bugger! Looks like I'm bang to rights."

We all laughed, but Dotty hadn't finished being serious. She had a twinkle in her eye.

"Talking about risk, this thing between you and Patrick. You're a married woman, Maggie, this could end in disaster for you."

Maggie appeared quite taken aback, but it was impossible to take offence at whatever Dotty said. She thought about it for a moment before replying.

"You're right, Dotty, but don't think for a second that I don't have my eyes open. I didn't intend for any of this to happen; it just did. There's something between us that's bigger than both of us. I've experienced nothing like it before, and neither has Patrick, but don't think it doesn't torment me every hour of every day. I remind myself I was never happy in my marriage, I tell myself it was always a mistake, but still the torment never goes away. I just have one overriding fear. If I had the strength to walk away from Patrick, I'd probably never feel this way again, and I would spend the rest of my life regretting it."

"For what it's worth, Maggie," I said, "I think you should follow your heart whatever the consequences; but how can you be so sure it isn't just a wartime infatuation?"

"Do you think we haven't considered that? You know how Patrick's brain works; he thinks of everything. We've made the decision that we'll wait and see what happens after the war, and if we feel the same, then I'll get a divorce."

"There's not a shred of doubt in your mind, though, is there, Maggie?" I said. "You're doing the sensible thing by not rushing into anything, but you've decided, haven't you? It takes a lot of courage to make a decision like that, I do admire you for it. Let's drink a toast to Maggie and Patrick."

We all raised our glasses, and Maggie looked positively relieved.

"I've been wanting to tell you about this for ages. It's been so difficult trying to pretend it was something other than it is. I'm pleased it's all out in the open."

Dotty was looking more mischievous than ever as she turned towards me.

"So let me see now. Fi can't live without Johnny, Maggie can't live without Patrick, and we all know about me, so what is it you can't live without, Lily?"

"I think I'm a bit like you, Dotty, I need the challenge and the excitement. I need to be achieving something."

"Have you always been like that?" asked Fiona.

"No, certainly not when I was a schoolgirl. It probably started when I went to work for my Uncle George."

"Tell us more, Lily. How did you get started on your career?" asked Maggie.

"Not much to tell, really Maggie, I'm sure you wouldn't be interested."

"No actually, Lily, I *am* interested, please tell us," she said.

"Well, really it's entirely down to my Uncle George."

"That's Uncle George who isn't *really* Uncle George, that's right, isn't it, Lily?" said Dotty beaming.

"You're right," I said smiling back at Dotty. "He was like a second father to me, and he took it upon himself to further my education. He arranged for me to go to boarding school. And then when I didn't want to go on to university, he offered me a job in his shipping agency. It was on my second day when he sat me down in his office. He gave me a cup of tea, and he talked to me like no-one had ever talked to me before. I'll never forget it.

He said, 'What do you think you would have achieved Lily, if I hadn't taken you under my wing?' Well, the only thing I was ever good at was singing. I knew apart from that I was just another no-hope East End girl, so I admitted it. 'And do you know why Lily?' he said, 'it's all about expectation. You looked at the girls around you and you saw your own future. You didn't expect to achieve anything in life, so you didn't try; you let yourself down! When I sent you to a boarding school, I made you promise to work hard, and to do it for me, do you remember?'

I remembered and told him I worked so hard at boarding school because I couldn't bear the thought of letting him down. That was when he said something which really changed my life. He said, 'You might have thought you were doing it for me Lily, but I only gave you the motivation, you did it for yourself. Everything in life you aim for is determined by your expectation of success; you mustn't let your self-doubts limit your expectations, Lily. You were born with a wonderful gift. If other people crawl, *you* can walk; if they walk, you can *run*; if they run, Lily, you can *fly*. The only thing holding you back is *you*. It's not the world you have to conquer Lily, it's your own demons'."

"Wow, that's a profound thing to say to a teenager!" said Maggie.

"It certainly was! It was the bit about how I had let myself down, and how I had to conquer my demons which seemed to get through to me. And so I've been trying to beat my demons ever since."

"Did you believe him?" asked Maggie.

"I did, I really did. I always trusted Uncle George implicitly. If he said it was, then it was. He taught me everything about the shipping business, and much more besides. His confidence in me seemed limitless. Every time a challenge presented itself, he would say 'you can do it, Lily,' and because I believed him, I did it. I quickly realised that I owed everything to George. I loved him like a father, and do you know what motivated me the most? It was the prospect of letting him down.

It never mattered what it was - if he trusted me to succeed, then I would move heaven and earth to achieve whatever it was. The prospect of letting George down was inconceivable to me. It was only much later when I came to realise the real lesson that he so skilfully taught me. George would have forgiven me anything; the real lesson was that I have to value myself, because then it becomes important not to let *yourself* down."

"Is this part of what motivates you here at Station M?" asked Dotty. "Is it all about not letting Edward down?"

"My word, you *are* being serious tonight, Dotty! I've not thought about it, but I suppose you're right. When Edward chose me for this role, he put his complete faith in me. So you *are* right, Dotty, I would go to the ends of the earth for him, I'll never let him down."

"Nobody can succeed at everything, Lily," said Fiona, "there must be many occasions when you might have done things better."

"Oh lots of times, but there's only been one significant occasion when I feel I've let someone down, and of all people that was my Gran. It was George who paid for my singing lessons and introduced me to the opera, but it's Gran who is so wonderfully talented musically. It's just luck that I've been fortunate enough to inherit some of that ability from her. She inspired me, she pushed and encouraged me to sing. According to Gran and my voice coach, I could have become a professional soprano if I had continued my training."

"Doesn't sound to me as if you need any more singing lessons, Lily," said Dotty. "I've never heard anyone sing like you."

"I wish it were true Dotty, but I'm a long way short of being an opera singer. When I started to work for George, my lessons became limited to when I visited Gran at the weekend, and eventually I was told I'd have to decide between a career as a singer, or a career in shipping. George was right, it's all about your expectations, and I wasn't mature enough to make that decision. All I knew was that I would have to disappoint either George or Gran. How many opera singers do you know who came from the East End of London? I could think of none, so I had no confidence; I just assumed I couldn't do it. That was when I realised how disappointed I'd made Gran. I'd failed her, let her down, and I've never been able to forgive myself for that."

"You're allowing an obsession to get the better of you, Lily," Fiona said. "When you sang 'Un bel di Vedremo' for Gran last Christmas, do you seriously think she was in floods of tears because you'd let her down? Her pride in you knows no bounds, stop being so hard on yourself."

"Maybe you're right, Fi, maybe I'm just still chasing my demons."

"I think you are Lily. If only you could see yourself as others see you, you'd love that person, Lily."

"We really are being serious tonight," Dotty said, "looks like Fi's got you there, Lily."

"Well, it takes friends like you to get through to me sometimes! I need telling, Fi."

"I'll tell you another thing Lily," Fiona said, "you need never worry about letting Edward down. You make such a brilliant team, the pair of you. I see it every day, and I swear sometimes I think you both share the same brain."

"Now there's a thought," said Dotty. "Is it your brain or His Lordship's that you share?"

"Seriously, Lily, how do you cope with someone who has an intellect like Edward's?" asked Maggie. "Or any of the boys in Hut 3 for that matter. Patrick's the same, they're all so damned clever!"

"I know what you mean, Maggie. I asked Edward once how the scrambler phone worked, and he knew all there was to know about it. They each have their own particular genius, but I think it often comes at the expense of something else. Edward appears to know everything, but then the next moment he can't see or understand something that, to you or me, is just obvious common sense."

"Yes, Patrick does that. We can walk down the road together, and whatever we see, he can tell me about it, and yet he's just as likely to fall down a hole in the pavement! He says I'm his eyes and ears in the real world."

"Oh, what a lovely thing to say, I think you'd better hang on to him, Maggie."

"I think I will, and will you hang on to Edward, Lily?"

"Oh dear, that's put me on the spot."

"Well, we all want to know," said Dotty.

"I think that's something private between Edward and Lily," said Fiona. "I don't think we need to know."

"But *I* need to know," said an increasingly mischievous Dotty.

"There isn't much to know," I said, "personal feelings and duty are different things for Edward. Above all else, he's the Ninth Earl of Middlebourne. It predetermined his future the day he was born."

"Come on, Lily, be honest. You're gooey-eyed over him, you always have been."

"Dotty, you're incorrigible."

"That's another big word I must try to remember. If it means that I need to know, then yes, I'm incorrigible. Come on, Lily, tell us."

"Oh, for goodness' sake, Dotty! I think he is the most wonderful man I've ever met - okay? I wish I could say there was more to it, but we have different futures ahead of us, so I try not to think beyond that."

I could see from the look in her eyes that Dotty wasn't about to leave it at that.

"And so where does Greg fit into this? You're gooey-eyed over him as well!"

Fiona interrupted on my behalf. "I work with them both every day, Dotty. I know this is not easy for Lily. I think it's best if you leave it at that."

Fiona had an air of authority about her. When she said it was best if Dotty left it at that, it wasn't a suggestion.

"When do you and Johnny plan to get married, Fi?" asked Maggie.

"He would marry me today, but I thought we should wait until after the war is over. But if he keeps asking me, I might have to change my mind."

"Well, why not?" I asked.

"I suppose it's silly really, it's his family you see. They're terribly well-to-do, and I just get the feeling they look down on me a bit. I can't bear the thought that they think I just need to snare him before anything….. you know if anything happened to him."

"I don't understand," said Dotty. "You never say arse, you say bottom, so you're also terribly well-to-do, Fi. What's the problem, how long does it take to organise a wedding, anyway?"

"Dotty, really! This is for Fi to decide," I exclaimed.

"No, I'm sure Dotty's right, Lily. His parents shouldn't intimidate me. It's his father, really; even though he's retired, he still insists on being called Air Commodore."

"But we deal with people like that all the time, Fi. Why should *he* intimidate you?" I asked.

"I don't know, he just does."

"Perhaps I should pay him a visit," Dotty said, with a menacing look.

"Don't you dare, you'd frighten the life out of him," replied Fiona.

"Just imagine if the silly man knew what you do here, Fi! The boot would be on the other foot."

"You're never intimidated by anyone, Lily. How do you do that?"

"If only you knew! I'm always being intimidated by people, it's an enormous problem for me. I just try hard not to show it. Normally, if I know what I'm talking about, that's enough, but there are some people - especially the military types - where I need something more. George gave me a wonderful piece of advice one day when I had to go to a meeting with a shipowner. He said I should imagine the person in a very compromised position, whatever suited that situation. You might imagine a very well-dressed formal man with no clothes on. One of my favourite visions was a revolting drunk who'd been sick; that always worked for me."

"I've seen you do that," replied Fiona. "Do you remember that ghastly man from procurement, the one who thought he was God's gift to women. He was trying so hard to flatter you, he was awful, and the look on your face - the poor man melted on the spot!"

"What did you say, Lily?" asked Dotty.

"I'll tell you what she said," replied Fiona. "She said, 'I haven't got time for this inane drivel Mr Broadbent. I'm sure you're charming, but I fail to see it. Would you mind leaving my office, so I can get on'."

We all sat laughing, which drew the attention of a man sitting at a table near to us. He got up and walked over to us. I think we all assumed our laughter had incurred his displeasure, and I braced myself to fend him off.

"Which compromising thought are you going to use, Lily?" asked Maggie. "I think the drunk covered in vomit sounds a wonderful idea."

The man came and stood at our table, and I braced myself for some kind of abuse.

"Excuse me, ladies," he said politely, "it's Mrs Heywood, isn't it?"

"Yes, it is," I replied curtly.

"I was in the pub the other night when you sang 'Over the Rainbow'. May I say you moved me to tears with your rendition? Is there any possibility you might sing it again for us tonight?"

"That's extremely gracious of you to say so, but I'm just having a quiet night with my friends."

"Come on, Lily, sing it for us again, come on," Dotty was not about to be refused.

One song turned into another, and then another, and I must say I really enjoyed it. I saved 'Over the Rainbow' until last, and my reception was almost the same as the first time I sang it. We left the pub on a real high that night.

Chapter Twenty-Seven
The Marriage Contender

The next time I sang that song was on Christmas Day, especially for Caroline as I had promised. My parents couldn't come to Gran's for Christmas, which was a total break with tradition. They needed to stay with Dad's sister, my Aunty Helen. She had been very unwell for some time; sadly they knew it was to be their last opportunity to see her. I didn't really want to break with tradition either, but Edward wanted me to meet his Christmas guests, and I seemed to be incapable of not doing what he wanted. I told myself it was just the one day, and I would go back to Gran and the girls for Boxing Day. After I'd accepted his invitation, I questioned why I did so. Not knowing any of the guests, I feared it would be a repeat of the previous New Year's Eve; I'd be ill at ease and feeling as if I was being put on display.

Florence was more excited about it than I was. She couldn't wait to get my fabulous evening dress out of the wardrobe.

"Which shoes, Mrs Heywood, I think these high heels?"

"If you say so, Florence."

"Your hair looks wonderful up like this. It really shows off your ruby earrings that His Lordship gave you."

"How did you know His Lordship gave them to me?"

"I couldn't think of anyone else who could have afforded them!"

"Well, you guessed right, they're lovely, aren't they?"

"I've never seen earrings like it, and they look so good on you."

"You're a real boost to my confidence, Florence."

"This necklace is lovely, but what you really need is a ruby necklace to match the earrings; perhaps His Lordship will give you one as a Christmas present."

"Do you know something about this that you aren't telling me?"

"Only that His Lordship asked me about your necklaces, that's all."

"Talking of presents, this one is for you, Florence."

"For me - is it from you?"

"Yes, of course it is, open it."

I knew Florence liked clothes. She had a good eye for fashion, but a girl from her background had little opportunity to express herself. So I had Caroline's dressmaker create a beautiful dress which she could wear for a special night out with her young man. I wrapped it in lovely Christmas paper, and could see she was very unused to being given nice presents. She kept looking at it and then glancing up at me, seemingly in disbelief that it was actually for *her*. Finally, she unwrapped it slowly and delicately, and I could see the excitement in her eyes. When she finally saw what it was, her reaction was one of the highlights of my Christmas Day.

"Oh my goodness! This is for *me,* you bought this for me?"

"Not exactly, no, I had it made for you especially. I took the measurements from your other clothes, so I hope it fits really well."

Florence was overcome. Obviously, she could never have looked seriously at such an expensive dress for herself but more than that, I doubt anyone had ever given her a lovely present before. The poor girl was speechless, her eyes welling up, and she didn't know what to do or say.

"Well, do you like it?"

Still unable to say anything, she just put her arms around me, and stood there crying on my shoulder.

"I didn't expect a reaction like this, Florence! I thought you would be happy."

"I am, Lily. This is me being the happiest I've ever been."

I made light of her remark, and her tears soon turned to laughter as she realised how she had reacted. The fact remained that her remark was very telling. The poor girl had come from a background where that kind of happiness was measured with a very short yardstick. Eventually, she must have said 'thank you' a dozen times.

"You must try it on."

"You mean now?"

"Of course I mean now, why not, you know you want to."

Not knowing what a teenager would like, I had taken the dressmaker's advice regarding the fashion and fabrics. When Florence put it on, not only did it fit her like a glove, it was perfect. When she saw herself in the mirror, I could tell she couldn't believe the reflection greeting her. As she looked at me, her eyes widened into the most wonderful smile, and then she turned to look back at her reflection. I'm not sure which of us was the more overwhelmed - Florence by the sight of her own reflection, or me by the sheer joy that her reaction had given me.

"Florence, you look wonderful, I knew you would. Seeing you standing there wearing this dress, well, you really look lovely."

"I still don't know what to say, Mrs Heywood."

"You don't need to say anything, Florence. You've made this such a happy Christmas for me."

And so there we were, both of us dressed up in our finery. Except she had nowhere to go.

"When is Harry home on leave, when can you wear this for him?" I asked her.

"I don't know, he's still somewhere in North Africa."

"Why don't you wear it for your Christmas lunch below-stairs?"

"No, I couldn't! Mr Jennings would go mad if I didn't have my uniform on."

"You tell Mr Jennings that I insist. If he doesn't like it, he must come and see me. But for goodness' sake, wear a pinny for the meal, and don't spill any food on it! Now, run along; oh and one more thing, when you have your Christmas lunch, you're not to worry about Mr Jennings; put on a little eye makeup, and some lipstick."

She hugged and thanked me yet again before she hurried off. I hardly recognised her as she walked away wearing the dress, looking so much more mature than her seventeen years.

"Have a wonderful day, Mrs Heywood," she said.

"I will, and don't forget what I said about Mr Jennings!"

As I approached the Drawing Room, I was unable to suppress a smile, thinking about Florence. Her reaction to my present really would be one of the highlights of my Christmas. She was not alone, however, in feeling good about wearing a lovely dress. I knew I would make quite an impression when I entered the Drawing Room. William smiled approvingly as he opened the door for me, and Edward sprang to his feet, greeting me with an enormous smile.

"May I be permitted to say, you look beautiful, Lily."

"I will permit you to say that Edward, as long as you mean it."

"Do you remember New Year's Eve last year when you walked into this room? You struck me speechless, and once again I made a fool of myself in your presence. I've been determined not to do that again."

"You're not very good with these things, are you, Edward?"

"You're right, I'm not, but be assured I mean it. You look breath-taking tonight."

"I think this is progress, Edward! Now stop smiling at me and introduce me to your guests.

As soon as the formalities were over, Jennings offered me a glass of champagne.

"Thank you, Mr Jennings. When you see Florence, will you make a point of telling her how lovely she looks?" I whispered.

"I don't understand, Mrs Heywood."

"Trust me, Mr Jennings, you soon will."

Edward looked at me in astonishment. "I won't even ask," he said with another enormous smile. He was always immensely considerate on occasions like that. I knew none of the guests, and his attention made me feel like a princess rather than his Chief of Staff.

The guests were all charming, but one was especially so. Lady Beatrice, daughter of Lord and Lady Stratton, was there. She was conspicuous for all the wrong reasons - I could understand why she was the frontrunner as far as Edward's likely marriage prospects were concerned. In her mid-twenties, she was excessively attractive and self-confident. Furthermore, I thought she was overly attentive towards Edward, so I immediately hated the woman!

I always felt on such occasions that I was something of a curiosity. I was dressed up to the nines but could see from their expressions I hadn't conformed to their stereotypical image of a Chief of Staff. To their credit, they were much more polite and approachable than the previous New Year's Eve guests. I was relieved, though, when luncheon was announced; small talk was always so difficult when I could tell them so little about what I did. Cook had prepared the most wonderful Christmas meal, and Jennings and the two footmen looked magnificent as they served us with grace and style. Jennings whispered in my ear as he topped up my glass.

"I carried out your instructions, Mrs Heywood, regarding Florence."

When he returned with my first course, I beckoned him to come close so I could whisper in his ear.

"Did you mean it, Mr Jennings, was it a sincere compliment?"

He had to restrain himself from laughing, but as always, he maintained his usual dignified splendour.

"Yes indeed, Mrs Heywood," he said, "I think you would approve of the outcome."

"Is there a problem I need to be aware of, Jennings?" asked Edward.

"Quite the reverse, My Lord. Mrs Heywood was just ensuring things run smoothly today."

Edward knew I had been up to something, but his complete acceptance of the way I treated his staff was very generous. Such a break with tradition was no slight thing for him. The guests knew I ran the household and knew Edward referred to me as his Chief of Staff. They also knew something unusual was going on at the Manor, something connected with the military. Beyond that, they knew nothing, which made me even more of a curiosity. I seemed to be the centre of attention, probably because Edward and Caroline never missed an opportunity to promote me. Lady Beatrice was slightly prickly, and I was slow to realise why. She had a good rapport with Edward - I had been trying hard to deny that fact - they obviously had a long-standing friendship.

"How long have you known Edward, Lady Beatrice?"

"How long have I *not* known him? And do just call me Beatrice. How long have you been here now, Lily?"

"It's about two-and-a-half years now, I'm surprised we haven't met before."

"Do you know, I haven't been here since last Christmas, I can't believe it. I've met Edward in London a few times, and he came to Stratton Hall during the summer for an all too brief visit. Whatever it is you do here, it has quite taken him away from me."

"I'm afraid it's the war," I said politely.

"I get the feeling you're not going to tell me exactly what it is that you and Edward do here. Edward certainly won't tell me."

"No, I'm sorry, I can't."

"Top secret, ah, how exciting! What I can't really under-stand is your position here, Lily. Edward says you are his Chief of Staff, but here you are like a member of the family."

"Yes, I know, I find it confusing myself at times. All I can say is that Edward and I work long hours, and we work closely together."

"I'm going to say something I probably shouldn't, so please don't take offence, Lily. When you say you work closely with Edward, just how close is that?"

Suddenly I realised the purpose of our conversation. She was not just a contender - she had serious ambitions towards Edward! She was younger than me, excessively attractive, and my hackles rose. She was also a Lady, and I was a member of staff, so I felt very much on the defensive. However, I remained determined not to do or say anything which could cause an embarrassment.

"I understand completely, Beatrice, I'm not offended. Edward and I do not have the kind of relationship that might be of concern for you."

"Now I feel a fool for asking, Lily. I'm sorry, but you see we are betrothed, and in these difficult times - well - you know."

"Betrothed, you mean you are engaged?"

"Not exactly engaged, no, but it's an understanding. I can't believe Edward has not spoken about me."

I didn't know what to say. My heart was racing. With hind-sight, she was not being objectionable. In other circumstances, I would probably have liked the woman, but at that moment I hated her even more. You only realise you've behaved irra-tionally when you return to rationality, and I was in such a turmoil! I managed to not say anything to make me look even more ridiculous, but I felt I had sent a clear signal to Beatrice, and possibly to other guests.

The kitchen staff had done a superb job producing a magnificent Christmas lunch, and Jennings and the footmen made everything even more impressive. I noticed how young Albert had matured into his job, and it was nice to see how Jennings had taken him under his wing. We all retired to the Drawing Room, where I made a point of asking Jennings to compliment the kitchen staff.

"Yes, indeed," Edward said, "please extend our thanks below-stairs."

"I think it's time to open our presents," Caroline said with an excited smile.

She picked them up from beneath the tree and handed them around the room, apologising that not all the guests had one. She handed Beatrice and me a little present each.

"I hope you like it, Lily," Caroline said.

As I pulled back the wrapping paper, it revealed a bottle of Femme de Rochas Perfume. I looked at it wide-eyed.

"Don't ask me how I acquired it, Lily, but I think you will love it."

Beatrice received the same perfume; she was equally thrilled. It was sublime; we both had to walk around the room as everyone wanted to smell the back of our hands. I hugged Caroline tightly, and thanked her as I handed her my present. I noticed Beatrice was not as effusive in her appreciation as I was. My present to Caroline was a pair of fine leather gloves, which she seemed to greatly appreciate.

Beatrice enthusiastically handed Edward a present.

"I do hope you like it," she said, as she sat back down again.

Edward smiled and spent a moment trying to guess what it was. When he finally pulled open the wrapping paper, it revealed a nice cardigan in autumn colours.

"How lovely, thank you Beatrice, I can always use another cardigan."

I watched intently to see how enthusiastically he might thank her, but he remained seated. I was still firmly locked into my irrational state of mind and felt like punching the air when I saw that!

I'd gone to an inordinate amount of trouble to find Edward's present. It was an exceedingly rare first edition book and had cost me an absolute fortune. He had more books in the library than I could throw a stick at, but he kept a small section for his obsession with rare first editions. I knew he would love what I had found for him. It was "In Our Time," by Ernest Hemingway, published in 1924, and only 170 copies were released and sold.

I had been so looking forward to giving Edward his present, but suddenly everything was different. The presence of Lady Beatrice had caused the magic to seep out of the book, taking my enthusiasm with it. I handed him the present without the generous smile that would normally have accompanied it.

As he peeled back the wrapping paper, it gradually revealed more of the book's title and author. He absorbed each detail in a process of discovery, becoming more and more animated with each revelation. Finally, he was quite beside himself. Jumping up, he came over to me and enthusiastically hugged me and kissed my cheek in front of his guests. This was being terribly demonstrative for Edward!

"Does this mean you like it, Edward?" I asked.

"Do I *like* it, Lily my dear, this is magnificent! What a treasure, thank you so much."

Turning the pages with reverence, he looked like a little boy with his first train set.

"I think he likes it," I said happily.

Beatrice sat impassively, but I knew she was seething.

"I hope my humble present to you can compare in some small way," he said.

He handed me a thin flat box from his pocket. I held it excitedly. Edward was staring at me, obviously waiting to see my reaction. Then he seemed to have second thoughts.

"Actually, it's only a slight thing. I intended to give it to you later; perhaps you might leave it for the moment."

I noticed that he looked uncomfortable, but I had no reason to think his request was serious.

"It's too late now, Edward, however small it is, you know I'll appreciate it."

As I pulled back the wrapping paper, I could see it was a jewellery box, and I looked up at him before I lifted the lid. It was the most fabulous choker necklace, pearls with a central ruby and diamond jewel which matched my earrings. I was completely taken aback; I just didn't know what to do or say in front of the guests. I just sat there, feeling almost paralysed with indecision. All I wanted to do was to throw myself into his arms and kiss him, but obviously that would not be the thing to do.

All the while, I was conscious of Beatrice looking at the necklace, and my reaction to it. I think it was the combined effect of the wonderful necklace, of not feeling able to express how I felt in front of the guests, and Beatrice. My eyes welled up, and I had to reach for my handkerchief.

"Thank you, Edward," I said, "I'm speechless."

I walked over to him and put my hand on his shoulder and kissed his cheek. It was utterly ridiculous; I desperately wanted to thank him like he had never been thanked before. Instead I gave him a genteel kiss on his cheek.

Beatrice opened her present from Edward, to find it was another bottle of expensive perfume. In any other circumstances, it would have been a lovely present, but having not asked his mother what she was giving Beatrice, it proved to be an unfortunate error. Beatrice was singularly unimpressed. She didn't move from her chair, and just politely thanked Edward.

"Look at what Edward has given me, Caroline, isn't it magnificent?"

"It's beautiful, Lily, and I can see what it means to you, my dear."

She unfastened the necklace I was wearing and placed Edward's present around my neck, something that Edward should have done. She squeezed my hand, and her lovely smile told a thousand words - if only I knew what they *were!*

Beatrice looked at the necklace. And if looks could kill, I would have died that instant. I thought she would storm out of the room, but to her immense credit, she didn't, though her displeasure was palpable.

I felt trapped in an inexplicable situation of my own making, as I stood there dressed in a fabulous evening gown, wearing diamonds, rubies, and pearls. I had become the only centre of attention in a room full of Lords, Ladies, and dignitaries, in every respect looking like the Lady of the Manor. In every respect but one - I was essentially a salaried member of staff, the woman from Stepney, an imposter. Sitting in front of me was Lady Beatrice, a very real reminder that there was no substitute for authenticity.

It was one of those excruciating moments, my inner demons having been given full rein to torment me. If the ground had opened up and swallowed me, I would have offered no resistance. I felt sure Caroline empathised with my position; I couldn't explain her immense kindness toward me in any other way. She noticed my moment of introspection, as she so often did, and once again, came to my assistance.

"Lily, you promised you would sing for me. Is now a convenient time?"

Caroline had metaphorically opened the ground for me, offering me a place where I could retreat and hide away from my insecurity.

"It is Caroline, I'd love to sing for you."

I eagerly grasped at her suggestion, and Edward escorted me to the piano. There was a hush in the room. I suspected the guests thought a woman from Stepney singing was probably an embarrassment to be politely endured, as they looked at each other with reserved smiles.

First, I told them the story about our wonderful night at the Forge Pub, and how Cole introduced me to his arrangement of the song. I think I might have deliberately misdirected them, leaving them expecting a bawdy pub sing-along!

"And so this is Cole's arrangement of 'Over the Rainbow' and - Lady Caroline - I would like to sing this especially for you."

It is hard to assess your own singing performance. It was difficult to capture the same emotion that Cole had created, but I put my heart into the crescendo, and when I had sung the last verse, there was a brief moment of silence, which I'd already learned was an excellent sign. The guests then rose to their feet and applauded rapturously. Beatrice remained seated and clapped politely while Caroline walked over and put her arms around me.

"Lily, you have made me cry, my dear. That was wonderful!"

Chapter Twenty-Eight
1944 The Opening Months

While the lot of the average person had not in any way improved, they welcomed 1944 with a feeling of optimism. For us at Station M, the optimism was rarefied, diluted by the certain knowledge that, if anything went horribly wrong, it was likely to be our fault. It was a period of introspection for us, a time when a single stray thought could easily develop into a debilitating self-doubt. These concerns surfaced daily, as everyone in Hut 3 sifted through their own particular thought processes. Every worry had to be considered on its own merit; nothing was ever dismissed. A typical occasion was when Corky was especially concerned about his geology reports. With the memory of the disastrous Dieppe landing fresh in his mind, he worried incessantly about every detail.

"I'm still not happy about the landing beaches, Lily. Everything I've got confirms my report, but as a geologist I need to see and touch it myself."

"Touch what, Corky, what are you talking about?"

"It's the beaches, the sand, I need to touch the sand."

"But you can't, so what's your specific concern?"

"I know what type of sand it is. It's been deposited by the rivers between Le Havre and Cherbourg. It's mainly quartz sand, with feldspar, limestone and shell fragments."

"What's the problem then, Corky?"

"It's the proportions, and that can change with a flood or a storm; too much limestone and it becomes soft. I need to feel it, I have to be sure."

"Okay, let's get some so you can feel it. I'll talk to Mac."

"I didn't think you would take me seriously, Lily, I should have known better."

"If you tell me it's important, Corky, then that's all I need to know."

I immediately found Mac and discussed it with him. He pointed out that he avoided landings near the invasion beaches - they were too open and exposed, even at night. He jokingly said that what we needed was a submarine to get divers ashore.

"Okay. I'll see what I can do, thanks, Mac."

"Where the hell are you going to get a submarine?"

"The Navy has submarines, I'll start there."

I would normally have spoken to Edward about such a matter, but he was in London at the War Office, so I asked Woody to explain to me what type of submarine I needed to ask for. He advised me that a midget submarine would be what we needed. He told me that SOE's Inter-Services Research Bureau had developed a midget submarine, but it was probably not suitable for sending divers ashore. After more consideration, he said what I needed was an X20 submarine; I needed the Navy.

"Thanks, Woody, at least I know what I'm asking for. All I have to do now is find one. Do you think that will be a problem?"

"I imagine asking the Navy to deploy one of its top-secret submarines might just prove difficult even for you, Lily!"

I worked my way through the Admiralty, but Station M's shroud of secrecy made life extremely difficult for me. It was all very exasperating, so I asked the head of SOE, General Gubbins, for advice. He was full of enthusiasm for the undertaking, but his suggestion only placed me back at the same department in the Admiralty where I had previously wasted half an hour. I was running out of patience.

Edward would have circumvented the bureaucracy by using his extensive connections, so I decided I had a contact and might as well use it. I went straight to the top; I sent a message to the Prime Minister via Elizabeth Layton. I needed an X20 midget submarine to send divers ashore to get sand samples from the D-Day landing beaches, and I needed it urgently. I received a message back.

"My dear Lily.

I am bereft that the lipstick which you so kindly planted upon my cheek is no longer with me. It is my greatest hope that when I next visit Middlebourne, you will honour me by replacing it.

Yours, Winston.

PS. You will have your sand."

On the 16th January 1944 Navy divers from an X20 midget submarine collected sand samples from the D-Day beaches. We rushed Corky down to Portsmouth to analyse the samples, and I slipped my personal message from Winston Churchill into a safe place to show my grandchildren!

-oOo-

As the winter turned to spring, our analyses concentrated more and more upon the German infrastructure, particularly transport and communications. Our part in the invasion was now clearly defined. We had identified the landing beaches, and now we needed to maintain surveillance. We had to be sure the German coastal defences remained unaltered, and where they reinforced any defences, we had to know every detail about it.

We needed to know about any alteration to German infrastructure, a key part of our function being the disruption of their transport and communications. Time-sensitive targets within the critical zone were our specific responsibility. Targets further away from the beaches were designated to the SOE F Section in conjunction with the FR. Some heavily defended targets, including within the critical zone, were to be dealt with by Bomber Command, or by Marines who would be parachuted behind enemy lines.

Our reconnaissance was always up to date - it had to be. Johnny Albright was flying over Normandy three or four times a week, and at the beginning of May he struck lucky when he spotted a high-ranking German officer in an open vehicle. Mac asked our agents on the ground to enquire about this officer, because Woody thought the appearance of such a high-ranking officer in a remote French village might be significant. Our agent quickly reported that the FR knew who this man was; he was Otto Schneider, SS-Gruppenführer und Generalleutnant der Waffen-SS. He had commandeered a remote chateau near Brutelles for his headquarters, and this chateau was centrally placed just two miles from the landing beaches.

This was significant - why had such a high-ranking SS officer set up his headquarters in this area? We thought it could only be to do with German defences against the invasion that they knew was coming. Within the week, we had reports of a general clampdown on the local Resistance movement. Six people were rounded up. They were interrogated and were eventually shot for being suspected members of FR. Communications with our agents immediately became extremely limited, so Woody was right to be concerned. Hut 3 went into an immediate huddle, as we all sat around a table together to discuss the matter.

"Do you think we're compromised, Edward?" Fiona asked.

"I don't think so. They know we are coming but obviously don't know where or when; otherwise we would see reinforcements."

"What about the six poor bastards the SS have tortured?" Patrick said. "We don't know what they knew, or what they might have told them."

"No-one in the FR has been told where or when the invasion will occur," Edward said, "so those poor devils couldn't have told them anything. The danger would be if they were aware of our agents, but we must assume they have said nothing, because the SS would have picked up our people by now."

"That's perfectly true, old boy," said Woody, "but I'm still concerned about this SS officer. His rank bothers me; I think they must have some suspicions to send an officer of that rank to an otherwise unimportant area, especially Schneider."

"Plus the clampdown on FR," said Rolo, "I think that confirms Woody's concern."

"We must reduce our activity in the area," said Mac, looking worried.

"Can we afford to do that, Mac," replied Patrick, "when we're only weeks away?"

"We have no option but to keep our heads down," Mac replied, "our agents mustn't be compromised."

"Even if we're not compromised," I said, "we still don't want an SS General right on top of one of the invasion beaches organising counter measures!"

"You're right," said Rolo, "especially a nasty bastard like Schneider; we need to kill him." His face was expressionless as he said it.

"A job for the Marines?" suggested Corky.

"No," replied Edward, "paratroopers are too obvious; it would give them vital minutes of warning. No, this is a job for you, Mac. It needs to be done quietly, moments before the invasion begins. His telecommunications can be cut, but his headquarters will have radio; we have to destroy that before they can raise the alert."

"Could we not just bomb the Chateau instead?" Fiona asked.

"We could," replied Woody, "but it's only a small target in the dark. The RAF could easily miss it."

"Can you do it, Mac?" I asked.

"I don't know, we need intel. Give me a detailed drawing of the building, and the whereabouts of all the personnel, and yes, maybe my agents can do it. This is the kind of thing we train for but without that kind of intel, I couldn't guarantee anything."

"Then we must get what you need, and fast. Who do we have there now, Mac?" I asked.

"I've got two agents only a few miles away. I must risk sending them a message."

Mac had steadily increased our number of field agents during the autumn of 1943. We had several agents seconded to us from the SOE F Section, including another woman. We now had ten operational agents, and our people rarely crossed the Channel on 'day trips'. Their missions had grown longer as they formed sustainable links with the FR. Two of these agents were posing as man and wife, living close by as a part of the French community. These were the agents Mac was referring to, and obviously the sudden change of circumstances had placed them in additional danger.

"If this operation is possible, Mac, will those agents carry it out?" I asked.

"Not by themselves, no, I'll need the help of the FR and at least one other agent. We'll need the best we have. They're not all trained to this level."

"You mean Dotty, don't you?"

"It has to be, Lily; nobody can bluff their way past a German guard like Dotty can, you know that, *and* she's highly trained for an operation exactly like this."

I didn't answer, but my heart sank at the prospect. It also meant that Dotty and the other two agents would be taken away from their planned sabotage at the onset of the invasion. This was principally to disrupt telecommunications and to sabotage some key parts of the transport infrastructure. Mac assured us that the French Resistance would be fully involved anyway. The agents' job was to lead the FR attack groups, and if the agents on the ground had confidence in their FR cells, then he would be confident as well.

I remained concerned; we had no option but to trust in our FR comrades but the wider the circle, the greater the risk. They knew an invasion was imminent, just as the Germans did, which was exactly why the time and location had to remain a secret right up to just hours before the invasion.

This was the role SOE agents played all across Europe. They armed, organised, and coordinated the local French Resistance movements. Their role was principally the sabotage of transport and communications all over German-occupied Europe. Telephone cables were a favourite target for one special reason - without telephones, the Germans had to use radio, and thanks to Ultra we could intercept these messages. The more they used radio, the more information we gleaned.

Road transport was sometimes clandestinely sabotaged by secretly greasing vital parts with abrasive grease, and by tampering with fuel. They disrupted train timetables, tracks were sabotaged, strikes were organised for railway and factory staff. Considerable planning and coordination went into ensuring that such attacks didn't draw undue attention to Normandy.

The key would be coordinating all the different French Resistance cells during the hours leading up to D-Day. The critical zone of the landing beaches and ten miles inland was our responsibility; beyond that, SOE agents by themselves were not numerous enough to cope with the scale of FR activity in the hours before the landing.

The problem was coordinating the various French Resistance cells when nobody could be told in advance about the time and location of the invasion. To overcome that difficulty, 'Operation Jedburgh' was formed. Three-man teams, comprising British, French and American Special Forces would be dropped into France in the hours leading up to the invasion. Their role was to work with the FR, coordinating targeting and timing.

The second layer of activity was the massive misinformation campaign, 'Operation Fortitude', codename 'Bodyguard'. It was vital for the Germans to remain convinced that an invasion would occur in the Pas-de-Calais, or possibly even in Norway. The key component was German agents who had been 'turned' during the MI5 'Operation Double Cross'. Agents such as Juan Pujol Garcia, code name 'Garbo', drip-fed misinformation to the German military command, indicating a landing at the Pas-de-Calais - or was it Norway?

To reinforce the probability of a Norway landing, they created a fictitious army in Scotland. Similarly, decoy tanks, aircraft, landing craft, transport lorries and barges were deployed along the Thames estuary and other places around the South East of England, to deceive German reconnaissance aircraft that the Pas-de-Calais was the invasion site.

The deception was immensely sophisticated, multi-layered, and elaborate at every level. Lieutenant M.E. Clifton James, an Australian actor bearing a remarkable resemblance to Field Marshal Montgomery, was employed to impersonate Montgomery in Gibraltar, misdirecting the Germans.

In the South East of England, General Patton was visibly placed in charge of the First United States Army Group, which in reality didn't exist. Our own contribution towards 'Operation Fortitude' was through Edward's association with the London Controlling Group. Although our contribution was only advisory, it was significant.

Those last weeks leading up to 'Operation Overlord' were the most stressful of my life; we all worried incessantly about every detail, and the tension ratcheted up until I could hardly breathe. Not least of my worries was Dotty's involvement in the operation we codenamed 'Top Hat', the elimination of the German SS General and his staff.

Agent Starling somehow obtained architectural drawings of the commandeered chateau, and close observation made clear the routine of the occupants. This was enough for Mac to make the decision that 'Top Hat' would go ahead, so - once again - the war had become very personal for me.

-o0o-

The final week before D-Day affected us all the same. We were terribly stressed, and I found the adrenalin seemed to heighten my senses. My mind would race from one thought to another. There was one personal issue which I had struggled with for many months. Usually I could put such thoughts to the back of my mind but during this stressful time, these uninvited thoughts would burst into my consciousness at the strangest times.

Greg and I continued to be more than just friends - when you've kissed a man on the lips more than once, you can't deny that you have some sort of relationship with him. The kind of relationship that we had was harder to define. I told myself it was our circumstances that came between us, but I was even unable to convince myself of that.

Fiona was now dealing with most of the estate issues which would have involved me with Greg. Not that I was deliberately avoiding him; it just made it easier for me to do so. However unfulfilled our relationship was, it undeniably existed. I was reminded of it every time I looked into his eyes.

One morning in the office, just five days before D-Day, Fiona had a message for me and in an instant what had been so troubling me, filled my mind once again.

"Greg left me a message for you. He wants to take you out one evening this week."

"I know he does; he's always asking me."

"I really don't understand, Lily, he's adorable, so why not?"

"Because he's adorable, I suppose! Trust me, Fi, it's taking a lot of willpower not to."

"What do you have to lose?"

"Everything or nothing, I'm not sure. It would undermine my authority in other people's eyes, and I just feel this ridiculous loyalty to Edward. If I slept with Greg, and Edward knew about it, I'd be absolutely devastated."

"What does that tell you, Lily, about you and Edward?"

"I wish I knew, but we don't have that kind of relationship, do we? Lady Beatrice made it clear that we never will."

"I can tell you what it means. Despite everything, you're hopelessly in love with the man, but unless there's a future in it, you're just wasting your chance for happiness."

"Best not beat around the bush, Fi, just tell me straight!"

"Well, someone has to, Lily, and if I can't, who can?"

"You're right, I know you're right, but I just can't help myself. I spend so much time with Edward. For goodness' sake, we dine together most evenings, we often have breakfast together, and we live under the same roof. I try to convince myself that it's the war which has thrown us together, that the war is the only thing keeping us together, and nothing else.

And then Caroline's so kind to me, and Edward gave me that wonderful necklace for Christmas, and oh, Fi, that Christmas! I couldn't bear it, Fi. Being nice to that woman was just awful. Oh, I just don't know what to think."

"I wish I could offer you some advice, Lily, but all I know of love is that it's simple and straightforward. I love him, and he loves me back; I can't imagine your torment. All that I can see are the two most desirable men I can imagine, and one way or another, they both want you."

"So what you're saying is that I'm spoilt for choice?"

"I know it sounds like that, but no, that's not what I mean. There's no doubt about the way Greg feels for you, and I can't believe Edward doesn't feel the same, despite this Beatrice woman. If only he wasn't so reserved!"

"I'm really beginning to wonder, Fi. I plucked up the courage to ask him about Beatrice, and all he was prepared to say was that any expectations were not of his making. That's what I hoped he would say, but then, when I asked him to elaborate, he just said it was how these things were done. He didn't seem to be at all enthusiastic, but then neither did he dismiss the prospect. There have been so many opportunities when he could have said something, and so many occasions when he really should have taken me in his arms and kissed me, but he never does. I begin to think he never will."

"Any man who gives a woman a necklace like the one he gave you, was trying to say something, Lily."

"I know, that's what I keep telling myself, *and* to do it in front of Beatrice! What was he thinking of!"

"From what you told me I don't think he was thinking - it's not at all like Edward to be inconsiderate. Beatrice must have been mortified."

"She was, Fi, believe me she was. So why did he do it? Is he telling me he loves me, or is he giving me a consolation prize because he'll marry her?"

"Nobody knows you better than I do, Lily. You'll do what you always do; you'll make your decision, and act upon it. I just hope you make the right decision; I'd hate to see you miss out on a chance of happiness."

"I *will* make a decision, Fi, and I desperately hope I don't regret it for the rest of my life," I said, reaching for my handkerchief.

"Oh Lily, I didn't realise you were so tormented; I just don't know what you should do."

Neither did I, and with all the stress of Station M around me, I kept trying to bury my torment beneath layers of far more important issues. Then, in the most unexpected moments - like on that morning in the office - those thoughts would draw back the veil I had draped over them, and my mind was once again full of indecision.

Fiona was right, I was hopelessly in love with Edward, but I also couldn't deny a magnetic attraction towards Greg. Perhaps that was some kind of love as well - I was beginning to think it was. I was so confused, but then the reality of D-Day filled my mind once again, and the two men in my life took a step back into the shadows.

I did go out with Greg that week; in fact, I made my decision, and we went out the next evening. He took me to a restaurant in Tunbridge Wells, and looked at me adoringly across the table, while I thought about what Fi had said.

"You're more preoccupied than usual this evening, Lily, what's the matter?"

"I'm sorry, Greg, I'm very stressed at the moment."

"The invasion, it's close, isn't it?"

"Where did you hear that?"

"Come on, Lily, for goodness' sake! Do you really think we're all in the dark?"

"No, I suppose not. You're right, it's extremely near now."

"Is this the end game, then?"

"Oh, I do hope so; if all of our efforts are worth anything, it should be."

"No, I didn't mean that. I meant is this the end game for *us*; is this when the war ends and you move on?"

"Oh Greg, I don't know, my mind is racing in all directions."

"All those thoughts racing around in that mind of yours, Lily; am I even one of them?"

I sat motionless for a moment; the wounded expression on his face left me feeling dreadful. My mind was full of my own torment, but I hadn't stopped to consider his.

"I'm so sorry, Greg, I've only been thinking of myself. You're not just one of my thoughts, sometimes you're the only person I can think about, but you deserve so much more than me."

"I'm not looking for more; all I want is you."

I had no idea what to say. He'd said nothing to me like that before; it almost sounded like a proposal. I reached out and held his hand across the table, and we smiled at each other. The waiter arrived with our main courses, and it diverted me from saying something that I might have regretted but so much wanted to say. It provided an opportunity to change the subject, which inevitably allowed Middlebourne back into our conversation.

"How's the cooperative running now, Greg?"

"It's working well. We can take on more after the war, but for now I can't cope with anything else. What I really need is an assistant, we must think about that soon."

"I agree, and you need someone who can grow into the job. Would you do something for me, Greg?"

"You know I will."

"Would you give Mary a trial, perhaps just the odd day to see how she gets on?"

"You mean the maid, what makes you think she'd be capable?"

"Trust me, Greg, with the right help she *is* capable. Did you know she now does the house accounts with her Ladyship?"

"No, I didn't know that. Why do I think you had something to do with it?"

"Maybe I did, but Mary needn't know that. She's a lovely young woman with a lot of ability, and it would make me really happy to help her realise her true potential; it's as simple as that."

"The assistant estate manager is traditionally a man, not a young girl."

"I know you're probably not comfortable with the idea, but would you try it for me?"

"All right."

"Is that it, just all right."

"If you think Mary can do it, then I've learned to trust your opinion, Lily. Besides, if it will make you really happy, then that sounds like something I should be involved with."

"I don't think you'll regret it. Leave it to me, I'll talk to Jennings and to Mrs Morgan."

Dining out in a restaurant was such a rarity for me during the war, and that was an incredibly special evening. I knew it would be the last such occasion before the entire course of the war would be changed. I tried to absorb every detail of the restaurant, of the food, of Greg sitting opposite me. I knew with D-Day just days away, we would never dine together again in those same circumstances.

Everything in my life was uncertain. I had not realised how desperate I was for something to cling on to, something of today, something that would be the same tomorrow. I wanted to believe that D-Day would be the sunrise of another day - a future where the sun continually shone. But there was no such certainty that I could cling to.

I had single-handedly shouldered every responsibility and stress that Station M could throw at me. I realise when I look back now that I had reached my limit. I desperately needed what I had so long denied myself; I needed emotional support. I needed intimate closeness with another person. I needed Greg.

I reached across the table and held his hand, and one of those sparks jumped the gap. I never cease to wonder how much of our communication is invisible to the outside world, especially that male/female thing. It happened in that moment! I felt it, I knew Greg felt it. I said it in my eyes, and his smile told me he felt the same.

We drove back to the Manor without saying very much; he just smiled at me. He was terribly polite and correct, stopping outside the Grand Entrance to the Manor, turning off the engine. At that point, he would invariably ask me if I wanted to go back to his cottage for a nightcap, and I always graciously declined. He turned to me that night and asked me again - I said yes!

Chapter Twenty-Nine
June 6th, 1944 D-Day

I opened my eyes the following morning to see him smiling at me. I instinctively put my arm around him, and we kissed. For a while I just existed in the moment, almost afraid of breaking the spell. What do you say the morning after a night like that? The words 'I love you' would be perfect, if only I could be sure they were appropriate.

"Have you seen the time?" I asked.

"Is it important, more important than this?" he replied.

It wasn't! We made love again, but this time we were both sober, and the previous night's outpouring of desire was replaced with something more considered but equally sublime. Eventually our heads fell back onto the pillows and we turned to face each other smiling. I didn't want to be the one to break the spell, but I had to.

"Have you seen the time now?"

"I'll make us some breakfast."

I borrowed one of his shirts and we sat at his kitchen table sharing some tea and toast. Neither of us said very much, but we hardly took our eyes off each other.

"I really need to go Greg; you know I do."

I got up from the table and walked around to where he was sitting. He undid the buttons on my borrowed shirt and put his arms around me. I held him close to me, forcing myself to look again at the clock.

"Really, I've got to go."

Reluctantly we both made ready to face the day, maintaining the spell between us until we stepped outside into the morning air. A last kiss goodbye and a new day began. Fiona was right; against the backdrop of all that had gone before, I *had* decided. I wasn't sure if it was joy that I was reaching out for, or despair I was walking away from. All I knew was that I had desperately needed Greg that night, I needed him emotionally and physically. My need was so great it was perhaps inevitable that its fulfilment would be a consequential moment.

I went directly to my bedroom in the Manor. I could hardly feel the ground pass beneath my feet. The last time I floated over the ground like that, I was wearing pigtails, performing cartwheels in the field behind Gran's cottage. Corporal Harris was on duty at the door, and I felt strangely guilty as I approached him.

"Morning, Mrs Heywood, you're up early this morning."

"Yes, good morning, Corporal."

"I wish I could feel as chirpa as you look, Mrs Heywood."

"Well, thank you. That wasn't a compliment, was it, Corporal?"

"No, just an observation, Mrs Heywood."

"That's okay, then."

My next encounter was inevitable, as Florence followed me to my room with my rather late morning tea.

"Morning, Mrs Heywood. Which of your suits would you like this morning?"

"I think the pale blue, with the two-button jacket."

"I like this one, the fitted waist really suits you," she said, as she laid the suit out on the bed. "Shall I do your hair for you now, while you drink your tea?"

"Yes, please." I sat at my dressing table drinking my tea

while she put my hair up. "Are you not going to ask me where I've been, Florence?"

"Not my place Mrs Heywood, it's not for me to know things like that."

She tried to return my smile, but I could see she was preoccupied about something.

"Is something wrong Florence, do you disapprove of me being away for the night?"

"Oh no, I wouldn't disapprove of anything you did, Mrs Heywood."

"What is it then, you're not yourself this morning, are you?"

"Nothing that you need to be concerned about, Mrs Heywood, I'll be all right."

"Florence, you're not all right, are you? I know you too well, tell me what the problem is."

With that, the poor girl burst into tears, obviously terribly embarrassed and not knowing what to do with herself. I jumped to my feet, put my arms around her and tried to offer whatever comfort I could.

"This is about Harry, isn't it, has something terrible happened?"

"It is, it's about Harry," she replied.

My heart sank, I immediately feared the worst. I assumed he must be badly wounded, or worse.

"Oh Florence, I'm so sorry, please just tell me, what's happened to him?"

"Nothing's happened to *him* Mrs Heywood, it's happened to *me*. I'm in the family way!"

"*You're pregnant!* That's exactly what I told you *not* to do, how could you be so silly."

I quickly realised the sudden shock of her announcement had made me overreact. "I'm sorry Florence, I didn't mean it like that; this is a bit of a shock. Are you sure; how many months are you?"

"Three months! I'm sorry; if only I had listened to you."

"Don't apologise Florence, these things happen, there's no point regretting it now. Are you sure about your dates?"

"Of course, it's the only leave Harry's had. What am I going to do, what's going to happen to me?"

"I could equally ask the same thing about Harry, what's he going to do about it?"

"He doesn't know yet."

"Okay, the first thing you do is write to Harry and tell him. I'm hoping that between you and Harry, and perhaps with the help of his family, you can find a way through this. I'll help you in any way that I can, you'll be fine, trust me."

"You can't help me, Mrs Heywood; when Mr Jennings finds out, I'll be dismissed."

"Don't tell him, don't discuss this with anyone else yet, Florence. We can keep this between ourselves for now, while you make arrangements."

She was right, the household would not support a pregnant housemaid. For some reason I felt very involved. I'd become extremely attached to Florence and knew she felt the same. I wasn't quite old enough to be her mother, but I felt extremely protective towards her. Until that moment I'm not sure I realised how close we had become.

I did my best to console her, though I wasn't sure in the circumstances what else I could do. For her part, she was simply relieved that I hadn't dismissed her on the spot. The poor girl was right to be anxious; life for an unmarried pregnant housemaid was not a happy one. She dried her tears and attempted a smile as she left me.

"Thank you, Mrs Heywood, I'm really sorry I've let you down."

"You mustn't think like that Florence, everything will be all right, I'll make sure it will."

As she walked away, I found myself wondering why I had said that. She wasn't my responsibility, but then again, I knew

I couldn't stand by and do nothing. She wasn't the first young woman to fall pregnant outside of marriage – who was I to judge! I just hoped her current difficulties would have a happy ending. I felt sure Harry and his family would do the right thing; it was too soon to be thinking the worst. She was so young to be thinking of marriage, but if Harry's family could take her in, they could build a life together.

I sat in front of the mirror thinking about Florence - in other circumstances, her news would have been a cause for celebration. I hoped this would be the outcome, and as I finished my makeup, I found myself smiling at the prospect.

Inevitably my thoughts returned to Greg, and in an instant my heart soared. I could still feel his arms around me, I could see his eyes looking into mine. I closed my bedroom door and made my way downstairs towards the Great Hall. When I entered the office, Fiona looked as if she'd hardly slept; those last days were certainly taking their toll on everyone.

"Morning, Fi. How are you this morning?"

"I'm not sleeping well, but I can see you've got a spring in your step this morning."

"Have I - I hadn't noticed?"

I was not about to discuss my love life with anyone, not even my closest friend, but it was amazing how the close bond between us three women joined us together. Fiona knew instantly that I had just spent the night with someone. A lovely warm smile spread across her face, as she interpreted the subliminal message that I hadn't even intended to send.

"Which of your two suitors was it?"

"Greg."

"Was it wonderful?"

"It was."

"Good, I'm really pleased. Now, you need to look at this data from the Met Office."

Fiona's discretion was admirable, but her concern about the weather was not just a distraction. We were all worried about the weather; it was most unseasonal. The combination of favourable weather and tide was out of Eisenhower's control, and it was also out of our control. They set the date for 5th June, but the conditions continued far from ideal. No-one in Station M coped well with a situation outside of our control; it was the nature of our business; we *had* to be in control.

I went over to Hut 3, and the weather was so unpleasant, they even had the stove burning, causing condensation to form in the corners of the windows. There was usually a buzz in Hut 3, as if all those intellects combined into one big electrical charge. It was notably absent that morning; they either sat in silence or, like Patrick, they paced up and down. I looked to see Edward and caught his eye on the far side of the room.

"Morning, Lily," he said.

The moment I looked at him a great wave of guilt and remorse flooded over me. My reaction took me completely by surprise. I felt as if I'd fallen into the sea and the waves were breaking over my head. The enormity of my situation exploded in my mind - I had betrayed him!

"Are you all right, Lily?" he asked. "You look terribly worried; try not to let the stress get on top of you."

"I'm sorry Edward…really…I'm sorry."

"What's the matter Lily, you don't have to apologise," he said, suddenly looking concerned.

I must have looked distressed because Edward came over and suggested I sit down. I put my hand on his arm; I just wanted to touch him, to feel a contact. I sat down and he pulled a chair close and sat next to me.

"This isn't like you, Lily, tell me what's wrong."

My first overpowering feeling was one of dread, I feared that I had lost him. My turmoil was that he was not mine to lose, how could I lose what I did not have? My second dread was that he would realise what I had done. Could he tell from my appearance, did I smell of Greg, did he see me coming from Greg's cottage? My mind became full of tormenting thoughts that only the guilty would obsess about.

"I just feel a bit under the weather Edward, I think I'll go back to my office and sit quietly with a cup of tea for a moment. I'll be all right, it's nothing."

"Would you like me to come with you?"

"No don't be silly."

I walked slowly back to my office, using the time to clear my head. I was sufficiently rational to realise that the situation was entirely of my own making, and one that only I could resolve. One of the most significant events in British and World history was about to unfold. I knew what I had to do. I had to find the strength to put my personal issues to one side.

During the next couple of days, the waiting was intolerable. We found time to worry about every detail. Dotty had been in France for weeks by then, and I realised I had not even wished her good luck before she went, which really troubled me.

Then, at the very last moment, D-Day was postponed, because the weather was ferocious. It was psychologically draining for everyone at Station M, so what that delay must have done to the morale of the troops who had mentally prepared themselves, I could not imagine.

The entire invasion now depended upon the Met Office, and on one man in particular, James Stagg, who had the un-enviable job of advising Eisenhower. Stagg predicted a small window of opportunity on the 6th June. It was far from ideal, but faced with a long-term postponement, Eisenhower took the biggest gamble of his life, and D-Day was now to be 6th June.

We could do nothing now but wait. Our agents were all in place, as was every agent in the SOE. The sheer magnitude of 'Operation Overlord' was difficult to comprehend. In total over two million soldiers, sailors, and airmen were waiting anxiously, just like we were. None of us discussed it, but I'm sure we all felt the same.

I knew I was about to be a part of something momentous. We were not just witnessing history in the making - we were a part of it; we *were* that history. I was both terrified and excited at the same time. Terrified that it could all go wrong, and excited that this would be the most significant day of my life.

Uppermost in my mind was 'Operation Top Hat'. I tried so hard to stay out of it, but now I found myself desperate to know the details of the operation. Mac understood my situation, having deliberately shielded Fiona and me from the detail during the preparation for the mission. I knew it was a high-risk operation, but I had to know.

I asked Fiona if she was aware of the details, and she said she'd been hiding from reality, the same as me. We agreed that hiding from the detail of the operation was irrational, so I suggested we both see Mac. We found him in Hut 5, and his first reaction was that I had been here before with 'Operation Skua'.

"You're both too involved. Are you sure you want to know?"

"I hear what you say, Mac," replied Fiona, "but it's an essential element of D-Day, we should know."

Reluctantly Mac showed us the plan of the chateau and the intelligence he had received. His operation was meticulously thought through, comprising a two-pronged assault. There were two targets: the chateau where the SS-Gruppenführer would be found and eliminated, and a separate building which acted as barracks for an attachment of supporting troops.

The plan was for Agent Sparrow to scale the outside of the building and gain access to the top floor where they believed the target would be found and eliminated. Agent Goldfinch would enter the ground floor and neutralise the radio room and its operators. Meanwhile, Agent Starling and eight heavily armed French Resistance fighters would suppress the attachment of supporting German troops.

The timing was important. Sparrow and Goldfinch would launch their assault to coincide with the first landings of the Pathfinder Paratroopers, just moments after midnight. Starling would launch the attack on the supporting troop barracks the instant they raised the alarm from the chateau. Fiona and I looked at each other.

"What could go wrong, Mac, what's your biggest concern?" I asked.

"My worry, as ever, is the unknown, but if all the guards are where we think they should be, then my primary worry is the supporting troops. We have the element of surprise, but if we give them time to mobilise, we would be heavily outnumbered."

"How do you rate the chances of success, Mac?" asked Fiona. "And tell us the truth."

"I wouldn't send them unless the chances were in our favour, you know that. Sparrow will get him; I have little doubt about it. My concern remains with the supporting troops."

"Thanks for being frank with us, Mac, we'll let you get on," Fiona replied.

We left Hut 5 and went back to our office, neither of us saying anything as we walked across the grounds. Eventually, we sat back down at our desks looking at each other.

"This isn't the Dotty we know, is it, Lily?"

"No, it's not. She's someone else when she's over there but beneath it all, she's still our Dotty. Please God, bring her back to us."

I worried about Dotty, I worried about D-Day, I worried about everything. I felt such an overpowering sense of guilt when I looked at Edward, and yet when I looked at Greg my heart soared.

That evening Greg came to the office, Fiona had already left. He put his arms around me and kissed me. He asked if I would be joining him again that night – I was powerless to say no.

-oOo-

None of us even attempted to sleep on the night of the 5th; we all sat in Hut 3 with the door open so we would hear any signals being received in the radio room. It was cold, and every so often a strong breeze would find its way into the hut like an unseen hand, disrupting someone's paperwork, causing it to flutter to the floor.

Rolo kept pacing back and forth to the communications hut. Every time he walked the few yards back, someone would ask him if there was any news, he would say no, and then five minutes later he would go back. We were all so tense, we seemed to have become locked in a compulsive and pointless cycle.

There was a clock on the wall of Hut 3 which we checked for accuracy earlier that evening but despite that, I continually compared the time with my watch; we were all doing it. Those last hours leading up to midnight seemed to drag by interminably slowly; we said little. We paced up and down; we asked Rolo every ten minutes if there was any news, and we kept checking the time, but none of these compulsive activities hastened the time forward. We all stood gazing at the clock, as the hour finally approached midnight. Edward looked at his watch for the hundredth time.

"It's just gone twelve, it's started," he said, biting his lip.

Nobody said a word, as we just continued to look at each other, each consumed in their own world of worry. I knew the first boots were hitting the ground in Normandy, and that the US and British Pathfinders were the first to parachute in. Their task was to light up the drop zones for the Airborne Divisions following on behind them.

Six Airspeed Horsa gliders would land near the bridges over the Caen canal and Orne river, which 180 men had the task of securing. We had identified those bridges as vital for the advance from Sword Beach.

Six SAS men would parachute near the town of Cotentin and falling from the sky with them would be 200 dummy paratroopers. The three-feet tall dummies had firecrackers attached to them. From a distance, the 'Ruperts', as they called them, would look and sound just like an invading force, their job being to create a diversion and confusion.

I also knew 'Operation Top Hat' had started, though I chose not to mention it, as I prayed that Dotty was safe. Rolo went back to the radio hut again. Susan the radio operator shook her head, no news. We all just moved about randomly, seemingly unable to sit or stand still. Fiona stood up, and sat down, and then stood up again.

"I can't bear it, I'll make us a cup of tea," she said.

"I'll help you," replied Maggie.

Nearly an hour ticked by until we received our first message from Station X. 'Bridges over the Caen canal and Orne river secured.' A little later, there was heavy fighting reported on the Cotentin peninsula. From that brief message, we assumed the airborne landings must have been largely successful.

I knew 'Top Hat' was probably still in progress, or perhaps it had already concluded. Then, at 2.25am, a single-word radio message came through from one of our FR cells. Rolo scrambled through his files to identify the codename, thumbing through the pages frantically.

"That's telecommunications successfully cut at Bayeux," he said breathlessly.

This was soon followed by several more single-word confirmations from FR. Saint-Lo, and Lisieux, all successful, but nothing about 'Top Hat'. Then there was news about railway lines being cut, and a transport depot destroyed; our agents working with the FR were reporting one success after another.

We knew that Caen was about to be bombed by the RAF at 3am. We had identified too many targets in this strategically important town for the Resistance to tackle it. This left us knowing that it would probably kill innocent French residents. It had been discussed, and now that it was about to happen, we said nothing.

More messages came in, mostly reports of objectives achieved, but not all airborne landings had gone smoothly. The 9th Battalion Parachute Regiment became scattered and could only gather 150 of their men out of 750, their mission to destroy the Merville coastal battery appearing at that stage to be in jeopardy.

"How serious is that Woody?" I asked.

"Very serious, we've bombed the hell out of it, but to no avail. This was our last chance to knock it out."

Then at 4am, we received a message from the FR at Sainte-Mere-Eglise, not a single code word, but three coded words - '*We are liberated.*' Sainte-Mere-Eglise was the first French town to be liberated during D-Day. It was not of strategic importance, but its symbolic significance did not escape Hut 3, and we all cheered as if D-Day was already over.

More splendid news was soon to follow this. Lieutenant-Colonel Terence Otway, with his vastly reduced force, had somehow captured the Merville battery. We later found that the cost in Paratroopers' lives was extremely high. It was an outstanding example of courage and bravery. Woody's relief was palpable – he'd been pacing up and down, fidgeting with his bow tie, and now he punched the air when we received the news. But still nothing from 'Top Hat'.

"Why have we not heard?" I asked Mac. "The operation should have finished a few hours ago."

"I know, I'm concerned. We should have heard."

It was practically daybreak, but low clouds obscured any rays of sunshine which might have brought us good cheer. The trees in the distance were swaying in a strong breeze - it didn't look like a good day for a beach landing. This was the moment when attention would be drawn to those beaches, as the RAF flew 1,136 aircraft over the coastal defences and dropped 6,000 tons of bombs. Warships bombarded defences with 15-inch guns, followed by bombers of the US 9th Air Force, who again dropped thousands of tons of bombs on the coastal defences.

We knew every square mile of the area like the backs of our hands, every strategic target. We knew where every element of the invasion was supposed to be, and what their objectives were. My head ached as I tried to absorb every detail coming in to us and could tell everyone else was the same.

Corky picked up one geology report after another, as if there was anything he could do now! Rolo never stopped thumbing through his codes and fact sheets. Woody worried incessantly about German troop build-ups and gun batteries, and Patrick was frantic, trying to get information to see if we had met strategic goals.

Mac was hovering between Hut 3 and the radio room, trying not to alarm me, but he didn't succeed. Edward amazed me, appearing outwardly calm. He had condescended to loosen his tie but otherwise he stood like the reassuring tower of strength he always was. Whenever nerves were frayed, his was the calming voice of reason.

Dawn finally broke over Middlebourne, just a faint glow of light against a leaden sky. The landings would soon begin.

Edward looked again at his watch. "6 o'clock," he said, "the rocket barrage has begun."

At that same moment, Susan handed a radio message to Rolo. He gave us all a thumbs up as he rushed back into the hut.

"Target eliminated, 'Operation Top Hat' successful!" he said.

I rose to my feet and looked for Fiona. As our eyes met, we both let out a spontaneous cry of 'yes.' I completely lost control for a moment and found myself jumping up and down with my hands in the air. Patrick gave me a hug, Edward punched the air, as Woody and Corky slapped their raised hands together. Mac remained in the radio room.

The next half hour was incredibly tense. The landings would begin at 6.30am and we knew Omaha Beach was likely to be the most fiercely defended. Woody had identified mines, barbed wire, and beach obstructions, not to mention the gun batteries that may or may not still be in place. What we did not know was that the American Forces were also battling against five feet high waves, which sank several landing craft. As time went on, we picked up various radio messages, all indicating extremely heavy casualties at Omaha, my heart rate increasing the moment we received any news.

"This is bad, isn't it, Edward?" I said.

"It is, this is what I dreaded."

Then we heard that just one of the amphibious tanks was ashore on Omaha, supporting the second assault wave. It knocked out one of the German 88mm guns which was pinning the troops down. The news from Utah Beach was much better - opposition was relatively light. We all breathed an enormous sigh of relief; this was the first hint of good news, but it was only a hint.

Information continued to come to us frustratingly slowly. The British and Canadian landings were due to begin at 7.30am, but it was not until 8.15am that we received the news that they also were meeting relatively light opposition on Gold, Juno, and Sword beaches. The second assault wave at Omaha Beach reported landing amid a terrible scene of destruction. Bodies littered the beach. More and more reports were coming in. The situation on Omaha Beach was not good - in fact, Woody called it disastrous.

"What's the worst-case scenario, Woody?" asked Fiona.

"The tide will come in, and if they can't overcome German resistance, the result is obvious."

"Oh, my God, this was our worst fear," Fiona said.

"I know the tide is against them, but let's not panic," replied Edward, "don't forget, our information is delayed; the situation might be improving by now."

Information was now coming in thick and fast about Omaha, and some good news arrived at 10.30am. Two American destroyers, USS Thomson, and McCook came close inshore and destroyed the German 75mm guns of Point de la Percee which were pinning down the landing force. Then we heard that the Airborne Divisions were involved in heavy fighting, and later that the 4th Division at Utah were pushing inland to join with the Airborne troops. A similar story emerged from the other landing beaches.

We were desperate for something to lighten the mood, and it came walking towards us in the most unlikely shape of Mr Jennings, being escorted by the military guard. He was being followed in a line by Florence, Mary, and Albert. They were all carrying large covered trays. The Intelligence Section was out of bounds for the domestic staff, which made the appearance of Jennings even more remarkable. I rose to my feet, rushing out to meet him, and could barely contain the smile on my face.

"I hope you will overlook this breach of protocol, Mrs Heywood," Jennings said. "I couldn't help but notice that you have been up all night. I assume this means the invasion, and I assume also that a hearty breakfast will be in order."

"You assume right on both counts, Mr Jennings. I can't thank you enough, bless you!"

"Is there good news?" he asked.

"The landings are in progress, but it's not all splendid news, not just yet."

We pushed the tables together, and they laid out a beautiful cooked breakfast. None of us had realised until that moment how hungry and thirsty we were. It was a tremendous boost to morale, just as we were flagging a little. Florence fussed around me, making sure I had everything I could need.

"Is there anything else I can do, My Lord?" asked Jennings, looking resplendent as usual.

"Jennings, this is absolutely marvellous, thank you, and thank the kitchen staff as well, will you?" replied Edward. "As soon as there is positive news from the invasion landings, I will personally let you know."

"Thank you, My Lord."

A few months before, Edward would not have dreamed of being so personable with his butler; I smiled happily, knowing that I had played no minor part in that transformation. Jennings ushered the staff out of the hut, and with a last conscientious look around to ensure we were all properly catered for, he gestured to His Lordship and departed.

"I've never had my breakfast served by a butler before," said a smiling Patrick, "I could get used to this!"

"Mr Jennings is magnificent, isn't he," said Maggie, "he's the consummate professional."

"He is, Maggie," I replied, "I can't tell you how much respect I have for him, and all the staff, they do a brilliant job."

It was truly a wonderful breakfast, but just as we were all enjoying having our spirits lifted, they were dashed and thrown to the winds. Mac hadn't touched his breakfast yet; he hadn't left the communications hut, which had not escaped my attention. I kept glancing in his direction, just too afraid to ask what his concern was. He trudged away from the hut; I saw him turn back and say something to Susan. I could tell from his face he had some terrible news.

As he walked into Hut 3 his eyes were on me, and then Fiona. I just knew instantly from his expression what it was. I sat rigid on my chair, unable to move. Mac looked at me and no-one else, his face contorted into a troubled expression.

"I'm so sorry, Lily, it's terrible news."

"Just tell me, Mac, what's happened?"

"Agent Sparrow has been captured by the Gestapo."

He was trying extremely hard to appear in control of the situation, but his expression and the look in his eyes told me he too was struggling with the gravity of the situation. My heart jumped into my throat. I wanted to scream, but I couldn't draw sufficient breath.

"Oh *no*! Oh dear God, *no*!" That was all I could say between brief gasps of air.

Fiona's reaction was the same as mine. The distressed expression on her face, and the look of horror in her eyes, only added to my anguish as she burst into tears and ran to my side. That was when I lost the last vestige of control that I was clinging to. I finally screamed, before breaking down into uncontrollable tears. Edward, bless him, stepped forward and put his arms tightly around both of us.

"This is awful news," he said, "what else do you know, Mac?"

"Message from Starling says the principal objective was a complete success, but FR suffered heavy casualties."

"What exactly happened, do you know?"

"It had all gone according to plan. Sparrow eliminated the target, but the German military contingent put up a stiffer resistance than expected."

"Do you know how Sparrow was captured?"

"Yes, Starling was clear about that. They had to retreat under fire, but Sparrow went back to help a wounded French fighter to safety, and their position was overrun."

I sat in a state of shock listening to Mac's account. I'd been there before, in that period when events are so terrible that your brain tries to protect you from the full horror surrounding you.

We trained every British agent to avoid capture at any cost; they knew capture would inevitably mean prolonged interrogation, followed by the firing squad. We all knew exactly what 'interrogation' meant, especially in the hands of the Gestapo. Nobody mentioned it, but we were all thinking the same terrible thoughts. Fiona was struggling desperately to stay in control - we both were - she only said one thing.

"You know what this means, don't you, Lily?"

My state of denial imploded - I knew exactly what it meant, and my world collapsed around me. I screamed again, shouting *no, no,* repeatedly.

"Come on, I'm taking you both into the house," Edward said with great authority.

I sat gripping the arms of my chair. Fiona sank to her knees and put her head on my arm. Edward knelt in front of us, hugging us both even tighter.

"Please let me take you both into the house," he said, "you can't continue here."

Those words 'you can't continue here' were the only words I heard. If I couldn't continue, I would let Edward down, I would let Fiona down, I would let down everyone in Hut 3. I looked up at him with my eyes full of tears, and I shook my head.

This wasn't the first occasion death had visited itself upon me. I had evaded death's outstretched hand before. I knew if I gave in, then I was giving up on life. Death's cold cloak was mine to endure, and endure it I must, but I vowed it would never break me.

To this day, I have no idea where that inner strength came from but somehow, I stepped out of myself and I took control of the situation.

"Come on, Fi," I said with a trembling voice, "thousands of people are sacrificing their lives today to give us back our freedom. We owe it to Sparrow to seize that gift; they'd expect nothing less from us. You know what we have to do."

"My God, Lily, me Mammy's feckin' proud of you," declared Patrick.

"I'll second that," said Woody, "this is why we *will* prevail today; no-one can defeat an unbreakable spirit."

Edward looked me straight in the eye, and said, "Woody's right, you made this day possible, Lily, your place is here. I'm so damned proud of you both."

It was immeasurably difficult to stay in control; we both teetered on the edge of the abyss all day. Somehow, I didn't let Sparrow down, and neither did Fiona. It was truly the longest day of my life, and it continued for us long into the evening.

When it was over, the course of the war had irrevocably altered and with it, the rest of my life.

Chapter Thirty
1980 D-Day Reunion

Charlie sat looking at me in amazement. "My God, Lily, I had no idea. My Mum has never spoken a word about this! To think all that went on in Middlebourne Manor, and nobody today knows about it. That's just incredible!"

"I suppose it is - it certainly defined the lives of everyone involved."

"So why have you not told anyone before?"

"Secrecy was paramount during the war. They classified restricted information into different levels, requiring various grades of clearance for personnel to see it. There were two secrets classified above everything else. One was Ultra at Bletchley Park, the other being the planning for D-Day. When you live in that secret world, it becomes a way of life. We just didn't talk about it, Charlie. Then when it was finally all over, it simply remained top secret; none of us talked about it."

"It was one of the most significant days in world history; the pressure on you all must have been enormous. I just can't imagine how you carried on. Knowing that Agent Sparrow was in the hands of the Gestapo, it must have been devastating."

"It was one of the most painful experiences of my life. Death visited itself upon me so many times during the war, first my brother, and then Gerry, it was awful. I thought I had experienced the final depth of my despair, but I hadn't. Death had one last exquisite pain for me to endure. Knowing death is in no rush to relieve someone from the pain of hideous torture, Charlie, that's a pain which cannot be described."

"And yet you all carried on."

"We did. I think each one of us lived our life through the brave souls on those beaches, feeling a responsibility for every one of them. Until the news of Sparrow, I'd never felt more alive, not before and not since. As soon as I knew what had happened, and that most likely she was being tortured at that very moment, well, it tore my heart out. I had no defence left, no means with which to protect myself from whatever appalling news came to us. As each item of dreadful news came in it added to that open wound, but I refused to give in."

"It's the most amazing story, Lily, and to think my parents were such an enormous part of it. Despite everything, D-Day succeeded, the invasion force got off the beaches."

"We all know that now, Charlie, but we didn't know it then. Omaha might have gone either way."

"When did you realise the landings were a success?"

"I don't think there was such a moment; any of the gains might have been reversed. The Mulberry harbours were on their way by the afternoon, one to be assembled on Omaha, in front of Colleville-sur-Mer. The other one was destined for Gold Beach, in front of Arromanches. This was the key to success, getting more supplies and reinforcements ashore. It really wasn't until the evening that things looked a little more secure. The last bunker in the Sword Beach sector wasn't taken until 6 o'clock in the evening and fighting continued right through the night; then it simply morphed into the Battle for Normandy."

"Was there at least a moment that evening when you allowed yourselves to celebrate?"

"Perhaps we should have done, Charlie, but none of us felt like celebrating."

We had all been awake for so long, and our only food had been that wonderful breakfast that Jennings brought us. The canteen finally brought us some hot food late in the evening, and Edward opened a bottle of whisky. All the while a constant stream of information came in. The fighting continued in all sectors, but we'd played our part, and there was nothing more we could do. I became delirious with tiredness and fatigue. Fiona felt the same, we couldn't function any longer.

We didn't have the strength to celebrate. Maggie kissed Patrick and said, "We did it, Patrick, we did it!" and Edward said, "Well done everyone, let's call it a night." We hugged one another, as we made our way out of Hut 3. I didn't go towards Greg's cottage; I wanted my own room. I didn't think Fiona would make it to Gran's, so I said she should stay there at the Manor. We walked with Edward arm in arm towards the Manor.

"Everyone has played their part," Edward said. "You have both made today possible, and in the circumstances, humbled us all with your extraordinary courage. None of this would have happened without you, so I thank you, both of you."

"It's been the best and worst day possible. I'm only glad it's over," Fiona said.

Edward hugged us both, holding me really close, and for the very first time we enjoyed being in each other's arms. Florence waited in the wings and came forward as soon as Edward had wished us goodnight.

"The first day is nearly over, Florence, we're ashore in Normandy," I said.

"Oh, thank God! The entire country should thank you; if only they knew what you and Miss Robinson have done here."

"They never will, Florence, and you must never say a word. Fiona is too tired to walk home. Would you prepare one of the guest rooms for her?"

"Of course. Have you got any night things, Miss Robinson?"

"I've got what I stand up in, Florence, I'm afraid."

"I'll fetch you a nightdress and some washing things. I'll be straight back."

Florence was wonderful that night; she helped us both to realise that life went on.

"So was that the end of your war?" Charlie wanted to know.

"There are never any certainties in war. We might have allowed ourselves a moment to think we could relax. Then, only days after the invasion on 13th June, the first V1 flying bomb fell on London. I actually saw the first one fly over us, heading towards London. The threat from the V1 and later the V2 was extremely serious; we knew so little about them. We desperately needed intelligence and counter measures. The Prime Minister asked that the best minds and field agents should be made available immediately; that was us, Charlie."

"You mean they gave Station M another operation?"

"We had proven ourselves to be a highly effective section of SOE and with our primary mission over, I suppose we were the obvious people. Mr Churchill gave Edward a simple instruction. He said, 'I don't care how you do it, Edward, just stop the bloody things!' We were charged with destroying crucial V2 production sites, and we did it, Charlie. Your parents did it, right in the heart of Germany."

"You must tell me what happened."

"That's another story for your mother to tell you. With my personal life in such turmoil it continued to be a hard time for me. I remained deeply involved with Greg, but all the while Edward filled my mind. I was being pulled in so many directions. So much happened to me during that final year of the war, but I will tell you about it, Charlie, I promise."

"You were in love with both of them, weren't you?"

"How can a woman love two men at the same time, Charlie?"

"I don't know, but you did, didn't you?"

"I suppose I did; heaven help me, I did!"

"I just had no idea about any of this, Lily, but why now, why are you telling me all this now?"

"You've got more of a connection to all this than you realise, Charlie, I couldn't have done it without your mother. That's why I asked you here today; it's our annual D-Day reunion. When it finally ended in 1945, we disbanded Station M, but we all kept in touch. When Maggie and Patrick got married Edward offered them the Great Hall here at the Manor for their reception. It just felt right that we should all be together again, so we decided to have an annual reunion. We have had a D-Day reunion every year since. We've lost our dear Woody now, but the rest of us are alive and well; the others will start arriving any moment. This is why I asked you to come this weekend."

"I thought you invited me so that you could give a lecture about my marriage!"

"Well, now that you mention it, I need to snap out of 1944, and your problems are a good antidote, Charlie!"

"For goodness' sake, Lily, I'm a married man with two small children!"

"All the more reason that you should sort your life out. You need to talk to me."

"Actually, after what you've told me about how you were tormented between Greg and Edward, perhaps I should. You're probably the only person who would understand."

"What are you going to tell me then, Charlie; are you finally going to divorce that wife of yours?"

"I'm telling you this in confidence, okay? I would never confide in anyone else. The fact is, I find myself in a terrible position; there's another woman."

"Are you telling me you're having an affair? *Charlie Bartlett*, I'm shocked!"

"Of course you're not; nothing I did would shock you."

"I'm not shocked about an affair, I'm shocked that *you're* having an affair. I didn't dream you would ever do such a thing."

"Neither did I, it just happened, and the thing is, she's

unlike any woman I've ever known, or likely to know. She has this way about her. She's exciting, she's intelligent, she has this amazing presence. Wherever we go, she becomes the centre of attention; she's just extraordinary. And as if that were not sufficient, she's the most beautiful woman I've ever seen."

"We're all beautiful to someone, Charlie. Sounds like she's turned your head."

"She's done that all right."

"I trust she's more than just a pretty face."

"Oh, she's way more than that, believe me. She fills my senses, and I can't imagine my life without her."

"You know what your trouble is, Charlie, you're in love with this woman. What's her name?"

"Joanna, and you're right, I do love her."

"Let me see if I've got this right, Charlie. You live a miserable life with Annie, your marriage is a disaster. Now you've found this amazing woman who you are madly in love with. Am I missing something here, or is this not the answer to your problem?"

"If only life was that straightforward. I have to do what's best for the children, and for Annie. As much as I love this woman, our relationship is anything but straightforward. Joanna really isn't like other women; I mean, she just isn't. She loves me, I have no doubt about that, but at the same time she is so driven. She's chasing some impossible dream and wants so much more from life than I can offer her. It's more complicated than I can possibly explain. The thing is, Lily, I have little time left, it's all spinning out of control. I think I'm going to lose her."

"Life has taught me many things, Charlie. One of them is that the love you're experiencing rarely comes your way more than once in a lifetime, so don't lose her, Charlie, whatever you do, don't lose her."

Charlie didn't answer. He was clearly in more turmoil than I had realised. He drew a deep breath and looked at me, starting to say something, when the footman walked into the drawing room followed by Maggie and Patrick.

"It's wonderful to see you both," I said, as we hugged each other tightly. "Maggie, Patrick, I'd like you both to meet my godson, Charlie. Charlie's staying with us for the weekend."

"At last, we get to meet you, Charlie," Maggie said.

"Lily has been telling me about Station M."

Maggie and Patrick looked at each other, and then at me.

"I thought it was about time," I said.

"An honorary member of Station M! You really are honoured, Charlie," said Patrick.

"Trust me, I feel honoured. What you guys did - I'm completely lost for words."

"Yes, it was quite something, believe me," said Patrick.

"This really is an occasion, Charlie," Maggie said. "Do you realise that, apart from the wives, you're the only honorary member of Station M?"

"Haven't you even told your children, have you really not said a word to anyone?"

"That's how it is," replied Patrick, "the only person I ever told is me Mammy, and I know she won't breathe a word!"

They talked between themselves, and I knew that I'd done the right thing to tell him. The next couple to arrive were Fiona and Johnny.

"Hello you two," I said, giving them both an enormous hug.

"Hello, Charlie! What are you doing here today?" asked Fiona.

Maggie was just explaining that I had told Charlie about Station M when Corky and his wife Beth arrived.

"Oh, it's so good to see you both, you look wonderful, Beth. This is my godson, Charlie."

They, too, were surprised to hear that I had taken Charlie into my confidence.

"Yes, I think it's probably about time," said Corky.

"I'm sure you're right," replied Johnny, "someone has to know before we depart this mortal coil, and Charlie's a good place to start."

Mac and his lovely wife Amanda arrived next, quickly followed by Rolo who never did find a woman who could put up with him. Rolo was the only one of us who didn't feel entirely happy about Charlie knowing.

"I'm sure you're all quite right," he said. "I suppose I'm just conditioned to treat our involvement as a state secret. I thought I would take it to my grave."

"I know what you mean, Rolo," replied Mac. "I don't feel the need to tell anyone about it, but maybe it's time we told our children."

Edward finally came rushing into the Drawing Room, full of apologies for being held up.

"Inexcusable of me, I know, local charity thing, just couldn't get away sooner, apologies to everyone," he said, breathlessly. "Hello, Charlie, I'm pleased you could make it this weekend."

"Hello, Edward," replied Charlie. "I don't know why exactly, but Lily has made me an honorary member of the Station M reunion. What you did here, Edward, what you all did, I'm really lost for words. I feel proud that Lily has taken me into her confidence. Did you know she intended to do this?"

"We discussed it, yes, and we agreed it was about time, and when you think about it, this is the perfect time, isn't it?"

We were nearly complete, just two more to arrive, and they were only half an hour late. I waited in anticipation of another grand entrance, and she didn't disappoint. Harrison announced them.

"Mr and Mrs Bartlett, My Lord."

She came striding into the Drawing Room, Robert on her arm, and with an enormous smile on her face.

"For goodness' sake, Harrison, they know who I am!" she said. "Never fear, I may be late, but Dotty's here. I've sent Albert off for some champagne, Edward, it's past the yardarm.

Give me a kiss, Edward - and Charlie - what the hell are you doing here?"

"Yes, hello Mother, hello Dad, it's a long story."

"I'll explain later, Dotty, after you've put Edward down."

"I'm not finished with him yet."

I put my arms around Robert and hugged him warmly.

"What's my boy been up to then, Lily?" he asked.

"He's a lovely boy, Rob. I just thought it was about time he knew."

"So you've told him?"

"Not everything, no. I thought maybe another time."

Reynolds, the butler, came in with a tray of champagne, and Florence poured the glasses, as she always does on these anniversaries. Albert Reynolds, Florence, and Mary the Estate Manager are the only remaining staff from the Station M days. They are also the only staff who ever attend the anniversary function.

It's the same every year. For that brief time, Station M is alive again. Middlebourne echoes with the sounds of the past, as we reminisce about that most important time of our lives. This year felt different, with our past now finally joined with the future. I'd chosen Charlie to be the first to carry our story on to the next generation. Florence poured his champagne.

"I had no idea, Florence; you've been here right from the start, no wonder you're so close to the family."

"His Lordship always insisted that I should say nothing about the past, but I'm pleased they've told you, Charlie."

"They're an amazing bunch of people, aren't they?"

"I've always thought so, and not least your Mum and Dad, Charlie. They're real-life war heroes."

"Are they? I didn't know, they've not told me anything."

Edward stood up, as was the custom, and tapped on his glass, to silence us all. He said much the same thing each year. He didn't need to say anything else, his few well-chosen words said it all.

"Ladies and gentlemen, we come together on this the anniversary of D-Day to honour those whose courage and determination turned the course of history. We salute all those who offered their lives so that we could enjoy ours in freedom. We also remember our own unsung heroes who did not come back: Merlin, Heron, Kestrel, Kingfisher, Jay and Swift. Finally, we remember our dear absent friend, Woody. Winston Churchill said we would receive neither recognition nor medals, but he also said, come the glorious day of celebration, no-one will stand taller. When I look around this room, on this auspicious day, I know he was right. So it is with immeasurable pride that I ask you to raise your glasses - I give you, D-Day."

We all raised our glasses in a toast before we then stood for a minute of silence. When we quietly resumed the conversation, Charlie asked Edward a question.

"Edward, I couldn't help but notice, you paid tribute to your fallen agents, but you didn't mention the most important one, Sparrow."

I took hold of Charlie's hand. "This is what I wanted you to know. She didn't die at the hands of the Gestapo, she made it back to us. Charlie, *your mother was Sparrow*, and your father was Goldfinch."

Charlie was aghast, he turned towards his mother.

"*You were Sparrow?* I just assumed your codename was Starling. You mean, the Gestapo imprisoned and tortured you?"

"Well, yes," replied Dotty, "but it's not something we talk about, is it Rob?"

"This is why I felt you should know, Charlie," I said. "I don't say this lightly because I know your parents have never spoken about it. What your parents did behind enemy lines has become legendary among the ranks of SOE. They are both war heroes many times over; Winston Churchill personally commended them."

"Lily exaggerates, Charlie. We just did what we had to do, that's all."

"He's your son, Dotty, and he deserves to know the part you both played, the *real* part."

"I thought it would die with us. You can't imagine how difficult it would be for me to relive those dreadful times. But perhaps Lily's right, maybe your generation should know what we went through. Even after what Lily's told you, you still don't know the half of it, Charlie. It didn't end with Operation Top Hat and D-Day. The final year of the war was the longest year of all."

"You absolutely amaze me, Mum, and you, Dad, you *all* do. Look at you all, you look like anyone else, but you're not like anyone else, are you, any of you."

"It was the war," Fiona said, "someone had to rise to the occasion, and it was us and people like us."

"Fi's right, Charlie," I said, "we all rose to the occasion, the whole country did. It was the girls in the munitions factories, the Land Girls, nurses, WRNS and WAAF. It was the boys in the Army, Navy, Merchant Navy, and the RAF. It was my Dad serving as an ARP Warden.

Every single person in Britain did their bit, which is why the British spirit could never be broken. Your generation needs to know the full story. I'll tell you about that final year, it was to be the longest year of my life. When your parents tell you what they did during the war, it's going to take your breath away. I am so proud of my generation, Charlie, and so should you be. It has been the greatest honour of my life to serve with these people."

Not The End

D-Day is over but for Lily the final year is the longest of the war. Her inspiring story concludes in **"None Stood Taller - The Final Year"**. Dotty has an equally remarkable story to tell. She pays the price for the freedom we all now enjoy. Her story is told in **"None Stood Taller - The Price of Freedom"** (October 2022) Charlie's story is of another time, it is told in **"Autumn Daffodils - Charlie's Story"**.

The Final Word

It is my greatest wish that this book, and indeed the series, will enlighten and inspire you as much as they have me. As a self-published author without the marketing reach of a publishing house, the success of these three books has been entirely due to the support of readers. Together the "None Stood Taller" series has fully occupied my life for three years, so please spare two minutes of yours and place a review on my Amazon or Goodreads page. We cannot exist without your support. Share your thoughts and comments with me, either through my website or email me directly. Now it's time for me to move on to another adventure

Come with me!

https://www.peterturnhamauthor.com
peterturnham.author@gmail.com

Principal Characters

Jack - Lily's Father

Pam - Lily's Mother

Linda - Lily's next-door neighbour and closest friend

Johnny and Adam - Linda's twin boys

Mrs Johnson (Ivy) - Lily's Stepney neighbour

Rose - Lily's Stepney neighbour

Alan - Linda's husband

Gerry - Lily's husband

Jim Smedley - Lily's cousin

Gran - Lily's maternal grandmother

Spencer Tracy - Gran's dog

Boris - Gran's cat

Mavis - Gran's sister, Lily's aunt

Mildred - Gran's sister, Lily's aunt

Dorothy Archer (Dotty) - Lily's great friend

Fiona Robinson (Fi) - Lily's great friend

Reg - Farmer

George Miller - Lily's uncle, mentor, and employer

Marcia - George Miller's secretary

John (Johnny) Albright - Wing Commander Albright

Lady Elizabeth - Lord Middlebourne's sister

Corporal Harris (Brian) - Corporal of the guard

Greg Norton - Estate Manager

Fuller - Builder

Robert Fuller - Builders' son

Mrs Morgan (Elsie) - Middlebourne Housekeeper

Jennings (Charles) - Middlebourne butler

Florence - Housemaid

Mary - Housemaid

Joyce Evans - Her Ladyship's Maid

William Evans - Footman

Albert Reynolds - Footman (later butler)

Caitlin - Scullery maid

Harold (Harry) - Florence's boyfriend

Betty and Tom Jennings - Butler's parents

Stan Golding - Farmer

Maggie - Photo reconnaissance analyst

Mac McBride - Head of Operations, Station M

Rolo - Boffin

Corky - Boffin

Woody - Boffin

Patrick - Boffin

Roberts - Estate lawyer

Rosemary (Kestrel) - Field agent

Roger - Pub landlord

Otto Schneider - Major General, German SS

Robert Bartlett (Goldfinch) - Dotty's husband - Charlie's father

Beatrice (Lady) - Marriage contender

Charlie Bartlett - Lily's Godson - Dotty's son

Prominent historical figures dramatised to add context to the period portrayed in this book.

Winston Churchill. Sir Winston Leonard Spencer-Churchill, Prime Minister of the United Kingdom 1940-1945 and 1951-1955. Popularly accepted as Britain's greatest ever leader, and the most inspirational voice of World War Two.

Elizabeth Layton. Elizabeth Shakespeare Nel (nee Layton). Winston Churchill's personal secretary, 1941-1945. The only woman present at the Yalta conference, where Winston Churchill proposed a toast to her.

Field Marshal Bernard Montgomery. Nicknamed 'Monty,' famous for the victory of El Alamein. Commander of the British Eighth Army during the campaigns in Sicily and Italy. Commander of all Allied troops during the Normandy landings before handing over to General Eisenhower in September 1944.

Louis Mountbatten, 1st Earl Mountbatten. Chief of combined operations in April 1942 and acting Vice Admiral. De facto member of the Chiefs of Staff. Became Supreme Allied Commander of South East Asia 1943-1946.

Field Marshal Alan Francis Brook, 1st Viscount Alanbrooke.

As General Alan Brooke, was Chief of the Imperial General Staff during World War Two.

General Dwight D Eisenhower. Promoted to Lieutenant General in July 1942, led the Allied invasion of North Africa ('Operation Torch') November 8th, 1942, and later the invasion of Sicily and Italy. Appointed Supreme Commander of the Allied Expeditionary Force December 24th, 1943. Gave the order to launch the D-Day landings on June 6th, 1944. Became the 34th President of the United States 1953-1961.

General Sir Fredrick E Morgan. Senior British officer appointed Chief of Staff to the Supreme Allied Commander March 1943. Morgan conceived the plan for 'Operation Overlord', and designated the Normandy beaches, for the greatest amphibious invasion in history.

General Sir Colin McVean Gubbins. Seconded to SOE November 1940, Gubbins became Head of SOE September 1943 when he replaced Sir Charles Hambro. He helped to transform SOE into a highly effective organisation.

Alan Turing. British mathematician, cryptographer, and pioneer in computer science. Synonymous with his work at Bletchley Park, Turing's contribution to the war effort, and to computer science was immense.

Captain Joseph T Dawson. An officer in the US 1st Infantry Division. Pinned down on Omaha beach during the D-Day landing, Dawson led his men up a narrow ravine and personally cleared the way through the German defences. He was one of the first officers to reach the high ground overlooking the beach. He was awarded the Distinguished Service Cross.

Lieutenant Colonel Terence Otway. Commanding Officer of the 9th Battalion, Parachute Regiment. In the small hours of June 6th D-Day, Otway parachuted into Normandy with the objective of taking the Merville Gun Battery. His 750 men became scattered and could gather only 150. Despite this, the assault upon the gun battery was successful. Of his 150 paratroopers 65 were either killed or wounded. Otway was awarded the Distinguished Service Medal.

Juan Pujol Garcia. MBE. Spanish spy who acted as a double agent for British intelligence, under the code name of 'Garbo'.

Cole Porter. Prolific American composer and songwriter, with over 800 songs to his credit. Notable songs: "Night and Day" - "Begin the Beguine" - "I've got you under My Skin."

Made in the USA
Monee, IL
05 March 2023

29183155R10256